INCIRRATA SECRET

INCIRRATA SECRET

ILLUSTRATED BY THE AUTHOR

VARTERELS' UNIVERSE
BOOK ELEVEN

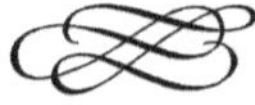

S.K. RANDOLPH

Cover and Illustrations by
S.K. RANDOLPH

Incirrata Secret: Illustrated by the Author (VarTerels' Universe Book 11)

ISBN
Paperback 978-1-962777-07-0
eBook 978-1-962777-34-6

Self Published by S.K. Randolph
CheeTrann Creations LLC
Suite 316-160
1410 Valley View Drive
Delta, CO 81416 USA

Web Site: www.skrandolph.com
Substack: skrandolph.substack.com
Facebook: http://facebook.com/S.K.Randolph11

Revised 2026

VU-130-J VU11-IS 260705-0256 | 240227 PibtA VUPt-2 | 6X9 428 0.75X0.5 .vellum

To JoAnna Pepe whose writing workshop in Traverse City, Michigan in the year 2000 lifted me up from the devastation of personal loss to the miracle of writing.

Thank you, JoAnna! Your loving support, as a friend and a mentor, gave me the courage to face a difficult time and to use the lessons learned to enrich my creative life. Because of you I found my writer's voice. I am forever grateful.

VarTereis' Universe ™
SCIENCE FANTASY

INCIRRATA SECRET

S.K. RANDOLPH

TOMORROW

Incirrata Secret

Prologue I

Tomorrow

Prologue I - Tomorrow

The Mocendi DiMensioner strode from the stable, his errand discharged. A triumphant laugh reverberated through the night. His black, purple-lined cape unfurled like a raptor's wings as he leapt into a shimmering vortex and vanished.

In the stable inside a filthy stall, a petrified child hugged her knees and sobbed. *So dark. So scared.* Her new prison, the second since her abduction, looked more frightening than the last. She swayed back and forth, murmuring a soft mantra: *My name is Penee. I am five sun cycles old. I love my birth-mate, Elf. I want my Aunt Rasi. I love you, Maman. My name is—*

A flood of recent memories left her panting: the burn of ropes securing her wrists and ankles; the sweet smell of something pressed over her mouth and nose; darkness; and, much later, hunger gnawing at her belly, waking her to the ink-black silence confining her.

Frantic to reclaim one pleasant moment since her abduction, she hugged herself and remembered B'hean.

The wall of her first prison shook. She scrambled away from the wall, her body trembling. Unfamiliar sounds——a low snort, muffled scuffling, a high-pitched squeal——triggered a desire to scream. She jammed a fist in her mouth and waited for a monster to emerge.

The distant screech of an opening door intensified her building terror. Stealthful footsteps sent her scooting back against the rough wooden wall. The top half of the prison door swung wide. She bit down on her fist.

Eyes and a nose appeared above the bottom half of the door. "Shh. I'm a friend. Don't make a sound."

Metal dragging over metal squeaked. The door opened a crack. A hand holding a lantern preceded an older boy into the musty prison. He set the lantern on the ground, latched the door from the inside, and remained listening. At last he flashed her a smile. Reclaiming the lantern, he knelt in front of her. The flame's flickering highlighted blue, blue eyes, eyes with sparks of amethyst like Maman's special ring.

"I tried to come sooner, but they stationed a guard at the entrance." He offered a tin container. "Drink."

She slurped the cool water until the burning dryness in her throat eased. Lips quivering, she tried to smile her appreciation. "Good."

He attached the container to his belt and withdrew an apple from his jacket pocket. "I know they haven't brought you anything to eat. Try this. Then I have to go. Wouldn't do to get caught, or we'll both be starvin'."

The first timid bite made her stomach rumble. The second, more aggressive crunch sent a spasm through her hungry body.

A thump preceding a sharp crack on the wall made her jump. She grabbed the boy's knee. "What?"

"It's alright. It's only a horse. Finish the apple."

Her brow wrinkled. She swallowed. "Where am I?"

"You're in a stable on the outskirts of Reachti."

Confusion left her shaking her head.

"You're on the planet of Soputto. Two turnings ago, a Mocendi brought you to the stable. I'm sorry I couldn't help sooner. What's your name?"

"I am Penee. I want Maman."

"How old are you, Penee?"

"Five sun cycles. Please. I want to go home."

He leaned closer. "Where's home?"

Penee thought hard. "A big stone house called Soasi."

A smiled warmed his eyes. "Do you know what planet?"

She nibbled her lip. Elf had told her. Why couldn't she remember? She thought harder, then blew out a breath. "TreBlaya." Her eyes questioned.

His filled with surprise. "TreBlaya's a long way from Soputto. I'll try to get help. If the men take you away, I *promise* to find you." He shot a look over his shoulder. "Finish the apple. I need to go. They're expected back soon."

She swallowed the last bite. He crammed the core in his pocket.

A scraping sound rounded her eyes in fear. She seized his pant leg. "What is horse?"

He looked perplexed. "You've never seen a horse?"

"No." The whispered word shook.

A finger to his lips, he tiptoed to the door, lifted the latch, and peeked outside. "Come here."

She scrambled to her feet. He took her hand. "I'm gonna show you a horse; then you have to come back here. Understood?"

She nodded.

He led her into a hall-like space with a row of doors on both sides. In the adjoining stall, an enormous creature turned soft brown eyes in their direction.

The boy scratched a white patch on the long face and pulled the apple core from his pocket. "Hold your hand out, palm up."

Curious, she did as he asked. He placed the apple core on her palm. "We're going to feed the horse. Don't be afraid." He cupped her hand in his. "She's gentle. Aren't you, B'hean?"

The horse's ears twitched. She lowered her nose. A warm puff of air tickled Penee's palm. Velvet-soft lips plucked up the core.

Amazement left a bright smile on Penee's face. "She is wonderful."

A flare of light outside the barn ended the moment. Men's voices floated down the stable's alley.

The boy urged her back to her prison and snatched the lantern. "You can't tell them about me, Penee. If they find out, we'll both be in trouble. Try not to be scared. I'll be close by." The door creaked shut. Metal scraped metal with a finality that made her sink down, her back to the wall.

B'hean's soft snort calmed her panic. She moved closer to the wall of the adjoining stall. "I will share memories with B'hean. She will help me remember."

Resting her hand on the rough wood, she whispered, "Elf and I played hide-and-seek in the Plantitarium on Maman's ship. He always found me. Do you think he will find me when he grows up? I miss him. I miss Maman. She hugged me. Her arms were warm. Her breath in my hair felt like your breath on my hand. She told me stories about another world." Soft sobs shook her. She stroked the wall's roughness. *B'hean is near. But I'm so, so afraid.*

Early the next turning, a man in the purple-lined cape appeared in her prison. A sickly-sweet cloth covered her mouth and nose. She woke to isolation and darkness on a cold stone floor in a tiny room with a heavy metal door, the sounds of B'hean a remote echo in her mind.

Knees hugged tight to her chest, she swayed back and forth. *I am Penee. I am five sun cycles. Where are you, Maman? Elf is——*

The familiar rattle of a key in a lock blotted out the past. A dull clunk, strident scraping, the key rattling, and silence returned.

She crawled to a metal bowl. A whiff of its foul-smelling contents turned her stomach. The key rattled. She gulped the bowl's contents, thrust it toward the door, and scrambled back to her corner. Rusty hinges groaned. Without a glance in her direction, a man retrieved it. The door slammed. As the key turned in the lock, nausea twisted her belly. A loud belch ricocheted off the walls. Her meal spewed over the floor.

Shivers careened up her spine. She draped a threadbare blanket over her shoulders, and tried to remember the other life, the one with a mother, a boy named Elf, and an aunt, the life that was happy until *The MasTer* appeared.

Unable to keep her eyes open, she curled into a grimy ball and slept.

Time passed, marked by the metal bowl's appearances and brief glimpses of the man. The turnings faded into long stretches of isolation, broken only by the tickle or sting of bugs roaming her body to leave their calling cards in small, itchy patches. Time slipped by without the sun or the moon or the stars to mark its passage.

The key rattling woke her. Torch light startled her. Her arm flew up to protect her eyes. She scooched backward, trying to hide.

A disgusted cough preceded a stifled question. "What *is* that stink?"

A second voice mumbled a response.

Disgust bristled in the first man's tone. "You left her wallowing in her own filth for how long?"

Another mumbled answer.

"I counted on you to take care of her." An accusatory snarl ended in a challenge. "You're certain about the eyes?"

"Yes, sir."

"I want her bathed, dressed in something decent, and brought to my quarters. Do *not* hurt her. Am I clear?"

More murmuring and a set of footsteps faded. The door opened wider. Large booted feet stopped beside her. A man yanked her to her feet. A surge of adrenaline lent her the strength to pull away. She dodged for the door. Strong fingers latched onto her hair.

"Let me *go*! Let *me* go!" Her knees buckled as she slapped at the hand.

"Stop fighting me, girl. If ya be good, ya might get yer freedom."

Her flailing arms hesitated. *Freedom?* She knelt, panting.

The guard released her hair, and, keeping her at arms' length, hauled her to standing, "No more fightin'. Do what I tell ya." He wiped his hands on the seat of his pants. A sniff wrinkled his nose. "Don't be touchin' me." His face screwed into a mask of distaste. "You be as filthy as a dung heap. Stay behind me."

She watched him marching ahead. Shaky legs carried her one step, two steps, three steps. Her legs buckled. Hard stone bit into her kneecaps.

Swear words gushing, he averted his face, scooped her up, and stalked along the passage. A well-aimed kicked opened a rough wooden door. He walked out into a beautiful sun lit day.

. . .

Eyes squeezed shut against unaccustomed brightness, Penee gulped in fresh, flower-scented air, listened to the chirp of a bird, and savored the gentle breeze cooling her skin. When the crunch of boots on gravel ceased, she peeked from beneath half-closed lids at the short, round woman who gazed at her from behind wire-rimmed spectacles.

"Dearie me, dearie me." The woman shook her head. "Bring her in and get yourself gone, Potts."

The guard carried Penee through the kitchen to a room with a tub of perfume-scented water steaming in the corner. He set her down and gave her a stern look. "Don't make trouble, girlie. Mistress Teesh will help ya get cleaned up." He escaped, muttering to himself about dirt and filth and stink.

The woman stripped the rags from Penee's emaciated body. "Ya poor dear. Men just don't know nothing. Look at ya—— filthy—— starving—— half eaten by bugs..." Gentle fingers examined Penee's tangled, dirty hair. "Least, ya donna got head bugs." She nudged her toward the tub. "Let's get ya scrubbed up."

Several soapings later, Penee stood clothed in a flowered frock and white pinafore, her curly hair drawn back with a bow, her feet in ruffled socks and shiny shoes. Mistress Teesh turned her to face a mirror.

Penee frowned at the unfamiliar, pale face. One warm green eye with speckles of gold and one cool blue eye, looking much too big above hollowed cheeks, stared back at her. Hands clutched behind her back, she gazed up at Mistress Teesh.

The woman drew a sign in the air and planted a tender kiss on each cheek. "The El Stroman prophecy is true."

A younger woman escorted Penee from the kitchen area through a big house. Left alone in a dim room, Penee climbed into an armchair and dozed. Background voices crept into a dream of her and Elf hiding from their maman, of smothered giggles, and jumping up and shouting 'boo'. Desperate to hold on to the happy fragments, she squeezed her eyes tighter.

An eager voice outside the door penetrated her consciousness. "I'm telling you, she is the *one*."

"*If* she is, I'll decide what to do." The reply, delivered in a calm, well-measured tone, edged her back toward the dream.

"But, Skultar, if her parents are who we think they are, she is *your* cousin. *You* can't harm her."

"Shush. We must see for ourselves, Osstol."

Penee held her breath. Her heartbeat quickened. Instinct-inspired fear kept her in the armchair, feigning sleep.

The speakers entered the room. The owner of the eager voice puzzled out loud. "Whatever made the Mocendi kidnap *her*?"

A protracted silence preceded Skultar's clipped reply. "Rebels kidnapped her from TreBlaya. I paid him to rescue her. It's most disappointing that the rebels didn't capture her birth-mate, too. At least, we have the girl."

"What if she isn't *the one*?"

Carpet-muffled footsteps moved her direction. "I believe it is time to wake her, don't you?"

The powerful presence of the voice's owner so close chilled her. A cool hand brushed her arm. She stifled a shiver and sat up. Beady, dark eyes stared straight into hers. Nostrils in a long, pointed nose flared.

His companion gasped. "The Matriarch's Eyes!"

Her observer raised a hand for silence.

Penee, her thoughts masked as Maman had taught her, concentrated on smoothing her pinafore over her skirt.

The narrow-faced man's features hardened. "I am your cousin, Skultar Rados. This is my nephew, Osstol Lurst. How are you feeling?"

She studied a button on his vest. "Do I have to go back to *that* place?"

Her cousin put long-fingered hands on the arms of her chair. "You are safe now, Penesert. I will not allow them to take you back." He straightened. "My housekeeper will escort you to your room." He pulled a fancy cord by the door. "She will serve you something to eat. I want you to sleep well. We will talk more in the morning."

A soft knock announced the housekeeper's arrival. "Girda, this is Penee. Please take our young guest to her room. You alone will see to her needs. Tell *no one* of her visit. Am I understood?"

"I understand, sir." She guided Penee through a labyrinth of hallways to a narrow, staircase. At the top, they entered a small, elegant room where Girda led her to a table by the window. "I know you're hungry." She set a steaming bowl of broth in front of her. "Eat slowly, or your tummy will rebel."

Almost swooning from hunger, Penee inhaled the tantalizing aroma. Her first sip made her entire body respond. Giddy with delight, she licked her lips. "It is so good. Thank you." She finished the small bowl of broth and pressed a hand to her stomach. "My tummy feels warm." A yawn brought tears to her eyes.

Girda prepare the bed. "I think it's time to rest, don't you?"

A nod accompanied a hiccuped sob. "Will they take me away if I fall asleep?"

Girda unbuttoned Penee's frock and laid it on a chair. A soft cotton nightdress took its place. "I promise, no one will disturb you tonight." She helped her onto the enormous bed, plumped the soft pillows, and tucked a handmade doll beside her beneath the silky bedding. "Is there anything else you need?"

Again, tears gathered. "I want to go home." Penee brushed a tear away. "I want Maman."

The housekeeper pulled a chair to the bedside. Her sad expression made Penee's tears fall faster.

"I won't see her ever again, will I?"

Girda brushed a curl from Penee's forehead. "I don't know, little one. Would you like me to stay until you fall asleep?"

Penee nodded. Her eyelids drooped. Sleep crept closer. Thoughts of her cousin's narrow, satanic features chased it away. She shuddered. *I think you are an evil man, Skultar.* A whimper of dread escaped her quivering lips. *I think you are like The MasTer.*

She peeked from under her lashes. The woman sat in the chair, tears slipping down her cheeks.

Penee clutched the soft blanket. *What will happen tomorrow?*

P enee gazed out the window at the manicured gardens surrounding her proxy parents' home. *Just over nine cycles ago, two men abducted me from my home on TreBlaya. Almost eight sun cycles ago, Skultar Rados brought me here.* Her jaw tensed. *Today is my fifteenth birth-celebration. For the second time, I will say goodbye to everything and everyone I know and love.*

She traced the pattern of a small spider's web glistening in the outside corner of the window. Memories of the turning she arrived wove their own web around her.

Several turnings after Skultar rescued her, Girda delivered her to his study. Her cousin's stern expression made her shake inside. "I am taking you to stay with distant relatives who will raise you." He leaned down to look her in the eye. "You will behave and make me proud."

After several long hours in his horse-drawn carriage, they pulled up to the manor house on a large country estate. Skultar descended. An older couple hastened to meet him. They talked in subdued voices with occasional glances in Penee's direction.

Skultar, who stood with his back to the carriage, turned. "Penee, it's time to get out."

Unable to move, Penee cowered in the corner. Her heart pounded her ribs so hard she could barely breathe.

A woman's soft voice penetrated her growing panic. "Barlet, take Skultar inside. I know you have business to discuss. Penee and I will join you in a while."

The carriage squeaked as she climbed up to sit on the bench seat. "Everything is going to be alright, Penesert. No one here will harm you. When you're ready, I will show you your new home."

Penee peeked from under her lashes. Gentleness and caring, reminding her of Maman, steadied her tumbling emotions. She opened her eyes to study the woman next to her. "My name is Penee."

The woman smiled. "I am Coranna." She helped Penee from the carriage. "Shall we explore the house or the barn first? We have goats, chickens, and a cow with a new calf———"

"Do you have horses?" Penee's cheek grew hot. Her lips trembled.

Coranna squeezed her hand. "We have horses." She beamed. "Barlet purchased something special just for you."

"He did? What is it?"

"He bought you your very own pony."

Penee searched her proxy mother's face. "Pony?"

Coranna's eyes twinkled. "A pony is a small horse."

A surge of delight chased Penee's shyness into hiding. She clapped her hands. "Can we see it? Please?"

Penee leaned her forehead against the glass. The pony was only the first of many surprises her proxy parents had in store for her. *Coranna and Barlet have been so good to me.*

A message received yesterday morning had flipped her life upside down. Skultar would collect her by mid-turning tomorrow.

Hands on her hips, she rounded on the upheaval in her room. Clothes strewn across the bed and piled on chairs underscored the changes to come. Wadding up a summer blouse, she hurled it across the room. His personal message to her had been short: "This is a permanent change. Winter clothes are all you need to pack." Coranna had supplied her with new boots, several pairs of warm pants, and a fur-lined jacket. Penee assumed Skultar ordered her to do so.

Sadness descending into panic carried her around the room. A sketch drawn by her tutor, a rock found in the garden, a feather from a Soputton grey heron magnified her increasing sense of loss. She picked up a portrait of her proxy parents. Their beloved faces triggered a plethora of emotions. *You have loved me, taken care of me, and seen to my education.* Memories of her time with them overpowered her. *Your sympathetic support helped me to recover from being torn from my home and family.* I wish I didn't have to leave.

When Coranna and Barlet shared the news of Skultar's plans, her proxy mother's eyes glistened with tears. Barlet had been stern and remote, a clear sign the news disturbed him.

Penee kissed the portrait and tucked it in a safe corner of her trunk.

To stem a rush of rebellion, she marched from one side of the room to the other, pondering her relationship with her cousin. Over the past eight cycles, he had remained pleasant but inaccessible. On his occasional, uncomfortable visits to the manor house, he had all but ignored her. She stopped by the window to study her reflection in the glass. Fingering her long caramel-gold hair, she frowned. "Skultar insisted I keep my hair long." Her eyes narrowed. "He demanded I wear an eye patch whenever I leave the grounds." She scowled. "A rare occurrence. Will I always be Skultar's prisoner?"

She opened the window to better absorb the beauty of grounds. "This is my home. I love it. Where are you taking me, Skultar? I dislike you. You don't like me. Why the sudden desire to have me under your nose?"

Another tomorrow filled with uncertainty. She shivered.

E vening meal with her proxy parents had left everyone disheartened. Penee excused herself to retire early. She woke to the knowledge that the fateful turning had arrived. The aroma of the morning meal, delivered to her room, made her feel sick. An attempt to eat made it worse.

Dressed for the changes to come, she wandered downstairs, hoping to steal a few minutes with Coranna. Unable to find her, Penee headed for her room, disappointment dragging at her heels.

Barlet's study door opened. "Penee, please come in and sit down." He closed the door behind her and sat at the desk. "I believe you know we don't want you to go." His sadness was palpable. "Coranna could not bear to say goodbye." He placed a pocket blade on the desk. "She asked me to give this to you. It belonged to our son. We have never mentioned him because his loss has been unbearable. Your presence in our lives eased our sorrow, Penesert. Always remember we care about you." He tapped the blade. "Don't tell your cousin you have this." His somber gaze held hers as he rose. "Remember, I built the secret room in the lakeside cottage for you. If you ever need it, use it." He hurried from the room.

Penee sat for a time, lost in thought. For her thirteenth birth-celebration, her proxy parents had taken her to the cottage, one of the rare times she had left the estate. Barlet had shown her a door secreted behind the gun rack in his trophy room that afforded access to hidden rooms beneath. *Someday, I may need to take you up on your offer.*

She picked up the folding knife, pressed the button, and stared at a blade as long as her palm. *My knife...* Closing it, she shoved it in her new winter boot. Voices down the hall drifted her way. *Skultar——*

Defiance overflowed. She snuck out a side exit and made her way to the stables. Her chestnut mare nickered as she entered the stall. Penee rested her forehead on the horse's face. *What if we just ride away, Genie?* Her shoulders drooped. *Where would I go? I've only been outside the grounds twice.*

Skultar arrived in the doorway. "I don't have time for your games, Penesert. The carriage is waiting."

She folded her arms. "I'm fifteen. I'm old enough to make choices for myself."

Danger, like the snap of a whip, crackled around her cousin. Beady eyes held a stark warning. He loomed over her. "I am your guardian. You are alive because I rescued you. Come now, or I will have my man drag you."

Genie pranced sideways. Penee curled trembling hands into fists. "But, Skultar, I love my proxy-parents. Why must I leave?"

He shot her one last warning glare and stepped into the barn's alley. A stocky, muscular man took his place.

Rebellion dissolved in the sting of defeat. She skipped out of reach. "I'll come." Head high, she marched after her cousin. When she was safely inside the carriage, he joined her. Swallowing her pride, she produced a tentative smile. "Where are you taking me, cousin?"

He glanced her direction, then out the window of the motionless carriage. "At this rate, nowhere."

Although her curiosity demanded satisfaction, her cousin's inscrutable expression kept Penee silent. Her emotions held in check, she sought a glimpse of her proxy parents. The carriage jerked into motion. Barlet with a sobbing Coranna watched as it rolled down the long drive.

Heart aching, she refocused on the world outside. A twinge of long-ignored interest surprised her. Excitement made a furtive appearance. *I'll get to see new things.*

· · ·

Skultar's unapproachable demeanor throughout the long ride held all questions at bay, so she watched the world go by amazed at everything she saw. The carriage turning onto a narrow country lane erased Skultar's air of disinterest. A mantle of authority replaced his traveler's lassitude. His expression enlivened with interest.

Penee inhaled a quiet breath. Rather than make herself a target, she kept her face to the window.

They arrived in a cleared field at sunset. A sleek, gleaming craft resting at its center caused her to heartbeat to quicken. Her gaze darted to her cousin's face. He ignored her and prepared to descend.

The driver opened the carriage door. Skultar exited and strode to meet a uniformed official. Penee climbed down. Two more uniformed men stacked their luggage on a hand cart to transfer it to the strange craft. The driver stowed the steps, closed the door, and tipped his hat in farewell. "Have a good jump."

"Jump?"

He gave her cousin a quick sideways glance. "Ya be going on a space jumper."

Before she could ask what that meant, the driver climbed to his seat, grabbed the reins, and set his team in motion.

"Penesert, come." The note of authority in her cousin's voice brought her rebellion slamming to the surface. Lips pressed tight to stifle a defiant retort, she followed him across the field. A steep ramp carried them into the underbelly of the craft. Skultar, as though forgetting her presence, spoke with a uniformed officer. A younger man escorted her along a passageway. By a rectangular panel inset into the wall, he tapped a green square. A door slid aside.

"This is your cabin. Governor Rados asks that you remain in it at all times. The trip will take two turnings."

"Please. What is a space jumper?"

He glanced toward the open door. "You are on a jumper shuttle, a craft that uses space portals to diminish travel time."

Confusion almost left her speechless. "Where are we going?"

The man studied her. "To a Soputton moon. Skultar Rados is the new governor of the Penal Colony on TaSneach. Sure hope you like winter." A whistle blared. "Enjoy your trip." He hurried away.

The door closing left Penee alone in a small gray-green space, trying to make sense of what she had learned. "A penal colony on a moon?" Anger close to boiling, she glared at the entryway. "Someday, I will escape your control, Skultar Rados, and my life will be my own."

The following two turnings, Penee saw neither the young man nor her cousin. The hours slipped by. On the dawn of the third turning, a whistle broke the monotony. A sharp knock announced the younger man's entrance.

"Time to disembark." He handed her a warm coat with a hood and a pair of thick mittens. "Governor Rados says to hurry." He stepped into the companionway.

Penee donned the coat, pocketed the mittens, and scurried to keep up with her winter-clad escort. Her cousin awaited her in the jumper craft's cargo hold. He greeted her with a grim stare. "Behave and you can join me in the main house." Turning to a man waiting by a control panel, he nodded.

The ramp doors opened. Winter wind blew a flurry of snowflakes into the cargo bay. The younger man pulled his hat lower and headed down the ramp.

Penee followed him into a world of white, a world so cold it made her teeth chatter. Her heart sank.

And tomorrow begins.

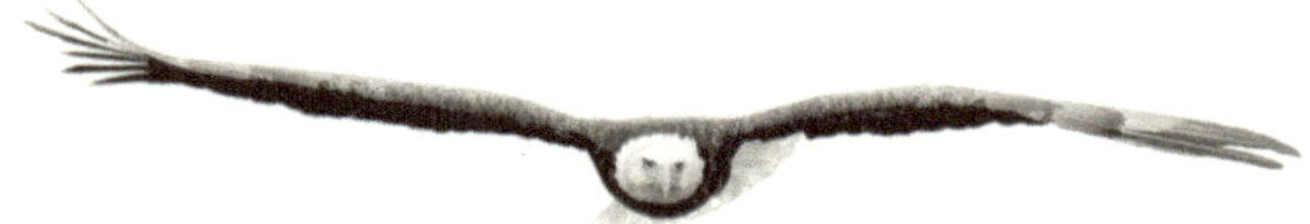

Incirrata Secret
Prologue II
Snowscape

Prologue II - SnowScape - 1

They are coming for you, Troms el Shiv. I have to find you first.

Penee stared between the ice-encrusted bars of her cell window. Soputto's ever-winter enshrouded the penal colony in shoulder-high drifts. Icicles as lethal as unsheathed daggers camouflaged windows and doors. *I'd be a fool to tackle this blizzard.* She dried sweat-dampened palms on the seat of her pants. *Yet, it offers me the greatest chance to succeed. Best of all, Skultar won't expect me to try anything.*

A guard in the compound hit a patch of ground ice, fought for purchase, and landed in an awkward heap. Another time she might have cheered. Today, anticipation of what was to come left her shivering. *What if I fail? What if I've missed something that will catch me unawares? Skultar will lock me away forever.*

Tugging a blanket over her shoulders, she shook her long, caramel-blonde hair back from her face. *You control my every move, Skultar Rados.* She gazed out the window. Frustration turned to a sigh. The previous night, her cousin had caught her listening at the study door. This morning, he had demanded she tell him what she had heard. She played dumb. His obvious annoyance provided her with a moment of triumph. The sting of his hand on her cheek and her immediate removal to the cell block canceled it.

Will ever I learn not to cross you? She grimaced. *When I do, I end up doubly trapped.*

Behind closed lids, she tried to picture her birth-mate, Troms el Shiv. They were only five the last time they had been together over thirteen sun cycles ago. She had given him his nickname, Elf, when she couldn't make her tongue form the name Troms el Shiv. He had called her Penee because Penesert was too hard to say. Both became terms of endearment when they were together. Memories of Elf's gentleness and his laughter made her heart ache. The overheard conversation about his potential capture had left her scrambling like the guard on the ice.

I can't let them get to you first.

What she had learned in the library after her cousin had gone to bed the previous night scared and excited her. A map of the Soputton moon, TaSneach, where the Penal Colony was located, showed a clear route to the space shuttle station. Penee estimated the two turning ride in a snow rover would take her three times longer to reach on foot, if she reached it at all. She ignored her nagging disquiet. *I'm trained to survive in TaSneach's ever-winter terrain. Skultar saw to that.*

Her gaze drifted from the window to the locked door. *If I wait, they'll capture Elf.* Angst spiked the hair on her neck. *We'll be at the mercy of Skultar forever.* She ignored her doubts, hurried to the rough-hewn door, and rapped several times.

The key clattered in the metal lock; the door creaked open a crack. A single blood-shot eye peered at her.

"Whatcha want?"

"I want an audience with Governor Rados, Jonto."

"*He* don't wanna see ya. Said to keep ya locked up 'cept for piddle breaks. Ya need to go or not?"

"Tell my cousin I'd like to apologize."

The eye blinked. The door slammed shut. A key rattling in the lock was Jonto's only response. Tugging her blanket tighter, she moved to the window. He waddled from the prison block, pulled his coat tighter around his pudgy body, and made his way, one plodding step at a time, to the main house.

The entrance opened to his knock, shut in his face, and left him prancing from one foot to the other. His breath gathered in a cloud around him. Fluffy snowflakes fell faster. He glared over his shoulder, caught her eye, and made an obscene gesture behind his back.

The door opening brought him to attention. He nodded and slogged back the way he had come. His key rattled in the outside entrance. Feet stamping and a string of angry expletives accompanied him down the dark corridor. More rattling and the cell door opened. Red-rimmed eyes glared. "Governor Rados says ta let ya sleep on it. If ya promise not to cause more trouble, I'm to take ya to the main house after mornin' meal." He wiped his runny nose on a sleeve. "Now's the time if ya gotta go."

A lascivious leer and the smacking of his lips made her consider blackening both his eyes. She hid the urge behind a sweet smile. "Please, Jonto. I'd appreciate it."

The guard gave her a long, hard glare. "No tricks." His grip on the club at his waist tightened. He yanked the door wide to let her pass.

She sucked in a breath, squeezed by him, and hurried across the hall into the latrine. Danger-sensitive instincts prickled up her neck. She cracked the door ajar. "I'll be a bit."

He scowled. "Come get me after ya finish." He shuffled down the hall.

Ear pressed to the door, she strained to hear movement. Satisfied, Jonto had reached the office, she knelt to remove a broken floor stone from beneath the sink. The knife from her proxy father went into her boot. A small vial she had taken from the infirmary and a key disappeared into her pocket. After replacing the stone, she did her business. The reflection of her sullen face in the metal mirror above the sink made her cringe.

"You won't fool him with that look." She schooled her expression to calm. Inhaling a deep breath, she walked down the hall.

The odor of Human filth assailed her as she stepped into the cellblock office. Jonto ogled her from behind the battered desk, a bottle of Soputton whiskey at his elbow. He raised a glass. "Have a seat."

She pulled up a chair and sat down. A casual glance skimmed by his keys on a filing cabinet, then came to rest on his face.

His complexion, already flushed from the heat and thoughts she could only guess at, turned redder. "Ya do what I say, and I'll make sure the governor sees ya tomorrow."

"If I don't?"

An ugly sneer distorted the plain features. "If ya don't, I'll see to it ya get punished good and proper."

Penee looked him in the eye. "If we're gonna play, you'd better pour me a glass of whiskey."

Doubt overshadowed the bravado on the pudgy face. "Ya ain't kiddin' me, are ya?"

Relaxing in her chair, she shrugged. "You have the upper hand, Jonto. I know when I'm beat." She smiled. "You taught me that."

Somewhat flustered, he rose. "I'll get ya a glass."

Her eyes glued to his stooped shoulders, she withdrew the vial, broke it over his whiskey, and slipped the tiny pieces in her pocket.

A swaggered waddle brought him back to the desk with an empty glass. Whiskey splashed into both. A pudgy hand set one in front of her. He lowered his bulk into the chair and raised his glass. A triumphant grin bared his decaying teeth. "To good times." He took a gulp, swished the liquor around his mouth, and swallowed.

With a nod, she took a sip. "Where d'you get Soputton whiskey? Sure is delicious."

He picked up the bottle. "The Gov' takes care of his staff. We gets a bottle twice a moon cycle, more if we do good."

He poured another shot of the amber liquid. His eyes widened. Awareness crept over his features. "I don't feel so great. What ya—" The words slurred. The glass tipped. Whiskey pooled on the well-worn desk. His cheek hit the surface with a dull smack.

Penee jumped to her feet, cleaned up the mess, and put her glass away. Jonto's keys in hand, she hurried to her cell. Two pillows created a body like mass under the blankets on the cot. A glance around the cell made her bite her lip. "It'll have to do." She turned off the light, shrugged on her heavy jacket, and stuffed her long braid under a black, woolen cap.

A quick peek out the window assured her dark clouds and falling snow obscured the wintery landscape of TaSneach, Soputto's largest moon. The only lights, one in the guardhouse by the gate and two in the upper story of the main house, left the penal colony in shadow. She stood in the hall, absorbing the quiet. Trepidation mixed with excitement made her giddy. A long, calm breath slowed her pounding heart. An exhale set her in motion. The cell key turned in the lock. She listened, heard nothing to alarm her, unlocked the back door, and returned the keys to the office. A cautious survey of the snowy terrain turned up nothing alarming. She slipped into the darkened compound.

Frigid temperatures kidnapped the oxygen from her lungs. Cold burned her eyes. The temptation to wait until spring made a fleeting appearance. *I have to find Elf first.* The scattered remains of the broken vial disappeared in the drifts as she crept along the compound wall. A glance back assured her the blowing snow obscured her footprints. She searched the enclosure. No one else had ventured into the lousy weather. Her goal, a large warehouse across the way, looked dark and forbidding. Key in hand, she sprinted to the rear entrance and unlocked it. Inside, she strode between shelves to an area filled with stacked boxes.

A door creaked open. Light flooded the space. She ducked behind a stack of boxes and squatted in a shadowed corner, her heart pounding. Panic ordered her to run; common sense held her motionless.

A voice called out. "We know you're in here. Come on out."

Military boots hitting the stone floor covered her startled inhale. *How did they find out I was missing so soon?*

Abrupt quiet pressed her lower.

An exit door on the far side of the building flew open. A flurry of snowflakes preceded by a blast of arctic air swirled in the wake of a man's dash into the night.

Guards poured from the building. Penee held her breath. The furtive tread of boots so close she could feel their vibration suspended her exhale. Her cousin's expensive cologne permeated the cold air. She forced herself to fade, to become her environment, a skill she had learned from Elf.

Footsteps retreated. Air whispered from her overtaxed lungs. The lingering aroma of sweet spice triggered memories she wished to forget.

At last the overhead lights dimmed. The door closed. She waited, a shadow, unmoving and invisible.

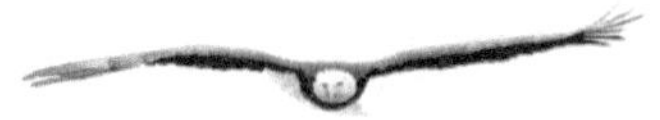

Prologue II - SnowScape - 2

Cold creeping into her body forced Penee to standing. When no alarm sounded, she stamped the numbness from her feet and legs and rubbed her aching arms. Pale-blue lights positioned on the interior walls of the warehouse highlighted her misty exhale. She shoved a box under a high window, climbed up, and peered out. Clouds, heavy with snow, obscuring the light of Chearra, Soputto's red moon, threw a starless mantle of black over the compound.

If I'm going, now's the time.

She moved a box with a blue circle obscured in its logo into the light, withdrew her knife, and slit open the top. Dressed in the gray and white polar gear and insulated boots she had hidden earlier, she slipped her knife into a hidden pocket, pulled the fur-lined hood of her polar suit over her woolen cap, and tucked renegade wisps of hair out of sight. A face covering masked her features. Insulated polar mittens hid her feminine hands. Her pack strapped on, she slipped out into the night.

The crunch of marching feet on snow brought her heart to her throat. Guards in polar gear came to a halt, broke formation, and began a search of the grounds. Torn between retreat and losing her chance at escape, she hesitated. A figure rounded a corner and walked toward her. Fight or flight fought for supremacy. *I'll just have to fake it.*

He halted at her side. Amethyst-blue eyes fastened on her face stirred a memory she couldn't quite grasp.

A whistle shrilled through the night.

He shoved a pair of night goggles in her hand. "Put these on."

Her instincts warred. *Do I trust him?*

"No time to debate." He held out a hand. "Give me your pack."

Guards running from every direction assembled at the compound's center. She donned the goggles and shrugged off the pack.

"Hide in their midst." Her companion pushed her into motion.

Falling in behind a running guard, she joined their formation. A second whistle sounded. The guards sprang to attention. Imitating their stance, she held her breath.

A shaft of light shot across the compound from the front door of the main house. Skultar, draped in a fur cloak, stalked toward them and spoke with the captain.

The Governor's heavy-lidded eyes inspected the group. The surrounding men tensed. Penee, grateful for her tall stature, stared straight ahead. A man arrived with a scent hound. Skultar offered him one of her scarves. The handler unclipped the leash. The trained dog sniffed the feet of each guard. Penee sucked her energy inward.

The scent hound paced her row twice, stopped by the man to her right, and growled.

Skultar strode down the row. He fixed a penetrating gaze on the man. "Remove your goggles."

The guard complied. Skultar side-stepped.

The dog's ears perked up. A sharp bark echoed through the night as it shot across the compound. At a sign from the captain, the handler gave chase.

With military precision, Skultar marched to the front of the formation.

"My cousin has escaped. *I* want her found. The man who brings her to my quarters *unharmed* will be well-rewarded."

The whistle shrilled. Amidst the chaos of scattering men, Penee made her way to the far side of the warehouse and stopped to collect her scattered wits. *How do I escape with guards everywhere and morning approaching?* She pulled the brim of her hood lower. *I take a chance and wish for luck.*

Joining the search, she traversed the compound, dodged into the shadow of a low hanging roof, and glanced at the sky. The intermittent snow of earlier fell in earnest. Random flakes turned into thick flurries. The air, opaque as white silk curtains, grew colder. Winter winds whistled between the buildings. Muffled footsteps faded into the distant.

A familiar figure ducked into view and motioned her to join him.

She hurried to his side, accepted her pack, and fastened it in place.

He gripped her arm. "We need to go. Skultar will discover all too soon that you're still missing. He'll order the guards to keep searching. They won't be happy about it."

She removed his hand. "I don't remember asking you to join me. How do I know I can trust you?"

"I haven't given you away yet, and I have no intention of doing so." He removed his goggles and face covering. The amethyst-blue eyes fixed on her face did not waver. "I told you I'd find you."

A distant memory surfaced—a boy who helped her a long time ago. Penee blinked. The past evaporated into the man in front of her.

He replaced his face gear. "One person escaping in this weather might make it. Two escaping doubles the chance of success. I can help. I'll explain everything when we're safe."

Penee stifled a sarcastic response. "We need to put some distance between us and the compound. Any ideas?"

"Follow me." At a little-used gate, he produced a key, unlocked it, and ushered her through.

Shoulder-high drifts covering the terrain made escape seem impossible. Through goggled eyes, she picked out the sagging roof of a building. Her companion trudged ahead of her. "I'll take the lead. Stay close." He forged the way to the old barn, swung a loose board to the side, and angled his body through the opening. She sidled past him. He wedged the board back into place. Two horse hounds greeted them with soft whines and noses, sniffing.

Amazed, she ran a hand over long silky fur. "Where? How?"

He placed a saddle over the largest hound's back. "I knew, after what you heard last night, you wouldn't wait long to attempt an escape. I figured we'd need transportation. Saddle up. It won't be long before the guards are out in force."

Penee held his commanding gaze with a questioning one of her own. "You were there?"

"I was. I promise I'll explain. We need to go."

Penee stored her questions away, secured the final strap on the saddle, and turned to find her companion's intent gaze watching her every move. A memory flashed. She pursed her lips. "Can you at least tell me your name, or do I call you stable boy?"

A satisfied laugh rustled his face covering. "About time you remembered. Name's Den." He grabbed his mount's reins. "This is Sager. Your hound is Tiza." He helped her to mount, shouldered the barn door ajar, and sprang into the saddle. Sager nickered and leapt through the opening.

Penee patted Tiza's side and slapped the reins. The lithe animal sprung into the winter blizzard. Eyes squinted in the cold winter light, Penee urged her after Sager. A siren whined. She thanked the storm gods for the snow covering their escape and their tracks.

Morning on TaSneach brought a modicum of light to the wintery terrain. Snow-heavy clouds the color of her maman's pewter bowls soaked up the dawn. Penee stole a glance at the sky. Fatigued beyond memory, she clung to Tiza's saddle. Some distance ahead, Sager and Den plowed through the waist-high drifts, forging a trail that lasted barely long enough for Tiza to bound through. Wind and snow erased their tracks, imprisoning them in white-out conditions.

A swirl of blinding white isolated her from Sager. Tiza floundered. Penee flew from the saddle, hit a high drift, and sank into a world of white. Soft snow closed over her head. Her hip hit solid ground. A muffled bark faded into profound stillness. A low hum took its place. She struggled to find her footing. Hands gripping her shoulders drug her upward. She broke the surface in the glare of headlights on a parked snow crawler, a guard on either side of her.

Penee stared into the face of Skultar Rados.

His expression held no warmth. "You are becoming quite tiresome, cousin." He scanned the snowscape. "I know someone helped you to get this far. Who?"

She fastened her attention on his sardonic features and concentrated on masking her thoughts.

Skultar glowered. "You can make this easy, or you can make it hard. Which will it be, Penesert?"

Her stony silence and blank expression inspired a flash of anger on his narrow features. With a steely gaze hinting at the unpleasantness to come, he motioned the guards to bring her along.

One gripped her arm. The other followed close behind. At the snow crawler, they shoved her into the back seat and sat on either side of her. Skultar climbed into the front. The engine purred to life. Wide tracks gripping the snow moved them toward the penal colony.

Penee stared at her hands. *One step forward and three steps back. Now what?*

Prologue II - SnowScape - 3

The blizzard conditions hampered the snow crawler's ability to navigate the winter terrain. Skultar ordered his men to make a detour. Penee felt a spark of hope as they pulled up to a base camp a half a turning's journey from the Penal Colony.

Skultar disappeared into a low building and reemerged looking somewhat less grim. After a brief discussion with the driver, the snow crawler crunched its way to a stop by a large, polyhedron-shaped tent. A soldier opened the door, jumped to ground, and assisted her from the crawler.

Skultar escorted her into the tent's warm antechamber, studied her for a long moment, and began removing his polar gear.

Mulish and leery, she folded her arms.

"Remove your gear, cousin. We aren't leaving until the weather clears. "When she didn't move, an intolerant gaze raked her face. "If you'd rather be stubborn and swelter, that is your choice. I'll see you inside."

Biting back an antagonistic response, she kicked off her boots and stripped off her polar suit. With a nod of approval, he ushered her into an elegantly furnished tent.

"You'll find suitable clothing laid out behind the screen."

She glanced at the hand gripping her arm.

The grip tightened. "Please don't make me regret not leaving you to freeze to death."

She mustered the meekest expression she could manage. "Thank you, cousin. I'm grateful you saved me."

The intensity of the eyes locked onto hers communicated volumes. She lowered her lids, an attempt at humility, and hoped he did not sense her boiling hatred.

With a grunt of satisfaction followed by a final warning look, he released her and crossed to the brazier at the center of the tent.

Behind the screen, she hung her prison clothes on hooks above the mosaic. An inventory of the clothes provided thrilled her. She slipped on warm leggings, a robe, and fur-lined slippers. With the luxurious feel of rich, silky cloth caressing her skin, she joined her cousin at a table set with china fit for a RomPeer.

The crystal goblets at their places glowed a deep, ruby red. Skultar lifted his wine to the light. "I suggest we both behave as adults." His eyes narrowed. "Let's attempt to have a conversation that does not end in yelling. I don't wish you ill, Penesert. Tell me why you constantly try to escape my care."

Penee examined the etchings on the fragile crystal glass.

Moments from her childhood filled her consciousness. The turning of her kidnapping, the last time she had spent with her mother and birth-mate, had been filled with camaraderie. The recollection of Elf's delight when she accomplished something with his help triggered a rush of deep sadness. Although they had only been five, they understood the importance of their shared destiny.

She gazed over the rim of her glass at her cousin. "You refused to return me to my home, to all I loved and understood. How can I not resent you?"

Skultar sipped his wine and set the glass on the table. "Do you know why I rescued you, why I had you brought to my home?"

"Some say you wanted to hold me for ransom. Others suggest you would be happy if I were dead. Something about me threatens your power. What is it, Skultar? Why do you keep me hidden on Soputto's moon? I am, after all, a Pheet Adolan woman with no power. I cannot rule. So, what is it about *me*?"

Inscrutability sculpted his aristocratic features. He rose to prowl the tent. Taller than average and slender, he reminded her of the great egret. When he turned, his narrow face reflected a moment of anguish before it went blank. The nostrils of his long nose flared. His lips vanished into a frown, then parted in a sigh.

"I am not an evil man, Penee. I rescued you from a prison cell, made certain you were cared for and well-educated. Your need to rebel, to escape my protection, has given me no choice but to hide you away."

Indignation bubbled up. Skultar's exasperated glare kept her silent.

"Do you think I enjoy having to earn a living in a penal colony on a frigid moon controlled by a foreign government? I'm as trapped as you are. Pheet Adole are hunted by an enemy who want us dead—who want *you* dead." He lifted his glass up in the light. "Our grandfather was the RomPeer of El SyrTundi on the planet of El Stroma. Eleo Predan filth destroyed our home. They murdered my family and yours. A process called Protariflee created you from an egg and a sperm carried in the womb of an Eleo Predan host mother. Your birth-mate is Eleo Predan. By accepting you as my ward, I have kept you alive." He tossed back the rest of his wine.

Penee stared at the ruby liquid in her glass. Conflict reared its head. The wine shimmered. *My mother loved me. Elf would never want me dead.* She sipped wine and thought about the overheard conversation, the reason she had attempted to escape. *You cajole, Skultar, yet I hear the lies in your voice. I know I am a threat to you.* She placed the elegant crystal on the table. "Where do I sleep?"

"You may rest on the cot behind the screen. I suggest you eat before retiring. The food at this outpost is excellent."

Penee fingered the fork by her plate. "I'm not hungry." Her stomach growled.

Skultar laughed. "I believe your belly has other ideas." He picked up a small bell.

A hand pulled the entrance curtain aside. Succulent smells preceded a servant into the space. He set an enticing array of items on the table, bowed to Skultar, and departed.

Before the curtain closed, Penee glimpsed Den in the background. Heart pounding, she turned her attention to filling her plate.

After an excellent meal, Skultar left to attend a meeting. Penee prepared for bed. Elusive sleep left her stretched out on her side, staring at the elaborate pattern on the back of the divider screen. An idle pursuit to calm her noisy thoughts turned serious. The mosaic's random design proved not to be random at all.

Careful not to give herself away, she strained to detect anything indicating her cousin had returned to the tent. Intermittent creaks and groans, the muffled sound of wind, and an occasional hiss from the fire in the brazier were all she could hear. Skultar had not returned.

She sat up and pushed aside her prison garments. Concealed within the wooden mosaic, small abnormalities connected, forming a map of the camp. Penee sucked in an excited breath. Ivy-like leaves wound from the main tent between several other structures and ended past the camp's perimeter. A tiny blue star glistened on a white mosaic tile. Not sure the map was meant for her, she scrutinized every inch of the screen. Wedged in a crack near the bottom where it curved around the head of the cot, she discovered a folded piece of paper. Muffled voices and muted footsteps on the carpeted floor sent her back to the cot, the paper clutched in her hand.

The soft tread of her cousin's slippered feet stopped beside the screen. His cologne scented the air. She gave a small sigh and shifted on the cot. When he moved away, she forced herself to remain still. Sounds of his preparations for the night drifted into eventual quiet. An occasional snore suggested he slept. She almost smiled. *If I can feign sleep, so can Skultar.*

Adrift between slumber and wakefulness, she gave him time to tire of listening and fall asleep. Oppressive silence filled the tent. Curiosity won at last. She unfolded the paper. *Do nothing until he leaves you in the morning. Rest.* The words dissolved; the paper vanished in a puff of gray vapor.

Mouth-watering odors woke her to the sounds of Skultar moving about the tent. He rapped on the screen.

"Wake up. We have a guest joining us. I'll be back with him in one quarter circle."

Dressed in her luxurious new clothes, she calmed her dislike of Skultar and stepped from behind the screen. Her cousin's continued absence was a relief. Maybe he was too busy to join her. A peek beneath the silver lid of a chafing dish steaming on a side table made her stomach respond with a deep rumble.

Skultar ushered a thin, stooped man into the space. "Penee, this is Furrnoce. I will leave you to get acquainted." Within the swirl of his fur-lined cloak, he departed.

The man bowed. Shrewd eyes held her gaze a moment too long. The subtle tingle of a mind probe prompted a warning shiver. Controlling the impulse to mask her thoughts, she focused her attention on food. Another rumble in her belly helped to establish her lack of interest in anything but the meal.

She moved to the side table. "I suggest we serve ourselves."

He reached for her elbow. Instinct sent her a step backward.

The shrewd gaze raked her face. "Please go first, my dear."

A servant entered to remove the lid from the chaffing dish. Steam wafted upward. Succulent aromas beckoned.

She held out a plate. Deep blue eyes with amethyst sparks met hers. Her tension eased. She smiled at Furrnoce. "This smells divine."

The servant filled Furrnoce's plate, followed them to the table, and filled their glasses with juice. In the tradition of the Pheet Adole, he addressed the male. "Do you require anything else, SorTech Furrnoce?"

A fleeting frown creased the man's brow. "Leave us."

The servant bowed and retired.

Penee savored a delicious bite. "I've always been curious about SorTechory."

Furrnoce's eyes narrowed. "If you were male, you could pursue it. As it is, you must hide your gifts."

She lifted her glass and sipped the sweetness of pears. "Throughout history the Pheet Adole have murdered women with mystical talent. I'm grateful to be ordinary."

He laughed. "Ordinary? Have you not looked in the mirror? Nothing about you is ordinary."

Puzzlement furrowed her brow. "I am not of peasant stock if that's what you mean."

The SorTech finished his meal and patted his lips with the napkin. "Skultar told me you were good, Penesert." He pushed back his chair. "I suggest we get to work."

She painted on a bland smile. "Work?"

A small squat man entered with a large, black box. He set it on the chair and removed the front cover to expose a panel of knobs and buttons. With a reverential bow, he departed.

Furrnoce placed a patch on his temple. His penetrating eyes fastened on her face. "Let's discover just how talented you are."

Penee remained in her chair, arms folded across her chest. "I am a Pheet Adolan woman with no sorcerer's talent. Do what you must do."

The tingle of SorTechory crept up her spine and spread throughout her body. A surge of current electrified her mind. Her thoughts curled into a nugget of consciousness. Childhood memories brought tears to her eyes.

Furrnoce turned knobs and pushed buttons until she wondered if she could continue to hold him at bay. A fist hit the top of the box. "Stop fighting me."

More current pierced her mind. She came to her feet, let out a soft whimper, and stumbled to her knees. Another jolt of the SorTech's energy surged through her. Gasping, she grabbed her head. A scream of pain laced with anger burst from her throat. She hit the carpeted floor of the tent, motionless. Techno energy melted from her mind. She restrained her desire to leave the SorTech mindless for the rest of his existence.

Skultar hurried into the space. "What did you discover?"

The sound of the lid snapping into place preceded Furrnoce's frustrated response. "She is either what she seems—a woman with no power—or she is far more talented than either of us expected."

Loud footfalls stopped just inside the entrance. "We have trouble headed this way. You'd better come with me." The footsteps retreated.

Skultar nudged her with his toe. "What about her?"

Furrnoce snarled. "Leave her. She'll be out for a while."

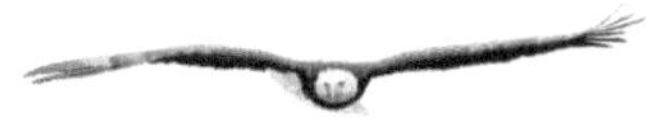

Prologue II - SnowScape - 4

Penee waited until retreating footsteps had faded into the faint howl of the TaSneach winds buffeting the polyhedron.

The soft pop of pressure changing in the tent kept her prone.

A male figure, dressed for arctic weather, ducked into the main tent, dropped her polar gear onto a chair and hurried to her side. Strong hands helped her to sitting. Den's startling eyes searched her face. "Can you stand?" His hand gripped hers.

Temples throbbing, she came to her feet. The tent spun. When it stabilized, she glared at The Box. "SorTechory." A deep breath steadied the shaking in her limbs. "How long do we have?"

He shrugged. "A herd of mammuthun cows is on a warpath, heading straight for the outpost. Couple that with the blizzard reaching its peak; add problems with the communication equipment to the list; and I think they'll be busy for a while." He handed her a glass of juice. "Drink this. Then change into your polar gear. We need to leave as soon as you can manage it."

"Leave in a blizzard?"

He took the empty glass, thrust her gear into her hands, and motioned her toward the screened area. "Horse hounds thrive in this kind of weather." He gave her a small push. "Go. The more time we have before they discover you're missing, the better our chances."

Sluggish but determined, she kicked off the fur-lined slippers, stripped off her borrowed clothes, and pulled her polar suit over her more serviceable penal clothing. After stowing her knife in its hidden pocket, she pulled on her winter boots, and emerged from behind the screen. Den waited by the door, her face mask and snow goggles in his hand. She settled them in place, tugged her hood over her wool hat, and pulled on her mittens. They slipped from the tent, their presence obscured by blinding snow and howling wind.

Den shepherded her to a low, snow-buried building a short hike from the main camp and urged her through the door ahead of him. Tiza, already saddled, pressed her nose into Penee's mittened hand. Den tossed Penee her pack. "Hurry."

Sager blew out a cloudy, snorted breath. Den led him to a second door. Moments after he mounted, Sager leapt into the blinding whiteness.

Penee swung a leg over Tiza's back. The hound launched into the whiteout. A backward glance showed blizzard-blown snow obliterating everything. She, Tiza, and their companions were as invisible to the outpost as it was to them.

Darkness crept upon them with no break in the wind, snow, or diving temperatures. Den reined in Sager and waited for her to come alongside.

"We need to find shelter. Big crater up ahead. Stay close. Trust Tiza. She has great instincts." He switched on a blue light attached to the back of his hood. "If you lose sight of this, keep yelling. I'll find you." He turned on her hood-lights, one green one in the front and a red one in the back.

"Let's go." Den nudged Sager in the ribs.

Penee patted Tiza's neck. "Go on, girl. Don't lose them."

The trek to the crater was quick; the journey down the slanting side— laborious. Frigid cold numbed her hands. Her face tingled beneath her mask. A blast of wind plastered snow on her goggles. A frantic swipe of her hand left her staring at featureless terrain obscured by blowing snow. The wind's howling refrain, the only sound, amplified her growing panic. Air hissed from her lungs. *Where are you, Den?*

Nerves steeled, she focused on Tiza. The horse hound plodded onward. Den, hood-lights gleaming, stepped into sight, grabbed Tiza's reins, and guided her through a snow-obscured opening. Darkness like a living thing closed around them. A whispery whine drifted toward them. Tiza's soft bark answered.

A short distance ahead, the world of winter misted away, taking Penee's fear with it. Sager stood in the light of a blazing fire, his saddle steaming beside it. A stooped figure wiped him down with a furry pad.

Amethyst blue eyes gleaming, Den helped her to dismount. Questions shouted for answers. She glanced at Den's chiseled profile. *Can I trust you?*

He guided her to a low bench then led Tiza to Sager's side, removed her saddle, and went to work rubbing her down.

Penee pulled off mittens, removed her face gear, and unfastened her hood. While the fire's heat warmed her extremities, she observed the old man working with Den. His bald head gleamed in the firelight. Snow white hair falling from just above the ears was drawn back into a thin queue. A single, white braid hung from the chin of his clean-shaven face. A twisted spine robbed him of height, although even a straight spine would not have brought him above Den's shoulder. They worked in congenial silence.

Her puzzled gaze wandered their surroundings. Rough-hewn wood defined the walls of what seemed to be part barn, part cabin. Where the men worked, straw covered the ground. Near her, the raised stone fire-pit, surrounded by a hodgepodge of rickety seats, was built on a hard-packed dirt floor. The rest of the empty chamber gave her the feeling it waited to be defined. She looked up. No ceiling—only a dome of pitch-black obscurity.

The horse hounds, watered and fed, curled up near the fire. Den beckoned her to join him. "Penee, this is Irstant, my mentor and friend. He is glad you're safe. Let's take off our polar gear. Skultar cannot follow us to this place."

Irstant stared her direction, his filmy eyes unseeing. A brief smile tugged the corner of his mouth.

Den raised a brow. "He suggests there are better ways to ask questions than doing a mental probe."

Penee's cheeks flushed hot pink. "I am sorry. Can he...you hear me?"

"He can hear, but he cannot speak or see. Get comfortable by the fire, and he'll answer your questions." Den helped Irstant to a low seat close to the horse hounds, shed his winter wear, and sat opposite his mentor.

Penee draped her gear over a bench to dry. Warm for the first time since morning, she straddled a three-legged stool and gazed at their host.

The old man raised a scarred hand.

Den met Penee's questioning gaze. "Irstant has asked me to tell you a bit of his history." He stared into the flickering flames. "As a young man, he joined the Order of Esprow on the planet of Persow to train in the arts of DiMensionery. He worked hard, honed his talents, and rose through the ranks to the level of VarTerel." Den raised his eyes. "In this position, he worked with the Galactic Guardians to maintain Trilemma throughout the Universe."

Penee frowned. "Trilemma? I have not heard the term."

Den looked to his mentor, listened, and returned his attention to her. "Trilemma is the balance of good and evil. It pertains to Humans, planets, solar systems, and universes."

"But don't we want only good?" She squirmed to look at Irstant. "Wouldn't it be better to rid the universe of evil all together?"

Den shifted his stool closer to his mentor. "You may speak through me, my teacher." He looked at Penee. His face went blank.

"I will explain."

Changes in the timber and inflection of Den's voice took her by surprise. Her gaze flashed to the older man.

He tugged his braided beard. "Yes, Penesert, I can speak through another if permission is granted, but do it only to expedite a conversation. Let me explain Trilemma, so I may withdraw from Den's mind.

"Within the Inner Universe, the shadow side of nature is DosWah. DosWah is essential to the continued maturing of All. Light without shadow, or vice versa, creates imbalance. Light comes from darkness. From the midst of light, darkness appears. It is not *destroying* DosWah that is important. It is maintaining the balance of good and evil which allows the Universe to thrive that is vital."

"Thank you, Irstant. I believe I understand."

A shiver shook Den's shoulders. His features enlivened. For a short time, he stared into the fire, gold-orange flames warming the deep amethyst in his eyes. "I understand, Irstant." He took up the narrative. "Perhaps forty sun cycles ago, an evil force traveled across the DéCussate to the planet of TreBlaya."

Penee's pulse quickened. She searched Den's face. "The MasTer?"

He nodded. "Irstant appreciates your quickness. He knows this strikes close to home. The MasTer sought to become the supreme leader of the Inner Universe. His plan included stripping it of all good. He knew he could not touch the Galactic Guardians. But their VarTerels—that was a different story. One by one, his Mocendi captured, tortured, and murdered them. The MasTer's followers believed Irstant to be the last." He released a breath. "Unbeknownst to them, one more VarTerel fought for balance in the Universe, one who had grown up with Irstant on the planet of Persow. The VarTerel came to Irstant's rescue, but not before The MasTer's Mocendi had cut out Irstant's tongue and blinded his eyes."

Silence broken only by the occasional snap of the fire or whimper of a sleeping hound infused the small group. Penee's mind raced. She remembered little of her home on TreBlaya, but memories of Maman, Elf, and her Aunt Rasi were always with her. The woman she knew as Maman had spoken of a man, her birth-mate, who had escaped to the Inner Universe, a man for whom she had searched all her life.

"Is your friend alive?" Penee held her breath.

Irstant turned filmy eyes in her direction. Den answered. "He lives."

The old man's face grew sad. Den took a breath. "Your maman died, Penee."

She pressed a hand to her heart. "Did she live long enough to find her birth-mate?"

Den nodded. "She found him before she passed."

"Aunt Rasi?"

Sympathy filled Den's reply. "She has also joined the ancestors."

Penee moaned. Sadness as ferocious as the blizzard outside threatened to drown her. The need to be alone launched her to her feet. No visible exit route left her sitting back on her stool, immersed in her emotions. Overwhelming love for her mother and aunt surged through her. For the first time, she understood the emptiness that followed the final passing of a loved one.

Unable to vanquish her pain, she raised tear-damp eyes to Den's face. "I have no words for what I'm feeling."

Irstant's voice filled the space. "We Humans understand little of death except the void left behind. Those you love and have lost are with you every turning of your existence. The gift *you* can give to your mother and Rasiana, Penesert, is that of achieving your destiny, of becoming *all* you can be. Den and I are here to help you do so."

She wiped a tear from her cheek. "If I am to achieve my destiny, I *must* find Elf. I am certain he's alive. If he weren't, I'd know."

Low rumbling growls from the horse hounds froze the expression on Irstant's weathered face. Den supported him to his feet.

Irstant's unseeing eyes swept the area beyond the fire. His mouth shaped one word—Trouble.

Prologue II - SnowScape - 5

Den draped a fur cloak over his mentor's shoulders, tossed Penee her gear, and scrambled into his polar suit. With a quick scan of the space, he shouldered his pack.

Penee strapped hers on. "What about the horse hounds?"

"Saddle Tiza. I'll get Sager."

Irstant shook his head.

Den whistled. The hounds shrunk to the size of large dogs. Huddled next to the VarTerel, they snuffled the air. Penee hurried to Den's side. Sager growled.

A tremor rocked the space. Impenetrable darkness descended. Wind howled and silenced in an instant.

Penee ceased to breathe. Her heart's rhythmic tempo slowed. Pressure squeezing the sound from her ears radiated pain down her neck into her jaw. The smell of logs burning vanished along with the musky odor of damp fur.

Memories of her lessons on TreBlaya came to her rescue. Panic changed to a need for action. Her concentration sharpened. The soft sensation of shields surrounding her and her companions gave her a moment to stabilize.

"Well done." Irstant's voice murmured in her mind.

Den's hand on her arm and a horse hound brushing her side steadied her.

Penee stared between snowflakes the size of a saucer at an immense crater scooped from the moon's surface. Shimmering ice formations covered it from one side to the other. She released the shields. "Where are we?"

Den stamped his feet. An exhaled breath misted the air. "Soputtons call this Cratere le Cici. It is at the northernmost polar round of TaSneach."

"Are we here for a reason?" The cold caught the words, cracked them like thin ice on a pond, and scattered them in the wind.

Irstant made a gurgled sound in his throat. Not waiting for help, he plodded between formations.

His attention fixed on his mentor, Den explained. "His VarTerel's staff is hidden in this crater. We need to locate it. Look for a fist-sized crystal glowing at about my height. Take Tiza." He pointed. "You look that way. Shout if you find it."

She scanned the sizable area. "If I get lost—"

"Tiza will bring you to this spot. The sooner we find the staff, the sooner we can travel beyond Skultar and his SorTech's reach." He called Sager to heel and strode in the opposite directions.

Tiza barked

Penee scratched her long ear. "It's just you and me, girl. Lead the way."

The exuberant hound forged a pathway through knee-high snow over ice-covered ground. Penee trudged after it. One breathtaking sculpted formation after the other left her speechless. She stopped to stare in wonder at layers of lacy scallops forming a mountainous cone the diameter of the outpost tent. Tiza's bark prodded her along the fast disappearing path to a field of giant, iridescent-blue spikes gleaming in the wintery light. On the far side of the field, she halted, her startled gaze locked on a huge feline head with eyes as big as Skultar's best porcelain plates.

Breathless from the hike and the startling beauty surrounding her, she stood shivering from the cold. A spasm of fatigue doubled her over. Tiza's breath on her cheek acted like a rejuvenating tonic. Penee blew out a cloud of misty air and patted the hound. "Take me to the staff."

The beautiful head swept her direction. Pink-grey eyes stared into hers. She grew to horse size. The message was obvious. *"Ride."*

With a sigh of relief, Penee climbed onto her back. Tiza bound between intricate ice constructs resembling leafless deciduous trees. She galloped by a formation mimicking a stream rushing down a steep hillside and wound her way through a series of majestic frozen arches. The horse hound slowed to walk at the edge of an immense frozen pond. At its center, a circle of eight-foot tall, diamond-clear pillars surrounded an opaque column taller than a man. She slid to the ground, awed by the spectacular beauty.

Huddled close to the horse hound, Penee concentrated on calling Irstant to the pool. A light flared. The VarTerel materialized at her side.

Den on Sager flashed into sight and dismounted, his seriousness pulsating like a pounding heart. "How brave are you, Penee?"

Her questioning gaze darted to Irstant, whose slack features told her nothing. His filmy eyes did not blink. Inertia held him captive. He shook himself. His trembling hand offered her a crystal key.

Den's voice penetrated her confusion. "Only a woman can retrieve the staff."

Penee surveyed the pool. "How do I reach it? The surface is sheer ice."

"The key." Den's expression grew distant.

An exasperated breath fogged her goggles. With an impatient swipe, she turned to Irstant.

The key floated above his palm, rising as though lifted by the wind. *"Catch it!"* Irstant's mental command propelled her into an upward lunge. Her fingers wrapped around the key. Fiery cold blistered her palm. The crater blurred. The glowing column beckoned.

She focused on a spot beside it. White light blinded her. She blinked the brightness away to gaze in awe at the towering column. A shaft of sunlight shot through a break in the clouds, directing her attention to a solid ice chain draped like a multi-strand necklace around it. The key bit into her palm. A circuit of the column brought her to a solid ice padlock fastening the ends of the chain.

Unease gripped her. The hair on the back of her neck prickled. Her gaze darted over the pond. Furtive movement froze her into stillness. A shadowy, amorphous form oozed between the pillars. Its plaintive howl pierced her heart, freezing it. She crumpled to her knees. Hunger for power clawed her moral principles to shreds. The shadow loomed over her. Cold clutched her throat. An attempt to stand failed. Desire's claws worked to strip her of honor, integrity, and self. As though it belonged to another, her hand reached for the column.

"No!" She yanked it back, lunged to her feet, and, dodging the shadow, inserted the crystal key in the lock.

Heat raced up her arm and, pooling in her chest, thawed her frozen heart. Mental clarity reignited her sense of self. The shadowy form shriveled into a moaning heap. She turned the key. The padlock melted. Water dripping between her fingers sizzled where it hit the pond's solid ice surface. Effervescent steam concealed the column, the pillars, and the arches beyond. Winter winds whipped the vaporous haze into wisps that faded away. Penee stared in wonder at a hand-hewn wooden staff crowned with a glowing quartz crystal.

Beyond the pillar-enclosed space, the shadowy form regained its menacing stature, lifted its arms, and wailed.

Penee quaked with a hunger to hold the staff, to feel the weight of it, to wield its power. Her strength of will battling the shadow, she backed away. It fought to snatch control. She embraced her honest desire to return the staff to its true owner and opened her mind to the VarTerel.

Irstant's voice spoke through her.

> *"Staff of Light, the spell releases,*
> *Mending all our shattered pieces.*
> *A woman's courage has set you free.*
> *Return with power and speed to me."*

Quietude claimed the pool. Penee felt the VarTerel withdraw from her mind. The shadow misted into nothing.

She released a shuddering breath. Clarity as profound as the silence settled over her. The staff quaked. Radiance illuminated its crystal crown.

Irstant raised his arm. The staff, its blurred image streaming behind, streaked across the pool into his hand. Gnarled fingers clasped it. The VarTerel straightened to his full height. Dark eyes blazing with newfound sight came to rest on her face.

The once mute voice boomed. "Thank you, Penesert Tamahine el Stroma, for the strength of your integrity and the return of Usolamet. Trilemma reigns!"

Penee flashed to his side. Den, eyes shining, stepped opposite. Tiza and Sager loped forward and shrunk to waist high, expectant gray eyes on their master.

Irstant lifted the staff, then lowered it. "Skultar heads this way. Hold on to the shaft."

A bolt of lightning zigzagged the domed sky. Thunder rumbled. Dizziness hit so hard Penee doubled over.

Den's hand touched her shoulder. "Thinking backward in time will help you stabilize."

She swallowed the desire to vomit and tried to remember her walk through the sculpted ice garden. The queasiness passed. She straightened and gasped in wonder. A night dome sprinkled with stars surrounded them in all directions.

Usolamet dimmed. Irstant's spine twisted. His eyes filmed over. Den supported him with a hand on his elbow. His smile beamed. "We're in Mittkeer, The Land of All Time and No Time. Skultar does not have the power to follow us. He will know when he finds the staff missing we've used this route to escape."

Penee, her brain reeling, tried to sort through the rapid changes occurring in her life. "What's next?"

"We must deliver you to the people who will take you to meet the Universal VarTerel and to find your birth-mate."

She frowned. "I am not a package, Den. Even though Skultar forced me to be subservient, Maman trained my birth-mate and me to be self-reliant."

Irstant stirred and leaned on the staff. His stern features softened. Den nodded.

"Irstant is glad you are independent. Your destiny dictates that you have the courage to trust your instincts." He scanned the star-laden dome. "Right now, we must follow our guide or remain in Mittkeer forever."

He whistled. Tiza and Sager trotted ahead. Penee fell in beside the VarTerel, annoyed that he hadn't provided more information.

Irstant squeezed her arm. *"I will share more when we have reached our safe haven."*

The clarity of his words in her mind took her by surprise.

"You possess the gift of telepathy, Penesert. Once before, you heard me speak in your mind. You summoned me to the ice pool."

Memories caught her off guard.

The TreBlayan turning had been a memorable one. The MasTer's withdrawal and Maman's return had brought Aunt Rasi out of hiding. After celebrating with an excellent meal, Maman suggested a game of mental secrets. She had placed a thought in Elf's mind, then directed Penee to tell her what it was. Penee's excitement when she found it made her clap her hands and giggle. When she had shared the secret, Maman asked her to place a thought in Elf's mind. Several failed tries left Penee in tears. On the verge of giving up, she had fixed her thoughts on her love for Maman. Elf grinned. Maman beamed. Penee jumped up and down with excitement. She had used telepathy for the first time.

Happiness warmed her. She glanced at Irstant. *"Where are you taking me?"*

"For now, that must remain my secret." He plodded onward.

Penee brushed aside her irritation at his gruff reply. *"How did your staff become trapped in the column?"*

The old man kept walking.

Den's voice drifted through the eternal night. "Irstant was working with a mystic guardian on the planet of Persow when The MasTer's Mocendi captured him. Glorya's talents included psychokinesis. The moment he realized the Mocendi and their SorTech had found him, he sent a telepathic message to her. From her home in Rainbow Gorge, Glorya snatched the staff from his hand. Mindful of his instructions to hide it out of reach of all Pheet Adolan males, she fled to TaSneach, created her own sculpture in Cratere le Cici, and encased the staff in ice. After setting a seal that allowed only a woman to retrieve it, she got word to Relevart. Her message helped him to rescue Irstant. The VarTerel took his wounded friend to Soputto to heal. Before he departed, he told Irstant where to locate the staff and about the charm."

Irstant raised the subject of their conversation. The crystal Usolamet glowed. Sager and Tiza trotted to his side. His blind eyes glinted in the dim light. He planted the staff on the starscape beneath their feet. *"Hold on."*

Penee gripped the smooth wood. Den placed his hand above hers. A star shot across the night dome. Sager sniffed the air. The landscape of All Time and No Time blurred. A wave of nausea left Penee gasping. She sought a happy memory. Her stomach settled.

She pulled off mittens and goggles, shoved her hood back, and gazed in awe at yet another new environment.

Prologue II - SnowScape - 6

The first thing to register after her extended stay on TaSneach was the lack of snow. Penee unfastened the top of her polar suit and shaded her eyes to look up at a cloudless blue sky. A rush of impressions—damp air in her lungs, lots of greens and golds, the hounds barking up ahead, and a mix of intriguing smells—all left her grinning.

Irstant tipped his head to listen. A brief smile changed his features from serious to relaxed. With a contented sigh, he led the way along a faint trail toward the distant sound of falling water.

Penee trailed behind, soaking in the temperate rainforest's beauty and celebrating the lack of winter. The melodic whispering of a breeze traveling through the treetops mesmerized her. Long-held tension evaporated into the leaves' rustling chorus. Her worries hitched a ride on air currents that wound their way through mountain passes and over the towering peaks.

She picked up her pace as the sound of water grew more insistent. Not far ahead, Den waited with Irstant by a footbridge over a creek. The elder VarTerel leaned on his staff, his blind eyes shut, his expression peaceful.

Den's features had lost their harried look. He guided his mentor onto the bridge. "We'll be able to rest soon."

Penee didn't even try to suppress the grin pulling her lips taut. Thrilled to learn the end of their journey drew near, she ambled after them. Midway across the bridge, she stopped to watch water cascading down the side of a rocky outcropping into the creek. With childish delight, she leaned over the railing. Her soft laughter mixed with the gurgle of water wandering over and around rocks into the woods beyond. She stared ahead at the trees flowing down the majestic mountains to a small acreage of flat land reclaimed by mulch and moss, broad-leaved plants, and startling scarlet and yellow flowers. From the branch of a pine tree, a small gray owl hooted a welcome.

Irstant hobbled off from the bridge. Tiza and Sager ran from the woods to sit, one on either side of him, their warm gray eyes alert, their noses sniffing the air. He raised the staff. A glowing corona enclosed the crystal. The VarTerel's spine straightened. Bronze eyes gleamed. His vibrant voice rang out.

> *"Arise from places deep and hidden*
> *Into a present that's not forbidden.*
> *Emerge to bring your comfort here,*
> *That we may rest and find good cheer."*

Words took the shape of iridescent dragonflies, sailed high above the trees, and circled down into the glimmering luminescence rising from the forest floor. Log walls, a moss-covered roof, a broad porch with a swing solidified in the late-turning light. The hazy form of a wooden walk leading to a group of small outbuildings hovered above the mulchy ground and materialized.

Tails waving, the horse hounds loped along it. Barking an excited chorus, they trotted back to the front porch.

Penee gaped. "Oh, my..."

Den grinned.

Irstant held Usolamet higher. Love shining in his eyes, he gazed at the cabin; released a long, emotion-filled sigh; and lowered the staff. The moment the tip touched the forest floor, his vibrance dimmed. Bronze eyes clouded to milky. His spine twisted, leaving him stooped and shrunken.

Dwarfed by the world, he moved with ponderous steps onto the porch. *"Come in and rid yourselves of your winter gear."* Not waiting, he entered the cabin.

Penee exchanged a glance with Den, then jogged up the wooden stairs. The horse hounds flopped down by the porch swing. Tongues hanging from the sides of their mouths accentuated their smile-like expressions.

Penee hesitated at the door.

"Come in, Penesert. Nothing in my home will harm you."

The warmth in his welcoming words erased her reluctance. She stepped over the threshold *and* glanced behind her. "Where's Den?"

"I've sent him to bring Relevart's emissaries. They will return soon." He reclined in a comfortable chair by a wood-burning stove, already radiating heat into the room. *"You'll swelter if you don't remove your gear. You will find fresh clothes in the guest room down the hall. Change and join me. I know you have questions."*

In the small bedroom, she found pants, a shirt, and handmade sweater on the narrow bed. Sturdy hiking boots sat on the braided rug. With a growing sense of freedom, she stripped off her polar gear. While washing up in the attached bathroom, she glimpsed herself in the mirror over the sink. Her eyes narrowed, then gleamed. She fetched her knife, gripped a handful of caramel-blonde hair, and started cutting. With a triumphant laugh, she dumped her shorn locks in the trash. "You don't control me any longer, Skultar Rados." She dressed, peered at her reflection, and grinned. "I look great. Everything fits. It's a new beginning."

In the main room, she settled in an overstuffed chair across from Irstant. "Thank you for the clothes. They're a perfect fit."

The old man's wrinkles deepened. *"Den thought you might appreciate something unconnected to your cousin."* His gnarled hand smoothed the *unfinished sweater in his lap.* The click, click of wooden needles mingled with the occasional crackle of the fire in the stove.

A sense of peace settled over the cabin. Penee ran her fingers through her short curls, smiled, and absorbed her new surroundings. Log walls joined to a roof supported by sturdy wooden rafters gave the illusion of openness to the large main area. Shabby but comfortable, the meager furnishings were arranged to accommodate the needs of someone who could not see. A bookshelf full of books, several small paintings, a picture of an older woman, a rifle hanging on the wall, and a fishing pole leaning in the corner lent a homey feel to the room.

Penee ran a hand over the sleeve of her sweater. *"You made this sweater, didn't you?"*

He nodded. *"Knitting helps me to concentrate."*

She settled more comfortably in her chair. "Tell me how you met Den."

The rhythmic clicking paused. Blind eyes blinked. The old man sighed and resumed knitting. *"When my friend rescued me from The MasTer's Mocendi, he brought me to Soputto. Den's mother, Miram, offered to take care of me. At that time, Den worked at the stables in Reachti, the capital of Igan. One turning, Miram arrived at my tiny hut in Til-a-Bah Park with an urgent request. For her safety and Den's, she needed to leave Soputto. I promised to take care of her son."*

"Has he been with you since then?"

The soft click of wood hitting wood accompanied Irstant's telepathic reply. *"Den, then sixteen, proved to be quite an asset. From the time I first met him, he exhibited mystical gifts. His talents were many. I offered to train him in the Arts of DiMensionery. We have worked together ever since."*

"When did you move here?" She glanced out the window. "This is Soputto, isn't it?"

Click, click, click... *"Yes. We are in the Wildwood of Astong. One turning, Den went to the village for supplies. While he was there, a villager informed him that strangers were in town looking for me. We decided it would be safer to move away from people our enemies could cajole, bribe, or frighten into giving us away. He found this cabin and brought me here."* Click, click, click... *"I taught him how to weave a charm to make it invisible whenever we left it or trouble approached."* He held up the unfinished sweater. *"I am making you a special sweater to match your eyes."*

"What do you know about my eyes?"

"Ah, my dear, your mismatched eyes, one blue, one green with gold specks, were famous before you were born. The Pheet Adolan Mocendi are divided into those who wish to end your life and those who wish to preserve it."

"The MasTer's Mocendi—" She swallowed a burst of anger. *"Do they want me dead?"*

"They wish to find you and make use of your talents."

Torn by a rush of mixed emotions, she pressed her booted feet to the floor. "Are my eyes why Skultar has kept me hidden?"

Irstant replaced the sweater in the basket and hoisted his twisted body to standing. *"Please let the dogs in."*

She opened the door to find two eager horse hounds waiting to enter.

A snap of Irstant's fingers brought Tiza to his side. The hound guided him to the corner of the room and nudged him with her nose.

Irstant crouched to lift a floorboard, exposing a hole underneath. Tiza snuffled inside it. When she raised her elegant head, she held a leather tube between her jaws. Gray eyes sought her master. Irstant replaced the board and climbed painfully to his feet. Tiza guided him to his chair, and, at his command, placed the tube in Penee's lap.

Irstant picked up the sweater and resumed knitting. *"Are you going to sit holding it all turning? Where's your curiosity, girl?"*

The tanned leather tube, not quite the length of her forearm, had seen better times. Scars at one end indicated someone had used a knife in an effort to pry the wooden lid free. Black streaks suggested fire had also been tried.

Penee held it up. "If fire and metal wouldn't open it, what do you suggest?"

Click, click... Silence. The old man's blind eyes turned in her direction. *"Force is never the key when working with enchantments, Penesert. What would your maman have done?"*

She remembered Maman showing her and Elf a leather-bound journal. It had a seal impossible to open except by— Penee smiled. "Maman would have allowed the object to tell her what to do."

Eyes closed, she cleared her thoughts. Attention fixed on the tube, she willed it to open. Nothing happened. A breath in slowed her growing frustration. She exhaled and let go of the outcome. Whispering a quiet pledge to honor the contents, she opened her eyes, and grasped the lid. It came away with a gentle twist. A parchment sealed with the Primal Insignia dropped into her lap.

She had seen the seal one other time. Eager to ask her cousin a question, she had entered his study without knocking. Skultar had been reading a document. He whipped it from sight, but not before she had seen the insignia. Less than pleased, he had sent her to her room with orders to stay there. Later that night, she had crept into the library. Dawn painted the sky coral by the time she found a reference to the seal. The following day when her cousin left the estate, she snuck into his study but found no sign of the document.

"Irstant, this insignia suggests the parchment is from El Stroma during the time of the Antediluvian Beings. How did you get it?"

He continued to knit. *"Examine the contents. Then we will talk."*

Someone had already broken the wax seal, so she unrolled the fragile parchment and read the precise calligraphic lettering.

THE AGE OF CONVERSION
CIRCA 100.09.001

A TURNING WILL COME WHEN THE PHEET ADOLE MUST
 CHANGE.
THEIR CULTURE AND VALUES WILL THEN REARRANGE.
A GIRL-CHILD BORN WITH THE MATRIARCH'S EYES
WILL HERALD THIS CHANGE IN THE PHEET ADOLE SKIES.

ONE BLUE EYE, ONE GREEN WITH SPECKLES OF GOLD
WILL BEGIN THE CONVERSION TO THE VALUES OF OLD.
AS A WOMAN FULL GROWN, SHE WILL LEAD AND AVENGE.
BUT WILL NOT CREATE HAVOC BY EXACTING REVENGE.

TO THE MEN WHO WILL HUNT HER AS A WOMAN OR GIRL
DO NOT MAKE THE MISTAKE OF HARMING THIS PEARL.
THE HAND THAT DOES ILL WILL DOOM ALL WHO INHERIT;
THOSE WHO TAKE CARE WILL CELEBRATE THEIR MERIT.

A SINGULAR WARNING TO PHEET ADOLE MEN
WHO THREATEN THE LIVES OF THEIR FEMININE KIN,
BEWARE YOUR SURVIVAL WILL BE AT THE WHIM
OF THOSE WHOSE VITALITY AND LIVES YOU HAVE DIMMED.

Penee lowered the parchment to her lap and clutched trembling hands to her chest. "Skultar knew this. He knew, and he kept me hidden." She raked her hands through her short hair. "What makes you so sure I am the one in the prophecy?"

Prologue II - SnowScape - 7

Irstant slid the wooden needle through the looped stitch. Ready to throw the thread, he paused. *"It doesn't matter what I think. It matters what your cousin and his associates think. Assuming you are the one..."* Several clicks followed. *"...what does Skultar have to gain by keeping you to himself?"*

She reread the prophecy. "The only thing that makes sense is that he wants to use my potential prestige to increase his own." Nibbling on her lip, she considered her cousin's decision to move to TaSneach, a colony of prisoners locked away in cells. They would never see her. "He can keep me hidden, so no one knows the prophecy has the potential to come true." Elbows resting on her knees, she stared at flickering colors in the window of the wood-burning stove. "He can't kill me, because his progeny will be cursed. But he can let someone else kill me." She straightened. "SorTechory. He can discover how much power I have, so he can use it to enhance his own."

Irstant inclined his head her direction. *"It appears your cousin has good reason to keep you to himself. What did he tell you of the Eleo Preda and what destroyed life on El Stroma?"*

"Only that they want all Pheet Adole dead, myself included."

"Do you know what destroyed life on El Stroma?"

"Skultar told me the Eleo Preda wanted to eliminate all Pheet Adole. They destroyed El SyrTundi to help achieve their goal." She frowned. "What are you getting at?"

Irstant placed the sweater on top of the basket. *"Lusktar Rados, your great grandfather, was the RomPeer of the Pheet Adole. He feared the power of the Eleo Preda, in particular, their longevity and their mystic gifts. He resolved to annihilate their race and culture. In retaliation the Vasro, a small band of Eleo Predan rebels, decided if their people could no longer live on El Stroma—many had fled to other planets—then neither could the Pheet Adole."*

Penee squirmed to the edge of her chair. "This is insane. My cousin tells me the Eleo Preda want us dead. You tell me the Pheet Adole want them dead. How do I extract the truth from the fabrications?"

Irstant maintained a thoughtful silence. He folded his hands in his lap. *"History, like anything else, is a matter of perspective. Historians bias it toward the perceptions of the time and the different cultures they represent. Your cousin's story is probably the one he learned from his parents and teachers."*

"So, what makes your version any truer than his?"

"Ah. That's the critical question, isn't it? If I were not blind, we would travel back in time so you could see for yourself. As it is, you will have to wait until you meet your mother's birth-mate to unravel the truth."

Penee slid the rolled parchment into the tube. "Is my mother's birth-mate the friend who rescued you from the Mocendi?"

Irstant's filmy eyes narrowed. *"Your mother's birth-mate is The Universal VarTerel. Relevart was smuggled to Persow as a small boy in the guise of Charid Darine. The couple who owned the farm adjacent to my father's adopted him. Catha, a mystic wise woman, often visited our farm. One turning, she brought Charid with her. While we got to know each other, she spoke at length with my maman. It seems she had sensed my gifts and suggested that Charid and I study the Arts of DiMensionery together."* He picked up his knitting, settled it on his lap, and slipped a needle through a loop.

Penee listened to the rhythmic click, click, click and watched the sweater grow along with her impatience.

At the end of the second row, Irstant lowered the needles. *"The choice to become a DiMensioner is an enormous commitment. One must take an oath to honor the life of all living things, to fight for justice and truth, and to serve mankind by defending and maintaining Trilemma throughout the Universe. I hesitated. Charid, with wisdom far beyond his sun cycles, convinced me to train with him. We became fast friends. At our initiation to VarTerel he was given the name of Relevart and I was named Irstant. We often worked together."* A grimace turned to a sad smile. *"The Mocendi captured me because I refused to listen when he told me they were near and I should leave at once. You see the results of my egoic stubbornness."*

Stitch by stitch, he cast off the last row, tied a knot, stuck the needles through the ball of yarn, and held up the sweater. *"What do you—"*

Both hounds came to their feet, noses pointing to the door. The sharp sound of hooves on the bridge quaked through the clearing.

The sweater dropped to the ground. Irstant came to his feet. *"My Staff!"*

Penee's eyes flew to Usolamet, leaning in the far corner. Tiza's growl deepened. Intent surging, Penee reached for the staff. It flew to her hand. Irstant grasped it. Tiza and Sager flashed to their side. The stove went out. The room wavered.

Penee gripped the staff tighter. Irstant's hand on her arm silenced her. Imitating his blanked mind, she held her breath. His telepathic words whispered, *"Repeat after me."*

> *"Time Distortion, transform our place*
> *Hide us deep within your space*
> *Obscure our presence and our thought;*
> *Do not allow us to be caught."*

Sucked backward like fluid through an upside-down funnel, their miniaturized bodies shot up to the wooden rafters and squatted behind a brace. Penee stared down at the vacillating scene below them.

Horses whinnied. Porch steps squeaked. The door burst open. Three undulating figures strode into the room. Two uniformed men began a search.

Their leader, clothed in the black and purple of a Rompeerial Klutarse, swept his piercing gaze from one side of the room to the other before pressing his lips together in a skeptical frown. The astute gaze made another pass, skimming the room from floor to ceiling. Narrowed eyes stopped on the brace opposite theirs. Perplexity deepened the furrows in his brow. He pivoted to stare up at their hiding place.

His sudden movement stirred the atmosphere into undulating ripples that spread outward to brush the walls and rebound.

Frustration clouding his expression, he wheeled to face his men. "Anything?"

A round-faced soldier scowled. "Nothing except dust and mouse turds. No one's lived here for a long time."

"Check outside, just in case."

The men departed. The Klutarse made a final slow inspection of the room, contemplated the rafters, and strode onto the porch.

Time ticked by. Horses snorting, snatches of conversation, and the dulled clattering of hooves over the bridge brought a sigh of relief from Penee. She glanced at Irstant.

He stood, head tilted and blind eyes closed. At last, he raised his staff.

> *"Distorted Time, set us free*
> *Place us where we ought to be*
> *Send us back to size and time*
> *With gratitude and thanks sublime"*

A subtle shift warmed Penee's heart. The cabin blurred. A breeze ruffled her short curls. Conscious awareness returned. She stood on the solid wood floor, her gaze fastened to a dimming Usolamet. Irstant turned filmy eyes in her direction.

"You did well, Penesert. I can see why Skultar is hungry to learn how talented you are." He yawned. *"I could use a nap."*

She guided him to his chair. "Your staff came to me. How?"

Her mind filled with his delighted chuckle. *"You called it. It responded. That is a first, my dear. We had best discuss your training, but not until I rest."* He held out the staff. *"Please put it in the corner."*

She leaned the staff against the wall and turned to find sleep had claimed him. Snuggling into her chair, she reviewed what had just occurred. *I have questions, Irstant.*

A soft snore, his only response, reminded her it had been several turnings since she had slept. She bent down to scratch the ear of the hound sprawled at her feet. "Warn me of trouble, Tiza."

The hound licked her hand and rested her elegant head on furry paws.

Penee's fatigue-heavy lids closed. The beginnings of sleep transitioned to dreaming. Images of a large lagoon laden with clouds and the bulbous body of an octopus swimming, its long tentacles trailing behind it, filled her with a sense of peace. A tingling sensation starting at her elbow traveled the length of her forearm, and changed to a sharp, blistering burn. She wanted to scream but couldn't find the sound.

Tiza woke her with a soft whine. Pink-gray eyes gazed into hers.

Penee sat upright, her heart pounding; her arm pressed to her chest. "I had the strangest dream." She shook her head. "I wish I could remember it."

Irstant sat, his hand on Sager's long neck. *"All is well, Penesert. Den arrives soon with Relevart's emissaries."* He patted the horse hound's head. *"If you have questions, now's the time to ask."*

She rubbed her arm and refocused her thoughts. "Please explain what just happened."

Irstant grew serious. *"I created a time/space distortion."*

"But we got smaller. How?"

He smiled. *"We didn't grow smaller. The time/space distortion sucked us back into another time and dimension."* His smile widened. *"I returned us to this time and place when we were safe."*

Penee shook her head. "Oh, Irstant, you make it sound so ordinary, so everyday." She leaned closer. "I want to learn more about DiMensionery. I want to understand my gifts and how to use them. Will you teach me?"

The filmy eyes glistened with tears. *"My time is short, Penee. Mairin and Lanli will take you to Relevart. He will see to your training."* Unabashed, he let the tears tumble down his weathered cheeks.

"I am so sorry, Irstant. Is there anything I can do?"

He picked up the sweater. *"You can humor an old man. Put this on next to your skin."*

She took it from his aged hands, laid it over the arm of her chair, and smiled at herself as she turned her back to the blind VarTerel. Stripping off her shirt, she slipped on the sweater. The moment it touched her flesh, it shrunk to skin-tight. Like a chameleon's scales, the colors morphed to flesh tones and the rows of stitches merged to a fine mesh.

She turned to find Irstant standing, staff in hand. *"Tell me, Penesert, how does it fit?"*

"It fits like a second skin." She marveled at the silky texture. "Why did you knit it for me?"

He reached out. *"Give me your hand."*

As their palms touched, Usolamet glowed. Irstant's seeing eyes shone with the brightness of bronze-circled obsidian. His spine aligned; his voice filled the cabin.

"In another time on another planet, soldiers heading into battle wore chain mail armor. I knitted this with spun silver graphene and fashioned it after that earlier garment. It will protect you from not only weaponry, but from Mocendi DiMensionery. Wear it always, Penee. Wear it knowing I honor the part you must play in El Stroma's return to life."

Usolamet dimmed. Irstant's eyes filmed over. *"Put your shirt on. We are about to have company."*

Penee prepared to guide Irstant onto the porch. The instant the door opened, Sager dashed across the bridge. Tiza waited with contained impatience. Irstant felt his way to the swing. As soon as he sat down, the extraordinary animal sprinted after her friend.

Penee leaned the VarTerel's staff against the wall and stared over the bridge. "Have you met them, Irstant?"

"Many sun cycles ago." He tugged his braided beard. *"I helped them outwit a Mocendi who sought to destroy them."*

She forced deep, even breaths. "So, I can trust them?"

"Only you can make that decision, Penee. You have good instincts. Use them. Mairin and Lanli approach the bridge."

Tiza bound into the clearing and gave a sharp bark. She sat close to Irstant, her eyes alert, her ears lifted.

Den followed Sager across the bridge, scanned the chaos of prints on the ground, and hurried to the porch. His worried gaze locked on Penee. "Who was here?" Without waiting, he turned to his mentor. "Are you alright?"

The old man nodded, his attention on the couple arriving at the end of the bridge.

Alert and motionless, they surveyed their surroundings. The woman, in her late middle years, crossed the clearing ahead of her companion. Long, silver-blond hair hung in a single braid over her shoulder. Extraordinary eyes glowed sapphire blue in the filtered forest light. Her tall, well-built spouse held back, his demeanor alert, his light blue eyes watchful. Both exuded the vigor of persons half their age.

The woman greeted the VarTerel with a brief touch on the arm. A warm smile brightening her beautiful face, she turned. "Penee, I am Mairin; I am so glad to meet you."

A spontaneous smile in response left Penee somewhat bemused. *I trust you already.*

"Good instincts." Irstant's soft telepathic chuckle surprised her. She smiled and observed Lanli's approach.

With the confidence of a trained warrior, he jogged to the porch. "Hello, Penee. I'm Lanli. We are grateful to Irstant and Den for helping us to find you." He shook hands with Irstant. "It appears you've had visitors. I suggest we go inside. We all have stories to tell." He exchanged looks with Den.

The younger man handed Irstant his staff, called Sager to heel, and trotted back across the bridge.

Once inside the cabin, Irstant started the fire in the wood-burning stove with the snap of his fingers, settled in his chair, and rested a hand on Tiza's head.

Lanli pulled his chair close to the VarTerel. Mairin and Penee joined them. Without preamble, he began.

"We had trouble on the way. Mairin spotted a man on the shuttle craft whom she had seen earlier in our journey. She mentioned him the first time she noticed him, but we thought he had gotten off in Roahymn."

Mairin chimed in. "His energy pattern caught my attention. Although he tried to hide it, he broadcast the signature of a SorTech. Twice during the first leg from RewFaar to Roahymn, I felt the tingling sensation which accompanies the use of The Box. SorTechory is difficult to disguise; doubly so if the SorTech's ego gets in the way."

Lanli took up the tale. "We didn't see him on the next leg, but Mairin detected the use of SorTechory at least twice. We recognized him during our brief layover on Persow and knew he had discovered our presence. In Soputto, three men met him. One, a Klutarse, questioned him at length before leaving with his men. The SorTech and a companion found their way to our inn."

Irstant mouthed the word 'Penesert'.

Penee finished sharing what had happened at the cabin. "Do you think the Klutarse you saw was the one—"

Den strode through the door. "We need to go. We have company at the trailhead."

Amidst the apprehension exploding in the room. Usolamet glowed. Den's eyes narrowed. "Irstant, you can't make another trip through Mittkeer this soon. It will kill you."

The VarTerel grew to his full height. His deep voice reverberated. "We have no choice. We have all travelled Mittkeer's path. Gentlemen, this is a ladies' game. Prepare to protect the women. Penee, grip the shaft. Do what I tell you. Mairin, join her. Tiza, Sager, heel. Ladies, I grant you control of Usolamet. Picture Mittkeer! Take us there!"

Irstant released the staff. An energetic rush left Penee breathless and trembling. Mairin met her gaze with a nod. Usolamet dimmed. Irstant lost the luster of his VarTerel persona. His vibrant voice shifted to short telepathic messages.

Penee tightened her grip and concentrated on entering the endless expanse of the Land of All Time and No Time.

Opposite her, Mairin's beautiful eyes gleamed brighter. A rush of blood to her cheeks left her flushed and panting. Their eyes connected. The older woman's thoughts poured into Penee's mind.

A link so strong it sang through every cell in their bodies left them captured in a corona of color. The world of stars shot toward them. A writhing golden rope snaked through Mittkeer's portal, caught Mairin by the ankle, and yanked her backward. Lanli caught her arm and pulled her against his chest. The pain in Mairin's eyes shouted a warning. She let go of the staff. The couple skidded over starry night toward the gapping portal.

"Usolamet" rang through Penee's mind. She whipped around, aimed the crystal, and pictured a laser-like beam of light cutting the rope in two. Den

held her steady on one side, Irstant on the other. The rope glistened and snapped tight.

"Let me go, Lan." Mairin's voice shook. "Save yourself."

He held on.

Penee focused. Pain ripped through her arms. Heat blistered her palms. Her grip tightened. She aimed the crystal laser. Mittkeer tilted. The stars pulsed brighter then dimmed. Irstant's hand covered hers. Their combined power raced through Usolamet. A loud snap echoed. Sparks chased each other along the unraveling rope, gathered at the portal gateway in a cannon-ball cluster, and exploded with a resounding boom. The portal swirled shut.

Dense quiet—starless night—a soft sob—smoke roiling through No Time and All Time cloaked them. Irstant released Penee's hand and sank to the ground, his ashen face contorted in pain.

"Take command, Penesert."

Heart pounding, she lifted the staff above her head and envisioned the star-spangled beauty of Mittkeer. The smoke dispersed. The darkness dissolved into starlit night. Usolamet's glow rekindled. Penee blinked. Mairin's sobs claimed her attention.

A haggard, blood splattered Lanli cradled his life-mate in his arms.

Den knelt beside them. "How bad?"

"The rope injured her foot and ankle." Despair filled Lanli's eyes. "She's losing a lot of blood."

Den removed his belt and applied a tourniquet.

Mairin inhaled a ragged breath and slipped into unconsciousness.

Irstant struggled to stand. *"We must take her to El Aperdisa."*

Penee gasped. "TreBlaya?"

"Yes, Penee. Take us home. Follow the serpent's trail."

Eyes brimming with tears, she searched Mittkeer. A barren strip of midnight blue sketched a serpentine path through the backdrop of stars. Usolamet blazed brighter.

"Think us there, Penee. Lanli will help. He's familiar with the ship."

Memories of her childhood flooded her mind: Maman, Elf, Aunt Rasiana. Lanli's memories merged with hers. El Aperdisa took shape. The stars blurred. Irstant's presence kept her steady. A bright flash blinded her. When she regained her focus, she stood in the plantitarium, the plant-filled space on board her maman's living ship.

A male technician burst through the hatchway. Two guards took up positions, one on either side. The tech took stock of the scene in front of them "Who—where—how—"

Penee handed the staff to Irstant and faced the blustering man. "I am Penesert Tamahine el Stroma, daughter of Rayn Jaradee Palmira, birth-mate of Troms el Shiv. My friend is hurt. She needs immediate help."

The man's startled gaze moved from her face to Den then Irstant and stopped on Mairin and Lanli. His eyes widened. He tapped a sequence of numbers on a panel by the hatch. "Help is on the way. But you must stay here."

A tiny woman with a mass of short, fly-away, dark hair bustled into the plantitarium with two attendants at her heels. She went straight to Mairin's side. After a quick examination, she gave succinct orders, then introduced herself. "I am Healer Nylimar." She turned to Penee. "How long since the accident?"

"Little time has passed. Lanli can explain what happened."

An air-gurney arrived. With efficient professionalism, the Healer supervised the transfer of Mairin onto it and motioned Lanli to follow her.

Two guards, standing shoulder to shoulder, blocked the hatch. "They can't go anywhere, Healer Nylimar."

"I will take responsibility for the patient. She needs help today, not tomorrow. Let my assistants take her to the Med Sector. They will prepare her for surgery. I'll wait to speak with security."

Lanli cleared his throat. "Commander Odnamo knows us. Mairin and I met him before we departed to find Penee for the Universal VarTerel. Our surname's Nadrugia."

A guard stepped up to the communications panel, spoke briefly, and nodded to his fellow guard, who stepped aside.

The two healing assistants maneuvered the air-gurney through the hatch and down the companionway. Lanli followed.

Healer Nylimar smiled at Penee. "Don't worry. We took DNA samples from both Mairin and Lanli before they left TreBlaya. I'll know more about what I need to do once I review the test results. I'll keep you informed." She glanced at Irstant. "As soon as the head of security clears you, bring the old gentleman to the Med Sector. It looks like he needs attention. If you'll excuse me—"

A uniformed officer stepped through the hatch and moved aside to let her pass. He glanced from Den to Irstant and looked at Penee. "You told my men you are Elf's birth-mate, Penesert. Am I correct?"

"Yes, sir. I was kidnapped when I was five. I'm sure Elf will recognize me."

"Your birth-mate is on the way." The officer smiled. "But your eyes identify you. Please introduce me to your companions."

Her emotions in turmoil, Penee made introductions and moved to one side while the officer conferred with Den and Irstant. The hatchway slid open. Her heart jumped to her throat. It resettled as an Astican ducked through and straightened to its full height. Cherub-blue eyes searched her face. The silver-gray scales covering its winged body susurrated a shimmery song. Its wings fluttered. A smile of recognition lit the child-like features.

Penee gasped. "I remember you! You're Abarax. You were always near Maman unless *He* was there."

A long-fingered hand with silver talons pressed against his chest. "Penesert. You are a beautiful woman. Your maman would be proud. I honor you in her stead." Deep sadness misted its eyes. Again, the scales whispered their shimmery song.

The hatch, obscured by the height and breath of the Astican, opened. Penee held her breath. Abarax bowed. One long stride placed him beside Den and Irstant.

A young man walked into the plantitarium. He froze, his eyes wide with wonder. Penee understood. Her body refused to obey her. She pinned a hungry gaze on his face, soaked in the beauty of it—the dark eyes she remembered so well; the curly, wheat-colored hair; the warmth of his skin tone. His smile changed from anticipation to delight. He took a step. Her heart gave a leap. She met him halfway. Strong arms embraced her. Warm breath brushed her cheek. He held her at arms-length, hunger she understood shining in his eyes. Neither seemed able to speak. And then they were laughing.

He hugged her. "I thought I'd never see you again. I knew you lived. I hoped—" He gave her a lopsided grin.

She stepped back. "Troms el Shiv, I have missed you every turning since they stole me away."

The hatch whispering shut jogged them back to El Aperdisa and the present. Elf put an arm around her. They stood alone in the immense space filled with flora and fauna from their home planet, the planet they were destined to save. Penee smiled up at her birth-mate. She felt whole for the first time since her abduction.

Soputto
Dia Bandia
Nira
Laich Gea
STRAIT OF NÀGRI
Reachti
Canniple M.
Igran
Astong Wood

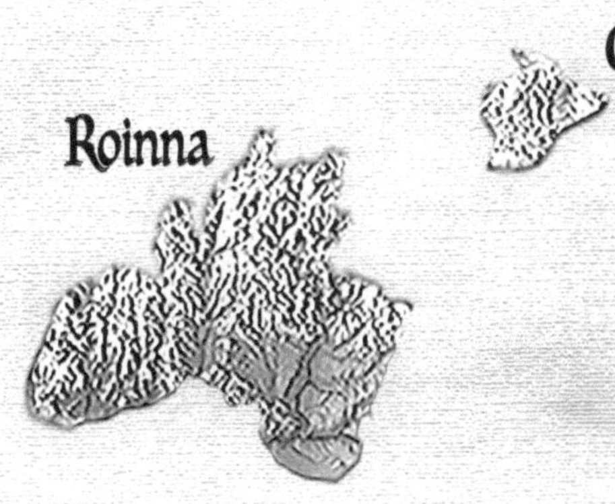

Sileah Mts
Rio Fóra
Dast
Lake Llyn
Baile
Neul Isle
Sea of
Canttila
Gach
Roinna

Prologue III

Secrets well-hidden, secrets unknown,
Many are searching, none are alone.
Seekers of power, regardless of kind,
Are willing to sacrifice body and mind.

DiMensioner-in-training Brielle Ralyn AsTar shifted her shape to a dune hawk and streaked over the Desert of Fera Finnero. Haunted by nightmares, she sought the counsel of her mother, Sparrow Lyn AsTar. *She will help me figure out what the terrified girl in my dreams is trying to tell me.*

The shimmering swirl of the desert portal gleaming below brought her to the ground in a long, easy glide. Human feet hit the sand. She whispered the Key to reset the portal's vibration for Myrrh and leapt into the dimensional gateway. Vacuumed space suspended her in time. Total silence pressed against her eardrums. Vibrant ribbons of color streaked through the blurred stars surrounding her. A shimmering fluorescent oval materialized at the tunnel's end. She braced herself and shot through the blaze of light into the Terces Wood.

Taking a moment to reorient, she absorbed forest noises, soaked in the beauty of ancient trees, and inhaled the scents of damp, mulchy earth. *I love Myrrh; I love the forest. It's so different from the desert on the planet of DerTah.*

Eager to solve her mystery, she began the trek to the Guardian's cottage. *I hope you can help me, Mother.*

As she rounded a bend in the trail, her father, Allynae Nadrugia, materialized, a finger on his lips. He clasped her shoulder. The forest blurred. Nemttachenn Tower enclosed them.

CheeTrann's ghostly persona solidified within a bluish haze. His bass tone rumbled. "Greetings, Allynae and Brielle. The enemy attempts to follow. Go. SparrowLyn awaits you in Meos. I will diffuse your presence."

Brie touched her heart. "Thank you, Sentinel of Myrrh."

He returned her honoring salute. His figure wavered, then reformed. "Teleporting leaves a psychic signature. I suggest you use the Intersect." The blue haze misted into nothing.

Her father urged her through the tower doorway into a grove of trees. Brie led the way to the hollow trunk which housed the Intersect entrance. Inside, she pressed the hidden lever, and they descended onto the subterranean platform. Together, they repeated the appropriate Key. Night and silhouetted tree roots blurred. Tunnel walls deep within the Dojanack Mountains solidified. They hurried along the torch-lit passage to the central square of Meos, home of the DeoNytes.

A slender creature covered with long white fur stepped from behind a carved fountain. Huge, pale blue eyes gleamed in a face as black as DerTahan obsidian. Brie waved.

Zugo, the son of the DeoNyte ReDael, sprinted to meet them. "Welcome to Meos, Allynae. Father sent me to bring you to the council chamber." He hugged Brie, his pale eyes sparkling with delight. "I'm so happy to see you!" Linking arms, Zugo guided her toward the chamber's double wooden doors. "Come tell me how you are and what brings you to Myrrh." He hugged her again. "I can't wait to hear."

When the doors closed behind them, he turned to Allynae. "Sparrow is meeting with father. They will not be long." His ever-present curiosity sizzled. "Let's sit and catch up while we wait."

Allynae paused by the door. "I'll stay here. You two have lots to share."

Brie noted the twinkle in his eye. "Thanks, Father."

Zugo hurried to the round council table and pulled out a chair. She slid onto it, her hand gravitating to the gemstone marking her place.

He sat down. "Tell me everything you've been up to." The eagerness in the DeoNyte's features blazed brighter.

Although his ever-present desire to know amused her, the jagged scars on his cheek and chest, permanent mementos of The MasTer's malice, sent a quiver of foreboding through her.

Zugo stroked his damaged cheek. "My father says the scars are an excellent reminder to temper my inquisitive nature." He rubbed his malachite place marker. "You look good, Brielle. How's DerTah? Are you a DiMensioner yet?"

"My initiation is several moon cycles away. DerTah's desert is hot—too hot most of the time." She smiled. "It's great to be home."

Her gaze darted to a wooden door across the chamber. *Please hurry, Mother.*

Zugo squirmed to see over his shoulder. "They'll be done soon. Tell me more about your training in DiMensionery."

She forced herself to pay attention to her friend. "Wolloh Espyro is a brilliant teacher. He's strict, demanding—"

SparrowLyn AsTar, Myrrh's Guardian, stepped into the chamber. Brie jumped to her feet. Her mother's serious expression transformed into delight. Without consciously moving, Brie found herself enveloped in a warm hug.

Sparrow kissed her cheek and held her at arms' length. "You are so grown up. I can't believe you're eighteen sun cycles." She clasped her hand. "I have something to show you. It may be a clue to your mystery." She turned to the ReDael, who had joined Allynae near the door. "We appreciate your help, Yookotay. Thank you. Would you care to join us?"

The DeoNyte ReDael touched his heart. "I am always honored to serve Myrrh's Guardian. Allynae and I will remain here in case of trouble. Zugo, I'm sure, would like to accompany you." He acknowledged Brie with a smile. "It is good to see you. You are always welcome in Meos, Brielle AsTar."

"Thank you, Yookotay. Wolloh sends his greetings and recommends an extra guard at the portal."

"I have given the order. You must hurry. Time is of the essence."

Sparrow led the way to a torch-lit passage. At an arched entrance, she pulled a curtain aside. "In you go."

Zugo hung back.

Brie entered. Three paintings sitting side by side brought her to an abrupt halt, her thoughts roiling. "How do you do it, Mother? How do you know the things you know? That's the girl, the one who has filled my dreams for the past several nights. I'm certain she's calling to me."

She moved closer to the first painting. A child with greasy, caramel-blonde hair crouched on a straw-strewn floor, a dirty fist stuffed in her mouth. A man's shadowy form towered over her. Memories of the terror in the child's muffled screams sent chills racing up her spine.

Canvas two portrayed the girl, perhaps her own age, dressed in winter clothing. Captured on a frozen pool's mirror-like surface, the paleness of her lovely face highlighted mismatched eyes—one cool blue, one warm green with amber-gold flecks. An ominous cloud hung over the pool.

The third painting depicted a miniature version of the adolescent girl hiding on a ceiling rafter. She peered down on a full-sized man with a balding head and long, narrow nose—the man who haunted Brie throughout the nightmares.

Brie hugged herself. "I don't remember ever meeting her. Who is she, Mother?"

Sparrow replaced the first canvas with a fourth painting. Brie gasped.

Floor-to-ceiling windows framed the view of a mountain lake. Like a mirrored reflection on the glass, the girl from her dreams stared at a silhouetted figure in a billowing cape, hovering above the water. Behind her, another girl with red curls gleaming around a sparsely freckled face peered over her shoulder. Chestnut-brown eyes, fixed on the hovering figure, glistened in the sun's light.

Brie stared at the canvas. "Who are you? Why are you in my dreams? And why are we together in Mother's painting?"

"Tell me how your dreams make you feel." Sparrow's quiet voice soothed her agitation.

"I experience her emotions: her fear, her desire to be free, her need to find something or someone—Oh!" Her hand flew to her heart. "You're Penee—

Elf's birth-mate! You need help." She turned. "Somehow, we're connected. I *have* to find her, Mother."

SparrowLyn, urgency flaring, gripped Brie's shoulders. "Your father brought you to Meos because Elcaro's Eye has foretold several things. You, Ari, Elf, and Penee are being hunted. All of you are important to the enemies of The Unfolding; but you, Brielle, and your growing power top their most wanted list. A Mocendi has picked up your trail. Go back to DerTah. Consult with Wolloh. He will know what you must do."

Allynae pulled the entrance curtain aside. "Trouble at Nemttachenn. Brielle needs to leave."

Before she could utter goodbyes, the cave vanished. Brie and her mother flashed into being at the Nervac Portal, deeper in the Dojanack Caverns.

Sparrow hugged her. "I've altered the portal's destination point on DerTah. You'll arrive near the Raptor Center at Shu Chenaro. I'll track you in Elcaro's Eye. Be careful, Brielle, and be wise."

Brie kissed her mother's cheek, whispered the Key to DerTah, and jumped into the spinning vortex. A blur of colors rushed by. Energy sped up, caught her, and expelled her through a bright, white circle. Her feet hit red sand. The startled squawk of a desert hawk dropped her to a crouch behind a prickly taccus tree.

1

Danger tainted the DerTahan desert air. Brie tingled with it, smelled it, tasted its bitterness. A slight rippling in the atmosphere became a spinning vortex. A man leapt to the ground, his purple-lined cape swirling around him. Narrowed eyes searched, paused at the barn, then the raptor center.

Drawing on her DiMensioner's training, Brie created a subtle shield and teleported to the inner garden. She entered her mentor's home through a side door. Light undulating at the end of the long hall brought her to a standstill. The Star of Truth shot a stabbing pain down her spine. She dodged into Shu Chenaro's library as the hidden panel on the back wall whispered open. Merging into the shadows tossed across the floor by book-filled shelves, she held her breath.

A stealthful step, drag, step paused. Clawed fingers gripped her shoulder. The tingling of a teleported shift took her by surprise. Flickering light from a lantern illuminated Wolloh Espyro's scarred profile.

"The enemy has found you, Brielle AsTar."

Staff in hand, her mentor angled his uninjured right cheek toward her. His hazel eye held a blatant warning.

Stebben Stol, Wolloh's assistant, materialized. He mouthed one word. "Mocendi."

Her mentor's expression held her silent. He gripped her shoulder. Shields surrounded them. The Temple of Nesune's dim interior flashed into view. A white stone walkway meandering from the concealed entrance arch to the Statues of Sinnttee at the far end gave off a greenish glow. Stebben urged them to quicken their pace along it.

Wolloh limped to a halt. "We are not yet safe. Our psychic signatures will lead them to us. We can escape their notice—"

Brie shot a horrified glance at the darkness bordering the walkway. She gulped a startled breath. "Not The Abyss of the Dead?"

Unfazed, he planted his staff firmly on the white stone. "Hold on to the shaft. *Do not* let go. Keep your fear at bay. Look nothing in the eye, and do your best not to swallow the darkness."

Stebben gripped the smooth rowan wood. Brie wrapped trembling fingers below his.

Behind them, the arched entrance to the Temple of Nesune irised open. A caped figure stooped to peer inside.

Wolloh urged them off the walkway. The Realm of SeDah, thick and black as molasses, closed over their heads. Lurid faces, mouths opened in silent screams, clustered around them. Whispering voices, pitched almost too low for the human ear, rippled the viscous blackness. "Brielle. Wolloh. Stebben. You belong to the dead."

From somewhere above them, a current surged downward, pressing them deeper. Wolloh's hand slipped over hers. He squeezed it. *"Hold on."*

Vacuous mouths breathed frost over her skin. Ice-encrusted eyelashes prickled her cheeks. Tears burned and turned to frozen droplets lining her lower lids. Frigid fingers encircling her neck triggered a desire to scream, to let go, to swim upward. Wolloh's hand kept her motionless.

The soft swish of death-infested night reverberated into silence. The Realm of SeDah flashed from inky black to Mittkeer's star-studded nightscape.

Nausea and dizziness sent Brie to her knees. To settle her stomach, she cast her thoughts back to a calmer time. Clean, cool air washed death's stench from her nasal passages and icy tears from her cheeks. A hand on her elbow helped her stand.

Wolloh's deformed smile warmed her. "You did well, Brielle AsTar. How do you feel?"

"A little shaky, but fine. Thank you for the help."

Stebben scanned Mittkeer's vastness. "Did we lose him?"

"For the time being." Wolloh gazed into the distance. "We must decide the safest place to hide until he gives up the hunt." His feathered brow fluttered above his cloudy white eye. The light from Vinredi, the crystal topping his staff, glimmered. His brow stilled. "I know just the place. Let us walk. When we are sure he looks in a new direction, we will project ourselves through time and space."

Brie fell in step at his side. Stebben matched his stride to Wolloh's. Stars glowed, constellations formed and faded, Mittkeer's eternal night filled them. Brie inhaled a quiet breath. *So where will we hide?*

On the planet of TreBlaya, restlessness escorted Relevart onto his favorite balcony at Soasi. His aged-wrinkled hands on the smooth, stone balustrade, he gazed at The MasTer's Pit of Death, where his birth-mate, Rayn, had met her demise. A group of Astican, magnificent winged creatures covered with silver-gray scales, worked tirelessly to smother the flames. *They will soon cover Rayn's ashes with rich, brown soil. Vegetation will decorate the surface, honoring her and those The MasTer sent to their deaths within the fire-filled chasm.*

Periwinkle's sweet scent floated over the balcony. A small hand touched his. His unease evaporated. "Good morning, Henrietta. I'm glad you're here. I have something to share." He regarded his life-mate. Amusement sparkled in his dark brown eyes. "I like your hat. Where on TreBlaya did you find it?"

A demure smile twinkled beneath the wide lavender brim. "A woman has her ways." She tipped her head to peek up at him. "Thank you. I rather like it myself." Her expression shifted to thoughtful. "You were looking most serious."

His hand engulfed her small one. "I've made a decision."

She cocked her head. "Would you care to share?"

"Unless my position as Universal VarTerel demands I use the Galactic Guardian's chosen title, Avlin Enus, I will keep the name Relevart."

The lilac and pink flowers on her hat bobbed above her playful expression. "I'm glad. You know *I* prefer your true name, Rethdun."

Relevart hugged her. "Rethdun is my preference, as well."

She wiggled free, removed her hat, and patted her white curls. "Hats do get in the way sometimes." Rising on tiptoe, she lifted her face.

He kissed her. "I love that you use Rethdun when we're alone, Henrietta."

Her soft laugh made his heart sing. He put an arm around her and returned his attention to the landscape. The colors and textures of healthy plants could be seen sprouting over the grounds, protected by Soasi's glass dome. Beyond it, he could pick out slender saplings. Greenery spotted the fire-blackened world.

Henri nestled closer. "TreBlaya is coming to life. I'm sorry Rayn's not present to enjoy it."

He inhaled her sweet scent. "Abarax and its fellow Astican have done well. Even the forests are regenerating. Soon, we Humans will no longer need to stay inside the dome."

She placed her hat on the balustrade and leaned her head against his shoulder. "Will Abarax travel to El Stroma?"

Grateful for her companionship, Relevart watched the subject of her question launch its seven-foot-tall, humanesque form into flight. Huge wings cast a shadow over the landscape. It hovered, then landed to confer with a fellow Astican. Silvery scales tossed the sun's light skyward. Golden curls gleamed in the TreBlayan sun penetrating the glass dome. Celestial blue eyes turned their direction. Abarax lifted a taloned hand in a salute and went about the business at hand.

Relevart watched with a slight smile. "Over the past moon cycles, it has proven to be a devoted assistant. I can understand why Rayn trusted it. If it wishes to accompany us, I will be happy to have it."

He transferred his attention from the Astican to his life-mate. "Vague childhood memories are haunting me, Henri. The harder I try to remember —" He shook his head. "Something blocks them. I wish I knew what."

Henri stepped away, withdrew her amethyst-rimmed spectacles from their special pocket, and settled them on her nose. Magnified violet eyes examined his face. "When my sister Mairin and I were girls, our mother gave us The Remembering Stone to guard. She told us it was from El Stroma. Her mother entrusted it to her. Mairin passed it to Almiralyn. She passed it to Brie. Last night I dreamt about the Stone...about you and Rayn as children. You must see Brielle before we travel beyond the DéCussate. I'm not sure why. I just know it's important."

He removed the large spectacles from her nose, kissed her, and handed them back. "Will you come with me to Shu Chenaro?"

"Do you think I would let you go without me?" She tucked the spectacles in their pocket. Retrieving her hat, she perched it at a cocky angle on her curls. "I feel certain Brielle is no longer on DerTah, Rethdun."

He stared at the landscape. His vision glazed over. "Ah. I believe you are correct, my dear. Come." He ushered Henri to the door. "We will take Ari with us. She should spend time with her twin. Rayn's living ship, El Aperdisa, is almost ready." His lips pursed. "Whether Brie will make the trip with us continues to be unclear."

•• ••

Wolloh absorbed Mittkeer's silent beauty. *I never expected to be the VarTerel of the Inner Universe. Thanks to Relevart's excellent training, I am well prepared to travel through both time and dimension.* He glanced at his companions. *The choice to bring you through Mittkeer was necessary. I promise to keep you safe.* Thoughts focused on their destination, he masked their presence.

Entering Mittkeer required a VarTerel's power. To his knowledge, neither the Pheet Adolan Klutarse nor their SorTechs had achieved this level of expertise. But times had changed. The Unfolding's completion had left the Universe, Inner and Outer, in a state of antithesis. Ancient texts suggested it would resolve into CoaleScence sometime soon.

His hazel eye focused on Brie. Her DiMensioner's talent surpassed his expectations. His lip twitched, tugging his scarred cheek taut. *If she joins the Order of Esprow, they will initiate her as a High DiMensioner.*

A thorough mental search of the Land of All Time and No Time produced nothing alarming. He raised his staff. The cocooning silence remained unruffled. No one followed.

"Hold on to me." The whispered words summoned his companions before fading into the never-ending night.

* * *

Mittkeer withdrew, leaving Brie and Stebben on either side of Wolloh. Dizziness made a quick appearance. Brie's slight nausea receded as walls and wooden beams undulated into being. The creak and groan of foundations settling solidified her return to the present moment. Instincts alert, she surveyed the room. A fireplace, bookshelves, cooking area, rough-built dining table—*No danger here.* She noted her mentor's knowing look, smiled, and peered out the window. "Where are we?"

He leaned his staff next to the fireplace. "We are on Persow."

Stebben's curious expression brightened with understanding. "Relevart grew up on this planet. Is this by chance his cabin?"

A wistful sigh escaped Wolloh's distorted mouth. "It is his home, the place where I trained to become a DiMensioner." Wolloh caressed his scarred left cheek. "I learned ego's hard lessons in this cabin, but not before the osprey tried to claim me."

Brie sank onto a chair. "Were you scared when your attempt to shift shape went awry?"

"The pain left no room for fright." He angled his good side to her. "I suggest we make a meal. I seem to recall a root and herb cellar at the back of the cabin."

Stebben retrieved a rifle from above the bookcase. "If you know where the shells are, I'll see if I can find something for dinner."

Wolloh rummaged in a drawer and held out a box. "Stay alert. Brie and I will see what else we can find. The cabin returns as it left, so I imagine the larder is stocked."

Brie left Wolloh to gather the ingredients for biscuits and went to explore the cellar. Herbs hanging in bunches from the low ceiling scented the air. Baskets of root vegetables lined the walls. On a shelf above, oil and vinegar prepared and bottled on Persow brought to mind a fresh salad.

While she collected vegetables to roast on the fire, she imagined Wolloh as a younger man and wished she knew more of his story. Perhaps one turning he would share.

The outer door opened, announcing Stebben's return. With her hip, she nudged the keep door ajar and entered the room to find him guiding a rabbit carcass onto a metal rod.

"I started a fire in the grill pit." He finished securing it and held up his kill. "I'll get this going. It shouldn't take long. The sun is about to set. Bring the vegetables and meet me outside."

While the men cooked, Brie explored. Built from fieldstone and stripped logs, Relevart's home sat at the foot of a domed mountain range. Trees flowing down smooth, rolling slopes bordered a sizable garden and formed forested areas on both sides of the cabin.

Thoughts of fresh salad made her mouth water. A search of the back porch produced a basket. Humming to herself, she filled it with lettuce, carrots, and round, ripe tomatoes.

The aroma of roasting rabbit caught by a breeze drifted past. A bird called. A squirrel scampered down a garden row, sat up on its hind legs, sniffed the air, and sprinted into the trees. Persow's sun perched on the mountain peaks, a jewel in a crown, golden light radiating upward.

Brie inhaled. "I wish this wouldn't end." A memory made hazy by time disrupted her peace. Before she could grasp it, it melted away, leaving her biting her lip. "What was that?"

Wolloh limped to her side. "Let it go, Brielle. The harder you think about it, the less likely it will be to return."

She studied the divided face. "Why Relevart's cabin, Wolloh? You could have taken us a dozen other places."

His hazel eye twinkled. "Let's eat. Stories are better told and heard on a full stomach."

When Brie and Stebben finished cleaning up, they returned to the living area. Wolloh limped to a chair by the fire and lowered his disfigured frame into it. "Brie, please go to the bookcase. Remove the three middle books on the second shelf. They cover a crevice in the cottage wall. Bring me what you find inside."

Brie removed the books. She found the crevice between two mismatched stones, withdrew a wooden box, and handed it to her mentor. "What's in it, Wolloh?"

"The answer to your question about why I chose the cabin. Let's see what it contains."

Brie pulled her chair closer.

Wolloh stared at the fire. A flame jumped, igniting a reflection in his hazel eye. A burning log snapped and crackled a cheerful refrain. He rested the small box on his knee. "I was here when Relevart opened this the first time." Lifting the lid, he withdrew a much-handled parchment. "Please read this, Brielle."

A poem written in spidery script held her quiet.

Stebben leaned forward. "Don't keep us in suspense."

She inhaled a steadying breath.

> *"Two held in one, two intertwined.*
> *Last representatives of their own kind.*
> *Two torn asunder and worlds apart*
> *Age, grow, and mature in their heart.*
>
> *The time draws near to play their role*
> *Rejoin together, return to whole,*
> *Two held in one, uniting what's true,*
> *Planet El Stroma created anew."*

A rush of emotion left her shaking. "It's about Rethdun and Rayn, isn't it?"

Wolloh removed the poem from her trembling hands. "Relevart said little after he read it, but I know it confirmed his feeling Rayn lived. Floree Mamdoti, the woman who helped smuggle Relevart to Persow, wrote it. Prior to leaving him with the family who raised him, she gave the parchment and the silver moonstone locket to a Persowan wise woman for safe keeping. When Rethdun turned twelve, his foster mother introduced him to the wise woman who presented him with the box and the key to unlock it. She advised him to hide it. He would know, she said, when to open it and remove the contents."

Stebben steepled his hands and tapped his chin. "We know about the birth-mates, so you must have another reason for choosing Persow."

Brie stared at the fireplace. Memories danced to the rhythmic, flickering flames: a pond surrounding a pink tourmaline throne, a moonstone path, the throne's coolness as she lowered onto it; the visions of the future...

She straightened. Her hand clutched the blue pouch that hung around her neck. The Remembering Stone's power responded to her touch. Her gaze darted to Wolloh.

He looked pleased. "Tell us what you remember, Brielle."

The smooth, blue stone tipped into her hand. She curled her fingers around it. "On ReNin RepPosu, the Throne of Destiny in the Dojanack Caverns, I saw the future. At the time, I remembered only those things important to Myrrh's survival." She held up the Stone. "This contains Relevart's childhood memories. It's important he reclaims them before he goes to El Stroma." She replaced the Stone in its velvet pouch. "How do we let him know?"

The cabin door burst open. A black and tan dog bounded into the room, gave a sharp bark, and rested her head in Brie's lap.

She scratched the warm nose. "Shyllee, I've missed you!"

"Have you missed me?" A deep laugh announced Ari's arrival.

After a sun cycle apart, Brie found herself enveloped in a fearsome hug. Laughing, she embraced her twin. "Where's Rel—"

Her great-aunt, staff in one hand and the other holding a lavender hat in place, toddled into the room. "Do I get a hug?"

Brie deposited a quick kiss on Ari's cheek and turned to embrace her Great-Aunt Henrietta. The wide-brimmed hat went flying. With a grin, she picked it up and held it out. "You're here, so Relevart must be close."

Henri donned the hat, tipped it at a coy angle, and greeted her great-niece. "Good to see you, too, my dear."

The Universal VarTerel materialized in the doorway. Thick, white hair framed his clean-shaven face. Unsuppressed pleasure twinkled in dark brown eyes.

Ari stepped aside. Wolloh rose.

Relevart shook his head. "Do not get up on my account, Wolloh." He studied Brie's face. "I understand you have something for me, Brielle AsTar."

She offered the pouch. "I am so glad you're here. The Remembering Stone contains something important to you."

He made no move to take it. "Please keep it for me. We have things to discuss before I lose myself in memories."

Stebben came to his feet. "How about something to eat?"

Relevart laughed. "You read my mind, Stebben. Or did you hear my stomach growl? I would love a bite. Henri?"

"Food sounds wonderful. Traveling through Mittkeer always makes me hungry."

Ari, hands on her hips, pretended to pout. "How about me? Do I get to eat?"

Brie laughed. "Yes, Arienh, I have definitely missed you and your appetite." She hugged her twin. "Come on, everyone. Have a seat at the table. After you eat, we'll share information."

2

Pretending interest in the adults' casual conversation, Brie listened with one eye on her sister. Something about Ari bothered her—something she could not put her finger on. Her twin's brusqueness and bawdy sense of humor remained unchanged, but Brie sensed a protective layer lingering below the surface, a wariness uncharacteristic of her boisterous identical twin.

As children, Ari had constantly reminded her she was the oldest and the boss. Her quick temper and sharp tongue had almost gotten her thrown in the Five Towers on several occasions. Quieter, gentler Brielle had always come to the rescue.

Brie glanced at Wolloh, who had remained by the fire. The brow above her mentor's hazel eye arched and lowered. She pushed back from the table. "I suggest we join Wolloh and share information."

Wooden chairs creaked as everyone left the table to resettle nearer the fireplace. Brie sat next to her aunt on the sofa, expecting her twin to join them.

Without a glance in their direction, Ari walked past. She lingered near the door, looking uncertain.

To the strains of the fire's crackling and the spicy aroma of cedar burning, Relevart revealed that Almiralyn and Corvus had unearthed the whereabouts of Vygel Vintrusie and Thorlu Tangorra. Vygel had refused to disclose where Relevart's son, Rethson, was hidden.

Ari shifted her restless gaze from the VarTerel to the door. Stubbornness tightened her jaw. She slipped away.

Brie's desire to understand her twin's behavior destroyed her ability to concentrate. She sighed.

Her aunt touched her arm. "Go. I'll fill you in later."

"Thank you, Aunt Henri."

Excusing herself, Brie stepped onto the porch. Ari sat on the step, an arm draped over Shyllee's back.

Brie sat down. "Are you going to tell me what's wrong, Ari?"

Her twin twisted a red curl around her finger, yanked it a couple of times, and let it slip free. "I will if you promise not to tell Wolloh."

"Is it that bad?"

"It's personal. If I share, you gotta promise it will remain a twin-secret."

Brie noted her sister's tight jaw and watched her blink away unshed tears. Twin-secrets had always been sacred pledges, promises that if broken would end their closeness forever. The Star's slight tremor flashed a warning. She rubbed her neck. "I promise, Arienh."

Defiance turned to frustrated tears. Ari raised her face to the sky. Cool moonlight heightened the pallor of her fair skin. An impatient swipe brushed the tears away. "Mairin and Lanli contacted Relevart before we left. They have found Penee. She'll be on TreBlaya when we get back." She stroked Shyllee's nose. "Elf will meet her without me. What if he discovers he loves her, not me?"

"Elf loves you, Ari. He has since the first time he saw you. Besides, loving you doesn't prevent him from caring about Penee. My love for Esán doesn't mean I love you less. Don't jump to conclusions. You'll make yourself miserable."

Ari folded her arms and glared at the ground.

Brie knew by her mulish expression she wasn't convinced. "Is that what you wanted to tell me?"

Ari gripped her arm. "Twin promise?"

The Star of Truth stabbed harder. Brie ignored it. "Twin promise." The pain increased. Covering a flinch with a coaxing smile, she waited.

Ari released her arm and stared into the night. "I overheard a conversation on board El Aperdisa." She grew quiet, then shrugged. "Two men were arranging a covert meeting. Their secretive behavior aroused my suspicion, so I arrived at their meeting place early and hid." She bit her bottom lip and shot Brie a sideways glance. "Remember, Brielle, you promised not to tell anyone."

Pain spread from Brie's spine into her ribcage. She gripped the edge of the step. "What did you hear?"

"I discovered the two men are Pheet Adolan spies who had infiltrated the crew prior to Rayn's death. Commander Odnamo doesn't know they're on board, and they've stayed out of Relevart's way."

Brie studied her sister. "Why were they meeting?"

"They have been ordered to kidnap—" She bit her lip and looked away. "Penee."

"Ari, tell Relevart. This isn't a childish secret. Someone could get hurt." Brie touched her knee.

Ari jerked away. Her jaw jutted forward. "I don't care if they take Penee. Maybe then Elf will remember he cares about me."

Brie gave her sister an incredulous stare. "I've never known you to be so thoughtless of another person's safety." She came to her feet. "Let's go tell Relevart."

"I'm not telling him or anyone else. If you break our twin promise, I will *never* speak to you again." Ari shoved past her. With Shyllee at her heels, she marched around the side of the house.

Footsteps on the porch stopped Brie from following. Relevart gazed down at her. "A disagreement?"

Brie stared after her twin. "I made a twin promise, Relevart. If I break my oath, Ari will never speak to me again."

He descended the steps. "I gather it is a promise you are uncomfortable with?"

The pain in her back pulsed. "It involves other people. If it were just about Ari and me—" She winced.

"The Star of Truth? What does it have to say?"

"It hurts so much I can hardly breathe." She looked away. "I don't know—"

"Look at me, Brielle AsTar."

The VarTerel's command rang through her head with such gentle authority she obeyed without question.

"Tell me what Ari shared. Tell me word for word. Leave out nothing."

Brie swallowed the rising lump in her throat. The words tumbled out. Relief followed by despair opened a floodgate of tears. "I don't want Penee hurt, but I love Ari. I am so..." She heaved a shaky breath.

Relevart's understanding expression became stern. "Arienh, I know you're watching. Please join us."

Shyllee trotted to her master's side. Ari emerged from the darkness. Her attitude wavering between stubbornness and guilt, she stopped in front of the Universal VarTerel.

"You understand your sister had no choice. She was duty bound to tell me your secret?"

Ari remained silent, lips pressed together and chin high.

Relevart's unyielding stare bored into her. "First, Arienh, Brielle's integrity and empathic nature would not allow her to ignore a threat to someone else if she could stop it. Second, and more important, she bears the Star of Truth. Do you know what would have happened had Brie refused to tell me?"

Her expression blanked.

"The Star of Truth would have drained her life drop by drop. Need I say more?"

"No, sir."

The sulky tone made Brie want to poke her.

Relevart's brows raised. "Ari, these men, who are after Penee, might also be after Elf."

Ari gasped.

He continued. "Both birth-mates could prove much more lucrative than having just one. If they were dead, it could solve a lot of problems for the Pheet Adole. If you'll excuse me, I have a quick trip to make. We'll discuss this further when I return."

Brie waited until the door closed to look at her sister. "Ari, I'm so sorry—"

"I'm not speaking to you, Brielle AsTar." Turning on her heels, Ari marched toward the back of the cabin.

Brie sank down on the step and dropped her face in her hands.

A whip-sharp bark brought her head up. Ari's angry voice filled the night. "Don't you dare hurt—" A startled scream propelled Brie to her feet. Panic carried her to the corner of the cabin. A firm hand pulled her up short. Stebben motioned her to stay put and ran toward a second muffled scream.

"Brie." Wolloh's voice stopped her from following. He waved her inside. "Stay with Henri."

"But, Wolloh—"

He placed a finger to his lips, handed her his staff, and shifted to an osprey.

She stepped into the lightless interior of the cabin. A whiff of periwinkle floated close. Henri drew her into the root cellar and whispered in her ear. "Shields."

Brie's shimmered into place. An eerie quiet engulfed the cabin. Henri sucked in a startled breath. Her wards evaporated.

A glowing line appeared beneath the cellar door. Stebben pushed it open. "It's safe to come out."

Henri stepped into the living area, a trembling hand pressed to her heart.

In the unexpected brightness, Brie gazed from her great-aunt's distressed expression to Stebben's. Emotions Brie found difficult to interpret ravaged his clean-cut features. Wolloh reclined in a chair, his scarred cheek pulled taut; his feathered brow low over his closed eye. Shyllee guarded the door.

Brie hurried to Wolloh's side. "Where's Ari?"

Stebben answered from behind her. "We were too late. They took her into Mittkeer."

She whipped around. "Who took her? I thought only VarTerels could travel through Mittkeer. I don't understand."

"They also have Relevart. He was on his way to El Aperdisa." Henri's voice trembled. "He managed a brief message—" She sagged.

Stebben hurried to her side and guided her to the chair.

Wolloh stirred and ran his uninjured hand through his hair. "If we do not do what they ask, neither Relevart nor Ari nor Elf will live to tell the story."

Brie rounded on him, fists clinched tight. "Why didn't *you* stop them? You're a VarTerel. You have as much power as Relevart." Yelling didn't cancel her desire to shake him. Blood rushed to her cheeks. Shame silenced her next outburst. She stared at the floor. *What am I doing?*

From beneath her lashes, she noted Stebben's momentary surprise and her great-aunt raising spectacles to rounded violet eyes. Wolloh's speculative glance brought another rush of heat to her cheeks.

Henri cleared her throat and lowered the spectacles. Focused on Wolloh, she mused, "The real riddle is why didn't Rethdun stop them?"

Wolloh pursed his lips. "He commanded me not to act. The question is, does he want us to rescue him?" His feather-like brow twitched. "Or do we wait?"

Henri perched her large-rimmed spectacles on her nose. Magnified eyes traveled from Wolloh to Stebben to Brie. "We will appear to wait." She took off the lenses and tapped them on her palm. "But we *will* investigate. Penee must not have tumbled into the trap. That means she remains on El Aperdisa."

Stebben looked almost bemused. "How do you know so much?"

"Relevart and I have few secrets. We read each other well. He shared his concerns prior to leaving TreBlaya." She tapped her specs once, twice; tucked them away; and became all business. "Brielle, wipe the anger from your heart. We will need to stick together if we are to unravel this mess. Wolloh, what were the demands? That should tell us a lot about whoever made them."

An almost smile tugged at Wolloh's cheek.

As she observed her mentor, Brie's anger melted. She pulled up a chair and prepared to listen.

In the land of All Time and No Time, the Universal VarTerel reviewed the emotionless message he had received, the one that persuaded him to lay his life on the line. Ari marched beside him, her temper held in check, but barely. Behind them, Elf plodded along between two men. The leader glanced over his shoulder, giving Relevart the opportunity to see blue eyes flecked with amethyst, eyes the VarTerel had first seen a long time ago.

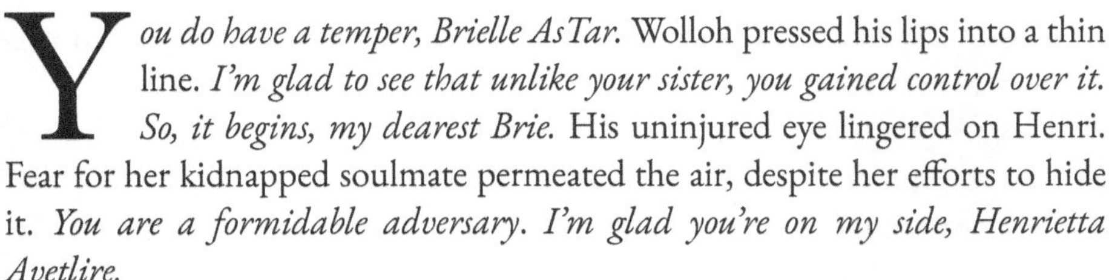

3

*Y*ou *do have a temper, Brielle AsTar.* Wolloh pressed his lips into a thin line. *I'm glad to see that unlike your sister, you gained control over it. So, it begins, my dearest Brie.* His uninjured eye lingered on Henri. Fear for her kidnapped soulmate permeated the air, despite her efforts to hide it. *You are a formidable adversary. I'm glad you're on my side, Henrietta Avetlire.*

He refocused his train of thought. "The Pheet Adole Klutarse kidnapped Relevart, Ari, and Elf. They hold someone or something important to Relevart—important enough he has put himself at risk to save it. What did he share, Henri, which might help us unravel the puzzle?"

"Only two names: Charid and Jaami. I know nothing of either."

Wolloh's agile mind wandered his memories. He rubbed his feathered eyebrow. "He never mentioned those names to me. Stebben, did you come across either of them in your studies of El Stroman history?"

"Nothing even similar."

Brie withdrew the Remembering Stone. "What if it's something from his memories?" She tipped the blue stone into her palm. "We could try to access them."

Wolloh refrained from touching it. "You are the guardian of the Stone. Since Relevart is not here, you are the only one who *might* recover his memories. The bigger question is whether the Klutarse know about the Stone's secret?"

Withdrawing her spectacles, Henri perched them on her nose and peered at Wolloh. "Relevart shared one other thing before our connection broke. The message was short: Two Mocendi battle; assassins gather. I'm not sure if he meant two individual Mocendi..." She shook her head. "That feels wrong."

Stebben cleared his throat. "Perhaps I can help. When all this began at Shu Chenaro, I had just returned from a visit to TiCeed, the capital of Geran province. While there, I learned several important things." He glanced at Wolloh. "May I share?"

"Please."

"The Mocendi are divided into two opposing groups. The MasTer's Mocendi, those who trained on TreBlaya, make up one group. El Stroman rebels who call themselves Vasro make up the other. The MasTer's Mocendi appear to have gone underground. What their intent is and who spearheads the group is a mystery."

Henri tapped her spectacles on her palm. "And the Vasro? What did you learn of them?"

"As a young man on El Stroma, Vygel Vintrusie was the Vasro leader. Under his direction, the Vasro seeded the storm clouds over El SyrTundi with deadly chemicals. The rebels, too, have gone underground. No one seems to know who their leader is now.

"The other tidbit I picked up is that Skultar Rados, Penee's cousin, has used his power, influence, and wealth to amass a group of Klutarse. He has augmented these trained Pheet Adolan assassins with the power of SorTechory. Rumor suggests he plans to use Penee's talents to enhance his power."

Wolloh's brows bridged his nose. "It appears your trip to Geran was worth the time." His brows snapped back into place. "We now understand Relevart's reference to two Mocendi battle and assassins gather." He gazed into the distance. *What is the best course to follow?* A mental scan of the fringes of

Mittkeer, including the forest surrounding the cabin, produced nothing to arouse his suspicion.

He focused his sighted eye on his companions. "Our enemies' attention appears to be elsewhere. I believe the next step, Brie, is for you to work with the Stone. What can we do to help, my dear?"

Brie pressed the blue velvet pouch to her heart. "Make sure I'm not disturbed. Aunt Henrietta, we share a bond with the Remembering Stone. Please be my personal guard."

Henri clasped her staff and stood beside Brie's chair. "I suggest you ask to see Rethdun's memories, Brielle. I'm sure the Stone knows him by that name. Tell me when you're ready. I'll construct our shield."

Wolloh nodded his approval.

❧ ❧

Brie tipped the blue stone onto her upturned palm. She whispered a quiet charm. The center glowed. "It has given its consent. I'm ready."

Henri raised her staff. Brie embraced the Stone's vibrance. Her emotions steadied. A rush of light stung her closed eyelids. Unabridged memories bombarded her. She silenced her ragged breathing, calmed her racing heart, and clarified her intent.

Show me only Rethdun's memories of Charid or Jaami. Images flickering fast forward slowed. A small boy listened to a woman he called Aunt Floree. She explained he couldn't be Rethdun anymore and asked him how he liked the name Charid Darine. Memories involving Charid and Floree sped past. Nothing referencing Jaami came to the fore. With a sigh, she released her connection to the Stone. The curtain of energy dissolved. Her eyelids fluttered open.

Henri sank into a chair. "What did you learn?"

"Charid is the name Rethdun used when he left El Stroma. Floree assumed the persona of his mother, Esta Mae Darine. I found no reference to a Jaami. Do you suppose he is someone Relevart met on Persow?"

Shyllee rumbled a warning growl. Wolloh put a finger to his lips. Attention glued on the door, he lunged to his feet. Stebben moved to his master's side.

Henri stood, her staff in hand. Brie hid the Stone in its pouch beneath her tunic.

Wolloh whispered instructions. "Henri, take Brie to Rainbow Falls at the back of Rainbow Gorge. Find a mystic named Glori. We will find you. Hurry!"

Brie linked elbows with her aunt. The rose quartz topping her staff glowed. The room vanished.

Plummeting water screened by shimmering rainbow colors heralded their arrival in the gorge. Henri urged her across a lush clearing to a churning plunge pool. A child of perhaps ten sun cycles, with ringlets as coppery as Brie's hair, beckoned them to follow.

Not waiting to see if they complied, she danced beneath a wall of forest foliage adjacent to the waterfall, jogged up a steep passage to even steeper stone steps, and skipped into sunlight and trees at the top of the falls.

As they blinked the dimness away, she urged them ahead of her into a cottage nestled beneath tall blue spruce trees.

A long, rainbow-striped cord appeared in her hands. She skipped rope to the rhythm of a chant.

> *"Cottage, take us far away,*
> *Where evil cannot cause delay.*
> *Hide us from all searching eyes;*
> *Wrap us in a safe disguise."*

The cottage spun faster and higher, so high, the waterfall shrank into invisibility. Golden radiance flared. The cottage resettled in a field of wildflowers. The child had vanished. In her place, the Galactic Guardian of the Fourth Galaxy from the Great Central Suns observed them with candid interest.

Henri tipped her head back. "Hello, Chealim. We are most delighted to see you."

He bowed his magnificent head. "It is good to see *you*, Henrietta, and you, Brielle Ralyn AsTar."

Henri put an arm around her. "You know my niece?"

"We have met. She is the reason for my visit."

Her aunt moved aside.

Brie's heightened senses magnified the stillness. Her shortness of breath tangled with the butterflies in her stomach. She wiped sweat-damp palms on her drango tunic and gazed into the intense blue eyes studying her.

The handsome features grew solemn. "Brielle, you are at a crossroads, one of those moments in life that change us forever. The Galactic Counsel has sent me to make you an offer. I encourage you to ask questions. You may take all the time you need to give me your response." A slight smile curved his generous mouth. "We are between moments. As in Mittkeer, you are in a place of no time and all time. Shall I continue?"

Her automatic reaction to any new situation—check the Star of Truth—occurred with such speed it took her breath away. Warmth flooded through her. She nodded.

"You have trained hard and have achieved the level of High DiMensioner in your work with Wolloh Espyro. You, your sister, Elf, Penee, and Relevart's son Rethson are key to the rise of a new cycle of growth in the Universe. As a result, there are those who would end your lives. Others wish to use your talents to enhance their own.

"To help ensure your destiny and, therefore, the success of the upcoming Cycle, the Counsel wishes to initiate you as the youngest VarTerel in the history of Universe." Dignity infused his words.

"Your Aunt Henri will tell you this is not a simple transition for the best trained. It magnifies your gifts and your personal deficiencies. You will, by necessity, learn control. If you accept this, you may tell only those with whom you are now working. It must stay a secret even from those you love and trust. Should you be foolish and entrust it to another, both of you will pay the consequences. Questions?"

Brie inhaled. "I have one question. Why me? Why now?" She shot him a lopsided grin. "Guess that's two."

"Why now? The Universe languishes between The Unfolding's completion CoaleScence, the phase of growth where that which has unfolded seeks to stabilize. Why you?" Light glowed around him. "Why not you, Brielle AsTar?"

Overwhelmed, she sought her great-aunt. The lavender rimmed spectacles lent deepening wisdom to her elderly features. Tears glistened on her wrinkled cheeks. "You alone must make this decision, my dearest niece. I pledge to support you in whatever you choose."

Brie returned her attention to Chealim. "I understand becoming a

VarTerel will magnify the skills I have mastered. VarTerel's travel through both time *and* dimension. What else will I need to learn?"

"If you accept our offer, you must take an oath to serve mankind for your lifetime and beyond. Forsaking the oath brings instant death. You will, like your Aunt Henrietta, your Aunt Almiralyn, and Corvus Castilym, report to the Universal VarTerel. I will not inform the Order of Esprow you are a VarTerel." He held open the door. "I suggest you take a walk and digest what we have discussed. I have things to share with your aunt."

Wandering outside, Brie tipped her face up to the mid-turning sun. The cloudless blue of the sky reminded her of Chealim's eyes. A stroll through tall flowers and grass reminded her of her first walk through the grasslands on Myrrh…to where it all began…to memories of Esán and Torgin, Buster's death, Skipt and Zugo, the battle at Nemttachenn, DerTah and becoming a Water ConDria, meeting Wolloh the first time. *So much has happened.*

She picked a shimmering violet flower and inhaled its fragrance. Her other hand clutched the Remembering Stone. The Star of Truth sent warmth skittering along her spine. *Ari will be furious.* She sighed. *Ari won't even know.*

Thoughts in a whirl, she made her way through tall grass to the cottage. When she reached the steps, she halted to stare into the distance, then crossed the stoop. At the open door, she breathed in the fragrance of wildflowers and stepped inside.

Chealim and Henri greeted her. Handing her aunt the flower, she faced the Galactic Guardian. "I've decided, Chealim."

"And?"

"Will I ever be able to tell the people I love most?"

"When the danger is past, we will celebrate your initiation with those you love."

"I accept the offer and the responsibility that goes with it."

Satisfaction intensified the fine lines around Aunt Henri's violet eyes.

Chealim offered his hand.

Brie took it.

4

In her entire eighteen sun cycles, Brielle had never experienced the emotional and physical awareness that washed through her when her hand rested on Chealim's. Joy, fear, excitement, and panic throbbed in her heart like drummers laying down a syncopated fill in a percussion solo.

Her body lost its strength, then surged with power. The world blurred before sharpening to such a degree tears spilled down her cheeks. Acute hearing left her ears aching from the sounds of flowers in the fields, birds overhead, butterfly wings beating the air. The scents of wind and sun and summer assaulting her senses left her panting. Her flesh tingled from the top of her head to the soles of her feet. An elated song filled her mind, her heart, her being. Then the cosmos became so quiet her inhale and exhale sounded like a tornado's rumbling. The world steadied. Her heartbeat slowed, and Henri's beautiful face came into focus.

Chealim continued to hold her hand. "How do you feel, Brielle AsTar?"

She attempted a smile. "Full. So full I think I might burst. Excited. Scared. Exhilarated—and yet calmer than I can ever remember."

He nodded and released her. "Until Relevart returns, your aunt and Wolloh will be your teachers. Stebben will also sense the changes in you. He possesses knowledge that will assist you. Listen and learn." He touched her temple. "I must leave. Should you need me, you will know how to bring me to your side." His image dimmed, then flickered back into focus. "One more thing, it is time to share the secret I gave you to guard on TreBlaya." Again, he tapped her temple.

Golden light blazed. The red-haired child waited by the door, a rowan wood staff in her hand. She held it out. "Chealim asked me to give you this, Brie. The stone crowning it is watermelon tourmaline from the Throne of Netydis and holds the secrets you learned there." She tapped the staff against the floor. It shrank to the size of a small dagger. "Chealim suggests you hide it in the box with the poem. You will know when it is time to claim it." Handing it to Brie, she held out her hands. "We must go. Wolloh and Stebben await you in the gorge."

They arrived by the waterfall at dusk. Glori bid them farewell and slipped behind the foliage curtain. Stebben stepped from the shadows. "Trouble at the cabin. Wolloh sent me to—"

Brie peered up at his worried face. "Wolloh?" Fear flew back at her. She gripped her aunt's hand. The next instant they stood in the woods at the garden's edge, a shield obscuring their presence. The back door opened. Shyllee bound into the trees. Wolloh motioned them away.

A hand gripped his shoulder and dragged him inside. The door slammed.

Henri clasped firm fingers around Brie's arm.

"Take Shyllee. Go." Stebben's urgent whisper melted into the emptiness he left behind.

Henri's staff appeared in her hand. Steely, violet eyes locked onto Brie's. The world blurred. They stood behind the foliage curtain at the gorge.

Glori, her small face filled with concern, beckoned them into the darkness behind the falls. "Relevart sent an urgent message: *'Find Penee.'* I don't know what it means, but I'm sure you do. Give me your staff, Brie. I'll hide it until you need it." She tucked it into a pouch at her waist and kissed Henri on the cheek. "Rethdun sent that to you. Mittkeer is empty. Go!"

The star-studded heavens embraced them. Brie's queasiness passed quickly. Next to her, Henri caressed the kissed cheek and murmured, "Now why would Relevart send the message and Rethdun send the kiss?" White curls bobbed. "Brie, what was the secret Chealim shared with you?"

"Jaami was a Persowan friend of Rethdun's. They studied DiMensionery together. I bet Penee knows something that will help. I say we go to El Aperdisa."

Henri beamed. "Spoken like a true VarTerel."

W olloh, tied to a chair in the cottage on Persow, peered up at the Pheet Adolan Klutarse standing over him. The man studied his disfigurement and grimaced with distaste.

"Tell me what I want, and I won't give you a matching cheek on the other side."

A second man, who had been guarding the door, stepped onto the front stoop. "Do your worst, Hossale. I'm gonna get some air."

Wolloh's good eye gleamed. He kept his expression blank.

The Klutarse leaned closer. "I have heard an osprey tried to claim your soul. It appears to have failed." He straightened, lifted his knife, and angled it until the light danced along the blade's sharp edge. A quick movement left a thin, blood-infused wound on Wolloh's cheek. "Tell me where—"

A yell. Then silence.

Dodging behind Wolloh's chair, Klutarse Hossale held cold steel to his throat. "What did you do, Wolloh Espyro?"

The door flew open. A trussed body crashed to the floor. A disembodied voice called out. "Release the VarTerel, and I will let you live."

Hossale gripped Wolloh's hair and jerked his head back. The blade pressed harder. "Show yourself, or I kill him."

Stebben stepped into view, his attention fixed on the Klutarse's face.

In one fluid movement, Hossale's arm went back, and the knife flew from his hand. Stebben flashed from sight. The next instant he reappeared behind the Pheet Adolan, clamped an arm over his windpipe, and squeezed his throat shut. Seconds later, he lowered the unconscious man to the floor and held out a hand. "I could use some rope."

Wolloh whispered a single word. The ropes restricting his wrists and ankles released and fell to the floor.

Stebben gathered them up and bound the Klutarse. He then lugged both men outside, rolled them off the stoop, and tossed the knife out of reach.

Back in the cabin, he examined the cut on Wolloh's cheek and another on his hand. "Why did you let him cut you?"

Wolloh sighed. "To give you time to do what needed to be done. Brie and Henri?"

"Safe. At least, they vanished into Mittkeer."

"Shyllee?"

"She left with them."

Studying his companion, Wolloh said, "I had no idea you knew how to fight like a Klutarse."

Stebben stared into the distance. Wistfulness glinted. "My father taught me to protect myself. I'm just sorry I couldn't save him and Momee the turning the MasTer's Mocendi came to our farm on Roahymn." He handed Wolloh his staff and helped him to his feet. "Can you take us through Mittkeer, or are you too weak?"

Wolloh waved a hand. A portal opened. Stars and midnight sky replaced the cabin. The quiet soothed his rattled nerves. Death had stared him in the face. Even knowing he could have ended the Klutarse's life did not distract from the memory of the knife at his throat.

He ignored the weariness weighting his body and raised his staff. "They will watch for us at Shu Chenaro, and I prefer not to leave a trail to TreBlaya. Let us confuse the enemy."

Stars and sky blurred together...

👁 👁

Relevart bided his time. Within a subtle, protective cocoon, he controlled the urge to consign those imprisoning him and threatening the lives of people he loved to another and deadlier dimension.

Forced to transport them through Mittkeer to a penal colony on the

Soputton moon, TaSneach, he had left a clue in Henri's mind. *Find Penee. She will know where to find me.*

A subtle mental probe had garnered him information important to his survival and the survival of Elf and Ari. As long as they were near enough, he could protect them. Wolloh, in the cabin on Persow, lay beyond his reach. But Stebben, a man of great ingenuity, hid close by.

A key rattled in the lock. A needle's sting in his arm demanded his complete attention. Metabolizing the immobilizing serum took time and concentrated effort.

A narrow-faced man stared down at him. "You thought you were invincible, Eleo Predan filth, but look at you now. I have Elf and Arienh. Soon, I will have Penee and Brielle. And last but not least, I will find Rethson, your son. They are the key. Behave, old man, and I will let you and those you love survive another turning."

The door clanked shut; the key rattled. Quiet descended on the cell. With methodical diligence, Relevart metabolized the serum into a harmless fluid. Paralysis fled. He lay perfectly still, staring at nothing, spittle leaking from his mouth.

Skultar's gleeful laugh floated through the barred window.

Relevart bided his time...

Brie paid close attention to Henri explaining the workings of Mittkeer and how constellations acted as beacons to the gateways leading into different worlds. She recalled the Dansgirl Nichi sharing how the Atrilaasu Dansmen on DerTah created songlines to chart the landscape of the Desert of Fera Finnero. *Songlines work there, so why not use them to help navigate the starry vastness of All Time and No Time?*

Henri pointed. "See that group of stars in the shape of a justice scale? That is the constellation Bilar."

"Bilar." Brie created a songline describing its position in the night sky.

Her aunt paused. "Are you ready to find Penee?"

Brie responded by clasping her aunt's staff. Shyllee sat between them. Profound silence turned to a faint hum. An interior space where plants covered the walls came into focus. A tall girl with an athlete's lean body and short, caramel-blonde hair stood tensed to fight. Confident mismatched eyes did not waver.

The quartz crystal on Henri's staff dimmed to a soft glow. "Penee?"

One green eye flecked with gold, and one blue eye narrowed. She remained silent.

Henri leaned on her staff. "I am Henrietta. Elf calls me Henri. This is my great-niece, Brielle. Relevart sent us."

The girl's obvious suspicion lessened. "You know Elf?"

Brie spoke up. "Elf made this hide-away when he was a boy. He hid you here, didn't he?"

A girl's silence remained unbroken.

Brie pointed at herself. "I'm Ari's twin." She made herself speak calmly. "We believe the Mocendi kidnapped Ari and Elf. We need your help to find them."

Penee slid the knife into a leather scabbard. "You came through Mittkeer, correct?"

Henrietta smiled. "We did. I'm guessing someone brought you to El Aperdisa via the Land of Time."

Circumventing a small pool, Penee knelt beside Shyllee. "Hello, girl. I knew you'd bring help." She scratched the dog's ears. "We can't talk here. Too many vents; too many enemies close by." She rose to look at Henri. "Can you take us to Rayn's chambers?"

Henri placed her staff between them. "Hold on."

Plant-covered walls morphed into Rayn's black-curtained chamber at Soasi.

Brie's memories enlivened with images from her earlier times on TreBlaya, of Rasiana and of Rayn's death.

Penee watched her with curiosity brimming over. "I know a safe place to talk. This way."

She disappeared behind the elegant obsidian throne that presided over the silent space. A panel slid aside. Shyllee disappeared into the darkness. Brie helped Henri down steep, stone steps to a narrow room. Penee lit a lantern and set it on the floor. The warm glow etched out a narrow cot.

"Please, Henrietta, sit."

Henri lowered onto it. With a sigh of relief, she leaned her staff against the wall. Brie made herself comfortable on the floor with Shyllee curled up at her side.

Penee sat on the bottom step. "Elf showed me this hideaway before they caught him. He prepared it in case—" She shrugged. "When the Pheet Adole Klutarse came, we couldn't get to it, so he hid me in the plantitarium." She looked sad. "I should never have let him leave to check on them. We'd still be together. Tell me how you found me."

Brie recapped what had happened on Persow.

Penee shook her head. "Are you telling me they have Relevart?"

Henri withdrew her specs and polished them on her shirttail. "They have Relevart. We aren't sure if they captured Wolloh and Stebben or not. What we do know is Relevart went of his own volition."

Penee's expression registered disbelief.

Magnified violet eyes blinked. "They threatened someone he cares about." Henri looked from Brie to Penee. "It appears we have stories to share. Tell us how you found your way to El Aperdisa."

Brie rubbed splayed fingers through Shyllee's long fur, her attention on the girl from her dreams.

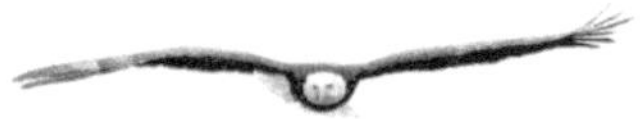

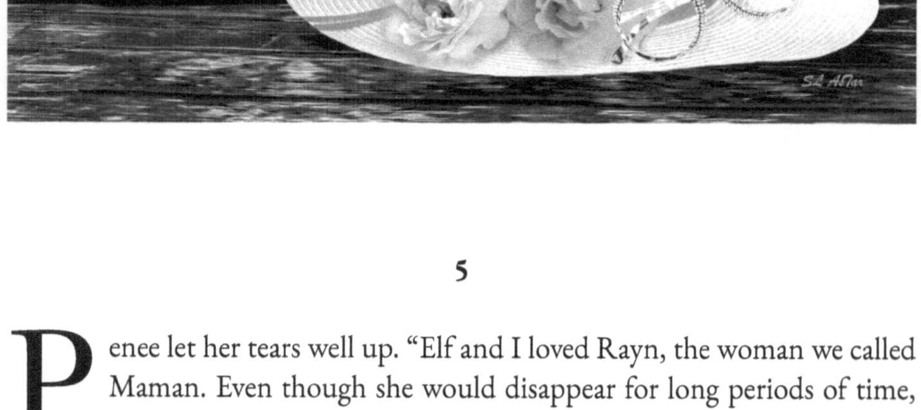

5

Penee let her tears well up. "Elf and I loved Rayn, the woman we called Maman. Even though she would disappear for long periods of time, we knew she loved us. Aunt Rasiana, Maman's best friend, always took care of us. When The MasTer's presence sent them into hiding, Rasiana made certain we were safe."

Anger sharpened her voice. "The MasTer doted on my birth-mate. He hated me. On my fifth sun cycle celebration, he hid Elf. I looked everywhere. I never saw him again." Defiance hardened her expression. "The MasTer left me prey to enemy Pheet Adole. They kidnapped me, bound me, and drugged me. I woke up in a stable, locked in a dark, smelly stall. I have no idea how long I huddled in a dirty corner, repeating my name like a mantra. One turning, a boy named Den snuck into the stall. He brought water and an apple. I remember he explained the scary noises in the stall attached to mine. He even introduced me to the horse, B'hean. With his help, I fed her the apple core."

Den's betrayal, when he changed his loyalty to Skultar Rados, battered her calm. She blanked her expression and took a moment to regain her composure.

"A few turnings later, a man in a purple-lined cape walked into the stall. I remember little until I woke up with a raging headache in a cell smelling of human waste and vomit. I wasn't there long. My cousin Skultar removed me. He took me to live with proxy parents whom I grew to love almost as much as Maman. When I was fifteen, Skultar arrived at their manor house. I told him I wanted to stay, that I was old enough to make my own decisions. Pitting my will against his, I soon discovered, would only make things worse. That's how I ended up in the penal colony on TaSneach. I now know he hid me away because a search had begun for the girl with the Matriarch's Eyes.

"My inability to curb my stubbornness turned life on TaSneach into a battle of wills. Brief stays in the main house always ended in much longer stays in a cell block. One turning, I heard two prison guards talking about the birthmate of 'the girl'. Skultar ordered him brought to Soputto. I swore in my heart I'd locate him first.

"Den helped me escape from the penal colony. We met up with his mentor, Irstant, a lifelong friend of the Universal VarTerel. He told me Relevart had sent a couple to find me. The Nadrugias hoped to meet us at his cabin on Soputto. Den, Irstant, and I traveled through Mittkeer to the cabin. Mairin and Lanli arrived with the Pheet Adole Mocendi at their heels. They caught up with us as we attempted to enter Mittkeer. Mairin was injured during the escape. Transporting her to El Aperdisa for medical care became our goal. She's in the infirmary. Lanli's with her."

The blood drained from Brie's face. "Wait. Do you say my grandparents are on the ship? The Mocendi injured Grandmama?"

Henri clasped her niece's hand. "Please, Penee, tell us how my sister is."

"After surgery to mend her damaged ankle and leg, the Geno Tech stimulated the regeneration of the tissue cells." She looked from one to the other. "The last time I visited Mairin, the Physio-Tech had begun the work to strengthen the injured leg."

The color flooded back to Brie's fair skin. "I'm so glad she's alright. Tell us what happened."

Penee scrubbed a hand through her shaggy hair, savored the freedom it represented, and shared the story. "When we entered Mittkeer, the Pheet Adolan SorTech couldn't follow, so he sent an enchanted rope after us. It trapped Mairin's leg. Lanli stopped her from being pulled from Mittkeer. With Irstant's help, I created a laser beam using Usolamet, the crystal topping his VarTerel's staff, to slice the rope. Our fight to free her from its coils injured her calf and foot. That's why Irstant helped me to bring us all to El Aperdisa. The ship has the best healing unit in the Inner Galaxy."

Comprehension flooding her mind, Henri placed her spectacles on her nose. "So, my dear, you *do* carry a DiMensioner's gifts, a rare occurrence in a Pheet Adolan." She chuckled to herself. "Rayn Jaradee Palmira, you were a genius." Her full attention returned to Penee. "Now we understand why your cousin is intent on tying you to him. Does he know how powerful you are?"

Penee patted her knee. Shyllee rested her beautiful head in her lap. "Maman taught Elf and me together. She made us promise to keep our talents a secret. My instincts alerted me that Skultar was the enemy. I remembered my promise. He is unaware of my gifts. But Irstant sensed them right away." She sighed. "The Klutarse captured him, too. He was not well the last time I saw him."

Brie leaned into the lantern's glow. "Do you remember Irstant mentioning the name Jaami?"

"He didn't mention it, but Den told me Jaami was Irstant's Persowan birth-name."

Henri straightened her spectacles to peer at her through the thick lenses. "How did you find out about The Matriarch's Eyes? It is a Pheet Adolan prophecy, is it not?"

Penee nodded. "Irstant shared a scroll containing the prophecy. It states that the birth of a woman with mismatched eyes will herald a change in Pheet Adolan culture. She will lead the Pheet Adole in a shift from a Patriarchy to a more balanced system. My eyes were famous before I was born."

Henri removed her spectacles and tapped her palm. "I see, I see, I see." She smiled. "Your mother planned this, Penee. Her sister Katareen was a specialist in DNA sequencing. They worked together to select and package specimens to transport from El Stroma to TreBlaya." She curled her fingers around the spectacles. "I believe, like you, Elf's heritage is significant."

The girl shrugged. "I don't know about Elf, but I came across another text in Skultar's library when I was researching the Primal Seal." She turned to Brie. "Twins born of Eleo Predan parents will assist the girl with the Matriarch's Eyes to prepare the way for the shift."

Brie's expression grew thoughtful.

Henri tucked her spectacles away.

Penee stroked Shyllee's head. Memories of Elf overwhelmed her. *I wish you were here, Troms el Shiv. At the very least, I wish I had some idea where they have taken you.*

Henri patted a white curl into place. "The puzzle pieces fit together. Brie, please bring Penee up to date on our adventures. We have important decisions to make."

While her niece shared their story and answered Penee's questions, Henri pondered the girls' tremendous potential. Hope glimmered. *We have a chance, Rethdun.*

She projected her thoughts outward. Two of Skultar's men popped up on her mental radar. Picking the weaker one, she used a subtle mental probe to search out information. The discovery they had orders to watch for Penee, Brielle, and herself did not surprise her. The fact she was the primary target left her frowning.

"Are you alright, Aunt Henri?" Brie moved from the floor to the cot.

"Skultar has men on board El Aperdisa. They are here to find us. I'm their primary target. They assume Relevart will be more cooperative if they hold me hostage."

"We can't let them capture her." Brie's attention riveted to her new friend.

Penee's eyes glazed over. Clarity returned. "The search has begun on the ship. They won't discover her on board, so they'll attempt to come down to Soasi."

"Can they teleport?"

"Most Pheet Adole are born without mystical gifts." She scowled. "One of these men is a SorTech. By connecting to The Box, he can travel scant distances."

Henri cleared her throat. "Excuse me, young ladies, I'm not the least bit addled. Perhaps I can contribute to the discussion?" She bobbed her head. "I've already contacted Abarax. He will derail their attempts to come to Soasi for as long as he can. Also, whoever built this room lined it with a material which obscures human energy. We're safe for a time. Shall *we* make a plan?"

"We didn't mean to ignore you, Aunt Henri." Brie's apologetic look spoke volumes.

Chagrin colored Penee's cheeks a rosy pink. "I'm so sorry, Henrietta. I guess I discounted you because of your age. I promise to be more aware."

"Thank you." Henri let a twinkle spark. "Teamwork is essential if we are to succeed." The spectacles appeared in her upraised hand. "The most important thing—rescue the Universal VarTerel." She tapped knee.

Brie nodded. "I'm betting Elf and Ari are close. If we rescue them, they can help rescue Relevart. Can you sense Wolloh?"

Henri touched the spectacles to her temple. At first, she could find nothing to indicate Wolloh existed. At a distance the casual observer might have missed, she picked up a glint of his energy. "He's alive. If I'm not mistaken, he's in a safe place. We let him be. If we can't rescue Relevart, the Universe continues to have a powerful male VarTerel."

She tapped her temple, nodded to herself, and put the spectacles away. Although the girls maintained a respectful silence, their need to be on the move sparkled like a firefly's vibrance. She glanced at Shyllee curled up at her feet. Leaning down, she scratched a black and tan ear. "I bet you're missing your master, aren't you girl?" She straightened to find both girls shaking their heads. "If you two don't calm down, they will find us by tracking your impatience. I believe I have a plan. My instincts suggest we start by rescuing Irstant. I'm certain he is why Relevart went with the Mocendi—as certain as I am that my life-mate could escape if he wished to."

Penee shot her conspiratorial grin. "If we remove all those he feels he must protect, he can escape on his own."

"If he needs help..." Brie nibbled her bottom lip. "...we'll have all the resources we need to rescue him."

Henri smiled her appreciation. "It seems we agree. Alright, ladies. Any idea how we find Irstant?"

Penee contemplated a spot on the floor. "Skultar would not keep him at the Penal Colony." Her gaze sought Henri. "My cousin is smart and cunning. He knows Relevart could tap into Irstant's energy and remove them both from harm's way if he were close by. I bet he's imprisoned Irstant in the cabin where Den and I met Mairin and Lanli. It's in the Astong rainforest on Soputto. Well-hidden and off the beaten path, it's easy to guard."

"You visited the cabin, right?" Eagerness animated Brie's question. "Tell us what you remember."

The description—a cabin backed by high mountains, surrounded by trees, and reachable only by a bridge across a stream—made a ground rescue seem almost impossible.

Brie wrapped a strand of copper-colored hair around her finger. A gentle tug slipped the ringlet off. She studied Penee. "Can you shape shift?"

Penee's astonished expression answered the question. She gulped. "I've never tried. Why?"

"I think flying's the best way to reach the cabin. If we all shape a Soputton bird to do our reconnaissance, we can figure the best way to rescue Irstant. I'm betting Aunt Henri can help you discover if you can shift."

Henri perched her specs on her nose and beamed.

6

A rush of goosebumps left Penee shivering. "It never occurred to me I might have the talent to shift shape."

Henri's twinkling eyes met hers. "We shall see what we shall see, my dear. Clear your mind."

Penee shut her eyes. Excitement stirred her thoughts into a whirlwind. She snuck a peek at Henri. Assuming Brie to be the stronger of the two, the elderly woman's true strength had surprised her. She wanted nothing more than to prove her abilities matched Brie's.

Henri stifled her concern. She sensed the strength of Penee's desire to shift but could not determine whether the girl carried the talent for changing shape. DiMensionery could be capricious. Not everyone carried every talent. Few were as gifted as Brielle or her Aunt Almiralyn. Thanks to

Relevart's birth-mate, Penee exhibited gifts not often found in a Pheet Adolan. *We shall see what you chose for her, dear Rayn.*

"You may open your eyes." Henri noted the uncertainty and the longing in the girl's posture. "Let's get to work, my dear."

"What do I have to do?"

"Stand up and rest your palms on mine. Keep your mind as still as you can."

Rising from the step, Penee inhaled a sustaining breath.

Henri smiled at the energy tingling between them as their palms touched. "Good. Close your eyes. If you feel any discomfort, tell me."

P enee jumped. Prickling reminiscent of SorTechory startled her. She fought the urge to break the connection, to yank her hands from Henri's. Trust and her need to know held her steady. More energy pulsed through her. She exhaled and centered her intent.

"Please look at me, Penesert."

Henri folded her hands in her lap. "Are you certain you wish to try shape shifting?"

Penee rubbed her tingling palms together. Brie's eager nod encouraged her. She grinned. "I do."

Seriousness cloaked the elder VarTerel. "Please, listen closely. Shape shifting, if done without thought and due respect, can end your existence by robbing you of your humanity or ending your life. You must always remember your shifted form is not who you are. You are a Human Being. Spending time in your human body is essential. Keeping your humanness uppermost in your mind is vital. Your failure to do this..." She shook her head. "Do you understand?"

"I do. I promise to be mindful."

"Good. Picture a Soputton bird, one you know well."

Sinking back onto the step, Penee cast her thoughts back to her time at Irstant's cabin and visualized the path through the woods to the bridge. Integrated into its environment, a small, gray owl had watched from a dead tree. She had almost missed it. Her lips twitched into a small grin. She straightened.

"The Soputton gecko owl would be my choice. Den told me it is native to the woods around the cabin. Like a chameleon, it blends in with its surroundings. I've only seen it once or twice, but I'm certain I can picture it." Eagerness fed her growing confidence.

Henri stood. "Brie, alert me to anything out of the ordinary. Penee, please stand."

Excitement propelled Penee to her feet. Brie's broad smile sent another jolt careening through her.

Henri settled her spectacles, her intense gaze fastened on Penee's face. "Settle down, girl. I need you focused. Let me know when you're ready."

Penee soaked in Henri's calming presence. She thought of her mother and Elf and the lessons they'd shared. Confidence steadied her. "I'm ready."

"Concentrate on my voice and follow my instructions. If your instincts tell you it's wrong, tell me. Understood?"

"I understand."

"Good. See the gecko owl in your mind; see every detail you can recall. When it is vibrant and clear, nod."

Penee marveled at the ease with which she pulled the details from her mind: the soft, gray feathers; the darker gray accents; the long, black feathers forming bushy brows over large, round black eyes. She nodded.

"Penee, feel its heartbeat."

A soft gasp escaped. "It is so much faster than ours."

"Stay focused. See if you can sense its brain."

Penee blinked, felt her breathing quicken. A shiver raced from head to toe.

Henri's voice penetrated her thoughts. "Can you hear me?"

"Yes."

"Good. Embrace the bird. On my count—"

A sudden rush of doubt doubled Penee over. "I don't think I can. I don't—"

"Look at me, Penesert." Henri's stern command shocked her like a bucket of cold water.

Shaking herself, she straightened to meet the older woman's gaze.

Magnified violet eyes stared straight into hers. "You have the gift, Penesert. You can dodge it, or you can embrace it. Make your choice. We have little time."

Determination swelled. Penee pictured the owl, felt its rapid heartbeat, and embraced its quick mind. "I'm ready."

"On my three become the owl. I will tell you when to fly. One, two, three—"

The shift, so subtle yet so fast, left no time to digest it. Small talons rested on the stone floor. The diminutive Henri looked gigantic. A voice whispered, "Stretch your wings."

The owl's back muscles rippled; its wings unfurled. The potential to take flight left them quivering.

"Good, Penesert. Fly to my arm."

Owl wings fluttered. She landed, swiveled her head one way and then the other, saw the delight in Brie's face, examined her reflection in Henri's specs, and ruffled her feathers.

Henri's voice demanded her attention. "Fly around the space. Land on the floor in front of me. Do not shift to Human until I snap my fingers."

The delight of her first flight in owl form filled her with joy. A yearning to perch at the top of a tree flooded her thoughts. Grasping the thinning threads of her humanity, she landed. At the snap of Henri's fingers, she shifted.

Human eyelids flickered open. Her heart pounded. "I did it!" Penee laughed. "I did it. I didn't think I could." Tears streamed down her cheeks. "Elf and Yanni would be so proud."

B rie viewed Penee's excitement with a fleeting touch of nostalgia. She recalled her first shift to Water ConDria. Cool water embracing her; thrilling sensations inspired by flight; fluid songs flowing from her throat all made the experience memorable. *Those first moments when the world of your shifted form embraces you are magic.*

Pleasure at both Penee's euphoric expression and her own delightful memories ended abruptly with Shyllee's deep-throated growl. Henri's smile froze halfway to being. Her finger flew to her lips. Brie grabbed Penee's arm. The panel slid open.

Abarax's cherubic features filled the opening. "Mittkeer, now!" He shrunk to the size of a small bat and shot down the stairs

Henri's staff materialized in her hand. Stars and night sky replaced the dim room. The miniature Astican landed on her shoulder.

Brie fought her slight nausea. Penee gagged. Shyllee stood guard, her attention glued to the open portal.

Henri flinched, swatted at something on the side of her neck, and paled. "Brie, Penee, help me."

Clutching the staff, Brie caught Penee's eye. *"Close the portal. Concentrate."*

A bubble of light filled the opening, swirled into a blur of stars, and vanished, leaving the Land of Time silent except for the quiet breathing of three women, a dog, and an Astican.

Brie returned her staff. "Are you alright, Aunt Henri?"

The specs had disappeared into their pocket. She rubbed her neck and tilted her head to see Abarax's tiny form on her shoulder. After a long moment, she looked at the girls. "They almost teleported us onto a jumper craft Skultar obtained from RewFaar."

Penee frowned. "I have to admit my cousin is resourceful. But *he* didn't stop the portal from closing. Who do you suppose did?"

Henri answered. "Abarax isn't certain. He's guessing Skultar's SorTech. The question is where to regroup?"

Inspiration infused Penee's features. "My proxy parents have a lakeside retreat on Soputto. I've only visited it twice, but I'm sure I can picture it."

Henri whispered a command. The rose quartz crystal on the top of the staff glowed. "Let's move deeper into Mittkeer. Once we're clear of TreBlaya's influence, Brie can help you take us there. The tracker beam's effect has left me feeling my age."

Shyllee led the way through the endless night. She looked over her shoulder, gave a sharp bark, and, feathered tail wagging, continued over the carpet of stars.

Dense quiet, as a tactile as a cool breath, caressed Brie's skin. "I am feeling a strange sensation, one I have not experienced in Mittkeer. Are you?"

Penee frowned. "You mean like something is touching your skin?"

Henri stopped. "They're tracking us. How?"

Penee grew stone-still. Her beautiful eyes hardened. "I was a child of perhaps ten sun cycles when Skultar brought a man to my proxy parent's home. He set up a surgery and drugged me. I woke up to my cousin telling Barlet, my proxy father, he would never lose me again. After he left, Coranna showed me a small incision in my neck." She touched the soft tissue behind her left ear. "On rare occasions, like now, it burns."

Abarax flashed to his correct size. Concern wiped everything child-like from his features. "I understand that on El Stroma the Eleo Preda had special birds called tukoolos. A Pheet Adolan jewelry maker invented a disc that helped the birds to form a link to a Human. The technician in the psych lab told me the Pheet Adole military adopted the technology. They took it a step further. I believe you have a stalker disc in your neck. If that's the case, we are at risk of discovery."

Penee pulled a knife from her boot and held it out to the Astican. "I suggest we remove it."

Henri held up a hand. "I suggest we think this through. Kneel, Penee, so I can get a closer look."

The rustling of the Astican's leather scales accompanied her examination. "Better hurry, Miss Henri."

Brie moved to her aunt's side. "How can I help?"

"Support Penee. I'll use my crystal to explore her neck. If I find the disc, I'll do my best to disconnect it." She touched Penee's shoulder. "This may hurt."

Abarax's scales whispered his concern. "Hurry. We must move soon."

Henri touched her staff's crystal termination to the scar.

Penee gave a sharp gasp. Brie squeezed her hand. The crystal burned brighter. Pain ripped through Penee into Brie. Their joint scream obliterated Mittkeer's overriding silence. Henri lifted the staff. A smoking black dot marred the termination, grew smaller, and puffed into nothing. The wound on Penee's neck reknit into a white scar.

Henri sagged. Her staff hit the starry ground. Abarax scooped her up. "We must go."

Brie helped Penee to her feet and retrieved her aunt's staff. "Picture the retreat, Penee. I'll do my best to take us there."

Penee gripped the rowan wood with trembling fingers. Color infused her paled cheeks. Pupils closed to pinpoints and dilated to normal. She gulped a breath. "I can help."

A breath later, they stood in the front room of a lakeside cottage.

7

The subterranean cavern in the Desert of Fera Finnero housed the Atrilaasu Dansmen in times of war. Wolloh knew this chamber well. He had almost died here. Corvus had used his raven power, the knife Efillaeh, and the Remembering Stone to bring him back from the vast Plains of Surazal, the Land of Undead.

He glanced at Stebben, who stretched out on a narrow bed, his chest rising and falling with the labored rhythm of a man fatigued beyond tired.

With a tentative finger, Wolloh traced the healing wound on his cheek, remembering the gentle touch of the woman who had performed the Atrilaasu healing rights. His distorted mouth curved upward. WoNadahem Mardree, the headwoman and Oracle of the desert tribe, held his heart and he hers.

Footsteps paused at the chamber entrance. Framed by the stone archway, WoNa's blind eyes gleamed in the soft light. Limping forward, he took her hands, kissed each palm, and pulled her into his embrace.

"Thank you, WoNa, for allowing us to hide here. I do not wish to bring trouble to Eissua, so we will not stay long."

Sensitive fingers caressed his features. Her lips left a light kiss on his. "I have men watching the portals. They report no strangers entering Fera Finnero. I believe you are safe—at least for a time."

She touched his injured cheek, then stopped to listen. "Stebben sleeps. Dare we slip away?"

Wolloh smoothed a curl away from her face. "Stebben and I must remain a secret. Only you, Narrtep, and Nichi are aware of our presence. Let's keep it that way."

She rested her head on his chest. "I understand. Nichi prepares a meal she will bring here. The three of us will dine together. Following our meal, I must attend a council meeting. The elders are curious about the need to oversee the portals. I will tell them I received word the Sebborr and the Mocendi have joined forces. We must put safeguards in place."

He listened to her footsteps retreat and turned to find Stebben awake and upright.

"How long have I slept?" He yawned.

Wolloh sat opposite him. "Almost a turning. Thank you, my friend, for lending me your strength."

Stebben bowed his head. "It is my honor." His gaze strayed to the entrance. "Do you ever wish you could stay with WoNa at the oasis and live a gentle life?"

Wolloh grinned. "What makes you think life with WoNa would be gentle? She is a powerful woman. I am a powerful man. Power brings with it complexities that can make relationships tangled and messy." He shrugged. "I believe we are living the life we are destined to live. Who knows what tomorrow will bring?"

A beautiful, young woman appeared in the doorway, carrying a food-ladened tray. Wolloh smiled at the subtle change in the room's atmosphere. Stebben hurried to her side, took the tray, and set it down. Warmth—more than that radiating from the fireplace—replaced the usual coolness of the cave. Stebben's hand brushed hers. A blush tinted Nichi's cheeks. Their growing connection enlivened the space, yet, neither appeared to recognize love's seed sprouting.

He stretched out on his bed, his thoughts filled with WoNa.

O n TaSneach, Relevart pretended a drug-induced stupor. Periodic visits by Skultar's SorTech, Furrnoce, provided him the opportunity to garner information. The man's egoic delight at believing he could control the Universal VarTerel made him an easy target for a mental probe.

Reminding himself ego had its positive side if used with awareness, Relevart plucked important information from the man's mind, adjusted the settings on the SorTech's Box, and created a psychic disturbance which obscured the SorTech's ability to obtain clear readings from his brain.

Skultar carried none of the gifts of sorcery, nor those of the mystics of the Eleo Preda. His instincts for detecting deceit, however, outweighed deficiencies in the Arts of DiMensionery. On his rare visits, Relevart became the drugged individual Skultar expected to see.

The cell had been peaceful for some time when Relevart had felt Skultar leave the Penal Colony. Furrnoce's arrogant presence entering the cell turned quiet to chaos. Careless hands checked his restraints and brought him around enough to eat. Weasel-shrewd eyes studied him. "Are you enjoying my drug?" Furrnoce laughed and ushered a tall, well-built man into the cell.

"The drug's wearing off, so be careful, Den. After he eats, tell the med-tech." The SorTech sneered at Relevart and took his leave.

Silence filled the cell until the footsteps faded. "I know you're awake." The straps restraining him loosened. Strong hands helped him to sitting.

Relevart blinked several times, licked drool from the corner of his mouth, and gazed into amethyst-blue eyes. His memories, like curtains parting, revealed another time and a boy named Den Zironho who offered to help Irstant in exchange for training in DiMensionery. Feigning a drug-induced grogginess, he sipped soup, chewed dry bread, and waited.

Den removed the tray. "The latrine's across the hall. Since you have no intention of escaping, I'll take you over. Then we'll talk."

He supported him to the latrine door. "I'll be right here. If I sense you even thinking of doing something ill-advised, I'll sound the alarm."

The door closed; a lock slid into place.

Relevart leaned on the sink. His legs wobbled like they were made from putty. His head swam. The urge to vomit gripped his stomach. An inhaled breath settled his belly. He did his business, splashed cool water on his face, and rapped on the door.

Back in the cell, Den helped him to walk several circuits before assisting him to the cot. Relevart felt leather straps chaffing his ankles and wrists and sighed. He met a studied look with one of his own.

"I know you recognize me, Rethdun. You mustn't give me away to Skultar. In exchange for your silence, I won't give you away."

Relevart remained quiet.

"I sense your speculation, so I'll tell you this much. My position in Skultar's household is complex. As far as he's concerned, I am his to command. We'll let him think that. I'll be telling him you are under the effects of the drug. I have exchanged the vials in the infirmary for something less incapacitating. Please don't let on its different, or we'll both suffer.

"At the moment, Ari and Elf are fine. They will remain so as long as you all cooperate. The twin is a spitfire. Hopefully, she'll behave." He crossed to the door and looked back. "I'll be nearby. I am watching, Relevart. Please don't make me regret trusting you."

A short time later, the med-tech arrived and gave him an injection. Den had told the truth. The medication did little to his system.

He woke from a light sleep to cold darkness and the odd sensation of no one monitoring his thoughts. His mind blank, he waited. No one came to check on him. The realization he had time to himself left him feeling lightheaded. With a grateful sigh, he allowed his thoughts to drift.

During a visit to Irstant, Relevart met Den Zironho in Reachti, the capital of Igran, Soputto's largest continent. At sixteen the boy had taken over Irstant's care from his mother. Smart, eager, and impressed by Relevart's position as VarTerel of the Inner Universe, he expressed his excitement at learning the Arts of DiMensionery and confessed a desire to be a VarTerel. As far as Relevart knew, he had been Irstant's apprentice and constant companion ever since.

Thinking about Den brought him to thoughts of Irstant. He could not pick his location from the SorTech's mind and wondered if the man even knew it. Unwilling to give himself away, he chose not to use a mental probe on Skultar. Instead, he waited from the opportunity to search beyond TaSneach.

Contracting and releasing the muscles of his arms and legs to increase circulation, he pondered Den's ability to short circuit his boss' acute sensitivity to defection.

A yawn turned into a stretch and the desire to move. He refrained from acting on it. His thoughts strayed to the escape of Henri and the girls from TreBlaya. Abarax deserved a pat on the back. The Astican had worked hard to prove its worthiness and to help Relevart hone its potential as a member of the El Stroman exploratory team. All Astican could change shape...few developed telepathic skills. Abarax's extrasensory abilities and his hard work enabled Relevart to warn him about Skultar's imminent arrival in orbit around TreBlaya.

Abarax warned Commander Odnamo. The ship El Aperdisa, now masked, would be difficult but not impossible to detect. RewFaaran advanced technology made it important to stay alert. Relevart crossed his fingers. With luck, Skultar would soon find himself wallowing in disappointment.

S leep heavy and desiring much needed rest, Relevart drifted. *I wonder how Lorsedi Telisnoe will react to Skultar's plans to kidnap his granddaughters?*

8

Brie helped Henri lie down on the sofa at the cottage and arranged a soft cushion beneath her head. "I wish we knew why you're so tired. I've never seen you like this." She scratched Shyllee's ears. "Watch over her, girl."

Relevart's dog licked Henri's cheek and stretched out on a hand-braided rug.

Brie crossed to the floor-to-ceiling windows and absorbed the peaceful beauty of the mountainside lake. Concern over her aunt's fatigue faded enough she even smiled when Abarax's hawk-sized form swooped by, its silvery wings beating a clipped pattern against the air. Circling upward, it alighted on the top branch of a tall evergreen and prepared to keep watch.

Brie studied her reflection in the window. Sudden understanding robbed her of breath. She pressed her hand to the pane. "These are the floor-to-ceiling windows from my dreams. Penee was calling for help. She's Elf's birth-mate.

She is Pheet Adole; he is Eleo Preda. Oh!" Her hand flew to her mouth and lowered. "Floree's poem—"

Henri's knowing expression reflected in the clear glass confirmed she had stumbled on the correct answer to the questions haunting her. Brie experienced a surge of love for her great-aunt, whose presence alone gave her the courage to seek the answers. She watched with a slight smile as Henrietta rearranged the cushion to protect her white curls and let fatigue-weighted lids close. Soft, staccato snores soon floated through the room.

Brie covered her with a handmade throw. Thoughts churning, she returned to the window. *We have to rescue Arienh, Elf, Relevart, and...*" Her warm breath fogged the glass. She wiped it clean, lifted her chin, and almost laughed. *I resemble Ari at her most obstinate."* A realization resonated through her. "I'm every bit as stubborn and even more determined, Arienh. I will find you."

Penee entered the room and placed a tray laden with individual cakes, dried fruit, nuts, and a steaming pot of tea on the antique coffee table. "You're looking overwhelmed."

"I'm astounded at the workings of the Universe, that's all." Brie faced her friend. "I had several dreams about you. In one you were a frightened child. Another showed you gazing at a portrait and crying. A third pictured you staring out of a barred window at a raging blizzard. I went to visit my mother in Myrrh to see if the fountain, Elcaro's Eye, would tell me who you were. A Mocendi had picked up my trail, so my father took me to meet her in Meos.

"Mother is an artist. Her paintings are prophetic. I don't know how she does it, but they show the past, present, or future, depending on what the situation requires. A recent painting depicted me with you, reflected in floor to ceiling windows. I knew I had to find you." She shook her head. "Now I realize a poem given to Relevart when he was only twelve sun cycles is as much about you and Elf as it was about Rethdun and Rayn."

Penee pressed her palms together. "What did it say?"

The image of the spidery script formed in Brie's mind. She recited the first verse.

"Two held in one, two intertwined.
Last representatives of their own kind.
Two torn asunder and worlds apart
Age and grow and mature in their heart."

Penee caught her breath. "Oh my. Is there more?"

Brie gazed over the lake.

"The time draws near to play their role
Rejoin together, return to whole,
Two held in one, uniting what's true,
Planet El Stroma created anew."

Penee's eyes glistened. "Oh, Brielle, Maman used to tell us stories about El Stroma and about our destiny. We knew she spoke the truth, but we were so little—" She brushed away a tear. "Who wrote the poem?"

"The woman who helped Rethdun to escape from El Stroma."

Penee licked tears from the corner of her mouth. "I'll think better on a full stomach. Let's wake Henri. Coranna always keeps the cupboards stocked, so I fixed a snack." Sinking into a wingback, she prepared to pour the tea.

Brie sat on the couch next to her aunt. "Aunt Henri?"

Henrietta yawned and pushed herself upright. After glancing at her niece and noting Penee's tear-stained cheeks, she focused her attention on the tray of goodies. "Just what I need to pick me up, sweets and a cup of hot tea."

Penee offered her a flower-covered mug. "This is Coranna's favorite china mug. Nira Porcelain is the finest china on Soputto."

Henri examined the pattern. "It is lovely, my dear. I understand why it's a favorite." She inhaled. "The tea smells wonderful."

Penee filled a mug for Brie. "Coranna is an herbalist. She grows her own herbs to make tea infusions. This is mint with rose hips." She picked up a handful of nuts, popped one in her mouth, and chewed. "Brie shared Relevart's poem. I knew Elf and I had a destiny—" She shivered.

Henri set her mug on the table, withdrew her specs, and handed them to Penee. "Try these. They may show you something."

She perched the spectacles on her nose. Magnified eyes rounded behind the thick lenses. "Elf. He's locked in a cell on TaSneach." Her brows snapped together. "It looks similar to the one Skultar used to keep me in." She lowered the spectacles and held them out. "These are amazing, Henri. Do you always receive answers to your questions?"

"You see what you are meant to see." Henri tucked them away and resumed sipping her tea.

Penee sighed. "Do you think we are clear of Skultar?"

Henri cradled her mug. "Before we left Soasi, El Aperdisa's captain informed Abarax a RewFaaran warship approached TreBlaya. Lorsedi Telisnoe, RewFar's Supreme Military Leader, has forbidden the use of RewFaaran ships against those who are preparing to rebuild El Stroma." She sipped her tea. "Skultar will soon be busy extricating himself from a situation he did not expect."

Brie set her mug on the table. "I'm glad Grandfather's soldiers won't harm El Aperdisa."

Henri looked thoughtful. "El Aperdisa will be just fine. What's important now is rescuing Irstant so Relevart is free to act. Penee, can you tell us where his cabin is in relationship to this cottage."

"Barlet keeps a map in his office. It will be much easier if you can visualize what I'm talking about." She strode down the hall.

Brie slid closer to her aunt. "You look worn out. Are you alright, Aunt Henri?"

"Traveling through Mittkeer is tiring. In the past, it has felt invigorating and magical." She squeezed the bridge of her nose. "Something is wrong in the Land of Time. Whatever it is saps my energy. It's the best way to get from one place to the other, but it doesn't feel safe." She patted Brie's cheek. "Don't look so worried, my dear. You, Penee, and I are smart and powerful. We'll figure it out."

Penee beamed. "Thanks for including me, Henri." She moved the tray to a side table and spread out a hand-drawn map so they could all see it. "It's time for a geography lesson."

"Soputto, the smallest planet in the Spéire Solar System, has three continents: Igran, the largest; Dast, middle-sized; and Nira, the smallest." She pointed at Dast. "Coranna wished for a private hideaway. The cottage sits on the western side of Lake Llyn, a respectful distance from populated areas. The Sileah Mountains border it on three sides." She touched a spot on Igran. "Irstant's cabin is here in the Canniple Mountains and the Wildwood of

Astong southeast of Reachti, the largest town on the continent. It's a bit of a flight from Dast, but achievable if we stop to rest."

Brie examined the map. "Could we teleport part way, Aunt Henri?"

Henrietta glanced up. "We don't want to call attention to ourselves. First, we need to know who is with Irstant. If Skultar left his SorTech, that is one thing. If he left his Klutarse, that's another."

Penee paced to the window, stared over the lake, then turned. "What if we send Abarax to do some reconnaissance? It's strong enough to make it to the cabin and back in a turning."

Brie grinned. "Brilliant idea. They won't be expecting an Astican. Even if they detect it, I bet they won't recognize its energy."

The Astican ducked under the head jamb of the door, glanced up at the high ceiling, and straightened to its full height. "You need me, Miss Henri?"

Brie provided a quick explanation. Penee described the cabin and pointed out its position on the map.

Abarax studied the detailed drawing, made the women promise to take care of each other, shrunk to the size of a hawk, and soared out through the open door.

"I'm curious to see what it discovers." Brie stifled a yawn. "I could sure use a nap."

A barax landed in the branches of a tall evergreen next to Irstant's moss-covered cabin. Below him, a man sat on the stoop whittling. The sound of water cascading down the side of a mountain mixed with the occasional call of a bird implied all was right with the world.

A second man stepped from the cabin, inhaled, and waved his companion inside. "Old man's sleepin'. Meal's prepared. Let's eat."

The door closed behind them as Abarax alighted on a branch brushing a windowsill. Inside, Irstant slept in a chair by the wood-burning stove. Blistered halves of a wooden staff lying at his feet suggested the men had attempted to destroy it. A tiny sparkle drew Abarax's eye. The crystal usually adorning the top of the staff had rolled beneath the old man's chair. Filing the information away to share, Abarax continued to study its owner.

Henri had explained that Irstant could neither see nor speak. Even so,

Abarax felt his power. Its scales ruffled and resettled. The old man did not sleep. He waited.

Abarax turned its attention to the two men sharing a meal at a small table. Neither carried the energy of a Klutarse or SorTech, nor did there appear to be a Box anywhere in the cabin.

"Beware. Klutarse close-by."

The telepathic thought flooding Abarax's thoughts triggered his lift into flight. It made a wide circle of the clearing, came to a rest behind a curtain of witch hair moss, and masked its mind.

Mounted on a majestic roan horse, a man traversed the track through the trees. Bringing his mount to a stop at the far end of a rustic bridge, he surveyed the area. Intelligent eyes skimmed the trees and swept over the fast-moving creek to the cabin.

He urged his horse into an ambled walk. The muffled clip clop of hooves, a soft rhythm on the damp wood, ended as it stepped onto the mulchy soil. The Klutarse dismounted and looped the reins over a bush. With a final piercing scan, he disappeared inside.

Abarax remained hidden. The echoed remnants of the Klutarse's strength pulsated through The Astong. Its gradual withdrawal brought a sigh of relief from the creatures living close by. Nature bustled once again.

Abarax, its scales reflecting the colors of water and foam, rocks and fallen branches, put a safe distance between it and Irstant's cabin and then soared upward. Over Igran's desolate eastern plains, it reclaimed its natural size, pressed powerful wings against the air, and set its sights on the lakeside cottage. Soon, the Sea of Canttila glistened beneath it. The Soputton sun hovering above the horizon tinted the thick fog obscuring Neul Isle's topography a soft shade of coral. A sweeping arc carried Abarax toward the continent of Dast. Land looming prompted a shift to a smaller form. Ignoring the beginnings of fatigue, it streaked inland. The moon, TaSneach, crested the Sileah Mountains as Abarax swooped over the lake.

Coranna and Barlet's lightless cottage detoured it to the top of a tree. Profound stillness held it motionless. A man draped in a calf-length black cape strode onto the terrace and stared at TaSneach's reflection on the lake. A breeze flared the bottom of the cape. The purple lining glistened in the moon's light.

The MasTer's Mocendi. Abarax silenced its thoughts and waited.

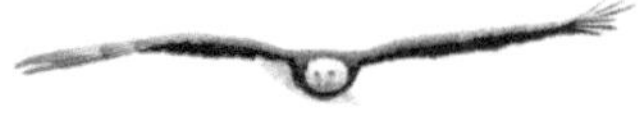

An urgent shake woke Brie from the first sleep she'd had in turnings. Henri, finger to lips, peered down at her and beckoned. Blanking her mind and obscuring her presence behind subtle wards, Brie tiptoed after her aunt to the room where Penee slept. One hand on her friend's arm and the other on Henri's shoulder, she waited. Shyllee, ears alert, stood beside Henri. They arrived in a tight, silent group in the boathouse a short distance along the boardwalk paralleling the lakeshore.

Penee woke with a start. Panic brought her upright. Brie's soft 'shh' held her quiet.

Henri's spectacles glistened in her hand. *"Brielle, Abarax has returned. Find it. I'll take care of Penee."*

To hide her presence, Brie shifted to a gecko owl and fluttered to an open window. A nod from her aunt sent her flying into the forest bordering the lake. As she landed in a tall, leafy tree, a flash of purple alerted her to mask her presence.

The MasTer's Mocendi rotated, his gaze darting from tree to tree. A mental probe sliced through the night. Dissatisfaction permeating the air, he pivoted in a swirl of black and purple, raised his hand, and opened a vortex. A final sweeping gaze and he leapt into the spinning gateway, closing it after him.

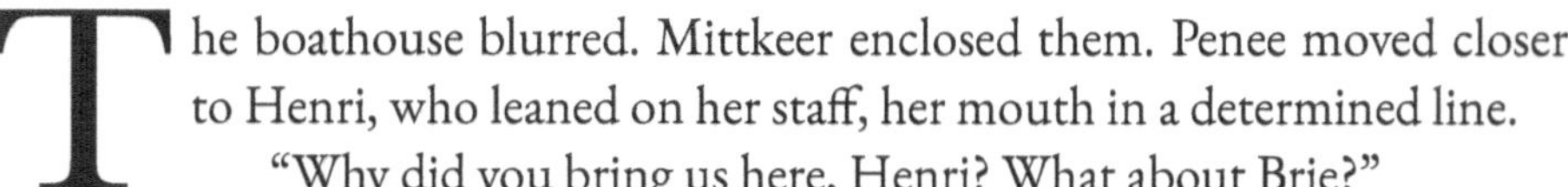

9

The boathouse blurred. Mittkeer enclosed them. Penee moved closer to Henri, who leaned on her staff, her mouth in a determined line.

"Why did you bring us here, Henri? What about Brie?"

The elder tucked her spectacles out of sight. "Thorlu..." She shivered. "Brie and Abarax are off to seek Irstant." Her jaw clinched.

"Are you alright?"

Henri ignored the question. "Let's walk."

Arm in arm, Penee walked at her side. Step by step, their pace slowed. Moment by moment, Mittkeer pirated Henri's vitality. Fatigue deepened the lines in her face. Pale blue lips pressed together in a thin line. Her usual robustness dimmed.

Shyllee whined.

The diminutive VarTerel stumbled.

Penee steadied her with a supporting arm encircling her waist. "Henri, help me understand what's happening."

A puzzled shake of her head bounced silver-white curls. "I wish I knew. Something in Mittkeer is pilfering my life force. I can't put my finger on what, so I can't stop it. We must get out, or it may trap us forever."

Collecting her panicking wits, Penee gripped the rowan wood staff. "What can I do to help?"

"Don't let go of my staff." Surprise wiped the fatigue from Henri's expression. "Rayn, Rayn, you worked a miracle."

"What happened, Henri? You look much better."

"Your strength has enhanced mine, but only for the moment. We must leave Mittkeer." Her voice trembled. "I can't take us. Listen carefully. Picture somewhere safe. Fill yourself with its image. When you're ready, nod and *think* us there."

Penee's heartbeat quickened. "I'm Pheet Adole. There's only so much I can do."

Henri's shaking hand rested on her steady one. "Your mother bred you to your destiny. Think of a safe place before I can't help you reach it."

Penee's mind scrambled. *Safe? Where in my life have I been—* "I've got it, Henri. On three, give me whatever help you can." She forced her racing heartbeat to normalize. "One. Two. Three!"

The walls of a room enclosed them. Pain shot from one throbbing temple to the other. Nausea rolled through her like a tsunami. A moan of distress from Henri jerked her upright. Penee shoved her nausea away and assisted her companion onto the bed.

Hurried footsteps alerted her to company. Shyllee growled. The door flew open. Barlet, her proxy father, marched into the room. His wife peeked around the jamb. With a cry of surprise, Coranna joined him.

Tears of pain and relief streaming down her cheeks, Penee straightened. "I didn't know where else to go. Except for TreBlaya, this is the only safe place I have ever known." Neither spoke. She rushed on. "I know I have put you at risk. Say the word, and we'll leave."

Coranna brushed a tear from Penee's cheek and threw trembling arms around her. "We'll help. What's wrong with your friend."

Penee turned to find Henri as still as death. Blue tinted her lips. Shallow, uneven breaths rattled in her throat. Fear of putting her proxy parents in danger kept Penee silent. Concern for Henri loosened her tongue. "I have so much to share. But first, please help me save Henri."

Her proxy mother held out a hand to Shyllee. The dog's black and tan tail wagged. Coranna moved to the bedside, pulled a small notebook from her pocket, and scribbled. "Barlet, go to the herb hut and bring back what is on this list." She glanced at Penee. "Don't tell anyone we have guests."

A quick look passed between her proxy parents. Barlet hugged her and departed. As soon as his footsteps faded into the quiet, Coranna checked Henri and looked up at her proxy daughter. "You'd better tell me what's going on. Neither Barlet nor I will give you away. We'll do our best to protect you both."

Penee sank into the chair by the bed. "When we left here almost five cycles ago, Skultar took me to a penal colony and locked me in a cell. I escaped and, with help, found my birth-mate, Elf. Skultar kidnapped him, one of Henri's granddaughters, and an injured VarTerel to use against Relevart, the Universal VarTerel." She gave the astonished Coranna a moment to absorb her story.

Her proxy mother gazed down at the elderly woman. "And who is Henri?"

"Henrietta is Relevart's life-mate. Skultar wants her so he can keep Relevart in line. Coranna, my cousin isn't the only one after us. It's complicated." Footsteps on the stairs interrupted. "I'll share more when I can."

Barlet strode into the room with a basket of herbs. Coranna went to work mixing a nostrum which she administered a drop at a time. A hint of color returned to Henri's cheeks. The blue faded from her lips. Violet eyes blinked and focused first on the ceiling, then on the woman holding her wrist between cool fingers. She mouthed the word 'Penee'.

Penee moved to Coranna's side. "I'm here, Henri. This is my proxy parents' home. We're safe."

Coranna covered her patient with a light blanket. "You need to rest, Henri. We will be near." She organized several small bottles on the bedside table. "I'll give you two a moment. Don't tire her any more than she is, Penee." She slipped into the hall.

Penee kissed Henri's cheek. "Sleep. I'll check on you in a bit."

Henri's eyes closed.

Penee tiptoed from the room and followed Coranna downstairs.

Her stepfather met them in the study. He looked from one woman to the other. "I am not one of Skultar's lackeys. I promise, Penee, not to give you away. If we are to help, however, I must know what's going on."

Coranna sat next to him and slipped a hand into his. "Fill us in, Penee."

At the lakeside cottage, Brie tipped her owl head and watched the Mocendi disappear into the swirling vortex. Peace settled over the lake. The call of a night bird shrilled. A fish jumped nearby.

A miniature Abarax landed on the pitched roof of the cottage. Moonlit blue eyes gleamed. *"Henri?"*

Brie lifted into flight. Her circuitous path ended at the boathouse. She flew through the window and shifted. Henri and Penee were no longer there.

Where she had last seen them, the Mocendi gazed at her, a brow arched. Charm laced with malice oozed from his half smile. "You're surprised? After all, Relevart banished us to a hideous dimension. You believed we were trapped their forever." Rage-fueled arrogance blistered the surrounding air. "Relevart only thinks he is all powerful."

Brie schooled her expression to neutral. "Hello, Thorlu Tangorra. What can I do for you?"

He took a menacing step. A miniature Astican landed on the rafter above him. Brie held her ground.

"I owe Relevart a visit. Where can I find him?"

"I understood Almiralyn and Corvus were taking you to him."

Thorlu folded his arms across his chest and snarled. "Tell me where he is, Brielle, and I won't hurt your sister."

The threat made her suppress a shiver. Wishing she could dissemble, she sorted the truth into snatches. The Star of Truth gave a slight stab. "He is in Spéire Solar System near Soputto." It eased.

Narrowed eyes held her for a long moment, then blinked. "Rumor has it you have found Elf's birth-mate. Where is she?"

A wave of relief made her feel giddy. "I don't know."

"I know someone is here with you. Tell them to show themselves."

Her attention riveted to the Mocendi, she responded. "I don't see anyone but you."

The Mocendi moved. Their chests almost touched. Her skin crawled. "Thorlu, if you want to see Relevart, you will need to find him. He can answer your questions. I cannot."

Thorlu grew pensive. "You have changed since we last met." A penetrating appraisal raised the hair on the back of her neck. "Something has changed." He reached to take her arm.

Her shields shooting into place stopped him. His hand brushed the barrier. He flinched and jerked it away. "You will come with me even if I have to render you unconscious."

The flutter of wings announced the arrival of a bird-sized Astican on the floor between them. Abarax flashed to its full height. Celestial blue eyes in its stone-cold seraphic visage glared at the Mocendi. Taloned fingers gripped Thorlu's throat. The color drained from his face.

"Abarax, do not kill him."

The Astican's rosebud mouth worked. Its scales susurrated a chorus of resistance. Releasing the Mocendi, it let him fall to the floor, nudged the body with a toe, and shot a petulant look in Brie's direction.

Brie looked up at the pouting face. "Thank you, Abarax. Please only kill if there is no other way."

She glanced around the boathouse. A coil of rope hung on a nail on the wall. "Grab the rope. We'll tie him up."

She tied the last knot and recited,

> *"Ropes be tight and keep him caught*
> *Hold him firmly with your knot*
> *When I'm gone, set him free*
> *Erase all memories of me."*

She studied him for a long moment. "The ropes won't keep him long, but at least they'll slow him down."

Abarax followed her onto the walkway. She looked up at the haggard face. "When was the last time you slept or ate?"

A shrug shook the enormous body. "I will manage."

"You keep watch; I'll fix food. We both need to be alert and strong for what is coming." She angled her head to see it better. "What do Astican eat?"

The tired features softened. "Fix me what you fix yourself." It grinned. "Only more." It sniffed the night air. "Morning comes. We must go before full light."

Brie hurried to the cottage. Coranna had left the larder well-stocked. A quick inventory resulted in two bowls, one large, one smaller, filled with home-canned meat and vegetables. Carrying them onto the terrace, she set them on a picnic table.

The Astican joined her. His first bite produced a grin. "Excellent food."

She chewed a succulent chunk of meat. "Coranna is a superb cook."

They ate in silence, watching the light warm the tops of the mountains. After they had eaten their fill, Abarax went to check on Thorlu. Brie cleaned up, making certain she left the kitchen the way they'd found it.

The Astican waited on the terrace. "He is unconscious but won't be much longer. We need to get a head start, so he cannot track us."

Brie shrugged on a supply filled knapsack. "How far?"

"It is a goodly distance. You may ride on my back most of the way."

"But, Abarax, I am too big—"

The ring of leather slapping leather announced the appearance of a ludoc cat, reminiscent of the one in the Tinga Forest in Trinuge. Silver-gray scales covered its body and wings. The facial features retained a hint of the Astican's cherubic appearance. It whipped its extra-long tail. She grinned in amazement. Scrambling on its back, she pressed her knees into its side and clutched thick, narrow scales forming a row of hand holds over its shoulders.

It crouched. *"I go."* The two words preceded the unfurling of huge wings. It launched into the air. Wind tugging her hair and pulling at her clothing, reminded her of riding on the back of a Pentharian. The lake dropped away beneath them. A burst of exaltation surged through her. *I'm glad Shyllee stayed with Henri.*

The Astican banked away from the mountains and swept toward the sea. Brie knew they would reach Igran all too soon. A breath of fresh air reminded her to enjoy the moment. The future would unfold in its own time.

10

Excitement mounting, Brie peered ahead at the continent of Igran cresting the horizon. Abarax's ludoc form flew with renewed vigor over the glistening Sea of Canttila toward the fast-growing land mass. Huge, gray wings carried them along the curve of the rocky shoreline to the mouth of a creek emptying its gurgling fresh water into the salty sea. Four legs touched down on sand and ocean-smoothed pebbles. The ludoc furled its wings and swung its massive head in her direction. The words *'break time'* chimed in Brie's mind. Happy to rest, she slid to the ground and stretched her tired muscles.

Abarax's height dominated the landscape. Its scales whispered their shimmery song. Seraphim-blue eyes gazed down at her. "We are at the edge of the Veld of Igran. Villagers say it is the home of a race of carnivores. Soputtons steer clear of it, and so shall we. Rest, Brielle AsTar. I will keep watch."

She needed no further urging. Her pack tucked under her head, she curled up on coral-tinted sand. To the sounds of creek and ocean merging, she slipped into a dreamless sleep. Too soon, the persistent sound of leather slapping leather woke her.

The Astican sat on a rock, munching bright-colored flowers from a pile next to it. "We must make plans. This creek leads to Irstant's cabin. Two soldiers and a Klutarse guard him. The VarTerel only appears to be in an exhausted sleep." Abarax licked its lips. "He awaits his chance. I suggest we give it to him. One more thing—they have tried to burn his staff. They broke it in two. The crystal is under the old man's chair. We must not only rescue him, but the pieces of his staff."

Brie rummaged in the pack for food. Abarax offered her a yellow flower. "These are nasturtiums. Their stems are filled with vitamin-rich honey. The flower petals will provide you with an energy boost. Eat. Then we must go." He studied her with interest. "I sense in you the power of a VarTerel, Brielle AsTar."

She took the flowers and nibbled a petal.

"You do not have to tell me, Brielle, but..." It studied her, its cherub features more serious than she could ever remember. "What I need to know is if you can enter Mittkeer? If you can't tell me, how do you suggest we escape? And where is the best place to hide Irstant?"

Her promise to Chealim made her avoid his question. "If he isn't hurt or drugged, he may have ideas. I think we should fly to the cabin to assess his state and see what his guards are up to. Hide the backpack near the creek, so we have supplies if we need them." She popped another flower into her mouth. Savoring the sweetness, she shifted to a gecko owl.

Abarax stuffed the pack in the upper branches of a tree, shrunk to match the owl's size, and led the way along the meandering course of the stream.

As she followed the Astican, Brie marveled at the diversity of the Wildwood of Astong's temperate rainforest. The sun slipped lower. A chorus of cascading water grew to a crescendo. The sounds of men's voices sent the Astican into the trees. Gecko owl feathers changing to match the greens and browns of the forest, she landed beside the small Abarax on a sturdy, leaf-covered branch a short distance from the cottage.

Two men, their horses saddled ready to travel, huddled near the stoop, arguing.

"I'm telling you he's dead. He's not breathing. There's no heartbeat. No one can fake *that*."

A second man placed fisted hands on his hips. "What if the old man's fakin' and gets away? Governor Skultar will have our heads."

"Old man's not going anywhere. If the gov wants the body, we can send someone to pick it up." Disgust dripped from each word.

A man, dressed in the black and purple uniform of a Klutarse, exited the cabin. "Stop the arguing. Irstant is dead. We no long have a reason to hang out here."

He marched down the steps, collected his horse's reins from the first man, and mounted. Not waiting for his men to respond, he nudged the horse into a walk. At the bridge, he looked over his shoulder. "See you in Reachti."

Speculative glances darting to the cabin and back to the bridge, the remaining men climbed into the saddle and urged their horses forward.

The sounds of the forest gradually returned to normal. A telepathic messaged whisper through Brie's owl mind. *"Stay."*

Abarax flew in the direction they had taken. Brie made a mental search of the area. Nothing stirred outside the cabin or in.

A man-sized Abarax materializing beneath the tree brought her to the ground in human form. The Astican preceded her to the stoop. It pushed the door ajar and peered inside before ducking into the interior. Brie waited, impatient for a signal to join him. When it didn't come, she entered and gave herself a moment to adjust to the dimness. Abarax stood, stone still, in a doorway across from her. She tiptoed to his side.

Inside the rustic room an elderly man lay on a cot, milky white eyes staring. Blue lips, in harsh contrast to the man's paleness, gaped open. The chest neither rose nor fell.

Brie took a step and froze. The old man blinked out of sight, leaving only an empty cot surrounded by dumbfounded silence.

Taloned fingers clasped her arm and propelled her into the clearing. Hidden behind a tree, they watched the cabin waft from solid to opaque to nothing.

The puzzled Astican regarded the abundant overgrowth. Gold and red flowers mingled with large leafed plants and fallen tree trunks covered with moss. "What happened?"

"I'm not sure." Something prompted her to explore. An auditory search identified only forest sounds: cascading water, the gush of the creek under the bridge, birds exchanging songs, a breeze traveling the treetops. Nothing Human came to her attention, nothing indicated anyone lingered near. Remembering that Relevart's cabin could fade when not in use calmed the tingle of fear. A flicker of light beneath a golden yellow flower enticed her to venture from behind the tree. Caution in the form of Abarax's hand kept her motionless.

"What is it you sense, Brielle AsTar?"

The light winked. *Usolamet.* The word whispered through her mind. She caught her breath, crossed to the plant, and pushed the leaves away. Nestled half-hidden in a bed of moss lay a clear quartz crystal. Abarax peered over her shoulder. "Is it the crystal from Irstant's staff?"

Brie held it up. "Usolamet is its name." She pushed aside soft soil. Beneath it, she discovered the blackened halves of the rowan shaft.

Handing the crystal to Abarax, she stood. A piece of the shaft in each hand, she hefted their weight. "Why would someone remove Irstant and the cabin and leave behind his staff and crystal?"

Furrowed brows aged Abarax's guileless features. "Is it not true a VarTerel's staff magnifies his abilities? Would Irstant have left it behind?"

Her full attention on the scorched pieces of rowan wood, Brie fit the ends together. A loud crack echoed through the trees. Light exploded, robbing her of sight. Heat raced up her arms and pooled in her chest. She blinked against the lingering brightness, saw the staff made whole, and smiled.

Abarax helped her to balance the glowing crystal on the top. Tendrils of rowan covered in tiny leaves wove an intricate pattern, cocooning it. Power shot down the shaft to the earth and back. A final leaf wrapped around Usolamet. The profile of a gyrfalcon, etched in relief on the wood by an invisible artist, emerged.

Brie raised it to the heavens. Tears spilled down her cheeks. "Usolamet has rendered the staff whole. Until we find Irstant, I wield its power in his name."

She lowered it. Danger sizzled in the clearing. The faint shimmering of a forming vortex hovered at the center of the bridge. She grabbed the Astican's wrist and raised the staff. The forest blurred; the mouth of the stream poured into the sea.

"Abarax, get the pack. We don't want to leave anything behind."

She glanced back along the creek. As though sucked through a straw, the water receded. "Quick, Abarax! We need to go."

The Astican sprinted to her side. Again, she gripped its wrist. Sunlight and ocean vanished into the star-studded landscape of Mittkeer. The endless stars blurred into the terrace of the lakeside cottage on Dast.

A wave of exhaustion left Brie sagging against her companion.

Abarax held her steady. "Are you alright?"

She leaned on the staff. "I guess I'm not used to channeling so much energy." A deep breath of fresh air eased her fatigue.

A long taloned finger pointed at the cottage. "Why here?"

"We have to find Penee and Aunt Henri. The last time I saw my aunt, she was feeling ill. She knew Penee had the power to help her, so she told me to rescue Irstant. The cottage belongs to Penee's proxy parents. She felt safe here. If she had to choose somewhere else safe to take Henri, where would it be?"

Silver-gray scales shivered and rustled into place. It shrugged.

"Coranna and Barlet raised her. I'm betting she would go to their manor house."

It cocked its head. "We do not know this house." Understanding dawned. "Ahhh, that is why we are here. You think we might discover a clue to where it is?"

"I do. In order to take us there through Mittkeer, I need to find something that will stimulate an image of house or the grounds." A shiver skittered up her neck. "We need to hurry."

The side door opened. Penee, her expression stricken, motioned them inside. Locking the door behind Abarax, she faced them, her famous eyes filled with dread.

Brie looked beyond her. "Where are Aunt Henri and Shyllee?"

Penee placed a finger on her lips. She hurried them along a hallway to a room hung with Barlet's hunting trophies. She crossed to a gun-case against the inner wall, slipped her hand behind it, and pushed. The case slid aside; a panel opened inward.

"You'll need to shrink, Abarax, it's a tight fit for Barlet."

The Astican shrunk to several inches high and perched on Brie's shoulder. Penee descended a cramped staircase, waited for Brie to move past her, and pulled a lever. The case slid into place and the door swung shut, leaving them in a narrow passage. A short distance along it, Penee dodged through a doorway.

Brie stepped inside. A lantern's light fluttered and steadied. Penee stood in the center of a well-stocked hide-away. "Barlet never trusted my cousin, so he built this. I was thirteen when he showed it to me. It's lined with a special metal that will block anyone trying to find me using the tracker disc. He made me promise to use it if I needed to hide from Skultar or anybody else. I sometimes feel he and Coranna know more about me than they let on."

She dropped onto a stool, her shaking hands clasped in her lap. The stricken look returned. "Henri and I traveled through Mittkeer to their home outside of Reachti. When we arrived, she was ill. Coranna treated her with herbs, and we left her to rest. Shyllee's frantic barking a short time later brought us running. We reached the bedroom to discover that Henri had disappeared. The only thing to show she'd ever been there was this." She retrieved Henri's staff and held it up in the light. "Shyllee made sure I found it. I'm so sorry, Brielle."

Brie fought to control a riptide of emotion. She rested her forehead against the shaft of Irstant's staff, forcing air in and out of her lungs. A long breath brought her gaze to Penee's face. "Irstant vanished, too. He disappeared right in front of us. Abarax and I exited the cabin moments before it faded away. The only thing that remained was Irstant's staff. What's going on?" She looked from Henri's staff to Penee. "You used the staff to travel through Mittkeer, correct?"

"When Henri vanished, I knew I had to find you." Her shoulders drooped. "I asked Coranna and Barlet to take care of Shyllee, picked up the staff, and wished I could be in Mittkeer. The next thing I knew, I was there. Without consciously picturing the cottage, I arrived here." She yawned. "I did not understand using the staff would be so exhausting. Do you think Henri and Irstant are alright?"

A human-sized Abarax sank cross-legged to the floor and spread out its wings. "Whoever has them wants them alive, otherwise, why bother to kidnap them? We must discover who the enemy is. It is impossible to fight what we do not know."

Penee sighed. "I'm too tired. I can't think." She stifled a yawn. "Rest now, decisions later."

Pulling two bunks down from the wall, she placed Henri's staff on the top one, climbed up, and yawned. "Don't worry, Brie. We're safe down here." Curled onto her side, she slept.

Brie sat in the silence of the insulated room. Thoughts racing whippet-fast through her mind kept her from sleeping. Much too tired to sort through them, she stretched out on the bunk.

Abarax changed to a ludoc cat and curled up by the door. Its soft, purr-like snores, a comforting chorus, worked like a lullaby.

Brie rested her head on an arm. *I promise to find you, Aunt Henri.*

11

Relevart woke to the sense of something wrong. Forcing himself to lie motionless, he made a mental search of the compound. The Penal Colony guards and residents functioned as usual. Ari and Elf remained close at hand. Skultar had not returned with SorTech Furrnoce. Den slept in a room down the hall. Using his VarTerel's power, Relevart extended his search to include the planet of Soputto. Irstant's essence, usually strong at his cabin, had faded to a mere spark. He could feel Brie, Penee, and Abarax somewhere on the continent of Dast. Henri, like Irstant, was the tiniest blip on his radar.

He let his senses choose their own course. Realization crept into his knowing with the subtlety of a heartbeat. Time, the Dark Matter of the Universe—the glue keeping everything in its place—was seeping away. Within the boundaries of All Time and No Time, stars and constellations, galaxies and solar systems faded. Mittkeer grew smaller as he watched.

Den stirring in his room down the hall ended his exploration. Irstant had trained him well. The man was a talent—also an enigma.

Relevart slowed his racing heart and forced his breathing to normalize. Peering beneath half-closed lids, he discovered the subject of his brief reverie looking down at him. The man's demeanor was unreadable.

"You must be careful, Relevart. Had Furrnoce been close—" He folded his arms. "But then, you know he is on a ship traveling to TaSneach from TreBlaya." His expression grew distant. A tiny smile tugged but did not make it to fullness. "It appears Lorsedi Telisnoe has sent Skultar packing. I imagine he will be in a foul mood when he returns." White teeth blazed, a contrast to his tanned skin. "Ah, I talk too much. You must tell me sometime what increased your heart rate." Turning on his heels, he strode from the cell.

In the hidden room at the cottage, Brie woke with a start. Abarax slept soundly. Penee's change in breathing suggested she, too, stirred. *What woke me?* The urge to attempt a mental probe rolled her onto her side; the realization that insulated walls would keep her cocooned cancelled it.

Penee peered over the edge of the upper bunk. "Something woke me up. Did you feel it?"

Abarax stirred. Consternation shaped its ludoc features. It shifted to a miniature Astican and perched on Brie's shoulder.

She put a finger to her lips, stood up, and clasped Irstant's staff. Penee climbed down from the upper bunk, bringing Henri's with her. They hiked up the stairs to the secret door. Tiptoeing into the front room, they stood transfixed.

Eerie colors reflecting off the lake's surface refracted, shot upward, and exploded into showering fireworks-light. Where sprinkles of color hit the lake's surface, a misty figure billowed into being. Brie's breath caught in her throat. Relevart's gaze sought hers. Whispered words pervaded her thoughts. The figure melted away. Colored light morphed into opaline dragonflies, flying along TaSneach's diamond path, and then upward to vanish amidst starlight and moonbeams.

A massive, panther-like darkness prowled over the mountains, devoured the moon's reflected light, and obscured the world behind undulating, black clouds.

Brie's heartbeat thrummed in her ears. Her knees buckled. Penee kept her from falling. Abarax grew to human size, scooped her up, and carried her to the bunk in the hidden room.

The fight to steady her thumping heart left her shaking. She drew in a breath. With her exhale, she released her sudden loss of energy. A sigh left her staring up at the ceiling.

Penee knelt. "Tell us what happened."

She tipped her head. "Did you hear anything?"

"Nothing, Brie. I saw the light over the lake explode." She shivered. "I saw pitch black roll over the mountains and cloak everything in its path."

Pushing herself to sitting, Brie massaged her temples. What had Relevart told her? She hugged her bent legs and rested her forehead on her knees. The whispered words took shape. *"To save Henri and Irstant, find the time eater."*

Save Henri and Irstant? Time Eater? Her head came up. "Penee, you said Henri was ill, right?"

Penee moved to the edge of the cot. "Remember the turning we arrived at the cottage the first time? She couldn't stay awake. You left to find Irstant. Henri and I escaped the Mocendi by going into Mittkeer. I led us out because she was too weak. When we reached Coranna and Barlet's house, she passed out on the bed. The last time I saw her, she looked awful. What happened on the lake?"

Brie described what she had seen. "Relevart whispered a message. He told me that to save Henri and Irstant, we must find the time eater."

Abarax loomed over her. "What is this time eater?"

"I'm not sure." Staring into space, Brie let her mind roam free. "Ahhhh. Penee, the last time you were in Mittkeer, how did you feel?"

"Exhausted. All I wanted was to sleep. I still can't seem to get enough."

Brie pressed her lips together. "Me, too. Where would a time eater find the most time to devour?"

The sound of Astican scales ruffling and slapping into place filled the hidden room. Its speculation morphed to realization. "The Land of All Time. But, Brielle, I do not tire in Mittkeer."

"You don't manipulate time, Abarax. VarTerels do." She came to her feet and paced the compact room. Her mind fit fragments of memory together in a time-defined mosaic. A history of their trips through Mittkeer took shape. What she could not figure out...who became ill first, Irstant or Henri. At the end of her paced path, she marched back to Penee.

"Irstant wasn't ill when you first met him, correct?"

"He appeared to be fine."

Brie continued to pace and stopped gazing into space. "The first time I noticed Henri's fatigue, we had just arrived at the cottage. I noticed it in myself then and even more so after we returned to begin a search for you."

Penee tapped her chin. "It hit me initially when I took Henri to the manor house and again when I returned to the cottage. I controlled time during both trips because Henri couldn't." Her brow creased. "How did I do that? I'm not a VarTerel?"

"Rayn must have made sure you had the power to become one." Brie sat next to her. A yawn gave her a moment of quiet reflection. She wiped a tear from her cheek. "I believe the time eater is in Mittkeer. What do you think?"

"It's the only place we have all been." Penee furrowed her bow. "What is a time eater? How do we find it? Once we know what it is, do we destroy it?"

Brie smothered another yawn. "I need sleep. Let's nap. Abarax, please keep watch." She stretched out on her bunk.

Penee stood. A yawn caught her midway to the top bunk. She glanced down. "I hope this fatigue goes away soon." She sprawled on the bunk and fell into a deep sleep.

Abarax sat with his back against the door. "I believe we must go into Mittkeer to solve the mystery, Brielle. Sleep while you can."

Brie absorbed the calming darkness. The chorus of soft snores floating through the room lulled her to sleep.

Dreams tiptoed into her subconscious. Clouds obscuring the dreamscape misted into nothing. A huge hourglass hovered above the lake. Stars and constellations filling the top half quivered. Point-like particles of time dripped through the narrowed neck, splashed against the obsidian base, and misted away. Each drop vibrated the entire length of Brie's body. Each robbed her of seconds of life.

Relevart's essence creeping back into his body caused nerve endings to sting in response. He peered into absolute blackness. Cold crawled over his skin. Frigid air burning his lungs exited in a frosty cloud.

A key rattled in the lock. Lantern in hand, Den marched to the cot. "What have you been up to, old man? Your cell is an icebox."

Without waiting for an answer, he hurried away and returned with a glowing portable heat-emitter. After placing it near the cot, Den unfastened the restraints and helped Relevart to sit.

Icy tremors shook him from head to foot. He nodded his thanks. "S-s-skultar?"

Den took a hand between his and endeavored to restore the circulation. "Not back. Where did you go? I felt you one moment, the next…nothing."

Relevart reviewed his options—to trust or not to trust? A frigid spasm shuddered through him. "T-t-time leaks f-f-from The Universe."

Handsome features twisted in disbelief. Den's mouth worked around denial. He pressed his lips together. Acuity flooded expressive eyes. "That's why Mittkeer is so hard to travel through." He stared at the hand in his.

Relevart remained silent.

Den's penetrating gaze returned to his face. "So, who did you alert? Please do not dissemble."

The smack of boots against the stone floor of the passageway ended their conversation. Den released Relevart's hand, motioned him onto the cot, tossed a blanket over him, and faced the young guard entering the cell.

"Skultar is on the way back. He wants you in the Communications Center, like yesterday." The guard scowled.

Den waved him from the cell. "Tell him I am on the way."

The sound of running feet retreated. Den buckled the straps and leaned over Relevart. "Keep your secret for now, VarTerel. Furrnoce will be back soon. You'd best prepare for The Box."

The door clanged. The key rattled. Silence returned to the cell.

12

Penee woke from a deep sleep, fighting to remember. Pitch black hid her surroundings. *Where am I? Who am I?* The rough length of a staff pressed against her back. A crystal's faint hum assaulted her ears. *Why do I have a staff?* Soft snores drifted upward, dissipating and repeating at equal intervals. *I'm not alone. Who?*

Shaking off the befuddling effects of sleep, she forced herself to awaken fully. Prickles of fear tingling up her neck brought her upright. Her head swam. She rubbed her temples. *What's going on? What's wrong with my memory?*

A vague remembrance claimed her. *Oh!* She released the breath. *I am Penee. I'm safe. This isn't a prison.* Memories trickled back a piece at a time. Her confidence returned. *Barlet built it. I'm at the cottage.*

Another muffled snore penetrated the stillness. Penee heaved a relieved sigh. *Brielle and Abarax.* Snatches of conversation from earlier in the turning reminded her of time eaters and Mittkeer.

She crept down the ladder, leaned Henri's staff next to Irstant's, and stood listening.

A hand grabbed hers and pulled her down onto the lower bunk. Bedding shifted. The bunk squeaked. A body squirmed closer. "Who are you? Where are we?"

Penee slid to the floor. Feeling her way, she found a lantern, flicked the switch to ignite the wick, and adjusted it to a low setting. Angling it toward the bunk, she caught a flash of coppery-red and a lightly freckled face. Bewilderment kindled in chestnut brown eyes. Slender fingers clutched a handful of curls.

Leaning into the dim light, Penee waited.

Recognition registered. "Penee. Why am I so confused?" She glanced toward the door. "Abarax?"

Penee looked amused. "Sound asleep." Amusement melted into concern. "I woke up confused, too. We are in Coranna and Barlet's hidden room."

Brie threw the covers aside. "I remember discussing something important before we fell asleep. Why don't I remember what it was?" The twin reached out, ran a finger along the rowan wood of Irstant's staff, and blew out a breath. "We were discussing the time eater. Does it eat memories—"

A snarl startled them. Abarax loomed, red eyes glowing in the cherubic face. Fangs sprouted where its upper canine teeth had been. Rustling scales scattered droplets of blood on the floor.

Penee pulled Brie away from its reaching talons. "What is going on? This room is supposed to be impenetrable."

Brie grabbed Irstant's staff. Usolamet glowed. A bubble of light enveloped the Astican in a soft glow. Fangs withdrew, irises turned to blue, silver-gray scales quivered and crooned a rustling song.

Abarax yawned and looked from one girl to the other. "I was dreaming. Oh!" He looked chagrined. "My dreams can sometimes take on a life of their own." A groan escaped the rosebud mouth. "Did I hurt you?"

Penee stood. "No, but I think you stole our memories."

Chagrin preceded a stifled groan. Abarax touched her temple. Memories hit like a tidal wave. She almost laughed with relief.

It turned to Brie, tapped her temple, and sank cross-legged to the floor. "I am so sorry."

She tensed, blew out a breath, and looked at the Astican. "Why now, Abarax. You've slept close to us before, and we've been fine."

It tugged a golden curl. "It only happens when I am extremely tired. Do you suppose I, too, am affected by the time eater?"

Brie gazed at Usolamet. Her eyes glazed over. "It is not the time eater affecting you. It is the leaking away of time, the loss of universal dark matter." Her voice sounded distant and strangled.

Penee touched her knee. "Hey? Are you alright?"

Brie gave a full-bodied shudder and clutched Penee's hand. "We have to find the time eater. If we don't hurry, we will all cease to exist."

Penee's heart grew cold. "How can we stop it? We don't even know what it is."

Brie released her hand. "But we know where it is. All we have to do is find it and lead it away from Mittkeer."

Scales fluttered. Abarax shrunk to human size. "I suggest you send me into Mittkeer. I will discover what is eating time. We can then decide what must be done."

A barax, in the form of a winged ludoc cat, watched the portal to the cottage vanish with only a slight shiver of misgiving. Brie and Penee tracked it. They would remove it from Mittkeer if the need arose.

Eternity enclosed it. No Time and All Time ushered it forward. Feline paws padded through the unending star-studded night. Abarax's alert, predatory senses found nothing alarming. Brie's cautionary reminder—don't call attention to your presence—tempered its desire to take flight. Its gaze sought the specific constellations she taught it to keep in sight.

Its ears twitched. A slight deviation in the silence prickled the nape of its neck. An almost undetectable ripple vacillated through the fabric of time. Abarax crouched. A conscious thought changed the cloudy appearance of its gray fur to night sky. Wary but curious, it waited.

The shimmering outline of an immense moth emerged from a chrysalis of moonbeams. Starlit wings unfurled, gleaming like phosphorescence on the Canttila Sea. Segmented antennae quivered above hexagonal eyes composed of iridescent, diamond-bright bumps. A long, aqua, tongue-like proboscis extended, sucked in stars, and recoiled to its resting place.

Abarax stiffened. The creature's inquisitive gaze brushed over it. Translucent wings wafted, bringing the moth closer. Its proboscis flicked out and in. Multi-faceted eyes came level with the ludoc's. Abarax unfurled ludoc wings to hover, ready for flight. Pale green wings fluttered, lifting the moth high. Their gazes locked. A high-pitched squeal split time in two. The ludoc's rumbling purr wove it back together. Ludoc cat and moth, both creatures of the night, flew side by side, swooping, circling, soaring, and gliding in wide, fluid patterns.

Abarax's heart beat to a new rhythm. Its ludoc form glided to a landing. The moth hovered. Diamond bright eyes glistened. Abarax whipped its long tail back and forth. Its pink tongue licked its nose. It tasted time, threw its head back, and howled.

◗ ◖

Brie jumped up from the couch in the front room. "Abarax found the time eater. It's tasted time. I'm bringing it back."

Penee grabbed Henri's staff. "I'm ready to help."

Brie trained Usolamet on the closed portal. It swirled open. She whispered the Key of Withdrawal. Abarax's ludoc form flashed into view. The closing vortex cut a high, plaintive shriek short.

A dismayed howl shook the huge cat. Abarax materialized on hands and knees. It sat back on its heels, wings quivering a frantic song. Caught off guard, it blinked several times. The rosebud mouth went flaccid.

Brie glanced at Penee and back at the Astican. "Abarax?"

It rose to its full height. "I found the time eater." Taloned hands pressed to its heart. "I tasted time. My heart wanted to stay, to join La in Mittkeer's eternal trap. Thank you, Brielle AsTar, for bringing me back."

"La?" Penee blurted out the single syllable. "Who or what is a La?"

Abarax settled cross-legged on the floor. "La, a nocturnal moth, is the time eater—not because she covets time, but because she's trapped in eternity." A shudder rustled its wing scales. "We flew together through the Land of All Time." It quivered with emotion. "She shared her story." Sadness crept over its cherubic features.

"She was sucked into Mittkeer during Arienh's kidnapping on Persow. A SorTech promised if she would bite two older Humans—a man and a woman—he would grant her immortality and release her back on Persow. She did what he asked. He did not return.

"La grew hungry. She soon discovered she could assuage her hunger and her sense of doom by eating time. Imagine her surprise when she grew bigger, lost her authentic form, and merged into the endless night sky. Eternity alone held no charm. The idea terrified her. When I found her, she had transformed into a moth bigger than I am."

Anguish-filled eyes beseeched the girls to understand. "We recognized in each other a kindred spirit, a commonality as winged, nocturnal creatures. I didn't want to leave her. If you agree, I will bring her to you. I promise there is nothing malevolent about her."

Penee scrubbed her short hair into spikes. "How do you know she wants to come?"

"Did you not hear her scream of anguish when the portal closed behind me?"

R elevart slowed his heart rate and allowed spittle to drip from the corner of his mouth. Skultar Rados was on the way to pay him a visit. The Pheet Adolan's return had created chaos in the TaSneach Penal Colony. Den had kept his distance.

Voices in the hall grew louder. Relevart prepared to observe his adversaries.

The rattle of the key in the lock and the squeak of the door opening escorted Skultar and his SorTech into the cell. A med tech trailed them.

Skultar's anger raged. He rounded on the med tech. "I want him awake; I want coherent. How long?"

"The drug will wear off by tomorrow morning."

"Give him something to counteract it, you fool."

The med tech blanched. "It will kill him if I mix this drug with anything else."

Skultar spoke through clenched teeth. "Get out of my sight, you worthless piece of—"

The med tech dodged into the hall.

Skultar reined in his fury. "Furrnoce, see what you can discover. Report to me within half a chron circle." He strode into the hall and turned. "Death is not the goal. Dead men can't answer questions. I want answers." He marched down the hall.

Den arrived, followed by a guard carrying The Box. Placing two chairs side by side, he helped to set it up. When everything was arranged to Furrnoce's satisfaction, Den prepared to take his leave.

The SorTech's egoic smirk beamed. "Please stay, Den. It will do you good to see a master at work." He pressed a small pad to his temple, touched a button on The Box, and glared down at Relevart. "Has he been like this the whole time we've been gone?"

Den remained by the door. "He came to once. The med tech upped his dosage to keep him under longer. I'm afraid he may not be of much use to you."

Furrnoce scowled. "I'll be the judge of that." He scowled at his subject. "Let's begin, shall we?"

Relevart remained unresponsive to the persistent tingling of SorTechory. Furrnoce's arrogance turned to frustration. Nothing he tried provided him with the information he sought.

He yanked off the patch and shook his balding head. "Skultar will not be pleased. The old man's drugged to the point of uselessness." He snapped the cover on the box. A cold angry glare fastened on Den. "When he revives, send for me." Chin high, he marched from the cell.

Den waited until the outer door closed. He moved to the window and observed the stocky SorTech plodding through calf-high snow to the Governor's house. At the entryway, Furrnoce squared his shoulders and disappeared inside.

Smiling to himself, Den approached the cot. "Well, old man, you seem to have foiled *his* plans. What now?"

13

Penee observed the conversation between Brie and Abarax and could not contain a rush of jealousy. She had spent her early childhood with Abarax, yet he seemed more loyal to Brielle. Another twinge tightened her throat. *Just like Elf is to Arienh.*

Elf had explained that his love for Ari did not detract from his delight at having her back in his life. Learned distrust of people kept her from believing him.

Her attention drifted to Brie. *Ari is your identical twin. I can't compete with her coppery hair and chestnut eyes.* She slipped into the hall. At the top of the steep stairs, she hesitated to consider the advisability of leaving the secret room. With a shrug, she pulled the lever and made her way to the front windows. Streaks of lavender and salmon tinted the lake's unruffled surface. It occurred to her that life, like water, was in constant flux. She glimpsed her reflection. A wish that she had not cut her hair made a fleeting appearance. An ironic grin replaced a grimace. "I love my hair short. I wouldn't keep it long to please Skultar. Why would I keep it long to impress Elf?"

The differences in the men made her shake her head. An image of Den came unbidden. The sting of betrayal bit hard. He had deceived Irstant and her.

Blowing a mist on the window, she printed his name. "Where are you, Den? Are you with Skultar, doing his bidding, being his hatchet man?" An angry swipe obliterated the letters, but not the hurt.

"Do you always talk to yourself, Penesert?"

The voice in the room behind her froze her to the spot. Her gaze darted to Thorlu Tangorra's reflection. A series of actions shot through her mind.

"Please do nothing silly. I would hate to hurt you."

Her mind went blank. She faced him. Defeat in her expression, she buried her power within the turmoil of emotions enshrouding her.

"Tell me, my dear, where are the twin and the Astican? I have a score to settle with them." He tossed one side of his cape over his shoulder. Loathing distorted the handsome visage. "They left me tied up in enchanted ropes."

"Hello, Thorlu." Brie's soft voice came from behind him. "I'm glad you enjoyed the ropes."

Thorlu's gaze hurtled in her direction. "Come out so I can see you, Brielle."

Brie appeared half-hidden in shadow. "Perhaps you should leave, Thorlu Tangorra before you become tangled in ropes once again."

His attention split between the girls, he continued to edge backward. "I have a proposition to present to you." He made a quick scan of the room. "Where is that Astican?"

Brie shrugged. "Not here, I'm afraid."

Thorlu's guard relaxed. He gave a smug laugh. "I have information regarding your aunt's whereabouts. If you and Penee come with me, I will take you to her."

Her thoughts masked, Penee marveled at Brielle's calm. Specter-like, the twin moved through the shadows until she stood to one side of the windows. Their eyes met.

"If I believed you knew anything about Aunt Henri, Thorlu, I would consider your offer. As it is, I am certain you're lying."

The Mocendi's handsome features twisted. "I'll make you pay, Brielle AsTar."

Behind him, a portal opened. A large moth darted to his shoulder. He yelped in pain.

The moth shot upward.

Thorlu rubbed his neck. "What..." He choked, staggered, fell to one knee.

Abarax stepped from the portal, caught him, and lowered him to the floor. Satisfaction flashed. "Enough, but not too much. He'll be out for some time."

Brie grinned. "Nice work." She offered Penee Henri's staff. "Thought you would want this. We'll leave soon."

Penee tore her attention from the moth on Abarax's shoulder. "You know that's a Luna Moth, don't you?"

The Astican bowed his head. "I do. May I introduce La, our time eater?"

Pale green wings quivered.

Penee peered at the moth, raised her brows, and put some distance between them. "Coranna informed me that, in a big enough dose, their bite can kill. She also told me the venom can only be neutralized in one place on Soputto."

Abarax adjusted his size to straddle a straight-backed chair. "I do not fear La, Penesert. We are kindred spirits. She will not bite me, nor will she bite either of you."

Brie sank onto the couch. "I trust you to warn us if things change, Abarax. How did you persuade her to follow you from Mittkeer?"

"I did no convincing. I told her of you and of Penee; I explained Mittkeer's importance to those who work for balance in the Universe. She came with me of her own accord."

Penee sat in a wing-back chair and propped her feet on a footstool. "Can she return the time she stole?"

The moth's wings fluttered. Its proboscis licked the air.

"She did not intend to *steal* anything. With our help, she can return time to Mittkeer."

Penee kept her disbelief to herself.

Thorlu's heavy breathing, the only audible sound in the room, underscored the silent contemplation of its other occupants. Brie fingered Irstant's staff. *I wonder where they're hiding you and Henri? Did whoever moved you know of the luna moth's bite?*

Penee regarded La, her expression troubled. "Luna moths have the shortest life cycle of any moth on Soputto. Does she realize by giving back time, she will end her life?"

Pale green wings palpating the air lifted La into flight. She came to rest on Brie's shoulder. The Star of Truth pulsed. A soft wing brushed her cheek. Offering her hand, Brie smiled at the slight tickle of moth feet against her skin. She examined the almost translucent wings and admired the intricate eye spots detailing the lower set. Her head tilted. "I understand. I'll tell them."

Brie switched her attention to Penee. "La has existed an eternity in Mittkeer. She is ready to live and die in the way nature intended. Her only stipulation is that we take her back to Relevart's cabin on Persow, where she emerged from the cocoon and dried her wings."

Penee covered her face with her hands. Heaving a sigh weighted with dread, she dropped them to her knees. "I cannot go into Mittkeer if it will drain my energy. We don't know what we'll find on Persow. What if this is a trick arranged by my cousin?"

La's wings fluttered. Brie listened and explained. "We'll be fine. La will return the time she has taken to Mittkeer as soon as we enter. She knows nothing of Skultar. Furrnoce was the Human who stranded her in The Land of Time."

Penee made a restless circuit of the room. "Anyone else hungry?"

An affirmative chorus sent her off to the kitchen. She returned with a plate of treats and placed it on the table. "Help yourselves."

Brie popped a grape in her mouth. "Thanks, Pen."

Abarax crumbled a piece of cheese and offered a tiny piece to La. She ignored it and fluttered to a landing on Penee's hand.

Penee lifted her to eye level. "You are a beautiful thing. I hate to think of you dying."

A soft squeak accompanied La's return to Abarax's shoulder.

In a companionable silence, they had finished eating. After cleaning up, Brie glanced at Thorlu. "Any idea how long he'll be out, Abarax?"

"La says a turning, perhaps more. She was careful not to kill him." The Astican shot Brie a meaningful look.

She beamed. "Thank you, Abarax." Holding Irstant's staff in one hand, she offered the other. With a gracious bow, the Astican clasped it.

Penee retrieved Henri's staff and rested a hand on her shoulder. The cottage blurred. Stars winked into sight. La flew ahead; transformed into an immense, translucent moth; and uncoiled her proboscis. Stars, galaxies, solar systems, and constellations spewed across the heavens. A new moth-shaped constellation formed in their midst. The two brightest stars highlighted the position of the eye spots on the lower wings.

⁂

The return of time's Dark Matter to Mittkeer sent an influx of revitalizing energy surging through Relevart. Cells tingled, muscles trembled, eyelids twitched. His heartbeat danced in his chest and settled into a normal rhythm. Details flooded him with information.

The activity in the Penal Colony increased. Skultar paced his office, marched to the window, and directed a speculative stare across the compound at Relevart's cell block.

Den came to his feet in his quarters; inhaled a deep, rejuvenating breath; and smiled. "Time returns." The smile vanished. *Will Skultar's dulled suspicions awaken?*

A subtle mental search confirmed his supposition. *Furrnoce's on the way.* He unlocked the cell and strode to Relevart's side. "Be smart, old man."

A scurry of footsteps ended at the cell door. The SorTech rushed to his side. "What are *you* doing in here?"

"My job. Checking on the prisoner—as I believe you are?"

Furrnoce glowered, stalked to The Box, and affixed the patch on his temple. The hum of SorTechory vibrated, rolled through the cell, and formed an invisible aura surrounding Relevart.

The Universal VarTerel remained unresponsive.

Furrnoce upped the power and peered at his subject. "Respond, Eleo Predan filth." When nothing happened, he wheeled on Den. "Bring me the girl."

Den feigned surprise. "It's my understanding you may not interrogate Ari and Elf without Skultar in attendance."

Fury turned the SorTech's cheeks fiery red. His fists clenched and unclenched. Full lips held back a stormy retort. With an angry snarl, he slapped a patch on the VarTerel's temple. "You will tell me what I want to know or—"

Skultar marched into the cell. Danger bristled. "I hope you aren't planning to harm the Universal VarTerel, Furrnoce."

The SorTech licked his lips. "I only want to provide you with the information you need, Governor Rados."

Skultar straightened his long spine, fixed his unyielding gaze on his lackey, and flared his nostrils. "Leave. I will see you in my office later."

Furrnoce scurried from the cell.

Skultar removed the patch from Relevart's temple and slapped it on top of The Box. He rounded on Den. Intense scrutiny gripped him like a strangle hold. Beady, black eyes bored into him. "Thank you for reminding Furrnoce of my orders." Skultar's countenance relaxed into a bland expression. "Perhaps a promotion is in order." He glanced at Relevart. "No more drugs or SorTechory. When he regains consciousness, call me."

Quiet settled over the cell. Den placed The Box on the floor and moved the chair closer to the cot. Relevart regarded him with interest. "A promotion?"

Den looked amused. "I've been out of favor of late. I can't imagine I will be *in* for long. Do you have a plan, old man?"

Relevart blinked. "If I felt sure Henri and Irstant were safe, I would remove the young people from harm's way. As it is—" He shrugged.

Den's gaze held his. "Furrnoce is on the defensive. Skultar is on the warpath. Perhaps now would be an excellent time to act. Waiting will only create a panicked situation down the road." Den rubbed his chin. "Time revitalizes Mittkeer. You are safe to go, old man. What do you need to make it happen?"

"A diversion may be necessary. Help if you can. Don't put yourself or your position at risk." Relevart frowned. "I believe your boss is about to summon you."

Den stood, moved the chair, and replaced The Box. Without a backward glance, he left, locking the cell behind him.

Relevart curled his fingers into fists. Awareness of something momentous rose in his mind and floundered. He searched, but to no avail. His hands relaxed. *It will rise again; when it does, I'll be ready.*

14

Brie raised her staff. La shrunk to her normal size and fluttered through the portal from Mittkeer into Persow. The domed mountains of Relevart's home materialized. Hidden in the shadows of a moonless night, Brie stared across the garden at windows glowing with light and smoke drifting from the chimney.

Abarax stepped up behind her. Penee clasped her hand. "Who do you suppose is in the cabin?"

"Shhh. We're about to find out."

The silhouette of a tall, well-built man filled the open doorway.

Brie urged her companions into the shadows. "Stay hidden. I'll see what's going on. If I signal trouble, or I'm gone too long, go to Rainbow Gorge. I'll find you."

Penee's hand on her shoulder gripped harder. "You can't go in alone."

The Luna Moth fluttered to the crystal crowning Irstant's staff. Brie pointed. "I won't be."

Penee released her. La settled where her hand had been. Brie looked up at the Astican. "Take care of Penee, Abarax."

Navigating between rows of late summer vegetables, she made her way to the back door. At her approach, the man moved aside. She entered the cabin and turned to find him regarding her from vibrant amethyst-blue eyes, his thoughts well hidden. Lantern light highlighted his dark, wavy hair and magnified his breathtaking good looks.

He offered a hand. "It is good to meet you, Brielle AsTar. I am Den Zironho, Irstant's apprentice."

She ignored the hand. "From what I understand, you are far more than an apprentice. Why are you here?"

A charming smile made butterflies collide in her stomach. "I see that our mutual friend has shared her misgivings."

Brie kept her guard in place.

He moved to the table, pulled out a chair, and sat observing her. "Please join me." Ignoring her hesitation, he continued. "My role in the current drama is complex. Someday, I'll share with both you and Penee. Right now, I'm here on Relevart's behalf."

The Star of Truth sent a flush of warmth down Brie's neck. La fluttered to Den's hand.

He observed the moth with interest. "Is this perhaps the reason time leaked from Mittkeer?"

Brie sank onto a chair on the opposite side of the table. "How did you know about the loss of time?"

He shook his head. "I must depart soon. We can small talk, or we can discuss why Relevart sent me."

"Shall I invite Penee to join us?"

"I'd rather your *friends* did not see me, Brielle. Listen closely. Relevart plans to remove Ari and Elf from Skultar's jurisdiction to a safe place. You, Penee, and Abarax must create a distraction to keep Thorlu and others focused away from TaSneach. See if you can draw their attention to all the most obvious places Relevart might hide—here, Irstant's cabin—"

His attention wavered. He came to his feet. "One more thing, use your skills to help Penee take the lead. Be careful. And do not get caught."

The portal into Mittkeer opened. Den leapt into the beginning swirl of the vortex.

Brie called after him. "What about Irstant and Henri?"

He turned and waved. The portal vanished.

Alone in the lantern's light, Brie sighed. "Training to be a DiMensioner was much less stressful than life as a VarTerel." She opened the door to find Abarax crouched, ready to barge in. Penee waited in the shadows, holding Henri's staff like a club.

Abarax straightened. La flew to his shoulder. Brie grinned at Penee. "There are more effective ways to use a staff, you know."

Penee scowled and lowered it. "I did what came naturally. Can we come in?"

Brie stepped aside. "Take a seat. I have a message from Relevart."

Chairs scraped the floor. Attentive stillness settled over the room. She presented the details of his instructions.

"You haven't told us who brought the message." Distrust brought Penee to standing, her palms pressed against the tabletop. "If the man in the doorway was Den Zironho, why are we trusting him?"

"I'm not sure trust is the right word. I prefer to think we're giving Den the benefit of a doubt." Brie pulled her curls aside to reveal the birthmark on her neck. "This birthmark is the Star of Truth. It is both a blessing and a curse. Because of it, I can't lie even when it would save a life." She sighed. "Or when it would keep me from losing my sister's trust. It warns me of danger and whether someone else is lying."

Penee sneered. "I suppose *Den* told the truth?"

"He didn't lie, Penee. He promised to explain why he is working with Skultar to both of us another time. The message from Relevart received a positive reaction from the Star. Please suspend judgement. I need your help."

Penee sank onto her chair. "I wish I could believe he is not the enemy. I want to understand why he betrayed Ari and Elf *and* Relevart." She shook her head. "Why he betrayed me."

Abarax traced the wood grain on the tabletop with a talon. "As one who has made the tough journey from enemy to ally, I suggest we give Den an opportunity to prove where his loyalties lie. Relevart trusts him. The reaction of The Star of Truth was positive." He held up his hand to provide a landing place for the Luna Moth. "La did not bite him."

"So, because a moth and a birthmark suggest he is trustworthy, we put ourselves and everyone else at risk?"

Brielle spoke with exaggerated calm. "No, we trust the message is real and we have a job to do for the Universal VarTerel, who believes that if you are to help change the course of history, it's time to develop your leadership skills." She stood up and motioned Abarax to join her. "We'll give you a few minutes to clear your head and decide where you stand."

Abarax preceded her onto the front stoop. La fluttered around him, her wings pearlescent in the light of the rising moon.

The Astican's wings quivered. "What do you think she will decide?"

"I don't know. Betrayal is hard to let go of." She thought of Ari and hoped that someday...

P enee sorted her way through a labyrinth of emotions. She had grown to depend on Brie's leadership. Sometimes she resented it, but most of the time she appreciated staying in the background. A thrust of negativity sliced sword deep. *You don't know how it feels to trust someone, Brie, and discover they're the enemy. You don't...* She pushed her chair back and came to her feet. *This isn't about Brie, Penesert.* She marched to the fireplace and back. *This is about you—the girl with the Matriarch's Eyes.*

She slid splayed fingers through her hair to the back of her neck. *Do I know enough? Skultar sequestered me most of my life. I'm not sure I'm ready.* Coranna's words from her childhood whispered through her mind: *Self-pity is a disabler.*

An unexpected dose of confidence stiffened her spine. She pressed her palms to her heart. "I will learn to lead. Brie and Abarax and, yes, even Den will teach me." Opening the door, she stepped into the moonlight. She gulped a breath. The porch was empty.

Soft voices drifting on the night air cancelled her moment of panic. La flew to her hand.

Laughter accompanied Brie up the steps with Abarax, a basket of vegetables in his arms, ambling behind her. "Hi, Penee, we've been harvesting in the moonlight."

Abarax showed her their bounty and entered the cabin with La fluttering after him.

Penee lowered onto the porch swing and patted the seat. "Join me, Brielle. I have something to say."

The swing creaked. Penee braced it with her feet and gazed up at the moon. "I am ready to let Den's behavior go for now. I'm also willing to take the lead." She glanced at Brie. "I'll need your help."

"I believe we'll make an impressive team, Penee. We'll do this together." Brie stifled a yawn. "I have just one request—actually two. I need a nutritious meal and a good night's slumber."

Penee pulled her to her feet. "Food and sleep. Sounds great to me. We can talk more over dinner." She stepped inside. La fluttering around the Astican's head. "How long does she have?"

Abarax held out his hand. His blue eyes sparkled as the Luna Moth alighted. "She has discovered her time in Mittkeer increased her longevity. She would like to help make trouble." The smile lines framing his mouth deepened.

La flew to Penee's hand and flicked her proboscis out and in. Multifaceted eyes gleamed. She emitted a small series of squeaks.

Penee laughed with delight. "I understand her! She told me she will not kill, but she will make our enemies sleep and forget." She lifted the moth eye-high. "I accept your offer."

La fluttered to the back of a chair. Penee rose. "Let's fix a meal." She yawned. "We eat. We sleep. *Then* we make plans."

❧ ❧

Brie sat on the porch swing, sipping steaming tea from a heavy pottery mug. A gentle breeze tossed sleep-messy curls to frame her face. A flock of birds swept by, touched down in the treetops, and sang a chorus of welcome to the morning. Peacefulness hugged her like a dream.

Penee stepped onto the stoop, yawned, and plopped down next to her. "I slept." She grinned. "I mean—really slept—all night. You?"

Brie cradled the mug between her palms and savored the aroma of mint and roses. "I don't remember the last time I fell asleep without dreams of people or events interrupting. I feel rejuvenated and ready for the turning." She offered her mug. "Tea?"

"Thanks, mine's steeping. Any idea what's next?"

Staring over the mug's rim, Brie considered her question. "I guess I'm not sure how to create a distraction when Skultar is on TaSneach, and we're on Persow."

Pain ripped down Brie's neck. The mug hit the porch. Her hand flew to the Star. She shoved Penee inside and slid the bolt on the door.

A human-sized, sleep-befuddled Abarax staggered into the room. La flew an agitated circle and fluttered to his shoulder. He mumbled through a wide-mouthed yawn. "What's going on?"

Brie peered out the window at a slight aberration in the atmosphere. "I'm not sure. Penee, grab both staffs. I think we're about to have company. Abarax, stay close."

The abnormality formed into a spinning, translucent vortex. Thorlu, cape flaring, leapt to the ground. Another portal swirled into being. A stoop-shouldered, balding man whose angry sneer locked onto Thorlu tripped, stumbled several steps, and jerked to a halt.

Brie murmured, "Vygel Vintrusie. How did you—"

Penee thrust Irstant's staff in her hand. "Thorlu gets around. The other guy—" She gripped Brie's arm. "You called him Vygel." She gulped. "The MasTer's Mocendi—his right-hand man. He's the one who took the baby Rayn named Rethson away. Didn't Relevart send both men to another time and dimension?"

"He did. My Aunt Mira and Corvus went after them, hoping Vygel would lead them to Rethson."

Penee's grip on her arm loosened. "Why is Vygel after us?"

"I don't believe *he* knows we're here." She kept her voice low. "Thorlu may have guessed. Let's see if we can hear what they're saying." She eased the window open.

Vygel's features twisted into a scowl. "Will you quit dodging me, Thorlu? I need information." He glared. "I even might have some you could use."

Thorlu stared down his nose and flashed a sarcastic smirk. "What makes you think I'm dodging you, Vygel Vintrusie?"

Vygel's homely countenance grew uglier.

Thorlu laughed. "You always were tongue-tied." He grabbed the edge of his cape and flipped it aside, exposing the deep purple lining. "So, Vintrusie, what is it you're after on this forsaken, insignificant planet?"

"I'm following you, Tangorra. Why *Persow*?" He glanced around, his gaze missing little. "What is this place? What are you—"

Thorlu threw up his hands. "For Emit's sake, calm down, Vygel." He became solicitous. "You don't look well, my friend. Perhaps you should sit down. Let's call a truce."

Vygel licked thin lips. "Why ever would I trust you, Tangorra?"

A graceful hand smoothed thick, wavy hair. "I've saved your life more than once, have I not?" Thorlu strolled to the stoop. His brows arched. He picked up a warm mug from the ground and shot a sharp glance at the cabin. His attention fixed on the door, he handed it to Vygel. "It appears we're not alone."

Brie pulled Penee closer and grabbed Abarax by the arm. Shields shimmered into place. The next instant they huddled in the forest. An agitated La darted from one to the other and landed on Brie's shoulder. Her wings shivered. Her worried thoughts flooded Brie's mind. Within a short time, Brie's soothing response calmed her.

Penee cast a worried glance behind her. "Why didn't we use Mittkeer?"

"Thorlu and Vygel mustn't learn we have that kind of power. If they find out, we'll be in even more danger than we are already. We need to separate. La knows the way to Rainbow Gorge. Take Abarax with you. I told her not to go straight to the falls. Don't stay too close together. I'll join you." She snapped her fingers. Both Henri and Irstant's staffs disappeared.

Penee gasped. "What did you do?"

"I sent them ahead. The wards should make it difficult to pick up more than one energy trail, but not if we have VarTerel staffs in our hands."

The wards wavered.

Brie whispered, "He's almost got us. Go!"

La flitted skyward. Penee shifted to a small forest hawk and followed a bat-sized Abarax. Brie shaped a Persowan falcon and soared back toward the cabin. From the top of a white pine, she observed the two Mocendi.

Thorlu stood in the garden, his DiMensioner's senses trained on the forest behind the cabin. He made a slow rotation, gaze searching every nook and cranny.

Vygel, in his clumsy though thorough fashion, searched the area on both sides of the cabin. When he found nothing, he limped down a vegetable row and stopped a scant distance from Thorlu. A silence bristling with mutual dislike stretched between them.

Their proximity magnified the glaring difference between the two men—one aging, clumsy, and homely; the other in his prime, elegant, and handsome. Thorlu, the smarter of the two, was a dangerous adversary. Brie could not fathom why *Vygel seemed* more frightening.

Behind her protective shields, she marveled at the delicacy of Thorlu's skillful search. Threads of silken energy extended from his fingertips, searching the trees, the air, the earth for any trace of who had been in the cabin.

Vygel opened his mouth.

Thorlu snarled. "Shhh, fool." He moved closer to the trees. "I've almost got it." A tremor shook him. He lowered his head, his concentration complete.

Vygel followed. He tripped, tried to right himself, and stumbled into Thorlu.

A series of expletives later, Thorlu righted himself and fought to recapture the fast-fading signature. Too late, trembling threads stretched outward. Too late.

He wheeled on his fellow Mocendi. "You are the stupidest man I know." He hit him in the chest with the palm of his hand. "I almost had it." He struck again. "We could have—" Rage left him shaking. His hand flew out. Vygel landed on his back in the dirt, scarlet faced and defiant. Thorlu stood over him. "Why you were The MasTer's righthand man is beyond me." He marched to the porch, gulping calm breaths of air.

An about-face and two long strides carried him back to Vygel's side. "Get up, fool. We might as well stay here and regroup. You must have something worthwhile in that ugly hide, or The MasTer would never have trusted you over me." He reached down, jerked him to his feet, and stalked past him into the cabin.

Brie remained in the pine until Vygel had slammed the door behind him. *If I didn't have places to go, I'd stick around for the fireworks.* She ruffled her feathers and launched into flight.

15

On TaSneach at the outer rim of the Inner Universe, Arienh AsTar kicked a metal chair across her cell. The clang of it striking the stone surface and its clattered skid across the floor softened the edges of her foul mood. She stomped to the window, fired the endless-white landscape a withering look, and groaned under her breath. "I hate snow. I hate ice. I hate white."

Flopping down on her bunk, she stuck her hands behind her head. It seemed to her that she had spent the better part of her life in this position, on this cot. The only break in the monotony of her existence was a SorTech who attempted to harvest secrets from her brain.

SorTechory didn't impress her; neither did Furrnoce. She'd been around her aunts, Mira and Henri, and her sister too long to allow a man with a patch on his head and a box full of wires to intimidate her. Still, she had learned not to fight it. The headache resulting from pushing back wasn't worth the fun of seeing Furrnoce break out in a sweat.

Rare visits from Skultar, a different matter altogether, left her shaking in her boots. No magic in the Governor's bones, but—he intimidated her more than she liked to admit.

She uncrossed her legs, re-crossed them with the other leg on top, and even found a smile. Den, the most fascinating of the three men who visited, intrigued her. He worked for Skultar, yet she sensed undercurrents in him of which the Colony Governor seemed unaware. Setting that aside, Den was nice to look at—tall, fit, warm brown skin, dark wavy hair, and the prettiest eyes she had ever seen in a man's face.

Wistfulness brought her upright. "So, what's up, Elf? Haven't seen you since Mittkeer. Are you dreaming about your birth-mate? Do you even remember I exist?"

Swinging her legs over the edge of the bunk, she leaned her forearms on her knees and interlaced her fingers. "Get over yourself, Arienh AsTar. Stop acting like a sappy teen-age girl."

An intuitive nudge brought her to her feet. The key rattled in the lock. Her stomach tightened.

Skultar pushed it wide, noted the upside-down chair, and cast a sardonic look in her direction. "Having a bad turning, are we?"

Ari folded her arms. "I have no idea about yours." She shrugged. "Mine stinks."

He pointed at the chair. "That is no way to treat someone else's property, Arienh."

She didn't move.

His jovial expression grew impatient. "Pick it up."

A slow amble across the cell brought a glint of anger to the man's predatory features. She set the chair on its legs. A guard entered, placed The Box on its seat and left. Skultar's malicious smirk sent goose flesh prickling up her arms. Moments later, Furrnoce shoved a boy ahead of him into the cell.

Elf's blank gaze met her startled look with one so unresponsive, it made her cringe.

Skultar shut the heavy wooden door and leaned against it. "I have a few questions, Arienh. Please be attentive. Should you lie, I cannot be responsible for the outcome."

Furrnoce placed the patch on his temple, adjusted the settings, and nodded.

Skultar lifted her chin with the tip of his finger. "Tell me how powerful your twin sister is."

Ignoring the urge to hit his hand away, she pressed her lips together.

Vice-like fingers squeezed her chin. "Answer me, Arienh, or your boyfriend pays the price."

Ari pulled her head away. "You are mistaken on two counts. I have *no* sister." She jerked a thumb at Elf. "*He* isn't my boyfriend." Her expression dared Skultar to suggest otherwise.

Furrnoce worked at the box. Tears dripped from Elf's chin. The SorTech adjusted a setting. The boy crumpled to the floor.

Observing her with a hint of glee, Furrnoce made another change to the settings. Elf's back arched. Muscles twitched. Ari forced her face to remain expressionless.

Skultar clucked and shook his head. "See what your stubbornness has done, Arienh?"

A whistle across the compound shrilled a rapid series of high-pitched notes. Skultar tensed. Pulling the door wide, he glared at Furrnoce. "Do nothing until I return. In fact, come with me." He waited for the SorTech to move past him. The door slammed shut; the key clicked in the lock. Muffled footsteps hurrying away left Ari on her knees, staring at Elf for the first time since their imprisonment.

She brushed blond hair from his forehead. "Elf? Are you all right?"

A hand pulled her closer. Elf winked, planted a soft kiss on her lips, and sprawled motionless on the floor.

The cell door flew open. Two guards marched in. Without a word, they carried Elf from the cell. The door slammed.

Ari, tears of frustration burning, flung The Box to the floor. Half-blinded by rage, she weaponized a chair and battered the SorTech's Box until both it and chair lay in pieces at her feet.

* * *

Elf paced his cell. His mother had bred him to lead. His Eleo Predan heritage contained a powerhouse of talent neither Skultar nor Furrnoce had discovered. He paused at the cell window. *Keep your temper, Arienh AsTar.*

An explosion shook the compound. Ari's cell window blazed. Sword sharp icicles scattered over the ground. Guards converging from every direction sprinted toward the cell block.

Elf swore under his breath. *What have you done?*

A surge of energy shook his cell. Relevart, with his staff in hand and Ari sagging against him, snapped into view. Ari, soot on her cheeks and eyes rounded in shock, sucked in a shaky breath. Elf slipped his arm around her.

Running feet pounded the stone floor in the hall. Relevart raised the staff. A portal opened. Stars rushed toward them. The cell grew small and distant. A fast-fading shout chased them.

Ari sank onto a carpet of stars and middle-night.

Elf knelt beside her. "What did you do, Ari?"

She shot him a tremulous smile. "I pushed The Box off the chair. When it didn't break, I grabbed the chair and hit the stupid thing again and again. The last time I must have broken something vital 'cause it exploded." Triumph made her eyes gleam. She glanced at Relevart's stern countenance. Chagrin took its place. "I'm sorry, but Furrnoce made me so mad."

A silent Relevart continued to regard her.

"I thought he hurt Elf. I thought—"

Relevart's expression remained unrelenting. "You did *not* think. If it weren't for Den, you would be facing Skultar, not sitting in Mittkeer. Please learn to control your temper." The hint of a twinkle made an appearance. "The explosion created a great diversion."

Elf noted Ari's relief and helped her to stand. "Where do we go from here, Relevart?"

"We disappear."

Ari's chin jutted. "But, Relevart, I want to help find Aunt Henri and Irstant."

Relevart scanned the star-studded night. Ari hurried to his side and plucked at his sleeve. "What good will it do if we disappear?"

"The harder it is to find us, the easier it will be for Brie and Penee to find Henri and Irstant." The VarTerel picked up his pace.

Ari scowled at Relevart's back. Elf linked arms with her. "Our disappearance will act as a distraction. It gives Skultar and Thorlu and anyone else who is after us one more obstacle."

Ari nibbled her lip. "It divides their resources, right?"

He hugged her. "It does. Shall we catch up with Relevart and find out where he's taking us?"

She grinned. "Race ya!"

Relieved that her anger had passed, he sprinted after her.

R elevart strode through Mittkeer, pondering his options. Elf would keep Ari out of trouble, but only if she was involved in a way she felt was helpful. He stopped to allow them to catch up and caught himself smiling at their youthful exuberance.

Ari bounded to his side a few steps ahead of Elf, put her hands on her hips, and flashed a happy grin. "Beat ya, Troms el Shiv!"

Elf laughed. "Gotta admit you're fast." He sobered and turned respectfully to Relevart. "How can we help?"

Relevart raised his staff.

Elf gazed in awe at a long, elegant room with a fireplace at one end and reading alcoves tucked between the shelves of books lining the walls.

Ari absorbed the familiarity of the space. "Why the Reading Room, Relevart?"

"A luna moth has bitten your Aunt Henri and my dear friend Irstant. My job is to help Brie and Penee discover where they are hidden; yours is to research the moth, its venom, and a cure. Also, see what you can discover about Neul Isle on the planet of Soputto."

A slender creature with silky white fur and a delicate-featured black face entered the room.

Ari grinned. "Elae! How did you know we were here?"

The DeoNyte priestess honored Relevart with a hand to her heart. "The High Priestess of Canedari informed me of your arrival, VarTerel." She hugged Ari. "You are on Myrrh to do important research, so I volunteered to help. I am well versed in the Reading Room and library floors below it."

Relevart offered his palm. "You honor us, Elae. Thank you."

She touched her palm to his. "How long will you stay?"

"Only long enough to pay my respect to Myrrh's Guardian." His gracious expression changed to one of delight. "Hello, SparrowLyn."

The Guardian hurried across the Reading Room. "Welcome to Myrrh,

Relevart. Thank you for bringing me such a marvelous surprise." She opened her arms to receive her daughter's exuberant hug.

"Mother, I didn't expect you to be here. I've missed you so much." She wiggled free and pulled Elf forward. "You remember Elf."

Sparrow offered her palm. "Troms el Shiv, welcome to Myrrh."

Relevart cleared his throat. "Elae, I am leaving Arienh and Elf in your care. Perhaps you could show them to their rooms while SparrowLyn and I catch up." He rested a hand on Ari's shoulder. "No one must know you're in Myrrh." His stern expression underscored his next words. "Not even Zugo, Ari. Stay within the boundaries of the Cave of Canedari. I'll be back when I can." He nodded at Elf. "Take care of her. Off you go."

Ari paused beside her mother. "Will I see you later?"

Sparrow gave her a quick hug. "You'll know when Relevart departs. Come and find me in Veersuni, so we can catch up."

Elf took Ari's hand. "Come on, I'm excited to explore. Is it true the Evolsefil Crystal is in Canedari?"

Relevart noted Sparrow's wistful look as they walked to the door. "Your girls are growing up. I imagine it's exciting and a little sad. Since I have not had the privilege—" He let the sentence go unfinished. "Where can we talk?"

Sparrow led the way to Veersuni, the sanctuary that had once housed the fountain, Elcaro's Eye. Stained glass cast soft-hued patterns on the carpeted floor. The comfortable furnishings, which had taken the place of the fountain when she returned it to the Guardian's cottage, were arranged around the room. Sparrow selected a grouping by the window.

Relevart sat in silence, contemplating the expanse of stained glass covering the entire wall of Veersuni. Sparrow stretched her arm along the top of the curved couch and studied his profile.

He sighed and leaned his staff on the neighboring chair. A quick summary of what had occurred over the past few moon cycles brought a frown of consternation to her lovely face.

"It sounds as though half the Universe is hunting the girls and Penee and Elf. How can I help?"

"You can help Elf keep Ari busy. I need it to appear they have disappeared from the Inner Universe."

"What about Brie and Penee?"

Relevart waved a hand. The stained-glass color floated to the opposite side of the sanctuary, leaving clear panes of glass and a breathtaking view of the Universe. His hand rested on Sparrow's. "We all have our individual destinies. Brie and Penee must go a direction none of us can follow. The best we can do is support them and keep them as safe as we can without interfering." He squeezed her hand. "I must be away. When I have news to report, I will contact you via Elcaro's Eye." As he rose, colors returned to the window.

He lifted his staff. Mittkeer's cool quiet embraced him. For a long moment, he remained undecided. "Where to begin the search?" Scanning the heavens for a particular constellation, he murmured, "First discover what may have transpired without my knowledge." Bilar's scales of justice appeared in the distance. "Learn more of Den and his role in this." He stroked his chin. "How do I disappear so completely not even Den can pick out my signature?" His grandsire's memories suggested a solution. His pace quickened.

Constellations shifted. A new one caught his eye. "Ah. A luna moth—a reminder of the importance of time." He strode toward it. A shimmering rainbow, water rushing over a cliff, and a cottage nestled between lush blue spruce trees came into focus. The stars of the ages flashed from sight.

16

Sparrow absorbed the quiet of Veersuni. Any way she looked at it, her daughters were at risk. Realizing the folly of her parental desire to keep them out of harm's way, she forced herself to view them from the perspective of Myrrh's Guardian, a role new to her, one she had not accepted without misgivings.

Content to be a mother and a visual artist, she had lived a quiet life with the twins in Idronatti, the only city on the planet of Thera. Quiet, that is, until the turning Allynae, whom she had not seen in fourteen sun cycles, had appeared at her apartment door, bearing the message that the twins were in trouble. From that moment, her life flipped upside down. Less than two sun cycles ago, she joined Allynae at the Guardian's cottage, accepted responsibility for Myrrh's safety; and watched her daughters step into young adulthood.

Longing for more time with her girls overwhelmed her. *All children grow up and leave the nest. The twins left way too early.* She sighed. *It was the right time for them. Relevart's notion of individual destinies rings true, but it doesn't make it any easier.*

The light shifting in the stain-glass window gave her a moment's respite from restless thinking. An intricate mosaic design of gold and orange leaves scattering in the blustery wind and birds flying V-shaped formations on their way to warmer climates reminded her autumn drew near. Time seemed to pass much slower since her girls left home. She caressed a streak of gold paint on her palm. *Thank goodness I have my art.*

A soft knock focused her on the heart of her concern. Ari stuck her head in. "May I come in?"

Sparrow smiled. "I'm delighted we have time to catch up."

Ari plopped down on the couch, bit her bottom lip, and blew out a long, frustrated breath. "I have something to tell you." She tugged a tendril of hair, her expression a mix of petulant child and resistant adult. Throwing her hands in the air, she jumped to her feet, walked to the window's center, and appeared to study its design.

A rush of memories hit Sparrow: Ari's tantrums because Brie had accomplished something before her; her barrage of hurtful words when Brie received an award, and she didn't; her deep remorse when she realized she'd hurt her sister's feelings.

"Arienh, sit down. You need to tell me what happened. Whatever it is, we'll deal with it."

Red hair forming a halo of color, her eldest daughter whirled to face her. A rush of blood tinted her cheeks pink. Ari dropped her gaze and returned to her seat. "I'm the reason they caught Relevant and me. If I hadn't acted like a spoiled child, neither Elf nor I nor Relevart would have spent time in a freezing cell on TaSneach." A slight tremor in her voice magnified her obvious regret. "Irstant and Aunt Henri wouldn't be missing. Time would not have leaked from Mittkeer. We could have avoided all the upheaval had I not played into the trap." She poked herself in the chest. "Why can't I control my emotions?" She dropped her head in her hands. Lowering them to her lap, she looked straight at Sparrow. "The worst thing of all is that I could have killed Brie, and I didn't care."

"It appears you saved the actual reason until last. You aren't responsible for other people's actions, Arienh. You are responsible for your own. Tell me why you think you almost killed your sister."

Cheeks flushed scarlet, Ari related what had happened at Relevart's cabin, described twin promises, and explained why she had demanded one from Brie. "The worst part, Mother, is that I didn't care if the Star of Truth hurt her. I saw her flinch. I knew it burned." She leaned forward. "I—Did—Not—Care. All I wanted was Penee out of the picture..." Like a balloon with a small leak, she deflated, slumped back in her chair, and whispered, "I thought with her gone, Elf would love me." The tears came. "What I realize is he does love me. He always has. If it hadn't been for Relevart, the *most* important person in my life might not be here." Sobs shook her shoulders.

Sparrow restrained her need to touch her daughter and let her cry. As the flow of tears abated, she clasped a damp hand between hers. "Tell me when you're ready, Ari. I have a question."

Tranquility gradually returned to Veersuni. Ari hiccuped, accepted the handkerchief Sparrow offered, and blew her nose. Her mother's face, more serious than she ever remembered seeing it, almost undid her tentative calm. Crushing the hanky into a ball, she harnessed her emotions. "I'm ready, Mother."

"Please tell me why Brie makes you so angry, Arienh?"

Sparrow's gentle question took her by surprise. "I'm not angry with Brie; I'm angry at myself."

Her mother remained silent. That her candid expression held a hint of understanding and nothing resembling judgement served to spring-board Ari into a search of her first memories of Brie. Self-honesty, never easy for her, sent her in a quick-paced circuit of Veersuni. She stopped in front of the window. The colors flew to the opposite side of the sanctuary. Moon, stars, and the vastness of space acted like a panacea. The angry undercurrents of her feelings dissolved into the realization that as much as she loved her twin, she hated the way Brie's serene and sometimes placid personality magnified the negatives in her own.

She returned to her chair. "Brie is so perfect, Mother. She always sees the good in people. She's never mean. I've only seen her lose her temper one time.

Everything she does makes my rowdy, abrasive personality seem worse. Her life is so much easier. Why?"

"What makes you think Brie's life is easy? Consider what it must be like to be the bearer of the Star of Truth. How often do you monitor your thoughts and feelings before you respond? Brie must be conscious of every word, thought, and action. She doesn't have the leisure of making mistakes. If she does, pain is her reward. Minor lies hurt. Lies about important things bring death to her doorstep."

Ari pulled a long curl straight and let it go. "Truth is such a personal thing, isn't it? What is true for me is not true for Brielle." She stretched the curl. "I see the world as simple strands of good and bad." The curl bounced back. "Brie has to navigate every bend and curve. I never knew, Mother. I just reacted. Why do you suppose she was born with the Star?"

Sadness encased her mother like a chrysalis. Ari clasped her hand. "What is it?"

Sparrow shivered, hugged herself, and met Ari's gaze. "I can't tell you why, Arienh."

"But you know, right?"

"For Brie's safety and the safety of those around her, the Galactic Guardians swore me to secrecy."

Ari frowned. "How can I help her if I don't know what she's dealing with?"

Sparrow rose, waved the stain glass color back to the window, and pulled Ari to her feet. "You can help by doing the research Relevart asked you to do."

"I won't tell—" Ari clamped her mouth shut and hugged her mother. "Thank you for listening and for understanding. Let's go find Elf and Elae."

Her mother hugged her. "It's time I got back to the cottage. I need to check Elcaro's Eye. If you need me, I'll know." She led the way into the Reading Room, hugged Ari one more time, and hurried down the Hall of Priestesses.

Ari stared after her. "I'll do Relevart's research, Mother. I will also find out everything I can about Brielle and the Star of Truth."

Relevart entered the cottage at the top of the falls to find Chealim waiting to receive him. The Galactic Guardian motioned him to a chair. "It is good to see you, Avlin Enus, Universal VarTerel. You look worn." He touched a fingertip to Relevart's temple. Fatigue fled.

"Thank you, Chealim. It has been a trying time. To what do I owe this honor?"

"The Council sent me to provide you with this." He placed a scroll on the table. "It is vital that Brielle and Penee find Henri and Irstant as soon as possible. The luna moth bite is only part of the reason they are trapped in oblivion. SorTechory also plays a part in their malaise. Brielle has the power to remove the enchantment, but only if she stays true to herself.

"You, Avlin Enus, must remain invisible to all who seek those you love. Follow your grandsires urgings." His immense presence filled the room. "Reclaim your childhood memories soon. They will illuminate your way. Take care, Universal VarTerel." Light spun a cocoon of invisibility and dispersed, leaving the spot he had occupied vacant.

Relevart, unmonitored for the first time in a moon cycle, listened to the sound of water plummeting over the falls. The distant vibration of the Remembering Stone alerted him to Brie's close proximity. The temptation to teleport to her side and reclaim his memories did not manifest into action. He picked up the scroll, untied the ribbon securing it, and unrolled it to find an almost blank parchment.

The ancient text in the upper left corner provided a clue. Find the correct words and a map will appear. A series of pictographs drawn across the bottom of the page were another story, one he could not decipher.

Taking care not to tear the fragile document, he secured it. *Another piece of the puzzle. Who would be the best person to unravel it?*

Gripping his staff, he stepped into Mittkeer, selected his course, and walked into the research area of the Galactic Library on Myrrh. Elae, Elf, and Ari sat at a long table covered with books, parchments, and ledgers.

Elae gasped. "Relevart! You always take me by surprise."

Ari came to her feet. "Is something wrong?"

Elf nodded a welcome.

Relevart handed the scroll to Ari. "I have an important job for you."

She untied the ribbon and flattened the parchment on the table so the others could see. "Most of it's blank. What is it?"

"The Galactic Council has provided us with an important clue to the whereabouts of Henri and Irstant. I need you to translate the pictographs. See if you can discover the sacred words to make the map appear. Make this your priority. I must go."

Mittkeer enclosed him as three heads bent over the parchment scroll.

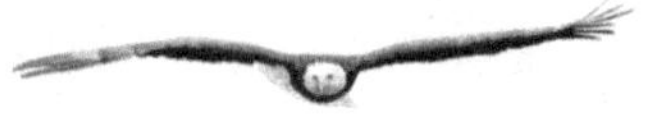

17

Brie perched in a blue spruce by Rainbow Falls, her keen falcon sight picking out the faint imprints of a child's feet in the sand at the edge of the pool. The trees and foliage bore evidence of summer's end. A brisk breeze ruffled her feathers and rustled the vines hanging to one side of the plummeting water. Penee, Abarax, and the Luna Moth were nowhere to be seen.

Glori walked from behind the curtain of trailing plants. No taller than a child of nine or ten, she wore a dress in autumn colors with puffy, elbow-length sleeves, a full skirt, and ruffled petticoats that fell to mid-calf. Ringlets tied back with a bright gold ribbon glowed a lustrous coppery-red. Only the wisdom she exuded belied her youthful appearance.

A disturbance in the bushes at the edge of the trees arrested her attention. "Come out, Vygel Vintrusie. I sensed your presence long before you reached the falls."

Gaunt-faced and awkward, The MasTer's Mocendi stepped from shadowed woods into the light of late turning. "Glori, I presume?"

The childlike wise woman studied him with interest. "You are a long way from home, Mocendi, or would you prefer Vasro?"

Bulging, bloodshot eyes blinked. "I am both, though I am here on Vasro business. Where is she?"

Glori tilted her head. Red ringlets cascaded over her shoulder. She tipped it the other way. "She?"

Vygel took an aggressive step. "Don't play games with me. The twin is here in this place." His piercing gaze snapped with desire. "I can feel *you*, Brielle AsTar, like I can feel *Him*. Show yourself." He darted forward and gripped the wise woman's child-sized arm. "I promise to hurt her unless you come out."

Glori flinched but did not break away. "Let me go, Vygel. You may find yourself—"

His large, callused hand stuck out with enough force to disable a grown man.

Brie materialized across from them. "Release her."

The Mocendi tossed the limp body aside. Hungry desire saturated his expression. Glee made him appear giddy.

Brie's wards shimmered into place. "Keep your distance, Vintrusie, until I check to make sure Glori is alright." She knelt beside the crumpled shape. A small hand gripped her arm. "Go. I can protect myself."

Brie helped her to her feet. "Can you walk?

"Yes, but I'm not leaving."

Vygel's impatience escalated into a flood of profanity. A hiss whistled through his overabundance of teeth. "Leave her alone, or I will end her existence."

Brie supported Glori to the curtain of vines. "Go. I will not allow you to fight my fight."

She rounded on her enemy. "What is it you want of me?"

Eagerness made him salivate. "Tell me which twin carries the secret—you or your sister?" He inched forward.

Brie held her ground. "What are you talking about? I don't have a secr—"

Pain exploded through her. The Star of Truth bit hard—bit with the power of an angry animal. The world spun. Strong Astican arms stopped her fall. Rainbow colors obscured the clearing.

Vygel's laugh of delight changing to a yowl of frustration was the last thing she heard before everything went black

P enee, in hawk form, perched amongst the gold-tinted leaves of a Persowan spena tree. Glori had asked her to keep watch. The wise woman had helped Abarax rescue Brielle.

Below her, Vygel Vintrusie threw back his head and howled in dismay. Pulling himself together, the Vasro glared at the spot where Brie had been. "I should have known you carry the secret."

Bushes behind him parted. "What *is* the secret, Vygel?"

The Vasro froze, his face the image of a child caught with his hand in the cookie jar. Thorlu Tangorra strode from the woods. "What secret would the girl not realize she knew? What secret, Vygel?"

Vintrusie growled, "If I'd wanted you to know, I'd have told you already."

Thorlu minced closer. "But, Vygel, you left me a trail to follow—a trail so clear I arrived right behind you." He clucked his tongue. "I'm shocked you hit the child. I had no idea you were *so* fierce or *so* unfeeling. The secret must be *very* important to you."

Vygel scowled and put distance between himself and his handsome counterpart. "Leave me alone, Tangorra. Her secret has nothing to do with you."

"Tell me, Vasro." Thorlu's teasing tone held a threat.

Vygel's back stiffened. "I will never tell you, Tangorra." He blinked and disappeared.

Thorlu swore under his breath, flung his cape up over his shoulder, and vanished.

In her aspen hide-away, Penee held herself motionless until she felt certain neither man would return. With the cool darkness of the early autumn dusk settling over the gorge, she soared upward. At the top of the falls, she landed in human form. The child-woman stepped from the trees. Penee took her hand. Firefly bright lights danced around them, spiraled upward, and faded, leaving them in a field of wildflowers beneath a mid-turning summer sky.

"Thanks, Glori." She peered at her face. "Vygel gave you one heck of a black eye."

Glori grinned. "My first ever." The grin turned grim. "And my last. Did you learn anything?" She moved past her, forging a path through tall, slender grass.

Penee plucked a daisy. "Nothing. How's Brie?" She glanced over her shoulder. Glori had vanished. "What is it about people lately? One minute they're under your nose, and the next they're gone."

She perched on the corner of the porch and gazed at the field of summer flowers. Childhood memories eased her frustration. *I love summer. Coranna and I used to pick daisies and sing a rhyming song.*

She plucked a delicate petal. "Den loves me." A second petal floated to the ground. "He loves me not." She glared at the flower, crumpled it, and let the pieces fall. "He betrays the ones who love him." Jumping to her feet, she ground its bedraggled remains under the heel of her boot.

Midway to the porch steps, she came to an abrupt halt. *What can be so important that not even Brie knows what it is?* She squinted in the bright summer light. *Or so dangerous?*

⁜ ⁜

Returning to conscious awareness hurt more than anything Brie had ever experienced. A throbbing headache made her nauseous. The muscles of her neck burned. Her body ached. When she forced herself to peek at her surroundings, everything in the room tilted. She groaned and squeezed her lids tight.

Gentle fingers brushed her temples. The pain in her head receded. Her body aches eased. Tears pushed against her lids.

"Brielle AsTar, you are safe."

The soothing voice chased away the last tattered edges of pain. She gazed into celestial-blue eyes. Hers widened. Pushing herself up on her elbows, she struggled to sit up on the bed.

Chealim's powerful arm supported her. He placed a second pillow behind her head and helped her to recline against it. "Lie still, Brielle. Allow your body to catch up while we converse." He lowered his muscular height onto a chair.

Vague memories taunted her, dodged, and pestered her again. *What caused the pain?* She winced and touched the Star of Truth. A haggard face skidded through her mind. "*Vygel...*" She forced herself to focus on the Galactic Guardian. "Did you rescue me?"

"No, my dear. Glori and Abarax brought you here. Penee stayed behind to eavesdrop. She learned little of consequence."

Brie reviewed Vygel's tirade in her head. "What secret do I carry, Chealim? What secret is so important the Star would react in that fashion to a lie I didn't even realize I was telling?"

Sympathy softened the Guardian's solemn expression. "I'm afraid it is one you must discover on your own, Brielle. How you handle it will define your destiny and is critical to the future of the universe."

A momentary flash of anger propelled her to sitting. "It is so important it could affect the lives of others, and you can't even give me a hint?"

"The Council knows it is a burden, but one you are well-equipped to handle. If it were not so..." He left the sentence for her to complete. "You have already proven your innate understanding of good and evil. This coupled with your personal integrity will provide the tools you require."

Frustration stung the back of her throat. She squeezed the bridge of her nose, lowered her hand, and looked at the Guardian. "What can I do to counteract the Star's response? I don't want to die for something I don't even understand."

He rose to his feet with the majesty of his kind. "You now realize you have a secret. That knowledge is your shield." His full height and presence dominated the room. "Trust your instincts, Brielle AsTar."

The radiant flash of his departure left her with questions unanswered and emotions at war in her heart. She sat in the quiet, fighting her rising anger. *I've spent my entire life stifling anything that might stimulate a response from the Star.*

She lowered her hands and traced the lifeline on her palm. *I remember Ari asking Aunt Mira if we are Human.*

"You are definitely Human, Brie."

Her gaze shot to the bedroom door, where Glori's petite face beamed compassion.

"You look confused. Can I help?"

"I doubt anyone can help," Brie grumbled. She rubbed her palms together. *I have more Ari in me than I thought.*

Glori scrambled onto the end of the bed and sat cross-legged. Child's hands smoothed the bedding around her. "Try me. If nothing else, I listen well."

Brie studied the pixie-faced wise woman. "I'm in turmoil, something so rare for me I don't have any idea how to untangle it. Do you know why Chealim came?"

"You have important things to accomplish, Brie. The Council did not want you harmed for something of which you were unaware."

"Yet, they left me in the dark." Brie hugged her knees to her chest. "Why leave me unprepared? Why not give me the tools to accomplish all these grand things? I hate being—" She stopped her tirade and gave Glori a rueful grimace. "Sorry. I'm not sure what to do next. A part of me wants to find Vygel and make him tell me what he knows."

Glori let raised brows speak for her.

Brie swallowed a laugh. "Not a great idea, huh? So, I have a secret I now recognize exists—one I will discover at some point along the way. I am responsible for helping Penee become a leader, for finding Aunt Henri and Irstant, for creating a diversion so Relevart can take Ari and Elf to safety—"

Glori raised her hand. "May I interrupt?"

"Sure, I'm just whining." Brie scooted to the edge of the bed.

The child-woman crawled to her side and sat with her short legs dangling. "You can cross the last item off your list. Ari and Elf are safe. You kept Vygel and Thorlu occupied, and your sister caused a ruckus by blowing up a SorTech Box so Skultar had his hands full." She gripped the side of the bed, swung her legs like a child of six, and grinned. "See. Life isn't so bad."

Brie couldn't hold back a laugh. "You sound like an adult and act like a child. The contrast is disconcerting." She sobered. "Do you have any idea where Elf and Ari are?"

"Even if I did, I would not feel good about sharing."

Brie thought a moment, recognized the wisdom in Glori's response, and chose another direction. "Thank you for saving me."

Glori winked. "It was Penee's plan. Thank her. Abarax and I just did what we were told. You have another question?"

Brie nodded. "We aren't on Persow, or at least on the same Persow as Vygel and Thorlu, correct?"

Glori halted her swinging legs and angled her head to see Brie. "We are in a parallel dimension. Although Thorlu and Vygel lack the power to access it, we have only a finite amount of time here."

"And if we stay too long?"

"We stay forever." The wise woman's childish expression turned forbidding. "Which might not be bad, except the dimension only includes the cottage and the meadow and trees surrounding it."

Brie sighed. "How long?"

Jumping to the floor brought the wise woman eye to eye with Brie. "With luck, we have until you decide what your next move is. I suggest you join Penee and Abarax, bring them up to date, and make a decision. While you do that, I will hold us to our place in time. Don't take too long."

Brie found Penee lounging in a large, overstuffed chair the airy main room. Abarax sat on the floor, scaled wings spread out around him.

Her friend jumped up, welcomed her with a hug, and held her at arms' length. "You look fully recovered. How are you feeling?"

"Confused, but good. Thank you for saving me. You, too, Abarax."

The Astican bowed his head. "It was my duty. Relevart asked me to keep you safe, Brielle AsTar."

A spark of humor sparked as Penee plopped back into the chair. "I'm glad it worked. Now what?"

Brie made herself comfortable on the sofa, where she could see them both. "What do you think, Penee? I'm still a little dazed."

"It appears I am not the only one who is being hunted. Whatever your secret is, my instincts are shouting that we need to put some distance between us and the two scoundrels stalking you. You have something they want—it won't take Thorlu long to discover what it is—and Skultar and the Pheet Adole Klutarse are after me."

Abarax looked from one to the other. "How does it feel to be the most wanted women in the Inner Universe?" His rose bud lips formed a teasing smile before he grew serious. "We must get you to a safe place—not the lakeside cottage."

Penee scrubbed her hair until it stood on end. "I agree. What about Irstant's cabin? Do you think they're aware of its existence?"

Brie turned as Glori joined them. "What do you think, Glori? Are Thorlu and Vygel aware of Irstant's hideaway?"

Glori pursed candy-pink lips. "The actual question is: Do they know about Irstant? They know Relevart. They are aware of Penee and Elf. If Irstant is an unknown, his place might be perfect, except for…"

"Skultar." Penee finished and scowled.

Brie brightened. "I got it! On DerTah, beneath the Cliffs of Tymine on the Isle of ZaltRaca, there's a terrific hiding place. Thorlu and Vygel have traveled to the island but never discovered the cavern. At least we could rest and make plans. The only problem is getting there. I haven't traveled through Mittkeer enough to be certain I can find the way."

Glori jumped to her feet, snapped her fingers, and handed Penee and Brie their staffs. "Form a circle around me. Hurry."

Shoulder to shoulder, they surrounded the wise woman, who spun, full skirt and ruffled petticoats whirling around her. Like a tsunami of stars, Mittkeer rushed toward them.

18

Molasses-sticky tension roiled through the Research Lab of Myrrh's Galactic Library. Ari muttered to herself while she sorted through a stack of parchments at one end of the table. At the other, Elae contemplated the comp-screen, tapped her cheek with a stylus, and scribbled notes on a pad.

The rattle of a scroll rolling onto the floor triggered a string of swear words. Ari crawled after it. Another hit her back and rolled to the floor. A third landed on the seat of the chair next to her.

She groaned. "Too many pieces of paper with little information." Rescuing the two scrolls from the floor, she returned them to the stack. Elae's worried gaze scrutinized the rolled parchments. "Look." Ari held up the third scroll. "No harm done. Where's Elf, anyway?"

Elae squeezed the bridge of her nose. "I sent him to find a book about the K'iin, a long-lost tribe on the Isle of Neul. The history of the island is fascinating. This tribe was known for the pictographic records of its past. Come here. I'll show you a representation of a K'iin codex."

Glad to take a break from the monotony of her pile of scrolls, Ari studied the pictures on her comp-screen.

"What am I seeing, Elae?"

"The K'iin illustrated stories and histories on bark fabric. Each panel of the codex, also called a screenfold, showed up to two stories or depictions. This one had twenty-four leaves or folds painted on both sides."

"Do you understand the pictographs?"

The DeoNyte enlarged the panel on the screen. "I believe this figure represents a K'iin Goddess of Small Creatures. The smaller ones beneath are the animals over which she presides." The DeoNyte sat back. "I'm hoping we might find pictos that resemble those on the scroll Relevart gave you."

Ari leaned closer. "Can you zoom out and down?"

Elae complied, her total attention fixed on the screen.

Her focus complete, Ari examined each pictograph on the panel.

"Hey!" The exclamation of excitement interrupted their intense concentration.

Ari shot Elf a dirty look. "By Emit, Elf, you could warn a girl."

Grinning, he held up a slim volume. "I found them! I found the symbols on the map." He caught sight of the comp-screen. "I found other books with codices from other tribes, but this one shows specific pictographs by the K'iin." He plopped down on a chair. His eager satisfaction magnified his delight. "I could study this all turning. It's fascinating." He looked from Ari to Elae. "Well? Where's the map?"

Ari circled the table and removed the map from the protective box Elae had provided. After placing a book on each corner to hold it flat, she moved to one side.

Elf opened the volume to a marked page and held it next to the almost blank parchment. Elae stood beside him with a pad in hand. Ari peered over Elf's shoulder, hoping against hope he had found something helpful.

SparrowLyn gazed at the fountain, Elcaro's Eye. Carved from the purest white alabaster in the Inner Universe, it made an impressive centerpiece in her cottage sanctuary. A statue kneeling on the rim, an exact representation of Myrrh's Guardian, always left her sober and thoughtful. "I am the Guardian of Myrrh, the last remnant of Earth." She moved to the window to absorb the beauty of the garden and paddocks, the pond and the Terces Wood. "I never saw it coming."

A gentle breeze tossed a chestnut tendril of hair across her face. She brushed it aside and listened to the soothing sound of water spilling from the statue's open palms into the fountain's alabaster basin. "I wonder how Brie is handling her dilemma? She is young to carry such a burden, but then she has carried it all her life without knowing it."

The barn door swung wide. Allynae ushered a younger man into the garden, pointed at the upstairs sanctuary, and ducked back inside. The tall stranger walked with a purposeful stride to the cottage, stopped beneath the window, and looked up at her.

"Oh, my!" She pushed the window wide. "Esán! Is it really you?"

His laugh of delight floated up to her. "May I come up?"

"I'll meet you downstairs." Glancing at Elcaro's Eye, Sparrow hurried to the kitchen.

Esán smiled as she entered the kitchen.

For a minute, she stared at the once bald boy who had become a man at least a head taller than her with shoulder length, honey-blond hair. "Has it only been two sun cycles since you left for seclusion at Timreh Pass? You look so—" She grinned. "Yes, Esán, you look grown up." A thought struck her. "Should you be here?"

He drew her into a hug. "The Quickening of the Seeds of Carsilem is complete." Releasing her, he gazed at her for a long moment. "Brielle is in trouble. I came as soon as I heard. I have another surprise." He pushed open the door.

Over six feet tall and handsome as his father, Torgin Whalend grinned down at her. "I understand Relevart needs some research done. I came to help."

Sparrow could not hold back the tears. Esán and Torgin had shared more adventures with her daughters than she could count. "How did you know the girls needed you?"

Esán pulled out a chair. "Sit. When Allynae gets here, I'll fill you in."

As she sank onto the chair, her life-mate and the father of the twins strode into the kitchen, shook Torgin's hand, and sat down next to her. "All we need is the girls to make life feel perfect. Barring that, Esán, tell us your news."

Esán took a moment to let his gaze roam the kitchen, to remember the changing color of its walls, the caw of the raven Karrew, and the countless discussions held at this table. He bent down to stroke the silky back of a smoky-gray cat.

"Hi, Majeska. Of course, I remember you."

An answering purr rumbled through the room.

Forearms resting on the table, he began. "The Seeds of Carsilem make me sensitive to those I love. In the last stages of their Quickening, they have increased my awareness of Brie." His focus shifted to Sparrow. "You know her secret." His held gaze hers. "So do I." He gave her a moment to digest what he had said. "Once the word is out, she will become a target for the Mocendi, Klutarse, and Vasro. That she is in the company of Elf's birth-mate compounds her danger."

Sparrow shot a glance at Torgin. "Do you—"

He shook his head. "I only know what Esán has shared to help me with the research Relevart needs done." He rocked back. "I'm almost as good at research as my father."

Allynae draped an arm across the back of Sparrow's chair. "Relevart knows the Seeds have matured, Esán?"

"He does. We've communicated regarding Brielle. He's given me permission to help, but only from afar. This is Brie's game and Penee's. They each have lessons to learn. I just wanted you to know I'd be close enough to help if the need arises."

The group in the kitchen grew quiet. Esán watched the walls turn from pale green to salmon. *Someday, Brie and I will have a kitchen with walls that change color.*

Sparrow leaned her head on Allynae's shoulder and straightened. "You're ready to go?"

"I'm taking Torgin to join Ari and Elf. Then I'm off to DerTah to confer with Wolloh. Elcaro's Eye will keep you informed of my progress." He pushed back his chair and walked around the table to give her a hug.

Allynae squeezed his shoulder. "Your father would be proud."

Esán's expression brightened. "Thanks. Come on, Torg. I'll race you across the garden."

Sparrow and Allynae stood arm in arm on the back porch, watching the boys race to the forest path beyond the barn. They turned to wave. Esán touched Torgin's arm, and they flashed from sight.

Sparrow experienced a rush of memories. "Who would have guessed that a sick, bald boy and a scared Idronatti kid would turn into such handsome, young men?"

Allynae placed a soft kiss on her lips. "Even boys grow up, SparrowLyn. They just take a little longer."

Laughing, she followed him through the kitchen to her artist's studio. "How did you know I needed to paint?"

He kissed her. "You have that look in your eye. I'm off to help Race with the chores." Another soft kiss and he was on his way.

Sparrow looked at the blank canvas on her easel. An image formed. She picked up a piece of charcoal and drew a long, curved line.

Ari's floundering concentration came to a standstill. Her mouth rounded in surprise. Framed in the doorway to the Research lab, a tall, good-looking man with warm-brown skin and summer-green eyes grinned at her.

"Oh! Oh!" Her chair crashed to the floor. "Torgin Wilith Whalend!"

He strode to her side, righted the chair, and hugged her. "Arienh, have I missed you." He grinned at Elf. "Hi. She running you ragged?"

Ari punched him in the arm, caught the wink he flashed at Elf, and punched him again. "You are such a Drotti."

Elf jerked a thumb toward the door. "Did I see Esán?"

"You did. He delivered me and is off to see Wolloh on DerTah."

Ari stuck out her bottom lip. "He didn't even say hi?"

Torgin hugged her again. "That's from Esán. I came to help with the research. Tell me what you need."

Elae walked in with Elf's slim volume in hand. "We need everything you can find on these six pictographs." She handed Torgin the book. "Elf, go with him. In the same area, see if you can find charts of the waters surrounding Neul Isle. Ari, I need you to find scroll number AX240. It should contain details regarding the K'iin."

Torgin followed Elf down an aisle lined with glass cases on both sides.

Elae sat down at her comp-screen and began a search for something else.

A ri watched the boys leave. "Would have liked to catch up." A glance told her Elae was deep in her research. Breathing a heavy sigh, she began sorting scrolls by number.

Esán stepped into the Nervac Gateway in the Dojanack Caverns. The dimensional tunnel enclosed him, held him suspended until it cannoned him through the portal onto the Desert of Fera Finnero. Skidding down the side of a dune, he remembered the first time he had encountered a Fire ConDra. Not wishing to meet another one, he melded into the desert sand. The heat of mid-turning filled his lungs and squeezed sweat from every pore. He shifted to a dune hawk and shot skyward. Within moments, he landed near the outcropping of rock at the end of Eissua Oasis.

A man stepped from the shade of a palm. "Wolloh asked me to give you this." Stebben Stol pressed something smooth and hard into his hand. "He said to tell you the portals of Mittkeer are yours to command. Give Relevart our best. Take care of Brielle." He turned and walked toward the sparkling water of the oasis.

Esán uncurled his fingers. The carved desert stone in his hand delighted him. *Mittkeer will make my job much easier.*

Stars and ever-night embraced him. Allowing the Seeds of Carsilem to plot his course, he began a trek through the Land of All Time and No Time.

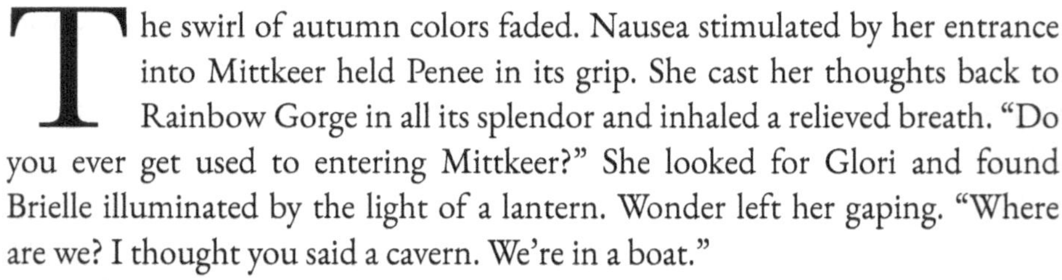

19

The swirl of autumn colors faded. Nausea stimulated by her entrance into Mittkeer held Penee in its grip. She cast her thoughts back to Rainbow Gorge in all its splendor and inhaled a relieved breath. "Do you ever get used to entering Mittkeer?" She looked for Glori and found Brielle illuminated by the light of a lantern. Wonder left her gaping. "Where are we? I thought you said a cavern. We're in a boat."

"This is a boat inside a cavern." Brie made a sweeping turn. "At least, it's the hull of a boat." She glanced around. "Looks like Bibeed has been keeping it stocked."

Penee roamed the space. Sand and time had worn rough stone smooth to form a floor. Cots arranged end to end drew her attention to the curved wooden sides of the boat. A table constructed of sun-bleached boards stood opposite a fire pit. Overhead, the wooden deck obscured the cavern ceiling. Splintered wood where the aft portion of the boat had been torn away rested against rocks piled one on top of another. The most fascinating thing of all was the beautifully carved figure of a woman, which lay to one side, La perched on her ear.

Abarax, his scaled body and wings sized to allow him to stand straight, observed the Luna Moth flutter around the cavern. "How did it get here—the boat, I mean?"

Brie thought back to her earlier visit. "I seem to recall the boat ran aground on the beach. The villagers hitched horses to it and dragged it beneath the cliffs so the Mocendi wouldn't find it. Someday, I'll introduce you to Bibeed and Cay. They can tell you the complete story."

Penee blinked as a tear-producing yawn blurred her vision. "I'll bet that was something to watch." A second yawn caught her midway to a cot. "Jumping dimensions sure takes it out of you. Are we safe? Can we rest?"

Brie stretched her senses outward. "We're safe for the moment, but we don't want to stay too long."

Abarax smothered a yawn. "La found a crevice big enough so she can fly outside. She says she'll be our guard."

After turning down the lantern, Brie curled up on the cot closest to the entrance. "Whoever wakes up first wakes the rest of us." Sleep snatched her before her head touched the pillow.

Penee yawned. "I'm usually the first one asleep. You're stealing my trick, Brielle." She tossed Abarax a blanket from the foot of the cot. "See you soon."

The Astican shrunk to the size of a small dog and cuddled within its folds. Snores drifted through the cavern.

Penee stared at the rough wood overhead and contemplated the events of the past few turnings. *Where do we go next?* She stroked the weave of the chain mail shirt Irstant had made for her. *I'll find you, Irstant. I promise.* Eyelids weighted with fatigue closed. Blissful dreams enclosed her.

The third turning of their stay on DerTah, Brie sat on the beach skirting the Cliffs of Tymine. Sounds of gulls and cormorants mingling with the gentle caress of the ocean breeze wrapped her in a blanket of serene solitude. Their urgent need to find Henri and Irstant had not waned. Fatigue made time to recoup vital to the success of their rescue mission. ZaltRaca, a small island off the coast of Geran Province, had proven to be the perfect resting place.

Obscuring the sun's brightness with a raised hand, she watched Penee dig DerTahan beach clams. Her short, caramel gold hair glistened in the sunlight. Tanned skin glowing with health made her mismatched eyes with their long, dark lashes even more startling. Brie had to admit she was beautiful. *I guess I understand Ari's fears about Elf.*

She picked up an angel wing shell, traced the delicate ridges with a finger, and thought about how much she missed Esán. *How would I react if you were Penee's birth-mate? I love you, Esán Efre? How much longer will you have to be alone at Timreh Pass?* Her thumb slipping over the smooth underside of the shell brought her to a realization: *I'm feeling less lonely since we arrived on ZaltRaca. It must be that I'm closer to you.*

She slipped the shell in her pocket and looked up to find Penee smiling down at her. "You sure had a dreamy look on your face. Do I know him?"

Brie laughed and climbed to her feet. "Nope. Maybe you will someday." She peeked in the basket on Penee's arm. "Yum. A tasty meal is on the way."

Resembling a couple of kids, they giggled their way to the boat-cavern. Inside, Penee set her basket on the table. "I vote we make plans in the morning."

Brie grinned. "Agreed. Let's get cookin'."

The choice to sleep unencumbered by decision-making gave them permission to relax for another night. After a delicious meal filled with lighthearted laughter, Brie observed her companions. Penee, more carefree than Brie could remember, hummed to herself. Abarax looked healthy and rested. Even the eyespots on La's wings seemed brighter.

Penee swirled the remains of the tea in her mug and finished it with relish. "I'm ready to bed down." She yawned, rinsed out the mug, and prepared for bed.

Not far behind, Brie made herself comfortable on her cot. The first turning of their stay, she had worn herself out worrying about the secret. The next morning, she had made a personal promise to give it a break. Now, as the time to look ahead drew near, anxious thoughts surfaced. With the angel shell next to her heart, she gave herself permission to rest.

She slept with the deep abandon of a child. Her hand hanging over the side of the cot rested on a soft furry back and coaxed her deeper into dreaming.

Tall white pines and beech nut trees surrounded her. The hoot of a small owl mingled with the gentle splash of water against the lake shore. The air smelled of spring. Tiny new buds formed a pale green mist on bushes and deciduous trees. The tranquility of the dream tempted her to stay, to leave behind the drama of her life.

Relevart walked toward her and ducked beneath a low-hanging branch. "Go to the lake cottage on Soputto. Use the secret room to hide your presence. Leave the Remembering Stone in the cookie jar in the boat pantry. I'll return it when I can."

"How do I know you're Relevart?"

An El Stroman galee materialized on the low-hanging branch, tipped its majestic head, and gazed at her from raptor-gold eyes. *"I flew with Rayn in this shape one last time before she died."* The thought brought the man into human form. "Thank you for safeguarding my memories, Brielle." His image dissolved in the gentle spring breeze.

The lick of a warm, rough tongue on her hand woke her. She came to sitting, touched the damp spot, and stared into the lightless cavern. The faint, musky odor of animal provided the only hint to the soft fur and wet tongue.

She made her way to the table and relit the lantern. Warm light washed over Penee. Abarax curled up in a pile of blankets. The animal, if it had been real, was gone.

Her dream nudged. The urgency in Relevart's voice spurred her into action. In the pantry, she found the pottery cookie jar. Removing the blue ribbon from around her neck, she tipped the Stone onto her palm. Lantern light intensified the smooth, blue, roundness. Tiny specks of gold twinkled to life. *I haven't been without you since Almiralyn gave you to me.*

After returning the Stone to its pouch, she held it to her heart. It throbbed; the Star of Truth twinged. *How do I ensure that Relevart is the only one who can open the jar?* The Remembering Stone's pulsing grew stronger. Sudden insight made her laugh. *Remember, Brielle AsTar, you are a VarTerel.*

She removed the lid from the jar and tucked the pouch inside. Lips pursed in thought, she pressed her palms to the jar.

> "Cookie jar, your lid stays tight
> Opening only to one who's right
> He carries power you will feel
> Only Relevart can break the seal."

The lid settling back into place left a tiny ache in her heart. With a touch of regret, she returned the jar to its place in the small pantry.

The gentle flutter of moth wings demanded her attention. La shared an image of Vygel at the cottage on the clifftop. Her mind filled with memories of her aunt hunted by the Mocendi. *I will find you, Aunt Henri.*

She hurried to Penee's side. "Time to wake up." She gave Abarax a gentle nudge.

Wide awake in an instant, he grew to human size. La flew to his shoulder. "We need to leave, Brielle AsTar."

Penee's yawn ended in a groan. "Really? Before breakfast?"

La chirped.

Penee, muttering under her breath, gripped the staff she had propped by the cot. "Where to?"

Irstant's staff in hand, Brie joined her. "Here we go. Abarax, hold on. Penee, are you ready?"

Her reply was lost in a vastness of stars swirling into stillness.

Brie searched the heavens, found the constellation Actias, the luna moth, and set their heading. She linked arms with Penee. "Once we are beyond the pull of DerTah, we head to Lake Llyn on Soputto."

Penee looked surprised. "I thought because Thorlu knows about it—"

Brie urged her onward. "I had a dream. I'll explain later."

From its perch on the peaked roof of Bibeed's residence at the top of Tymine Cliff, Relevart, in the form of a DerTahan black-headed gull, observed Vygel exit the deserted cottage and stride to the rim of the cliff. After a quick scan of the distant beach, the Mocendi shot a furtive glance over his shoulder, leapt into the air, and shaped a cormorant.

The black-headed gull soared clear of the cottage, swooped over the precipice, and glided to a landing at the ocean's edge. A short distance away, Vygel reclaimed his human form.

The chattery squawk of seabirds and the consistent rumble and splash of the incoming tide accompanied the Mocendi's awkward gait as he walked along the beach. He stopped to scan the cliff face. "Brielle AsTar, I can feel you." He sniffed the air and grimaced. "I smell Astican and luna moth."

Water rushing and gurgling around his feet and ankles spawned several profane expressions. An amused laugh close-by made him jerk his head to the side. Thorlu Tangorra's sneer brought a flush of heat to his cheeks. Dismay stretched his thin lips into a scowl. Another wave of saltwater sloshing over his boots and soaking his pant legs went unnoticed.

Thorlu glanced at Vygel's feet. "Move up the beach, Vintrusie. The tide won't hold back because The MasTer's Mocendi is getting his feet wet."

Vygel tromped to higher ground. "What are you doing here, Tangorra? I told you to leave me alone."

The gull pecked at a shell and waddled closer.

Thorlu squinted up at the cliff. "They are here. My question is, how did you know?"

"My question, Tangorra, is how did you get to DerTah?"

"How do you think?" His sarcastic laugh traveled the beach. "I was on the same space shuttle you were on, fool. You were just so distracted, you didn't notice. I even sat at the table next to you for meals, and *you* never realized I was there." He faced him. "If you have secrets you wish to keep hidden, I'd advise you to exercise some situational awareness."

A menacing step brought him nose to nose with Vygel. "And, Vintrusie, since we are not the only ones after the girls, *and* I deflected two attempts to trap you, I suggest you be more forthcoming."

The black-headed gull flew along the tide line, caught a small crab in its beak, and gobbled it down, one glistening eye trained on the men.

Vygel's pallid complexion bleached to almost translucent. His lower jaw jutted forward. He ran his tongue over his teeth, pressed his lips together, and glowered at the man whose gaze had returned to the cliff. He wiped a drip of spittle from his chin and opened his mouth to speak.

Thorlu shook his head and pointed. "Over there. See the irregularity?" He marched up the beach, threw a disparaging glance over his shoulder, and hissed, "You coming or not?"

Vygel slogged after him, his feet squishing in his sodden boots with each step. He stopped several feet from Thorlu and watched him examine the nature-roughened wall. A sneer of resentment made his already unattractive features repulsive.

A black-headed gull swept past him and landed nearby. Overhead, a large moth darted into a narrow crevice. The gull pecked at its breast feathers. *La will deliver my message.*

20

In the research lab on Myrrh, Ari studied her stack of scrolls. AX240 was not among them. She tossed her stylus on the tabletop. "I need a break, Elae. I'm going for a walk."

Elae glanced up. "Remember not to leave Canedari." Her attention returned to the comp-screen.

Ari bit back a retort. Grumpy muttering escorted her to the Reading Room. The door to Veersuni beckoned. Inside, an aimless circuit of the room let the sanctuary's serenity sooth her agitated nerves. Her wanderings ended at the spot that had once hosted Elcaro, the All-Seeing-Eye. *I know Mother needs the fountain at the cottage.* She sighed. *Just for today, I wish it were here.*

A flicker of light pulled her gaze to the stained-glass window during a pattern change. Autumn leaves turning to flurries of white birds darted over the ocean. Ari touched blue triangle. *I miss the sea. Someday, I'm going sailing again. Maybe Elf and I will even have a sailboat.*

She slipped from the sanctuary to stroll along the Hall of Priestesses' pristine length to the Cave of Canedari. Indecision stopped her at the double doors. The pull of the crystal heart of Myrrh nudged her through.

Evolsefil's beauty left her breathless. Seven feet tall with glittering gold filaments traveling from the solid-gold base to the tip made the entire crystal glow. Suspended amid the threads, a parchment scroll unrolled.

Ari strode across the stone floor. The number AX240 scribbled on a tattered corner pulled her closer. Crystal light illuminated faded black writing.

> "A secret held within a map
> Will prove to hold a hidden trap.
> Disarm it with this single word—
> ISHNAB—too loud to go unheard."

The black letters faded. Flame-red letters took their place.

> "If caught within the hidden snare
> By simply being unaware
> Repeat ISHNAB and then NABISH
> To free the spell like a slippery fish."

Ari's heart jumped to her throat. "What happens if they translate the symbols before I get back?" The question's potential answer sent her racing along the hall. She dashed across the Reading Room and down the steps to the Research Lab.

Torgin and Elae stood near the end of the table. Next to them, Elf, his hand resting on the blank center of Relevart's scroll, nodded. Torgin read from the slender leather volume as the DeoNyte Priestess drew symbols in the air.

Elf gasped. "I-I-I...

"It's booby trapped! **ISHNAB, NABISH! ISHNAB, NABISH.**" Ari's shout echoed through the halls of the Galactic Library, bounced back to the Research Lab, and wrapped Elf in a cloak of golden light. He snatched his hand free of the parchment's trap. The light settled over the scroll. Coastlines, valleys, mountains, and lakes appeared one sketched line at a time.

Elae leaned closer. "It looks similar to the maps I've seen of Neul Isle, but more detailed." She hurried to her comp-screen. "Look, there are significant differences."

Torgin picked up the map.

They moved as a group to the comp-screen. The maps were comparable, but the one on the scroll contained more detail. Several places were missing on Elae's map.

Ari sucked in a breath. "This is where Irstant and Aunt Henri are. I'm sure of it."

Elf nodded. "I agree. Brie and Penee need to see this."

Torgin rolled up the scroll and set it on the table. "But we don't know where they are and..."

"None of us can travel through Mittkeer." Ari finished the sentence. With a heavy sigh, she sank into a chair.

Elf sat next to her. "I'm betting Relevart knows we've discovered the key. While we wait, tell us how you found out about the map's hidden trap."

A short while later, the group stood in the Cave of Canedari, listening to Ari's tale. The faint imprint of the scroll's presence at Evolsefil's center, all that remained to confirm her story, faded as they watched, leaving only golden threads in the clear quartz.

Torgin and Elae, deep in conversation, walked toward the door.

Elf rubbed his palms together. "I'm glad you found it, Arienh. The parchment burned my hand as though it were on fire."

Ari slipped a hand into Elf's. "I was scared I wouldn't make it in time."

He glanced over shoulder. "Look." He turned her to Evolsefil.

In the crystal's depth, a male figure walked toward them. Ari's mouth dropped open. She clamped it shut and stared.

Torgin hurried back to her side. "How on Thera did he..."

Esán's wavering form solidified. "I became attuned to Evolsefil when I returned her to Canedari. She alerted me you found the key to the map." He held up the scroll. "I will deliver it to Brielle." His form dimmed.

"Wait!" Ari called. "Take me with you."

The image steadied. "I cannot, Arienh. You must stay hidden. You have important research to do." He faded. His voice echoed through Canedari. "I promise to watch over Brie and Penee."

Threads of gold vibrated into stillness. Quiet soaked up Ari's disappointment. She pulled Elf toward the door.

"I want to learn everything about the Star of Truth."

Torgin followed. "I'll research how the K'iin cured the bite of a luna moth."

Behind them, Elae whispered, "I'll do my best to keep you all safe."

The black-headed gull perched at the top of a large rock on the beach at ZaltRaca, observing Vygel Vintrusie and Thorlu Tangorra search the rough, uneven cliff face.

A grinding sound brought a shout of triumph from Thorlu. "Over here! I found an entrance."

Vygel peered into a dark recess. A section of the rock wall had swung inwards exposing a tunnel the height of an average-sized man that wound its way under the cliff.

Thorlu grabbed a kerosene lantern from a hook a short distance inside. A snap of his fingers lit the wick. He flashed a conspiratorial grin at Vygel and crept forward.

The gull waited long enough for the men to move out of sight, shifted to a small orange DerTahan fly, and shot into La's crevice. It arrived in the boathome as the younger Mocendi ducked under the ledge.

Lamplight cast a warm glow over the empty cavern. The fly made note of the dust on everything, the clean fire pit, and blankets folded at the end of each cot. No one appeared to have visited the boathome in some time.

Vygel muttered. "No one's been here."

Thorlu set the lantern on the table. "They were in this cave. I know it, and you know it. So where are they now? They couldn't have gone far."

Vygel's bulging eyes gleamed. He dropped awkwardly onto a chair. "You're the smart one. Where do *you* think they are?"

"We know the witch of Rainbow Gorge brought them to the cliffs through Mittkeer."

Fiddling with a button on his vest, Vygel shot him a triumphant look. "Witches can't travel through Mittkeer, so..."

"Who's the VarTerel? Penee or Brielle?" Thorlu stroked his chin. "I vote for Brie."

A gurgle of laughter burst from Vygel's throat. "See how smart you are? Now, where did they go?"

"No more games, Vintrusie." The taller man loomed over him. "Tell me Brie's secret."

Vygel launched to his feet and kicked his chair out of the way. "Figure it out, Tangorra. I have a jumper to catch." He grabbed the lantern and ducked under the ledge.

Frustration sent Thorlu chasing him down the tunnel. "When I get my hands on that girl, I won't ever take a shuttle again."

The fly followed them to the beach. Vygel dropped the kerosene lamp on the sand. With a final sardonic sneer at his fellow Mocendi, he stepped into a vortex that swirled shut behind him. Thorlu swore. A wave of his hand brought a portal into being. He leapt into its center, leaving the beach on ZaltRaca empty of Humans.

The fly shot skyward. Shifting to a gull, it swooped to a rock near the recessed opening. Time drifted by...time and the tide and the turning. Sunset streaking the sky with color brought Relevart back to his human form. He retrieved the lamp and walked into the tunnel. The lantern's wick sprang to light. Its warm glow preceded him, highlighting the ledge, and dispersing the cavern's darkness as he ducked inside.

The Universal VarTerel straightened, absorbed the absence of others, and placed the lantern on the table. "Alone at last."

From a rough-hewn chair, he inspected the place he had only seen through La's eyes. Now, he absorbed the peaceful uniqueness of the hideaway. His over-taxed nerves relaxed. Escape from TaSneach had been a strain on his reserves. The effort to neutralize the drugs in his system had taken more energy than he had expected. Unencumbered sleep tempted him.

His tired gazed came to rest on the pantry shelf. *Memories...now or later?*

He stepped over the wooden figurehead and hefted the cookie jar. The tingle of Brie's enchantment tickled his palms. A smile tugged the corners of his mouth. *You are fast becoming a power to be reckoned with, my dear.*

He set the jar on the table, sat down, and tapped the lid. A soft crackle released Brie's charm. A hiss accompanied the lid's removal. He withdrew a blue velvet pouch on its matching ribbon and held it to his heart. Long, steadying breaths prepared him for what was to come. The Remembering Stone rolled onto his palm. His fingers caressed its smooth, blue roundness. He tried to recall the turning he had filled it with his childhood memories.

A twinge of sadness left him thoughtful. *I wish you were with me, Henri.*

The insistent thrum of the Stone pulsed through his entire body. Images bombarded him. Rayn—her wavy, black hair; brown eyes outlined with black lashes; and an impish grin—brought tears. Childish giggles chased him along a pebble-strewn beach. The smell of fish roasting made his stomach rumble. The roar of water, a small bird caught in its fast-moving currents, a smoky galee's talons snatching it up and carrying it to safety left him panting. Rayn's shift from bird to Human when *he* called her name made him clutch the Stone tighter. A ramshackle homestead filled his senses with the smells of spices and cooking, the sounds of laughter and song, goats naying in an overgrown yard, a batch of kittens mewing, a fire crackling in the fireplace in winter, and the coolness of splashing in the creek in summer brought an outpouring of joy. Fear emanating from his maman and his Aunt Floree, a man named Kuparak, another named Mylos... So many memories overflowed both his mind and heart. When at last they faded, he curled up on a cot with the warm Stone next to his heart. A small boy with amber eyes, a beautiful girl reminiscent of Henri, and a bench by the sea filled his dreams.

He woke in the dimness of the boathome. The world he had always known now contained a richness of remembering that left him bathed in wonder. More memories rose to the surface, imprinted the gentle kiss of their reality on his heart, and provided the details he needed to create a timeline of his existence. Even his grandsire's memories, which had not vanished into the Stone, became more poignant.

Crossing to the table, he turned up the lamp, sank onto the chair, and fixed his attention on a figure materializing near the ledge. The wolf, Forêst, his grandsire's Familiar Spirit, gazed at him from lupine-wise eyes. Relevart felt a rush of love and gratitude. The wolf faded. Relevart sat steeped in the stories that were now his forever.

The need to breathe the fresh ocean air propelled him through the entrance into the light of a bright, sunlit morning. At the water's edge, a tidal pool called to the child in him. He knelt and peered at miniature sea life washed in by the tide: a crab; a tiny yellow and black striped fish; a slender, green, worm-like creature.

The breeze stilled. The surface captured his reflection. Wind-tasseled, white hair framed his face, highlighting eyes the deep honey-gold of amber, eyes that had been dark brown since his escape from El Stroma.

A laugh of delight chimed. "Henri, I can't wait until you see me!"

"You look happy."

Relevart came to standing, his arsenal of skills at the ready. A grin replaced consternation. "Esán. I almost banished you to another dimension. How did you find me?"

The younger man shrugged. "The Seeds of Carsilem direct my path. They brought me to you." He held up the scroll. "Your team of researchers unlocked the key. I thought you should see it before I take it to Brielle."

Relevart led the way to the opening in the cliff face. "You're familiar with the boathome. I suggest we go in, and you can show me what you've discovered."

R elevart had expected the parchment scroll to reveal a secret; he had not expected it to center on the K'iin, an indigenous people who had vanished over half a centurial cycle ago.

With a reminder to stay out of sight, he had sent Esán into Mittkeer. The boy's talents, formidable prior to the Quickening of the Seeds of Carsilem, had matured. Nothing good would come of their adversaries discovering the strength of his power or Brielle's or Penee's.

Even as he watched the portal into Mittkeer close, his senses trembled with the coming of change.

21

Brie leaned on the terrace railing, gazing across Lake Llyn at the snowcapped Sileah Mountains. Signs of spring—buds on the trees; mountain streams depositing snowmelt into the cold, clear water; and tiny green sprouts pushing up through rich black soil—made her heart feel lighter. Somehow she, Penee, and Abarax had missed the winter snows during their sojourn on DerTah.

They had arrived at the cottage to find Coranna, Barlet, and Shyllee waiting. Skultar and his SorTech had paid them a visit at the manor house. After threatening to make their lives miserable if they withheld information, he left Furrnoce to interrogate them. The SorTech had discovered nothing. The recollection of Barlet's obvious satisfaction at The Box's failure pleased Brie.

Coranna had made it clear Skultar knew nothing about the lakeside cottage, but expressed concern that discovery was in the wind. Rather than provide

Penee's cousin with a weapon to use against her, she and Barlet had made the decision to disappear. She suggested an invisibility charm for the cottage, kissed her proxy daughter a fond goodbye, and departed with her spouse and Shyllee in a closed carriage. If Penee knew their destination, she hadn't shared.

The soft swoosh of the door opening ushered Penee onto the terrace. She leaned on the railing beside Brie. "Abarax back yet?"

"Nope. It's kinda cute how it likes to fish. I never would have guessed at our first encounter that we'd become friends."

Penee flicked a small pinecone off the railing. "Is that when it chased you through the Tinga Forest on DerTah?"

Brie nodded. "We were being hunted by both the Astican and the Mindeco. It was pretty scary." She grinned. "Look! It caught something."

The full-sized Astican soared above the lake, a fish flapping in its taloned hands. La shot ahead. The tickle of her wings close to Brie's cheek made her laugh.

Penee studied the pale green moth. "I don't think she likes me."

La fluttered to her shoulder, flicked an antenna against her cheek, and gave a series of soft squeaks.

Penee held up her hand. La alighted on her thumb. "Thank you, pretty moth. I like you, too."

Abarax reached the terrace. A gust of wing-wind from his massive wings rustled the leaves on nearby trees, then ceased. The Astican held up a large, black fish with pale blue fins. "Dinner." Its smile stretched from ear to ear.

Brie caught Penee's eye. They oohed over the size of its catch, told Abarax what a great fisherman it was, and grinned at each other as it strode down to the cleaning station at the boathouse.

Penee lobbed another pinecone into the lake. "How long do you think Thorlu and Vygel will take to reach Soputto?" She shook her head. "Let me rephrase my question. How long until we're on the run again?"

Brie reveled in the Soputton sun and inhaled spring air. "They can't travel through Mittkeer, so they'll need to take an intergalactic ship to Roahymn and then a jumper shuttle to Soputto. How long it takes will depend on how long they have to wait for a ship. It only took them a few turnings to catch up with us on DerTah."

Penee stared over the lake. "How do we find Henri and Irstant when we're stuck here? I enjoy having down time, but what if they're running out of time? What if..." Penee's expression completed the sentence.

Brie pondered the question she had been asking herself. "Relevart would not have sent us to Soputto if he didn't feel it were important. So, what can we access from the cottage that we couldn't access on DerTah?"

Penee straightened to her full statuesque height. Her blue eye glowed bluer; the amber specks in her green eye glistened. She repeated something over and over.

Mesmerized by her intense beauty, Brie held herself quiet. Her thought process had given her a plausible answer. *What will you discover, Penesert?*

A scan of the opposite shoreline ended with Penee facing her. "We are closer than we think to the VarTerels. That's the most important reason Relevart would have sent us back to Soputto. Another might be Barlet's library. He has an entire section on the K'iin. I gather the tribe and the island have a fascinating history. If Henri and Irstant are on Neul Isle, the more we know, the better."

"I agree." Brie glanced beyond her and couldn't hold back a smile. "Our fisherman returns with his prize. What do you say to dinner, then research?"

In the darkness of the hidden room, Penee stretched out on her bunk and revisited the series of interesting facts they had uncovered in Barlet's Neul Isle collection. Clouds had not always enshrouded the island. Before the K'iin disappeared, its rugged beauty had been visible to anyone sailing by. The mystery of why the ancient tribe vanished and what created the island's cloud covering continued to puzzle researchers.

The K'iin, prolific storytellers and historians, had a written language, so it came as no surprise that she had unearthed an ancient map. Although timeworn and faded, it furnished a clear outline of the island's shape. What it did not provide was a sense of the terrain.

A robust yawn sent tears down her cheeks. She blinked them away and continued to review their discoveries.

A Stannag, a guardian spirit, combined with a creature endemic to Neul, protected the island and its people. In this case, the spirit had joined forces with an octopus known as a phantom incirrata that inhabited the bay at the island's center. She rolled onto her side. *So, where is the Stannag? If something had happened to the people, something might also have happened to their guardian.*

Another yawn nudged her toward sleep. The haunting image of an incirrata pulled her into dreaming.

Water bubbled to the surface, forming a frothing path that pursued the translucent creature that circled the center of the lagoon. Reflected clouds swirled in its wake. Its head broke the surface. Luminous gold eyes glinted. Jet propulsion thrust it forward in a long glide, its gray-blue tentacles fanning out behind it.

Penee woke to find the room illuminated by lantern light. Brie peered at her over the edge of the upper bunk. "Are you alright, Penee? You just made the strangest sound."

"A phantom incirrata appeared in my dreams." She rubbed her short hair into a tangled nest and blinked back tears. "It was so sad." She scooched to the end of the bunk, descended the ladder, and stood scratching her left forearm. "I'm sure it was the Stannag from Neul. We need to do more—"

"Shhhh!" Abarax achieved human height in an instant. Its warning look closed her mouth. La fluttered to her shoulder.

Taut with alarm, Brie gripped Irstant's staff. "Skultar is close. Come on. It's time to learn how to use an invisibility charm. Grab your staff." She raced up the stairs, pulled the lever, and dodged into the trophy room.

Penee jogged after her. "How much time do we have?"

Brie hurried onto the redwood terrace. A quick scan of sunrise-painted clouds brought a relieved exhale. "They're in a hot-air balloon near the coast of Dast."

"Why are we on the terrace?" Penee searched at the sky. "We don't want them to see us."

"I want you to see how the charm works. Stand beside me."

Abarax remained near the door, his gaze searching the heavens. La perched on his shoulder, proboscis flicking in and out.

Penee moved to her side. "What's do I do?"

"Repeat after me:

> *"Invisibility protect and shroud*
> *This cottage within your mystic cloud.*
> *Keep it hidden from all who seek*
> *Until our voices once more speak."*

As the last word faded, the cottage, terrace, and boathouse shimmered away, leaving them standing on a solid nothingness.

Penee gripped Henri's staff. "Are we invisible, too?"

Brie joined Abarax by the door. "We're only invisible if we're inside. It takes another charm to hide us, one that's more difficult to achieve." She gazed over the lake. "I suggest a cup of tea while we can. Happily, all aspects of the cottage are hidden, including the smell of smoke from the kitchen stove."

Abarax let them pass. "La and I will keep watch."

Penee trailed Brie to the kitchen. *How did Skultar find us so fast? Will he bring Furrnoce and The Box?* She hurried to catch up. "Can a SorTech break the charm?"

"Depends on his strength." Brie placed a kettle on the stove. "Can women become SorTechs?"

Penee set out mugs. "No. The principal reason the Pheet Adole developed Protariflee was to ensure that women did not have the genes for mystical talent. The RomPeer and his counsel couldn't control the lower classes, but they made sure upper-class women weren't able to compete with the male population."

Steam drifted up from the kettle's spout. The ringing of its tiny bell reminded Brie of the Wood Tiff Sibine. Smiling, she poured water into the teapot. "Rayn and Rasiana made certain you had the gifts you need to lead. I'm glad Skultar didn't discover how talented you are." She set the lid in place. "He'd lock you away forever."

Penee collected mugs and sat down at the table. "I am an anomaly. Time has passed." She shrugged. "Much has changed. Who knows? Perhaps I won't be the only Pheet Adole female with mystic gifts."

La flew into the room. *"Balloon on the horizon."* A circular route carried her back the way she had come.

Penee glanced longingly at the brewing tea and hurried after the Luna Moth.

Brie retrieved her staff from the corner, took a moment to determine if the invisibility charm remained intact, and entered the living space. With a mentor's eye, she observed Penee move into the shadows near the windows, Henri's staff in hand. *She is growing stronger and more confident by the minute.* A wave of nostalgia surprised her. *I wonder if Wolloh has enjoyed my progress as much as I'm enjoying Penee's?*

The tantalizing aromas of fur and earth tickled her nostrils. Glancing around for the source, she caught the glint of a leather cylinder resting on her favorite chair. A rush of warmth over her skin and a slight tingle from the Star assured her it was safe.

As she crossed to it, La landed on the top of Irstant's staff. *"Wicked man comes."*

Secreting the cylinder under the seat cushion, she made her way to Penee's side. Sun sprinkled the lake with tiny diamond lights. At the far end, a blue and gold hot-air balloon floated in the calm of morning. The deep hiss of its burner system traveled ahead of it over the water.

Abarax, its full height masking the door, stood, head bowed, listening. La fluttered from the Astican's shoulder to the girls and back to her friend.

Dread vibrated around Penee like a small tornado. Brie clasped her hand. "They won't see the cottage. I checked the invisibility shields. If the SorTech is on board—and I am almost certain he is—The Box might pick up powerful emotions. We must become emotionless nonentities."

The tension dissolved. Penee's energy merged into walls and carpets. Brie followed her example. A glance from Abarax showed it understood. Hushed emptiness permeated the cottage.

Outside, the balloon's repeated hiss grew louder. A single scope tela-lens glinted in the sunlight as it searched the shoreline. An updraft sent it higher, the roar of the burner echoed over the lake. The balloon ascended to hover. Another blast carried it over the invisible cottage and back toward the coast.

The Astican eased the door ajar, shifted to a bat, and followed.

La perched on Brie's shoulder. *"Abarax spies."*

Brie shared what she had found with Penee, retrieved the leather cylinder from under the chair cushion, and led the way to the hidden room.

Penee sat with her on the cot to examine the cylinder. "Where did it come from?" She shook it. What's in it? How do we know it's not dangerous?" Understanding left her nodding. "The Star of Truth, right?"

Brie touched her neck. "It gave no warning, only affirmation that all is well." She accepted it back, turned it one way, and then the other. "The question is, how do we open it?" A slight indent on the top snagged her finger. With a soft click, the lid flipped off. She removed a parchment scroll.

Penee peered over her shoulder. The map of Neul Isle glistened as though alive in the lantern's warm glow.

22

barax in bat form clung to the weave of the balloon's gondola. Sharp ears picked up an angry exchange.

"Why didn't you inform me that you perceived something?" The frustration in Skultar's voice, palpable in the air, hissed between clenched teeth. "If Penee was somewhere close by, she's now warned of our search."

"Whatever I felt was not Human."

The SorTech's defensive reply brought an explosion of anger from his master. "I asked you to inform me if you felt *anything*. I did *not* ask you to interpret or define what might or might not be down there, Furrnoce. If you can't do what I require, I'll find a SorTech who can."

A loud whistling roar obliterated Furrnoce's response. The balloon descended toward a vale between rolling, tree-covered hills, where the landing crew waited, eyes shaded from the mid-turning sun. Abarax let go of the basket, shot into the foliage of a tree, shaped a Soputton songbird, and continued to spy.

As the gondola touched down, the three crewmen went to work securing it, then helped the passengers disembark. The captain left his men to deal with deflating the envelope and escorted Skultar and Furrnoce to a tent near the mouth of the small valley.

Keeping within the shelter of the trees, Abarax flew to a tall pine.

Skultar rounded on the captain. "How soon can we go up again?"

"If the winds cooperate, we'll fly this afternoon."

Skultar scowled. "We need to go now."

The captain shook his head. "Even if we did, the winds would take us out to sea. Relax. We'll take you to the lake if that is where you think your girl might be located. Excuse me." He walked to the landing site and began directing his men.

A disgruntled glare bored into his back. "I knew I disliked him from the start." Skultar wheeled on Furrnoce. "Let's look at the map. You can show me where you *thought* you sensed something." He ducked into the tent.

A brisk breeze shook the pine tree. Across the clearing, the captain pressed a long brass object to his eye and scanned the sky. The crew folded the empty envelop. At a sign from him, they stuffed it into a canvas bag. Another gust stirred the air. The tent flap danced. Skultar appeared at the entrance, his thin lips pinched together. Ominous clouds gathered overhead.

The captain strode to his side. "Weather's changing. We won't be flying again today. You can stay here or retire to Bailé. I'm sure the food at the Inn is better than our camp fare."

Abarax cringed at Skultar's ugly expression. "We will go back to the village." Turning on his heels, he disappeared into the tent.

The look on the captain's face made Abarax want to laugh. Instead, it remained silent.

Furrnoce stomped outside, helped a crew member load The Box into the back of a horse-drawn wagon, and covered it with oil cloth to protect it from the weather. Skultar spoke with the captain and joined him on the seat next to the driver. A clicked message sent horse down rutted tracks toward the mouth of the valley.

Abarax, hidden within the trees, tracked them to a corner rounding the lake. From the top of a tall pine, it watched until the wagon emerged at the edge of the village, shaped a bat, and flew back to the women it had sworn to protect.

Brie and Penee sat at a table in the library, surrounded by piles of books and manuscripts. Outside, a storm raging over the mountains announced its imminent arrival with blustery winds chasing white caps over the lake. As restless as a hummingbird, La fluttered to the windowpane and finally landed on a stack of books next to Brie.

"Abarax knows how to take care of himself, La. Stop fretting." She bent over a book, comparing it to the map spread between her and Penee. "I can't find a way into the valley. It's surrounded by rocky cliffs. Are you finding anything of interest?"

Penee pressed her lips into a frown. "Since the clouds appeared almost half a centurial cycle ago, nothing has been written. What I have learned is that anyone who penetrates the mist is never seen again."

Brie thumbed through the book. At a page covered with representations of a screenfold created prior to the clouds enshrouding the island, she paused. "These pictographs suggest the K'iin were not the only inhabitants of Neul. One or two smaller breakaway tribes lived along the coast. It is unknown if they continue to exist, or if, like the mother tribe, they have disappeared."

A tree branch scratched the window. Abarax peered into the room. Penee hurried to the outside door, unlocked it, and pulled it wide.

A man-sized Astican filled the doorway, its blond curls tumbling in the wind, its blue eyes searching. Relief curved its rosebud mouth into a smile. "La." Stepping into the library, it nodded to each young woman, and then focused on the moth perching on its shoulder. "I missed you, too. I am safe." Straddling a chair, it arranged its wings and gazed at the papers littering the table. A brow lifted. "A new map?"

Brie nodded. "First, tell us if you learned anything."

It rested its arms on the back of the chair. "Not much. Skultar and his SorTech are at odds with each other. They're staying in a village called Bailé, unhappily the storm is brewing. I doubt they will fly for a couple of turnings. The SorTech thinks it sensed something near the lake, but not something Human." It laughed. "Skultar is not a happy man." Its brow creased. "Your cousin is dangerous, Penee. We must not underestimate him." It tapped the map. "Tell me of this map."

The storm raged for three turnings. Rain pelted the cottage. Wind whipped through the trees, reminding the buds of spring that nature was not always gentle. Spray from the lake beating the shore joined the rain in creating splattered patterns on the windows.

The cottage creaked and groaned. Penee paced. Anticipation tiptoed after her, dodged ahead of her, ambushed her at odd moments. Burying herself in research didn't help. Nerves taut with tension screaming to be released marched her around the library a third time.

She stopped by the table, drummed the edge with restless fingers, and muttered under her breath.

Brie placed a finger on the page of her book. "What's irritating you besides being cooped up?"

"Something's about to happen. I'm not sure what." Penee's fingers played their restless tune. "Can you feel it, Brielle?"

Brie marked her place and moved to the window. Overhead, the clouds looked less threatening. Occasional rays of sunshine glinting off the window suggested a break in the storm. "I'm uneasy for no reason I can put my finger on. Being trapped in the house doesn't help, but it isn't the reason." She twisted a long, red curl. "A storm of another sort builds, and not that far away. It may have something to do with your cousin. Maybe Henri and Irstant need us." Her brow creased. "To top it off, Relevart seems to have disappeared." She bestowed a rueful smile on Penee. "How's that for a long answer to your short question?"

Penee grinned. "I gather your answer is yes." Pressing her nose to the window like a small child, she peered up at the sky. "There seems to be a lull in the storm. I think I'll get some fresh air. Wanna come?"

"I'll finish reading this section; then I'll join you." Brie returned to the table. "Take Abarax with you in case our other storm breaks."

Penee nodded. "I'll see if our favorite Astican needs some fresh air. Don't work too hard."

Brie sat in the afternoon stillness, her mind racing. Skultar's presence close by wasn't the only storm brewing. Unaccustomed fury raged in her subconscious. "When did it start?" Her thoughts traced the thread of memory to its beginning. *The Secret! I noticed the rage building after Chealim told me I carried a secret I had to discover on my own.* She jumped to her feet. "I refuse to give in to this kind of anger."

As though in response to her pronouncement, the rain ceased, clouds dissipated, and sun poured in the window. Stepping into a pool of light on the library floor, she threw back her head and laughed. "Oh, sweet sunlight, I have missed you!"

A wave of uneasiness stole her delight. Earlier that morning, she had released the charm of invisibility. Maintaining it drained her reserves, something she couldn't afford to do. A frown creased her brow. "I think we might want to redo it."

La fluttered in front of the window. The small creature's erratic behavior sent a shiver thrilling through her. The Star of Truth stabbed a warning. She threw open the window.

La shot inside. *"Wicked men have Penee."*

Brie sucked in rain-freshened air. "Abarax?"

The moth trembled. *"Hurt."*

"I need you to hide, La. If you can, help Abarax. Don't let the men catch you."

A series of sharp squeaks faded as the moth streaked out the window.

Brie hurried to the table, rolled up the map, and slipped it into the leather cylinder. Footsteps pounded in the hall. *She* hurried to Barlet's desk and pressed a carved leaf in the decorative pattern. A drawer slid open. She placed the cylinder inside, pushed the draw closed and grabbed Irstant's staff. Shrinking to the size of a small Nyti, she shot to a top shelf.

The Library door flew open. Thorlu Tangorra shoved Penee ahead of him and pressed her onto a chair.

Tall, lean, and regal, Skultar Rados followed. His alert gaze came to rest on his cousin. "Don't do anything silly, Penesert. I may not want to hurt you, but..." He jerked his pointed chin toward Thorlu. "The Mocendi may have different ideas."

His attention wandered to the table. "You've been doing some research." He loomed over her. "Tell us what you've discovered."

Vygel Vintrusie, homely features brimming with excitement, walked into the library. "She's here. I feel her. Come out, Brielle AsTar."

Brie obscured her energy in typeset and paper, in words and author's thoughts. Vygel's excitement faded. "She was here. Now, she's…"

"Shut up, Vintrusie," Thorlu growled.

Skultar cleared his throat. "Stop acting like children, both of you." He gazed down at Penee. "Now, Penesert, tell us where your friend is and why the research."

The urge to strike out, to use her power, to end the charade held Penee rigid in the chair. Dislike churning in her stomach soured her saliva. Her gaze glued to the carpet, she forced a grimace of distaste into a noncommittal expression and refused to speak.

A gust of wind rattled the open window. Vygel stuck his head out and scanned the shore. He faced his companions. "What if she left by the window?"

Skultar gripped Penee's chin. "If you refuse to answer my question, I will turn you over to the Mocendi. It is up to you."

A taciturn silence, her only reply, brought a flash of anger to her cousin's narrow face. She remained immutable.

Skultar released her chin. "Your choice, my dear."

Penee folded her arms and stared straight ahead. A strong hand gripping the back of her neck yanked her to standing. Thorlu's other hand grabbed her arm, shoved her from the library, down the hall, and through the living space onto the terrace.

A reddish-blue smear marked the empty spot where Abarax had fallen. She yanked free of Thorlu and glared from one man to the other. "I don't know where Brielle is." She smacked Thorlu's hand aside as he reached to grab her. "Don't touch me, Thorlu Tangorra. I may not have your strength, but I know how to fight." She rounded on her cousin. "What is it you want of me, Skultar Rados? What is it you think I can do for you that you can't do for yourself?" She shot Tangorra a disgusted look. "Why join forces with rabble Mocendi?"

An arm clamped around her neck and pressed her airway tighter and tighter. Blood pounded in her ears. Tear-filled eyes rolled back.

"Tell us what we want to know, Penesert, or I will break your neck." Thorlu's voice growled close to her ear. "You mean nothing to me. I want Brielle AsTar." He squeezed tighter. "Where is she?"

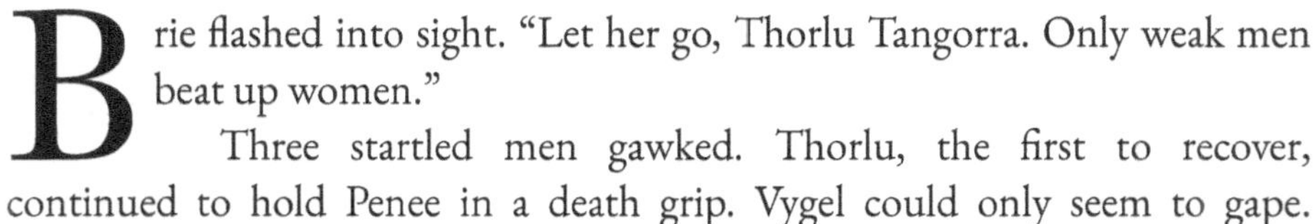

23

rie flashed into sight. "Let her go, Thorlu Tangorra. Only weak men beat up women."

Three startled men gawked. Thorlu, the first to recover, continued to hold Penee in a death grip. Vygel could only seem to gape. Skultar watched her, curiosity coloring his egret-narrow features.

Thorlu, his gaze locked on Brie, tightened his grip until Penee sagged against him. Flinging her limp body to the ground, he strode across the terrace. His arm whipped back. His slap met empty air.

Brie materialized several feet away, her focus on Vygel Vintrusie. Trapped between his fingers, a luna moth trembled.

His lips puckered in disgust. "I hate luna moths. Perhaps, I should smash this one beneath my foot, grind it into nothing but tattered green wings—"

Skultar and Thorlu surged toward her.

She whispered a charm. Irstant's staff snapped into being. She lifted it high. "Elibommi!"

The men froze in place. She swung the crystal tip toward Vygel, willing him to release La. His features twisted in pain, he placed the trembling moth on the railing and backed away.

The staff clattered to the terrace. Brie clutched at her neck. The Star of Truth sent blistering heat racing over her body. She dropped to her knees, battling the rage building inside her. Head thrown back, she screamed in agony; fought the demand to become the anger in a shifted form; and felt herself losing ground. She stared through a blur of tears at her hands reshaping. Her chest broadened. Strong muscular legs thrust her to standing. A triumphant shout chased over the lake, rebounded off the mountains, and hit the cottage, shaking it to its foundations.

Struggling to grasp her fast-fading essence, Brie saw Penee struggle to sitting, her expression panicked. Thorlu, Vygel, and Skultar sidled away.

A deep voice reverberated in the broad, muscular chest. "That's right, gentlemen. Stay back, or I will crush you like the vermin you are."

Rounding on the windows, Brie stared in shock at her reflection. A tall, dark-haired man with tawny skin and amber, hate-filled eyes glared back.

Brie grappled with the personality's attempts to obliterate her will to survive. A faint memory flickered. The Throne of Netydis—Fisaco, The MasTer's personality, looming—Chealim beside her. "Remember, Brielle, you have control." Confidence strengthened her resolve. She waited for the right moment to reclaim dominion.

The male persona growled. He shook himself, marched to Penee's side, and scowled down at her. "Had I known who you were, I would never have let you go." His gaze shifted to his adversaries.

Vygel bowed. "I honor your return, Master."

The MasTer's mouth twisted into a sneer. "You are nothing but a decrepit piece of scum, Vygel Vintrusie."

The elder Mocendi's mouth worked, then shut in a firm line.

Thorlu took a tentative step forward. "I believe we can come to an agreement that will suit all of us, Brielle."

The alien anger roiled upward. "I am not Brielle AsTar. I am The..."

Her returning strength yanked his attention inward.

Brie reeled The MasTer's personality in like a fighting fish. Second by second, she regained control. Smaller and smaller, weaker and weaker, his power floundered. Reel in and release. Reel in and hold firm. A distant scream of dismay heralded his final retreat. The shift ripped her subconscious into pieces. She slammed back into her own body. Firm hands gripped her arms. Her eyes opened to the menacing presence of Thorlu Tangorra.

"So, Miss AsTar, we all know your secret."

Skultar yanked Penee to her feet, sneered in Brie's direction, and spoke to Thorlu. "It appears we have what we require. I suggest a retreat to Reachti. We can take a shuttle from there to TaSneach."

Vygel shoved Thorlu aside. Brie yanked her arms free and stumbled backward. The MasTer's Mocendi placed himself in front of her. "The MasTer is mine. I knew the secret. You did not."

Brie picked up Irstant's staff. Her gaze locked onto Penee. A slight nod later, an unexpected jerk of her arm released Penee from Skultar's grasp. She dodged out of reach.

Brie pointed the staff. Wind cycloned around the three men. She chanted:

"I send these men to Tymine Cliff
Though space and time I cause a rift
Cyclonic winds carry them along
Cast them ashore where they belong."

Thunder rumbled. A zigzag of blinding light streaked across the sky. The men vanished.

The Star of Truth throbbed. Blood rushed through her veins and receded. Her flushed cheeks cooled. She released a shaky breath.

"You did well, Brielle AsTar."

The familiar voice brought tears of relief. She took Relevart's offered hand with her own delicate one. "You saw?"

His gentleness calmed her. "I did. Chealim will be proud. We were certain you would make the correct choice." Pride beamed. "And, you did."

"Will he, Fisaco, try to take over?"

"The dual personality's gene is part of you. Fisaco is always near, waiting to overcome the carrier. You proved your strength. Now, you must prove your ability to manage the personality. I know you will find a way."

He released her hand, withdrew a velvet pouch from his pocket, and held it out. "The Remembering Stone belongs to you. Thank you for guarding my memories." His amber eyes twinkled. "And for the charm to keep them safe."

She looped the blue ribbon over her head and tucked the pouch inside her tunic. "Thank you for returning it." Tilting her head, she studied his face. "I like your eyes"

He kissed her cheek and turned to Penee. "You continue to grow stronger, Penesert. Take care of each other." He flashed from sight.

Penee hugged her close. They stood, arms around each other, until their breathing calmed and their hearts beat a steady rhythm.

"What a secret!" Penee stepped away. "You carry The MasTer's gene."

Brie gave a shaky laugh. "I didn't mean to frighten you, Pen."

"*You* didn't. *He* did. What happened to our friends?"

"I created a time loop. They are back at Cliffs of Tymine on DerTah—at least the Mocendi are. I'm not sure where Skultar ended up. If I managed it right, they won't remember what happened. The loop will continue until one of them figures it out."

Penee grinned. "Excellent work! What now?"

Brie glanced at the lake. "I'm glad Abarax and La got away. I wonder where they are?" She yawned. "I need to rest."

Penee helped her to the hidden room. "Sleep. I'll find the Astican and the Luna Moth."

The panel slid shut. Brie lay in the silent darkness, her thoughts churning. *I refuse to live in fear that he will emerge.* A wave of loneliness washed over her. *Esán, I wish you were with me?*

A yawn caught her by surprise. Fatigue overwhelmed her. The earthy scent of animal musk and the warmth of a furry body next to hers ushered her into a deep sleep.

In the final moments of dusk, Penee paced the terrace. *Abarax and La seemed to have vanished.* Her gaze wandered the shoreline. *I can feel them, so where are they?* She rested her hands on the smooth wood railing. The sun descending below the horizon shot shining shafts of light from behind the mountains. As the light faded, a sliver of the moon TaSneach crested. She shivered. *I spent three sun cycles of my life up there.* Turning her back on the past and her time in the penal colony, she anchored herself in the present. *I have to find Abarax and La.*

Her thorough search of the area surrounding the cottage turned up nothing—no sign of either the Astican or the Luna Moth. Frustration laced with dread stalked the fringes of her thoughts. A search of the boathouse elevated her rising alarm. With a lantern held high, she walked along the shore. The shimmer of pale green wings caught her eye. Tiny squeaks guided her into the woods to a grove of Dast Oaks.

The human-sized Astican lay on its side, limp wings spread around it. Penee placed the lantern on the ground and knelt to examine what she could see of its body. With gentle fingers, she searched the back of its head. Her hand came away sticky with blood. On closer inspection, she found an oozing gash. She touched the Astican's forehead. "Abarax, can you hear me?"

The creature remained unmoving. La landed on her hand. *"Abarax come here, then fall down."*

Penee lifted the wing draped over its side. Nothing drew her attention. She sat back on her heels. "I am not sure what to do, La."

Taloned fingers encircled her wrist. Eyelids fluttered. The rosebud mouth pushed out the words "Alright. Need water."

Relief moved her to lean closer. "I'll be back."

The hand squeezed. "Brie?"

"She's resting. Don't move. I won't be long."

Penee hurried to the cottage. A quick check to assure herself her friend slept peacefully reinforced her sense of relief. The musky odor of animal fur tickled her nose. She whispered, "Whoever you are, you'd better take good care of her." A wet tongue licked her hand. A surprised squeal almost burst into being.

Her thoughts tumbling in several directions, she collected what she needed to help Abarax, glanced at Brie, and climbed the stairs.

At the top, she hesitated. *How do I know it's a friend?* She pulled the lever. *I sense it, that's all. A quick jog brought her to the front door.* My life is so strange. A soft laugh escorted her from the cottage.

She arrived in the grove to find Abarax upright, leaning against a tree trunk. She handed it a bottle of water. "Drink this. I'll take care of the gash." By the time she finished, her patient's color had improved. "How do you feel?"

"I am better." It gulped the rest of the water. The cherubic features turned evil. "When I meet Thorlu again, I will give him such a headache."

In that moment, Penee realized, not for the first time, how glad she was the Astican fought on her side.

＊　＊

The Galactic Library on Myrrh, empty of people for the first time in turnings, accepted the appearance of the Universal VarTerel without a ripple in its atmosphere. Relevart sank onto a chair and pulled an open book toward him. A glance at the title—*Myths Surrounding Mystical Birthmarks*—suggested it might provide what he required.

The table of contents guided him to a chapter on star-shaped birthmarks.

"Where's my sister?" The deep voice interrupted his concentration. Ari moved into his line of vision.

"Hello to you, Arienh." He spoke with a hint of humor.

Ari blustered. "You'd better not be laughing at me, VarTerel. Where is Brie? Is she alright? Can I join her? What about—"

"Whoa, girl, catch your breath. I'll answer your questions."

She plopped down on a chair. Petulance flared. Her gaze mellowed. "Sorry. I'm just frustrated being stuck on Myrrh if Brie isn't alright." She shrugged.

Relevart turned his book face-down. "You're here for a reason, Ari. So is Elf. Were our enemies to capture you, they would use you to gain control of your sister and Penee."

"So, they're more important than Elf and me?" Testiness tinged the question.

"At the moment, yes. What they must accomplish demands a lot of both of them. Their destinies are blossoming as we speak. Don't worry, Arienh AsTar, you are every bit as important to the CoaleScence as Brie. Your time has not arrived." He flipped over the book. "Besides, I need you to continue the research you're doing. Without it, your sister may fail. We can't afford to let that happen."

Ari sighed. "Tell me how she is, Relevart, so I can go back to work."

"Brie and Penee are fine. Their talents mature along with their abilities to make right choices."

She held up a journal, one he recognized. "I've been reading Rayn's diary." She tapped his book. "I've also been researching the Star of Truth."

He studied the eager twin. "Tell me what you've discovered."

The Star protects Brie from outside threats, but that's not all. It also protects her from threats within her own psyche." She traced an infinity sign on the tabletop. "I know 'the secret', Relevart." Relief mixed with sadness clouded her eyes. "Rayn carried The MasTer's gene. It skips generations." Her hand curled into a fist, then flattened. "This time it skipped three. I thought because of my temper I carried it. The idea terrified me. Now, I know Brie is the carrier. Unlike Rayn, she also carries the Star of Truth. Tell me she's discovered 'the secret'. Tell me she realizes she has the power to mold the gene to her needs."

"You've done well, Arienh. Yes, Brie knows she carries The MasTer's gene. Whether she will discover her ability to mutate, it is yet to be seen."

"But, Relevart, you can tell her; you can help her change it, right?"

He studied the twin's earnest face. "She must come to this understanding on her own, Arienh. *I* cannot interfere."

The hope in her expression died. She pushed the book away. "I need some sleep." She walked around the table. "Thank you for trusting me with this information. Please don't let anything happen to Brie."

"Your sister can take care of herself." He raised a brow. "Besides, her personal champion is close by."

Understanding flickered. A slight smile appeared. "I guessed as much. I'll see you soon."

Relevart watched her weave between cases of books. *You can help her, Arienh. I trust you will find a way.*

❦ ❦

Ari marched to her quarters, irritation beating against her temples like ceremonial drums. Her back against the closed door, she struggled to control her temper. An angry groan propelled her across the room. She grabbed a pillow and threw it with all her might. A second followed, hit the wall, and rebounded, landing at her feet. A vicious kick sent it sailing. Her red-faced image in the mirror pulled her up short. She inhaled, picked up a pillow, and hugged it to her chest. "Think, Arienh."

A review of her conversation with Relevart left a look of triumph on her face. *You can't help Brie."* She chuckled. *"But you didn't say I couldn't."*

Tossing the pillow on the bed, she lay down, her brows bridged in thought. *Brie and I share a strong psychic connection. It's proved useful throughout our childhood. Let's hope it will work across galaxies.* Sleepy but determined, she organized her thoughts and concentrated her attention on her twin. *Listen up, Brielle As Tar.*

Slumber lulled her into its warmth.

24

Brie awoke with a start. Urgency buzzed in her ears. Suppressed anger gnawed at her guts. Her feet hit the floor with a soft smack. *What was I dreaming?* Her brow furrowed. Fragments re-ignited. Vague, distorted images flickered into focus. She sucked in a startled breath. *Ari!* More disjointed fragments brought her to standing.

"Oh!" She hugged herself. *Thank you, Arienh.*

The Star of Truth centered her attention on an upsurge of internal anger. Not wasting time, she created an inner shield enclosing the ember of rage. At the end of the hall, she stared into a full-length mirror, and reviewed the few bits of information Ari had shared.

The MasTer's gene, full-blooded Eleo Predan, matched her own genetic heritage. *I am female, so it stands to reason the gene is also female this time around, which means I should be able to mold it to my own specifications.* She nibbled her bottom lip. *What if I infuse the gene with female energy? I wish I knew more. I wish—*

Spikes of pain shot from the Star down her spine. The shield encapsulating The MasTer's gene collapsed. Anger rushing up from her belly, gripped her by the throat, and shook her until she crumpled to her knees. Her hands flexed and grew larger. She clenched them into fists and fought to regain her position of strength.

Fiery pain blazed across her muscular chest. Powerful legs launched her to standing. Her reflection wavered. The MasTer's triumph-filled eyes glared back at her.

Focused on cajoling her fear into submission, Brie shielded her presence and waited for the right moment to catch him unaware. An unruffled calm overtook her.

He gazed at his reflection in delight, flexed his muscles, and laughed with total abandon. "Not even a VarTerel can keep me from manifesting. I will use your power, Brielle AsTar, to accrue a fortune; then I will crush the Galactic Council and all who follow their lead." He threw his head back. Another laugh filled the room. Footsteps on the stairs halted it mid-stream.

Penee faced him, seething with anger. "Release her."

He took a menacing step. "Ah, Penesert, do you miss your friend?"

She remained unmoving and silent.

"Get used to it. Brielle AsTar is no more. *I* am your master. *You* will serve *my* need."

Arrogance flooded through him. Brie wielded her marshaled strength. With the speed of a fast-approaching storm, she reclaimed her power, shook herself free of The MasTer's shape, and stood gasping for breath.

Red curls tumbling loose around her face, she hugged her friend. "I couldn't have done it without you, Penee. I needed him distracted. I needed him..." She doubled over, grappling with The MasTer's bid to reclaim control. Her friend's hand on her back leant her courage. She straightened and faced the mirror.

"You do not get to use me, Fisaco." She smoothed her hair and squared her shoulders. "You will stay bound by my strength until I can bring you to heel."

Her attention turned inward. She constructed a protective shield encircling the gene and sealed it by chanting,

> *"Cocoon of power hold this gene*
> *Within your walls 'til I have seen*
> *My way clear to use it well*
> *For good and not in evil dwell."*

The MasTer's tranquillized gene ceased its struggle. Brie breathed a sigh of relief, sank onto her bunk, and ran shaking hands through her hair.

Penee sat down beside her. "What just happened?"

Brie lowered her hands. "Ari tried to send a message to me. It came through garbled. I thought I understood, so I tried to transmute The MasTer's gene from male to female. Since it is part of me, I thought..." She frowned. "Somehow I woke Fisaco instead of infusing the gene with my female essence. I wish I could do some research, but I doubt Barlet has what I need in his library."

Penee came to her feet. "It's worth a look."

Brie's stomach growled. She grinned. "First, I need food. The battle with Fisaco wore me out." She smoothed her hair back. "Did you find Abarax and La?"

"I did. The Astican has a nasty gash on the back of its head. I'm glad I'm not Thorlu. The next time they meet..." Penee shook her head. "It's upstairs with La. I'll fix a snack. Take a moment for yourself."

After Penee ducked into the Trophy Room, Brie re-examined her reflection. "I have to discover a way to transmute the gene." She stretched out on the bunk.

The odor of musk wafted over her. Searching fingers found soft fur. Her ears picked up a faint animal pant. "I'm not alone. I'm safe. Whoever you are, thank you." Focusing her thoughts on her sister, she allowed exhaustion to overtake her.

A hand on her arm brought her to the surface. Penee peered at her. "Hungry?"

Brie sat on the edge of the bunk, yawned, and stood up. "I am starving!"

I n the living space, the Astican sat on a sofa with the ends of its wings draped over its knees. La perched nearby.

Abarax attempted a smile that never finished. A cringe drained the cherub face of color. "Good to see you, Brie." It smothered a yawn. "Penee won't let me sleep."

"Penee's smart. Concussions are nothing to fool with."

It regarded her with interest. "Penee says you carry The MasTer's gene." A touch of uncertainty glimmered. "Where is *he*?"

Brie sat opposite him. "I've put shields up around the gene. With luck, they'll contain it." She wrinkled her brow. "I have to discover a way to transmute it to female. Once I do that, I can create an alter ego that adheres to my moral principles."

The scales on Astican's wing fluttered and settled. "I like this female idea." It grew serious. "How did you know to change the gene?"

Brie looked pleased. "From what I learned, the MasTer's gene is male. With Ari's help, I realized that because I am female, I can infuse the gene with feminine characteristics. Unfortunately, I don't have enough information to ensure the effectiveness of the change."

Abarax looked surprised. "Ari helped?"

"We've always had a strong psychic connection. She sent me a dream message containing information from her research. Distance made it hard to decipher. Still, I could understand some of it."

Penee handed her a sandwich from the tray on the table. "Eat, Brielle. You need your strength."

Brie chewed and studied Penee. "Do you and Elf share a link?"

"Birth-mates have different parents. We birthed from the same womb, but..." Penee shrugged.

A hungry rumble focused Brie on eating. She finished the last bite and patted her stomach. "That was delicious, Pen. Thank you."

After securing her long curls into a queue at the nape of her neck, she jumped to her feet. "I suggest we discover more about Neul Isle and the K'iin before our favorite adversaries arrive back on our doorstep."

Penee picked up the tray. "Irstant and Henri have been missing long enough. If they aren't on Neul, we need to refocus. Where's the map you found? Let's start with it."

"I hid it in Barlet's secret drawer."

"Great. I'll meet you in the library." She strode down the hall.

Brie offered Abarax a hand. "Come and help. I wouldn't want you to fall asleep too soon."

"I won't fall—" It stifled a yawn and, mumbling under its breath, allowed her to lead it to the library. La shot out the window, once more on guard. Brie picked up a book about Neul Isle, curled up in her favorite chair, and immersed herself in the island's history.

P enee surveyed the clean kitchen. Satisfied, she hurried down the hall to the library. Abarax raised its head and flinched. Brie continued to read. Tiptoeing to Barlet's desk, Penee removed the cylinder from the secret drawer, tipped the map onto the desktop, and unrolled it. After placing a book on each corner to hold it flat, she retrieved the older map she and Brie had found.

The rustle of wings settling accompanied Abarax to her side. "They look similar."

Penee examined every etched detail. Although the shape appeared to be the same, Brie's map provided information not shown on the ancient one Penee had unearthed. She studied the maps from the opposite side. Something about them nagged at her.

A soft squeak preceded La's arrival. The Luna Moth alighted on the ancient parchment, fluttered to the more recent map, and flew to Abarax's shoulder.

The Astican looked closer. "La says the map has a secret."

Penee examined the maps and shook her head. "Brielle, we need you to look at something."

Brie crossed to the desk. "What's up?"

"I'm not sure." Penee moved to the side. "Compare the maps. Tell me what you see."

A careful examination of the maps left Brie looking puzzled.

La touched down on each.

Penee frowned. "She touched down here and here. I don't see anything. Does she know something we don't?"

Brie laughed. "I'm sure she does." She leaned closer and studied each map. "Something is strange. I just can't quite grasp what it is."

A panted breath blew the antiquated map on top of its newer counterpart. The older parchment quivered, faded into the more recent map, and highlighted the outline of Neul Isle. The ancient ley lines on the combined maps gave off an iridescent glow.

"Oh my." Penee gripped the edge of the desk. "Are you seeing what I'm seeing?"

"Stay put. I'll be right back." Brie hurried across the room.

Penee glued her gaze to the map. "I'm not going anywhere!"

B rie stared out the window and squinted down the walkway. *Ahhh. I knew it.* Faint animal tracks retreated along the narrow beach. *I don't know who you are, but thank you.*

Rejoining her friends, she continued her examination of the maps. Guided by her VarTerel's intuition, she cleared the desk, removed the books from the parchment, and stepped back. Penee and Abarax followed her example.

"What now?" Penee's voice trembled with excitement.

Brie inhaled. "I'm uncertain this will work, but I'll try it." She drew a large, invisible circle around the parchment. In a soft whisper, she chanted a rhyme.

> *"A secret you hold, a secret to share.*
> *Guide us in knowing how to get there.*
> *We open our hearts and our minds to your need.*
> *Guide us by showing us how to proceed."*

Fog roiled over the map, swirled, and dispersed, exposing within the invisible circle a three-dimensional island in a sparkling blue sea. At the island's center, a large lagoon gleamed. A rugged landscape of mountains and plateaus, lowlands, marshes, and thick forests spread out from the shoreline. To one side, a small volcano gaped open-mouthed at the heavens.

Abarax whistled. "It is beautiful."

Penee clutched Brie's hand. "Look."

Water as still as smooth glass showed a cave burrowing beneath a small island. The water at the mouth quivered. A glistening, crystalline shape circled and dove.

"Was that the Stannag?"

Brie squeezed her hand. "Watch." Mist floated upward, hovered above the central lagoon, and morphed into a translucent woman. Luminous, fire-opal eyes glowed in a shimmering black face. A plethora of reddish-black braids the size of a little finger fell from a center part to below her waist. Teardrop-shaped opal earrings matched the full-length dress floating around her. Miniature sea birds, as though startled into flight, formed a glistening white cloud above her. A wave of her hand sent them fluttering to a landing along the shore.

A musical voice filled the library:

"I am Aahana, youngest daughter of Abellona, the Sun Queen. As is the custom to ensure the safety of this sacred Isle and the K'iin, at eighteen sun cycles my spirit and heart merged with Rina, the phantom incirrata, to become the Stannag Guardian of Neul. I left behind my husband and my baby. My heart broke. My tears wet the island without ceasing."

Her opal eyes glistened brighter. A tear slid down her cheek.

"The shaman of the K'iin took pity on me and worked his magic. Each moon cycle when TaSneach ripened into fullness, I placed my heart and soul in a crystal jar and crossed into a parallel dimension to spend time with those I loved. With the waning of the moon, I returned, swallowed my heart, my soul, and my sadness, and resumed my position as the Guardian of this sacred isle.

"Almost half a centurial cycle ago, someone betrayed me by stealing the crystal jar. My ghost tears obscured Neul in a thick fog. My anger quaked over the island. Enormous stones tumbled down the mountains, trapping the K'iin in a hidden valley." She grew taller. "Return my heart and soul to me, and I will help you free Neul and its people."

A trail of tears coursed down her cheeks and splashed on the water's surface. The tiny sea birds surrounded her, dispersed her misting form, and melted with her into the lagoon.

The three-dimensional island flattened into two parchment maps. Outside the window, trees shivered in the wind. A gust blew through the library, lifted the two maps, and released them to glide off the desk and onto the floor.

25

Penee, the first to move, picked up the maps and placed them side by side on the desk.

Abarax's silver-gray scales swished over its body, once, twice, three times. It shook itself and straddled a chair, its huge wings quivering behind it.

La circled her friend. When its scales ceased their trembling, she landed on its shoulder.

Brie contemplated the two maps. "We now know Neul Isle is our goal." She tapped her chin. "But before we do anything else, we must return the maps to Myrrh."

"Why Myrrh?" Penee sank onto a chair, rubbing her left forearm.

"The leather cylinder bears the seal of the Galactic Library in Canedari. The Research Lab beneath the Reading Room will be the safest place to hide the maps. Let's make a sketch to take with us." Brie rotated the map so they could all see it. "

The three friends got to work. Outside, the wind stilled. Tranquility descended. Only their soft breathing penetrated the quiet.

L a glided out the window. The sun had slipped behind the planet. Soon the moon would crest. Night, her time, made her happy. She flitted over the lake, her attention fixed on the sky. Nothing disturbed her. Peace reigned. Yet something had called to her, beckoned her into the subtle light of the turning's end. Caution kept her in the shadows. Her multi-faceted eyes dissected the world surrounding her. A slight aberration prodded her to explore.

From dim patch to dim patch, she made her way to a tree near the boathouse. A man's shadow detached itself from the building and crept up the steps toward her hiding place. He looked directly at her and held out a hand.

Nothing alarmed her. She alighted on his palm.

Holding her at eye level, he smiled. *"You are lovely."*

Her wings trembled in response. *"Who you?"*

"A friend of Brielle and Penee's. Tell them the loop is in motion."

"I tell."

The man melted into the woods.

P enee put the finishing touches on a sketch of the map, noted the things they wanted to remember, and handed the parchment map to Brie. "Are you certain you can send this to Myrrh?"

"We're about to find out." Brie placed the ancient drawing on top of it, rolled them together, and slipped them into the leather cylinder. Holding it up, she pictured the research room in Canedari's Reading Room on Myrrh. A whispered series of key phrases sent the cylinder through the Land of No Time and All Time. Wonder brightened her smile. "It arrived safely."

Penee, arms folded, regarded her with an arched brow. "What's it like to be a VarTerel?"

"I'm not sure how to answer that. It's a formidable responsibility, one I don't take lightly." Brie regarded her friend. "Sometimes, I wonder what it would be like to be normal, don't you?"

"I thought I was. I thought Elf was the only one with gifts." Penee sighed. "Now I worry that I don't know enough to accomplish what they expect of me."

Brie gave her a quick hug. "All we can do is live turning by turning and try to make good choices."

La's wings brushed her cheek. *"Time loop in motion."* She shot out the window.

Anticipation made Penee's palms sweat. "Did I hear her right—the time loop's in motion?" She wiped her hands on her pants and stared after the moth. "How long before they reach the cottage?"

"That depends on whether they have figured out they're trapped in a loop." Brie shrugged and moved to the window.

Penee joined her. "I can feel you thinking. What's up?"

"I believe we should fly to the village. If we arrive by the time the loop reaches it, we might even learn how Thorlu and Vygel hooked up with Skultar."

"Won't they feel us?"

Brie thought back to Wolloh's lesson on time loops. "Our part in the action hasn't begun, so they won't be aware of us." She nibbled her bottom lip. "It could be dangerous, but it might be worth it."

Abarax leaned its head on the back of the chair. "I cannot go."

Penee re-examined its gash. "I agree. La will stay here with you."

Brie looked over her shoulder. "Tell us how to find the village, Abarax."

"Fly south, paralleling the coastline." He squinted into the distance. "You will find the village called Bailé between two lakes."

Brie shifted to a Dast forest swift and flew out the window.

Penee kissed Abarax's cheek. "Thank you. Don't go to sleep." She shaped a Soputton swift and hastened after the youngest VarTerel in the Universe.

Bailé sat on the shore of the larger of two lakes. It boasted a main street lined with small businesses, a market square where farmers and artisans gathered to sell their wares, and a village monument circled by government buildings and a shrine to the local deities.

The inn, on the smaller lake, contained the only public eating establishment in the village. A tier of commercial buildings formed a boundary between Bailé and the farmlands stretching to the mountains behind it.

From her perch in a maple at the center of the market square, Brie observed a prosperous village, one more elegant than those she had seen on other planets. A flight over it had shown her clean streets and well-cared-for homes. She saw no run-down areas overflowing with squalor and no beggars on the streets. The Loch Inn, a spacious two-story building on a rise above the Cúpla Lakes, suggested wealthy guests patronized it this time of the sun cycle.

From her perch, she observed ambling foot traffic, the occasional horse-drawn buggy, and even one or two steam driven motor cars. A carriage rolling down the street caused an explosion of activity outside the inn. The driver reined in the team of four horses. A footman placed steps by the door and assisted a tall, blond gentleman from the carriage. A gawky, stoop-shouldered man several years his senior made an awkward descent. Both wore the black, purple-lined cape of a Mocendi DiMensioner. Everyone scurried to please them.

Brie tipped her swift's head. *"And so, they arrive..."*

Not long after, a wagon with Skultar and Furrnoce pulled up to the inn. A handsome, dark-haired man strode forward to meet them. The SorTech jumped to the ground, spoke to him briefly, and hurried to help their driver unload The Box.

The man assisted Skultar down from the wagon. "Two of The MasTer's Mocendi arrived a short time ago. They expressed an interest in meeting you."

Skultar's brow arched. "Mocendi." An evil gleam lit his eyes. "Well, well, well..." With confidence oozing, he walked into the inn.

An amethyst-blue gaze darted over the landscape, paused on their hiding place, and lowered. A half smile exposed even white teeth as Den disappeared after his master.

Next to her, Penee's swift form trembled. The Star of Truth pinched a warning. Brie whistled and lifted into flight. With Penee close behind, she raced beneath the clouds gathering overhead to the cottage on the lake.

Swift talons touched the top rail. Fluttering to the terrace, Brie shifted to Human.

Penee materialized and paced the terrace.

"You seem rattled, Penee. Is it Den?"

"I know you trust him, Brie. If he is on our side, why does he glue himself to Skultar?"

"I imagine he will share his reasons when the time is right." The Star burned. "The time loop moves this way. We need to go inside."

Penee pushed the door wide. "What if we teleport across the lake to hide until they're gone?"

Brie trailed her into the cottage. "We can't use any of our DiMensioner's gifts at this end of the time loop. Our options are to stay and watch or go to the secret room."

Abarax entered from the hallway. "It is good you are back, Brielle and Penee. La worried you wouldn't make it ahead of the men." He touched the back of his head. "I prefer to go to the hidden room. I cannot guarantee my behavior if I have to witness Thorlu getting the best of me."

Penee patted the Astican's arm. "I understand. I'm not sure I want to see Brie shape The MasTer either."

Brie looked from companion to companion. "The hidden room it is."

La landed on her shoulder. *"Wicked men on beach."*

Penee yanked open the library door. "Let's go!" She hurried to the Trophy Room and pulled the lever. The door slid open.

La darted down the stairwell. Abarax gripped its wings, lifted the tips, and made a cautious descent. Penee hurried after him.

Brie listened. A furtive conversation drifted down the hall. Mouse quiet, she jogged down the steps, closed the door, and sank onto her bunk.

Apprehension as tangible as the sun's warmth radiated from the four occupants of the hidden room. La flitted and fluttered from spot to spot. Astican scales whispered a constant uneasy song. Penee rubbed her hand over her short hair and muttered to herself. Brie lay back on her bunk and, using distance vision, followed the time loop's progress.

Like the reenactment of a play, Thorlu, Vygel, and Skultar moved through the actions of their previous visit. Brie saw herself change to The MasTer, glimpsed Vygel's excitement, and noted the curiosity in Skultar's face. Thorlu, the only one whose reaction was hard to interpret, held her attention. As she pointed the staff, understanding dawned in the handsome face. Before he could react, the men disappeared in a ball of bright light.

The Star of Truth jabbing erased her trance. A deep-seated throb of anger propelled her to sitting. She confirmed The MasTer's gene remained cocooned. The throbbing eased. Her rugged breathing normalized.

Penee knelt beside her. "Are you alright? What just happened?"

"I'm fine." Brie shuddered. "The MasTer stirred." She swung her legs over the edge of the bunk. "Thorlu knows about the loop. They are back on DerTah, but I imagine they'll return as fast as they can."

Astican wings ceased their nervous song. "Did you uncover anything helpful in Bailé?"

"We determined that Thorlu and Vygel went to the inn, hoping to connect with Skultar."

Penee added, "We also learned Den is still a member of Skultar's entourage." Her expression grew more agitated. "I don't understand why he continues to work with Skultar. He's playing a dangerous game."

Brie kept her voice emotionless. "He's a big boy, Penee. He can take care of himself."

Muttered vexation accompanied Penee up the steps, through the Trophy Room to the living area. She stood mesmerized by the reflection of the rising sun on the lake's mirror-like surface.

Abarax followed Brie into the room. "Are you certain you're alright, Brielle?"

"The MasTer's gene remains dormant. I just have to stay alert."

For a long, concern-filled moment, the Astican peered down at her. "What will Thorlu do with the loop?"

Brie considered the question. "This is my first attempt at creating a loop, so I'm not a hundred percent sure. Wolloh told me time loops are as individual as those caught in it. Thorlu knows I trapped them. If he dismantles it at the Cliffs on DerTah, they would start from scratch to get back to Soputto." She bit her lip. "He's smarter than that. My guess is he'll dismantle it when they land on the beach." Her eyes narrowed. "Staying at the cottage is dangerous. We need to leave."

Abarax frowned. "Can we use Mittkeer?"

"No DiMensionery." She glanced up. The sun slipped in and out of the billowing clouds scattered over the intense blue sky. Ideas bustled and sorted. "Penee, grab two packs. We'll meet you in the boathouse."

Penee sprinted down the hall.

Brie hurried outside. Abarax ducked under the door header and matched her stride. At the steps, she took the lead. Near the boathouse, a flash of orange merged into forest shadow. She stared after it and frowned.

The Astican joined her. "You look puzzled, Brielle AsTar."

"Did you see anything strange, Abarax?"

Its expression questioned.

She sighed. "I didn't think so."

Penee jogged to a stop and handed her a knapsack. "What's the plan?"

Brie scrutinized the Astican's cherubic features. "How are you feeling, Abarax? Can you row to the other side of the lake?"

"I can row."

"Good." She directed his attention to the opposite shore. "Penee and I will hike through woods and meet you at that stand of trees at the foot of the mountains nearest the shoreline."

The Astican's rosebud mouth rounded. "I'm the distraction. And La?"

"Since we can't use telepathy, she is our go-between. Come on. We'll help you push off."

The boathouse contained several dinghies, a large rowboat, and a lake-sailer with a single mast.

Penee preceded Abarax into the dim building. "I've never been on a sailboat."

Brie ignored the wistfulness in her voice. "We have little time. You've got the—"

"Map." Penee held it up.

Brie laughed. "You're getting to be as bad as Ari...always second guessing me." She untied the boat and handed the lines to the Astican. "Move her to the end of the slip, Abarax. Penee, help me move a dinghy into its place."

Penee grinned. "So Thorlu won't know a boat is missing. You are good, Brie."

Once they secured the dinghy, Brie took the rowboat's line from the Astican. "Get in, Abarax. When you're ready, I'll push you off."

The Astican shrunk to human size and settled on the center bench, set the oars in the oarlocks, and shipped them. "I am ready."

Brie tossed the line into the bottom of boat. A strong shove sent it gliding into the open. The Astican dipped the oars and skimmed over the water. *Take care of yourself, Abarax.*

A warm canine nose nuzzling her hand urged her to move. She jogged along the shore to a break in the ground cover. A single sidestep took her into the shelter of Dast pines. A patch of orange darted further into the trees. *I wish I knew who you were.* She put the thought aside. Penee's impatience titillated the air around them. Her need to solve the mystery would have to wait. With a glance over her shoulder, Brie took the lead.

26

Penee trotted along the rough track, her thoughts in a jumble. *Why is Den with Skultar? What does he hope to accomplish? Is he my cousin's man or not?*

La fluttered to her side. *"Wicked men beach."* She flew to Brie, repeated the message and shot back toward the lake.

Brie paused. Penee braked to a stop. "I understood we couldn't use telepathy."

"*We* can't. Only those La tunes into can hear her, plus her signature is so tiny—" Brie's eye's narrowed. "Thorlu's dismantled the loop." A finger to her lips, she pulled Penee behind a dense thicket of bushes.

The muffled tread of a man's boots skidded to a stop. Vygel's stooped silhouette took shape against a fading ray of sunlight. He bent to examine the trail; straightened and sniffed the air.

"Vintrusie!"

The shout, an annoyed command, brought him to his feet. Pivoting, he tromped back the way he had come.

La landed on the bush. *"Men see boat."*

A loud hiss and a concussive crack echoed over the lake.

Penee jumped. "Let's go." Motioning Brie to follow, she crept through knee-high undergrowth to a squatty beech tree. A quick search revealed a winding animal track, one she had discovered as a child. "This way." She led the way to the top of a gentle incline and hesitated.

The track which continued down a steep, rock-strewn slope, appeared to end at a wide-open expanse bordered by gnarled trees on three sides. At the center, a massive angel oak sent thick branches and roots in every direction. Mushrooms the height of small children nestled in colorful clusters in the crooks and gaps between them, grew on the roots and branches, and scattered over the terrain.

Penee tugged Brie's hand. "This is the Lêa of Beacáin. Barlet told me about it when I was a child. He made me promise to stay away from it." She shivered. "Tiny, winged creatures called the Fée live here. If they feel threatened, they swarm around your head, biting face and ears. They often leave those unlucky enough to survive their attacks blind and deaf."

"So why bring us here?"

"I've read the Fée sometimes help those in trouble who don't pose a threat. We aren't—"

"Over here!" Vygel's shout ricocheted through the forest.

Dread slithered over Penee's skin. She shuddered.

Brie pulled her closer, her expression grim. "He's found the trail."

One harried glance back the way they had come propelled them down the slope to the edge of the vast mushroom field. The ground trembled beneath their feet; air pulsated against them. A swarm of twinkling flecks of gold light swept from the branches of the angel oak and over the lêa.

Vygel, his Mocendi cape billowing, dodged through the trees approaching the top of the incline.

Penee fought her panic. "Vygel is closing in." She pointed ahead. "We can't go back, and we can't go forward."

Brie squeezed her hand. "The Star is quiet, so we must be safe. If we remain calm—"

"Stay where you are!" Vygel began a scrabbling descent down the slope.

The swarm picked up speed, flew earthward, circled the girls' ankles, and spiraled upward, forming a sparkling curtain.

Clinging to Brie, Penee murmured, "The Star says we're safe, the Star—" The world spun, tipped, and righted itself. Through the dispersing mist of twinkling radiance, she stared up at the underside of an immense mushroom cap. "Oh my!" She gulped in a breath. "Either they grew, or we shrunk."

Penee peered through the forest of stems to where Vygel's angular height dominated the landscape. "We shrank." She pulled Brie to crouch behind a huge stem. "Look."

A cascade of twigs and stones tumbling down the slope preceded two more figures. Their long shadows stretched up the rise behind them as they searched the Lêa of Beacáin.

Skultar side-stepped to a level spot. Thorlu skidded to a stop. "Where are they, Vintrusie?"

The older Mocendi grimaced. "They were right over there. Then a swarm of bugs came. The next thing I knew, they vanished."

Thorlu shook his head. "A swarm of bugs? Even you should be able to lie better than that."

Vygel bared his mouthful of yellowing teeth. "I'm just telling you what I saw."

"I'm going back to the cottage." Skultar pivoted to hike up the slope. "Maybe we can find a clue to where they're going in the library."

Thorlu's gaze swept from one side of the lêa to the other. "Bugs?" He gave Vygel's shoulder a condescending pat before traipsing after Skultar.

Vygel studied the ground where the girls had been standing. Muttering about making them pay, he retraced his steps. At the top of the slope, he turned. A mental probe reached out, searched, rebounded like a boomerang. A howl of pain exploded from his throat as he fell to his knees. Hugging himself, he sobbed.

Penee cringed and shot Brie a questioning look. Before either of them could comment, a sparkling, fist-sized creature fluttered to a stop. Hummingbird-fast wings kept it at eye level. Tiny, almond eyes in a pixie face blinked. *"Follow. Now."* Another blink and the creature shot between enormous, white muscaria stems and hovered, wings beating and impatience on the tiny face. With a soft cry, it darted further along a faintly glowing path.

Penee, with Brie at her heals, jogged through the dense jungle of roots and stems, never taking her eyes off their guide.

Soft rustling in the looming shadows brought Brie to a halt. Where the path behind her had been, tree roots crisscrossed one another, and towering mushrooms crowded close together. The forest and the heavens, hidden by the mysteries of the world surrounding her, had vanished. Vygel's anguished sobbing had faded into the distance. The Star's pulsing warmth flowed through her. *Thank goodness. Penee and I are safe.*

Her attention fixed on the spot of glistening color leading them away from danger, she ordered her thoughts. *Why is it helping? Where is it taking us? Can Thorlu, Vygel, and Skultar follow?*

Ahead of her, Penee held her fear in check and led the way without faltering. Brie experienced a surge of admiration and understanding. *Leadership is never easy.*

Their guide hovered as three more Fée caught up to it. A conversation ensued. Urgency filled their lilting language.

Penee stood motionless, but alert. "What did they say?"

A dragonfly zipped between stems to land on the flattish cap of a stocky mushroom. Its long, black abdomen quivered. Its segmented legs pushed its head higher. A puff of glistening particulates exploded around it. When they settled, Brie gazed at a tiny man sitting cross-legged where the dragonfly had been.

He cocked his head and studied her with unblinking round eyes. "They are discussing if they wish to pursue the men. Their goal is to get you to safety on the far side of the lêa, so they hesitate to leave and take action against them."

Brie drew Penee to her side. "I am Brielle. This is my friend Penesert."

A slow smile spanned the lower half of the man's round face. Pointed ears twitched. "I am Jinx, counselor to Bantina, Queen of the Fée."

"Why is your queen helping us?" Penee kept her tone humble.

The four Fée hovered closer, exchanged a series of melodious phrases, then shot away through the jungle of stems.

Jinx uncrossed his legs and jumped to the ground. "Bantina senses substantial power for good in both of you." He looked from Penee to Brie. "In this time of transition, it is a rare pleasure to meet a female VarTerel." The admiration in his gaze increased. "You have shown great wisdom by not using DiMensionery near the lêa. Within its boundaries, charms and spells can backfire and cause considerable harm to the user." His ears twitched. An impish grin made a momentary appearance. "One of your enemies has experienced the results." The grin vanished. "We must hurry. Bantina wants you free of the lêa before the red moon rises."

He led them to a clearing surrounded by clusters of yellow-gold chanterelles. "I will resume my dragonfly form. When the shift is complete, climb aboard. Sit behind the thorax in back of the wings. Hold on tight."

Glistening particles enshrouded him. The gleaming shape of the dragonfly materialized at the clearing's center. Brie helped Penee mount and scrabbled up behind her. Shimmering wings beat the air. Jinx rose above the mushroom jungle and whizzed toward the woods on the far side of the lêa.

Brie grinned. Riding on the backs of strange creatures had become part of her life.

Much too soon, Jinx landed amongst giant, gnarled trees. Brie slid to the ground to help climb Penee down. A swarm of fist-sized Fée enshrouded them, the hum of their wings growing fainter and fainter. Brie shot to her full height, gulping in air. Penee's yelp of surprise echoed through the trees. Together, they watched the tiny Fée zip from sight; a glistening black dragonfly skimming over the Lêa of Beacáin in their wake.

Penee tracked the dragonfly's progress until it became lost in night dimness. "That was so much fun!"

La fluttered to her shoulder.

Abarax stepped from behind an immense olive tree. Its concerned gaze scrutinized them. "You are fine?"

"We are." Brie smiled.

Penee stared up at its angelic face. "How did you know to meet us on this side of the lêa?"

It scowled. "After Skultar discovered the boat, which is now at the bottom of the lake, a dragonfly told La where to find you."

Brie observed the Astican with interest. "How did you escape?"

"I felt Thorlu dismantle the loop. When I heard the hiss of fire behind me,

I shifted to a bat. La and I flew into the woods overlooking the lêa in search of you. Did we hear Vintrusie yelling?"

"You did. Let's put some distance between us and our favorite three men. Can you fly us to the coast, Abarax?"

"Wait." Penee's brows knitted. "What about using DiMensionery by the lêa?"

The Astican tilted its head. "My shifting, Penesert, is not the result of DiMensionery. I change because it is my nature. Besides, we are far enough from the lêa." Its nose twitched. "I must find someplace to lift free of the trees, then I will carry you to the coast." It squinted. "Night is upon us. Jinx warned me to have you far away before the red moon rises."

La fluttered from Penee's shoulder to Brie's upraised hand. *"Stay. I seek clearing."*

The Luna Moth dodged through the canopy.

P̲enee sank onto a mossy root. Den's position in Skultar's entourage continued to nag at her. She stared at the tangle of branches overhead. *I want to trust you, but how can I?*

A shadow detaching itself from the growing darkness took the shape of a man. Deep amethyst eyes gleamed in the phosphorescent glow of moonrise. Abarax surged to his full height. Brie gripped his arm to keep him stationary. In slow motion, Penee came to her feet, her attention consumed by the presence of Den Zironho.

"You can trust me, Penee, because I *am* on your side." He turned to Brie. "I need your help, Brielle, but first..." He handed her a crystal quartz vial with a jeweled stopper. "Keep this safe. When you find Henri and Irstant, you will know what to do..." His attention wavered. A blink brought his focus back. "I have to reach Bailé ahead of Skultar. Take me through Mittkeer."

Brie tucked the vial beneath her tunic. Her flared nostrils picked up the aroma of his fear. "You can travel Mittkeer on your own. Why do you need me?"

"I hitched a ride on the time loop to get here. If I initiate a trip through the Land of Time, Furrnoce will sense it and tell Skultar. The SorTech can't monitor you. If Skultar discovers I have been anywhere but Bailé, everything I have worked to protect since I turned sixteen will be at risk. Please, Brielle. I wouldn't ask if it weren't the only way."

Penee tuned in to every word, watched every expression, and tasted the bitterness of his fear on the tip of her tongue. "Take him, Brie. By the time you return, La will have found a clearing."

Den kissed her. "Thank you, Penee. You won't be sorry, I promise." He offered Brie his hand.

She gasped it. Mittkeer's starry heavens embraced them.

Penee rubbed her tingling lips. "If you lied to me, Den Zironho, I will find you and—"

Brie stepped from a star-studded portal, her expression serious. "Furrnoce almost caught us. We can't use Mittkeer until we're clear of the continent of Dast."

La fluttered into view. *"Come."* Wings glowing pale iridescent green, she flew between trees and over stumps and dodged wispy curtains of hanging, lacy moss.

Penee swallowed her impatience. A stumble over a twisted root left her muttering under her breath. She came to a halt.

La landed on her shoulder. *"We here."*

Abarax disappeared behind a large pine. A deep laugh rumbled. "Superb work, La."

Penee walked into a clearing. A ludoc cat, illuminated by reddish moonlight, waited to take flight. She handed her pack to Brie. "I'll go first, then you can toss it up to me." The cat's hind leg formed a perfect step. She scooched along his spine to sit over its shoulders.

Brie, her backpack in place, tossed Penee hers, and crawled up behind her.

The massive ludoc head swung their direction. Unblinking gray eyes regarded them. The head swung forward. Back muscles contracted. With a downward thrust of the huge wings, they were airborne.

An adrenaline rush left Penee laughing out loud.

27

Far, far away on the last remnant of Earth, Ari sat alone in a corner of the Research Lab, books scattered all over the desk and light from the comp-screen glowing. Everyone had gone to bed. She continued to work. Brie had reached out in a dream. She needed more information on how to transform The MasTer's gene to assure she could maintain control.

Ari scanned her notes. They contained the data her twin required. The question that kept her from sleeping, eating, or being anything but bad-tempered—how to get the information to Brie?

Elf attempted to convince her to sleep on it. She ignored his pleading. *How can I rest when The MasTer's evil intent threatens the person I love more than anyone in the Universe?*

Restlessness carried her to Elae's comp-screen. She pursed her lips. *How do I get this information to the other side of the galaxy? Paper is not the media to use.* The glowing screen grabbed her attention. *A micro-recorder would be perfect. It's small and transportable.*

Seated in Elae's chair, she opened her supply drawer. Success made her giddy. *Calm down, Ari. You have work to do.*

She placed a tiny silver disc in the recording slot, set up the recording parameters, and clicked on the microphone. A short time later, she ejected it and tucked it in her ear to listen. With a triumphant laugh, she removed it. *It won't be long, Brielle.*

With the micro-recorder clutched in her hand, she hurried from the Lab to her room. An unsuccessful search left her brow furrowed in frustration. *Where did I put it? Ah ha.* A black velvet ribbon trailed from beneath her pillow. She pulled the black pouch attached to it free and tipped an orange agate cabochon onto her palm. A rush of happiness left her smiling. Elf had given it to her for her last Sun Cycle Celebration. She kissed it, put it down, and slid the micro-recorder into the pouch. *The question is, Brielle Ralyn AsTar, how do I get this to you?*

She picked up the agate and rubbed its polished smoothness with her thumb. *Esán Efre. If only I knew how—* "Oh! Got it!" Hurrying along the Hall of Priestesses to the double doors of the Cave of Canedari, she entered. Doubt throbbing in her brain held her motionless. *What can a crystal, even a super powerful one like Evolsefil, do to bring Esán here?*

A square panel in the floor slid open. Water lapped the edges. The Lake of Rorret's watery voice reverberated through the cave. "Evolsefil cannot come to you, Arienh AsTar. If you want help, bring the pouch." The lake withdrew. The panel closed.

Hope ignited, Ari strode across the stone floor. With gold threads glistening in its the glow, the Heart of Myrrh towered above her. Ari gazed at Evolsefil with a touch of wonder, remembering what it represented to those in the Clenaba Rolas System and to the Universal Crystal Web. She stepped between two smaller crystals at its base; pressed the pouch against cool, shimmering smoothness; and bowed her head. "Please help me reach Esán."

Tranquility soothed the ache in her heart. Fear for her sister melted away. A subtle vibration preceded coolness flowing over her hand, up her arm, and throughout her body.

"Look at me, Arienh AsTar."

Esán's stormy blue eyes stared into hers. His presence produced a wave of relief. Her gaze darted to her hand, encased in crystal. He removed the pouch and touched her trembling fingertips.

The coolness of the quartz crystal faded. Her hand slipped free. She pressed it, empty and throbbing, to her heart. "The pouch contains the information Brie needs to control The MasTer gene. Please take it to her."

He tucked the pouch in his pocket. "I'll deliver it as soon as I can. Take care of yourself, Arienh AsTar. I promise to protect Brie." A brisk salute and he misted away.

Blinding light concealed Evolsefil. Ari sank to her knees, rested her head on one of the smaller crystals, and sobbed.

Elf found her, embraced her, and let her cry. When the tears subsided, she shared what had occurred. He took her face between his hands, kissed her with such gentleness more tears welled up and spilled down her cheeks.

Hands continuing to hold her face, he kissed each tear until her laugh of delight filled the Cave of Canedari, and her heart brimmed over with love.

T he ludoc cat soared above the Soputton forest on Dast, its wings wide, its long tail trailing behind it. Brie grinned at the unrestrained joy in Penee's laugh and savored her own delight as Abarax winged its way skyward. To the North, TaSneach crested the Sileah Mountains on the far side of Lake Llyn. Moonlight inched down the mountainside. Soon, TaSneach would hover above the lake, and the red moon, Chearra, would begin its ascent.

Prior to leaving the cottage, she placed false clues on the desk, clues she hoped would confuse Thorlu and his companions.

Hopeful for the first time in turnings, she reveled in the beauty of TaSneach's light brightening the world. The Sileah Mountains loomed ahead of them. The cat soared up, skimmed their tops, and swooped over forested slopes that transitioned to well-kept farmland, then transformed into sand dunes bordering a wide expanse of beach.

Coastal winds tangled her hair and chilled her to the bone as Abarax swooped lower. A long glide through a well-protected, moonlit slack between dunes brought it to landing, its belly low to the ground.

Brie slid to the sand and caught Penee's pack.

Penee jumped down, hugged her, and laughed aloud. "That was wonderful!" She threw her arms around the ludoc's neck. "Thank you, Abarax."

La fluttered along the valley-like slack to Brie's shoulder. *"All safe."*

Woozy with fatigue, Brie managed a smile. "I'm thinking we gave Thorlu and gang the slip...at least for now."

The tension in Penee's stance melted away. "Hooray!" She hugged herself and grinned.

A cool breeze turned Brie's grin to a shiver. The night air chasing gooseflesh over her skin brought memories of Fera Finnero, the desert on DerTah. She yearned for the long robe WoNa had given her to protect her from the turning's heat and the chilly desert nights.

Abarax, in cat form, stretched out on the sand. *"We need sleep. I will keep you warm. La will warn us of trouble."*

Penee dropped to the ground. She positioned her pack to use as a pillow, curled up next to the enormous cat's side, and slept.

Brie yawned, removed her knapsack, and joined her. The ludoc's long, thick belly fur formed a warm blanket covering them. Its wing stretching over them created a shelter from the cool night air.

Fatigue, held at bay by the need to stay alert, washed over Brie with the force of waves at high tide. Sleep claimed her, cradling her in dreamless slumber. The cry of seabirds woke her to the sun rising above the horizon and morning's radiant glow tiptoeing up the side of the dunes.

The ludoc cat's low-pitched snore combining with Penee's higher tone created a murmured harmony that allowed Brie to relax. She crawled from beneath the wing into the open. An inhaled breath brought her to her feet. She walked onto the beach to take stock of her surroundings.

A horseshoe-shaped beach bordered the Sea of Canttila. Offshore, immense rock formations, scattered in random fashion and topped by undergrowth and stubby evergreens, left her breathless with amazement. The incoming tide, midway between high and low, sent lazy wavelets to lap the sand and retreat in a rhythmic sequence. To the South, the granite cliff face dropped from the headland straight into the sea. To the North, sylvan slopes of rolling hills bordered the beach in a long curve. The dunes behind her evolved from a band of arid land bordering the lush farmland beyond.

Her looked up at the sky and spread her arms wide. "Thank you for a beautiful awakening."

"You look happy, Brielle."

A sharp pivot brought her face to face with the man who had stolen her heart. "Esán! How did you find me?" Patches of orange, the musky animal scent, the warm nose nudging her palm crowded her mind. "You're the animal that's been with us the past few turnings. How did you get here? Wait! Have the Seeds of Carsilem matured?" Questions plowed into one another. She glared. "Say something."

Amusement flickered across his face. "I've been waiting for you to give me the opportunity." He pulled her into his arms and gazed at her with rapt attention. "I have missed you, Brielle AsTar."

Her heart thumped so hard against her ribs she was sure he could feel it. She shook her hair back from her face to meet his gaze with tear-brightened eyes.

He kissed her. "I've never known you to be so quiet."

Happiness left her giddy. "I'm so glad you to see you." Her desire to know more sobered her. "Please answer my questions."

His fingers intertwining with hers, he guided to her the foot of a dune. "Let's sit. We don't have much time. You and Penee must find Irstant and Henri as soon as you can. I hope what I am about to tell you will provide some helpful information." He gazed at the ocean.

"The Quickening Cycle for the Seeds of Carsilem is complete. I am free to move forward in my life, at least as free as the seeds allow." He turned to her, his expression one of compassion mixed with understanding. "Like you, I have responsibilities which take precedence over my personal desires. I realize you are a VarTerel, *and* I know your secret, Brielle. Relevart gave me permission to watch over you. I promised him I would not interfere. Your destiny impacts that of the Universe and depends on you achieving certain things on your own." He withdrew a flat, black stone the size of a gold coin from his pocket. Emotions flitted across his face. "Relevart gave this to me." He pressed into her hand.

She examined the carving of a fox within a star on the stone's surface. Choosing to remain quiet and allow Esán to tell his tale in his own way, she handed the stone back.

He held it up in the morning light. "This allows me to travel in Mittkeer. It helps me to maintain the shape of a fox so I can be near you, yet remain undetected." He slipped it into his pocket. "Questions?"

"If you're not supposed to interfere, why are you here?"

From his other pocket, he withdrew a black pouch. "I am delivering a message to you from Ari. What you do with the information is up to you. I do believe you would be wise to review it before you go to Neul Isle."

The tenderness of his kiss kept her quiet. "Your companions will awaken soon. They mustn't see me. I love you, Brielle AsTar."

His immediate shift to a red fox that faded into sand left her emotionally bereft. The warmth of a furry canine body pressed against her thigh soothed her sense of loss.

The rising sun created a sparkling path on the ocean's calm. Warm colors streaked the sky. She fingered the pouch in her lap. A sigh reestablished her desire to learn what it contained. She tipped the earbud onto her palm. *What have you discovered, dear sister of mine?*

A brief explanation preceded the scientific material Ari shared. Brie soaked in every word. The more she listened, the more agitated she became. She stopped the recording. *What is wrong with me? This will give me control; it will decrease the need to monitor the gene one hundred percent of the time.*

The growing unease building to anger sparked a moment of delight. *Ahhh, Fisaco, you realize your chances of using me are lessening with each word.*

28

Penee lay in the ludoc's shade, listening to the melodies of morning: the soft swish of water, the squawk of seabirds, the Astican's intermittent snores. Unafraid for the first time in many moon cycles, she allowed herself the luxury of an unhurried awakening.

From under the gray-scaled wing, she watched the sun rise, turning the ocean from pastel pink to salmon to blue. When wakefulness turned to restlessness, she tossed her backpack ahead of her and crawled into the open. Fresh sea air caressed her cheeks and ruffled her hair. With a soft laugh, she shouldered the pack and walked to the water's edge.

"All safe." La's message made her want to sing. Penee scanned the beach, picked out Brie sitting at the foot of a dune, and trotted toward her.

"Good morning, Brielle! What a beautiful day." Her friend's expression stopped her. "Why so serious?"

"Have a seat." Brie patted the sand. "I have something to share."

She plopped down facing her.

Brie offered the earbud. "Ari sent this to me."

Penee inspected it, then Brie. "And she got it to you...how?"

Brie laughed and held up the pouch. "It came in this via special courier. Have a listen."

A sea breeze stirred the air. Penee inhaled. "Your friend is back. I can smell his scent. Care to share who he is."

"Listen to the recording, Pen. My friend will reveal himself at an appropriate time."

Penee shot her a mischievous look. "Ah ha. It *is* a *he*."

Brie rolled her eyes.

"Alright." She put the earbud in her ear. When she finished listening, she removed it. "Epigenetics? Do you understand this?"

A convulsed gasping, Brie's only response, brought Penee to her knees. She gripped Brie's shoulders. "Brielle, don't let him take over."

Brie gasped again. Determination straightened her spine. White-knuckled hands clutched her knees. A deep breath steadied her. "I do understand it. I can and will do what needs to be done." She returned earbud to the pouch and pressed it into Penee's hand. "Please keep this safe."

Penee looped the black ribbon around her neck. "I promise." She helped her friend to her feet. "What now?"

They walked in silence to the slack where they had spent the night. The Astican, in its natural shape, sat with its wings spread out on the sand, looking out to sea. La flew from his shoulder to Brie's. *"You not good?"*

"I need everyone's help." She looked from friend to friend. "If we are to remain safe from The MasTer, I must alter the gene to reflect the moral integrity of a VarTerel. I will not allow Fisaco's renegade personality to control The MasTer gene."

She provided Abarax and La with a simple explanation of the material Ari had shared, then touched her neck. "With the Star of Truth's help, I believe I can make the genetic modifications required. To do so, I will need to go into a trance state. Any interruptions could cause Fisaco to usurp control."

The Astican's wings shivered over the sand. Luna moth wings brushed Brie's cheek. Penee rested her hands on her hips. "Are you sure you want to do this now?"

"Waiting will only make it harder, Pen. Besides, our enemies are on the other side of the mountains, but they won't be for much longer."

Penee smiled. "I like that you call me Pen." She sobered. "What do you need us to do?"

B rie understood her companions' apprehension. Had Esán not been so close, she might have abandoned her plan. His presence and her VarTerel's instincts intensified her desire to be free of The MasTer's hold on her. She reviewed what she had learned. *I can do this.*

"La, I need you to be our guardian. If anything worries you, report to Penee or Abarax."

The Luna Moth fluttered pale green wings. *"I guard."* She flew over the dunes to begin a patterned patrol.

"Penee and Abarax, surround me with your love and confidence. I don't know what will happen. Be prepared for anything. If The MasTer rises, don't interrupt my trance."

She sat cross-legged on the sand facing the Sea of Canttila. "Abarax, sit behind me at the base of the dune. Pen, I need you at this end of the slack."

When they had positioned themselves, La confirmed that all appeared to be quiet.

A slight breeze whispering across the dunes carried with it a hint of musk. Her confidence solidified. She concentrated on breathing in to heighten her confidence and out to release negativity. Only breathing mattered—in and out, in and out. The world faded. The Star of Truth grew warmer. The MasTer's gene trembled under her intense scrutiny. Spite, cruelty, dishonesty, aggression, and greed infused the gene. Anger festered like an infected sore.

Epigenetics attested to the fact that she could alter it. Ari's information described how to use the Star to help. With the lessons of Trilemma, that which integrates shadow into wholeness, in the forefront of her mind, she envisioned the character traits she wished the gene to have. Heat from the Star imbued her with the courage to move forward. She instructed it to use her body's histone response to tone down the negative characteristics inherent in The MasTer's gene and to amplify the positive qualities she valued as a VarTerel.

Fisaco's awareness of the work being done triggered more anger. Electrical impulses leapt from cell to cell. Hatred building like a geyser in her lower abdomen arched her spine. A howl of pain screamed up her throat into the morning air.

Stunned silence followed. She curled into a ball on the sand, covered her face with her forearms, and buried her fingers in her hair. The Star's throbbing encased her exhausted body in a chrysalis of healing. Hot, then cold, then hot again, she trembled from head to foot. Energy rushed over her skin. Tiny electrical impulses shooting through larger muscles left them quivering.

An arm reached out, palm up, the fingers curling and uncurling. The hand twitched, turned palm down, and stroked the sand. A leg straightened. She pushed up to sitting, moved her head from side to side, and in one graceful, muscle-empowered movement came to her feet.

Sea air filled her lungs. Sunshine warmed her skin. Acute sight absorbed the world in such detail, she laughed in delight. The lapping of waves on the beach, the squeak of a luna moth, and her friends' exclamations of surprise intermingling centered her attention.

Penee's astonished expression penetrated Brie's wonder-filled daze. The whisper of Abarax's scales, a sure sign of agitation, startled her into the realization that something unforeseen had occurred.

She looked from one to the other. "Are you alright? What just happened?" The timber of her voice, almost as deep as Ari's, stopped her.

Penee took her hands. "I give you permission to look into my mind. See yourself through my eyes."

Brie steadied her breathing and concentrated her thoughts. A woman's image came into focus. She regarded the amber eyes studying her. Short, black hair curled around bold features in the fair-skinned face. Her gaze traveled from the curls down her muscular body to her feet. She withdrew from Penee's mind. "I'm taller." She flexed her arms. "And stronger, too." Delight and confusion collided. "I didn't expect this. I assumed I was changing the gene, not creating a new me."

Abarax peered down at her. "My mistress could shift back and forth."

Brie glanced down at her body. "I should have figured that out." She hugged herself. "This is overwhelming."

A long stride carried her midway down the beach to a line of seaweed left by an earlier high tide. The gentleness of the water's quiet lapping helped to calm her apprehension. Regulating her breathing, she fixed her attention on her authentic persona.

At first, she experienced nothing. *What have I done?* A tingling sensation spread out from The Star. The shift came over her with the fluidity of water over ocean-smoothed stones. She held her breath and peeked at freckle-speckled hands. Copper curls tumbled across her face. The familiar feel of her own body brought a wave of relief. The Star of Truth grew quiet.

A rough tongue licked her hand. She lowered to her knees. Warmth soaked her side. Esán's closeness gave her the courage to accept a warm embrace from her companions.

P enee observed Brie's uncertainty. The urge to ease it prompted her to assume a leadership role. "Abarax, shrink and fly back toward the cottage. See what you can learn about Skultar and the Mocendi. Don't give yourself away. La will continue to stand guard here."

The Astican studied her, its expression questioning, then, in the form of a small bat, it shot over the dunes.

Brie, her expression distant, scoped up a handful of sand and let it trickle between her fingers.

Penee grabbed their packs and sat down. "We need food." She withdrew two pieces of mela, a round, red fruit endemic to Soputto, and held one out. "Eat this."

Brie brushed granules of sand from her hand, accepted the fruit, and took a nibbled bite. Hunger demanded more. She savored the juicy crispness of a bigger bite and gulped a long drink of water. "Thanks, Pen. I can talk now."

Penee set a canteen between them and bit into the mela's crisp sweetness. "Good. Did you expect to create another persona?"

"No. I expected the gene to alter, and it did. I'm not sure what stimulated the shift into a new form." She bit her bottom lip. "We have a new ally. I believe things most often happen for a reason, so she must play a role in the destiny we're sharing."

"Will she emerge on her own, or do you control her appearances?"

Brie touched the Star of Truth. "If the Star is any indication, I'm the one who calls her forth. We shall see."

Penee beautiful eyes gleamed. "She deserves a name of her own. Any thoughts?"

A human-sized Abarax landing postponed her reply. It strode toward them, its expression dour. La fluttered to its shoulder.

The Astican lifted its wings and sat down. "Skultar and the Mocendi are circumventing the lêa. Thorlu realized using DiMensionery too close to the angel oak had caused Vygel's extreme pain. He discovered that detouring around the lêa would be far safer than trying to cross it. Once they reach this side, he will scout ahead to find out what direction we took."

"Is Furrnoce with them?" Loathing left a sour taste in Penee's mouth.

"The SorTech arrived at the cottage right after Thorlu dismantled the time loop. He left The Box there, but he has a mini trans-receiver with him." Abarax scowled. "I dislike the sorcerer."

Penee tossed it a piece of mela. "Tell us how you learned so much."

A crispy crunch and loud chewing were the only response. It licked its taloned fingers. "More fruit?"

"Answer my question, and I'll toss you this one."

It grimaced. "I found them resting about half-way to this side of the lêa. Furrnoce was complaining about taking the longest path. He explained he had a mini box with him. Thorlu responded with a lecture on the Lêa. The sorcerer pouted like a small child. Skultar told him to stop it, or he would personally deliver him to the Fée." Abarax paused, its pleasure at the thought making it seem childlike. The cherubic features turned ugly.

"Their plan is to capture you both and use your power to attain their personal goals, the first of which is to destroy every VarTerel in the Inner Universe." A grimace of hatred made it more evil looking. La's appearance returned its cherubic innocence.

Penee walked to the tideline and back. "It will take them about two turnings to find this beach. We know Neul Isle is our goal. Using Mittkeer or accessing DiMensionery to get us there is not a good idea. What are your thoughts, Brie?"

"I suggest before we go anywhere, we make certain my new personality is our ally. I also want to establish that I can regain my authentic form without a problem. A few minutes of working with her is all I need to confirm my control. We can then determine our next step."

Penee shot her a sideways glance. "If you can't control her?"

"I'd prefer to remain positive. Ready?"

Penee crossed her fingers and held her breath.

29

Brie made note of the world around her. The coral specks on the cream-colored beach, the waters range of colors from turquoise to deep azure, and the rugged granite cliffs helped to register place. Blue, cloudless sky, a backdrop for a sun on its way to the horizon, established time. She held up her freckled hands, patted her long, red curls, and crossed her fingers. Smiles of confidence from her wary but hopeful companions affirmed their support. She closed her eyes.

A gasp of surprise from Penee and Abarax's scales humming as it attained its full height signaled her success.

She fingered her short hair. "I noticed nothing." Flexing her muscular arms, she walked along the beach, inventorying the differences in her body and her thinking.

La landed on her shoulder. An unexpected shiver ran through her new persona. The Luna Moth shot skyward.

Brie fixed her attention on the gene, searching for what caused the tremor.

Nothing suggested a problem. The Star remained unaffected, so she jogged back to her companions. "I need a name."

"You resemble my former mistress." Abarax turned shy. "Perhaps you would like to be named after her?"

Penee's mismatched eyes glistened brighter. "You do resemble Mother, but with fair skin. What do you think of Rayna?"

The Astican, tears brimming over, pressed his palms together in supplication.

A thrill of rightness transformed into surge of pleasure. "I am Rayna. Thank you, Abarax and Penee. What a lovely name! I am honored." She walked a few steps and turned. "Time to switch back." She closed her eyes.

The seamlessness of the transformation surprised her. The sight of the setting sun resting on the horizon line accompanied by the familiar sensation of self helped her to reorient. "Oh, my." A soft laugh escaped.

Penee regarded her with uncertainty. "Did something strange happen when La landed on your shoulder?"

Brie shook her long curls back from her face. "I experienced a slight tremor, but I couldn't find what triggered it." She frowned. "Until we're positive Fisaco can't control her, Rayna is an unknown."

Abarax shrunk to a less formidable height, intense interest in his expression. "You altered The MasTer's gene, did you not?"

"I did, but according to the material Ari shared, our personalities are polygenic. It's not just about *one* gene. Fisaco may be more multifaceted than we realize. Time will be our teacher." Her stomach rumbled.

Penee grabbed her pack. "I believe food is on our to-do list. What else?"

Brie gazed at the dark shadows creeping over the terrain. "We don't want to travel to Neul this late in the turning, and we're too exposed if our friends arrive without warning. The map of Dast showed two lakes within the trees at the North end of the beach. I suggest we camp there and replenish our water supply." She cast the Astican a coy smile. "Perhaps Abarax will catch us dinner?"

Scaled wings lifted and resettled. A grin of delight brought La to its shoulder.

A flurry of activity removed all signs of their brief stay. Abarax strolled behind them up the beach, using its wingtips to assure no footprints would give them away.

. . .

Dinner, a lighthearted meal, had been delicious. Abarax had proved once again its talents as a fisherman. Penee's harvest of edible roots and greens made a succulent addition to the spread.

The moon TaSneach arrived in the sky in time to bid them goodnight. Their goal was to awaken early to begin the long trip to Neul Isle.

Brie smothered a yawn. Grateful for the ludoc cat's sheltering warmth, she burrowed into its long belly fur. Sleep interrupted by dreams of Rayna and her Aunt Henri made her fretful. Snuggled close to the ludoc's belly, Brie's thoughts sought an answer to why her aunt wandered her dreams. Determination settled over her. *Today we travel to our goal.*

A mental review of the map of Neul Isle suggested the Forest of Deora might be a logical place to start the search for the VarTerels. Yet, Bolcán Murloch, the lagoon at the island's center, drew her with hypnotic power. She lay watching morning creep one patch of sunlight at a time into the forest and tried to decide which destination would be best.

Penee rubbed her left forearm and moaned in her sleep. Confusion-filled eyes blinked open. She regarded the arm as though it did not belong to her, cradled it against her chest, and maneuvered from beneath the ludoc's wing.

Brie scooted to her side. "What's with the arm?"

"In my dream, it kept burning. I'm not sure why." She ran a tentative hand over the forearm. "It seems alright now. I dreamt Irstant was trying to tell me something."

Brie climbed to her feet and stretched. "Aunt Henrietta appeared in my dreams. Wish we understood what they wanted." She scanned the area. "I don't see La. Wake up Abarax. I'll look for her."

In the hopes that their enemies would not see them, they had set up camp beneath thick-trunked evergreens. Brie shivered. "Bet the sun doesn't warm this place until late morning." Keeping within the trees, she followed the sounds of ocean waves to the beach. The immense rock formations pushing up from the sea filled her with awe. The closest one to her hiding place, only a scant distance off the shore, blocked her view of the rising sun. Rays of light shot from behind it in a pinwheel pattern. La's familiar shape danced from ray to ray as she descended from her perch on a stubby pine and flew across the beach.

She fluttered to Brie's shoulder. *"We go soon?"*

"Brielle!" Penee's alarmed shout demolished the morning calm.

Abarax shot to its full height, caught Penee as she fell, and eased her to the ground. Alertness cloaked it. Its acute gaze sought a cause.

Brie knelt beside her. La's wings beat a frantic question.

Penee mouthed one word. "Box." She lay quiet except for a hand. Minimal movements cleared a spot. With her finger, she scratched out the word, *pretending.*

Understanding dawned. Brie beckoned Abarax to her side and touched her ear.

The Astican, now human-sized, listened.

"Police the campsite. Make sure nothing's left behind."

It went to work.

Penee tapped the ground and scratched two more letters. *'Go.'*

Brie placed hands on her friend's temples. Penee slipped into unconsciousness.

Abarax handed over two packs. "Plan?"

"We fly to the rock formation furthest from the shore. I will bring Penee around, so we can determine what's next."

The Astican leaned close. "Why go to the formation?"

"Can't use DiMensionery on Dast. But we can offshore." She put on her pack, stood up, and reached for Penee's.

Abarax shook its head, slipped the pack onto its arm, and went to one knee. "Climb on. Put your arms around my neck. When I grow to size, brace your feet on my ribs. I'll carry Penesert."

Brie followed his directions. It lifted Penee and grew to its full size. After careful scrutiny of the beach and a *"safe"* from La, the Astican stepped free of the trees, launched into flight, and flew as far from the mainland as possible.

The thrust of its huge wings left Brie marveling at its strength and the smooth transitions from flight to hovering to its feet touching down.

A quick survey of their new surroundings and Abarax lowered Penee to the ground. Its height decreased.

Brie dropped between its wings. The Astican stepped to the side. Like the 'reveal' in a magic show, a spectacular view opened up. A slow rotation showed her the flattened top of a massive tower of rock. Moss and tall grass covered the ground. Sprigs of young evergreens moved in the breeze. Vibrant turquoise water circled their perch. In the distance, beach, dunes, cliffs, and trees gleamed in the morning sun.

Abarax's soft whistle of delight magnified her sense of wonder.

She touched Penee's temples. *Hope we're still speaking when you wake up, Pen.*

G rateful the seeker beam from The Box no longer buzzed in her brain, Penee opened her lids a crack. Brie knelt at her side. La flitted overhead, then flew out of sight. The Astican stood at her feet, gazing down at her from its immense height. She noticed Brie's contemplative expression. "Where are we?"

"We're safe. How do you feel?"

"I'm fine." Easing herself to sitting, Penee gasped. Astonishment left her staring. Ocean surrounded them. In the distance, the sand dunes, cliffs, and, at the opposite end of the beach, the evergreens formed a breathtaking panorama. "We're on a rock formation!" Memories snapped into place. "What did you do, Brielle? I told you to go."

"I rendered you unconscious to break the connection to The Box. Abarax transported you out of range, so we can establish what our best course of action is."

La streaked into sight. *"Bad men close to dunes."*

Brie, the first to move, pulled Penee to her feet. "Usolamet!" Irstant's staff materialized in her upraised hand.

Penee called Henrietta's. It flashed into being in her outstretched hand.

"Hang on, everyone." Brie gripped her arm. "It's time to go."

Penee clasped Abarax by the hand. Mittkeer embraced them. Dizziness overtook her. As Irstant had taught her, she focused on pleasant memories to help it recede.

The Astican, wings rustling, sniffed the air. "Your friend is with us, Brielle." Its mouth puckered in disgust. "So is something I do not recognize."

La landed on Abarax's shoulder. Her proboscis uncurled and flicked the air. *"Badness comes closer."*

Penee's nostrils flared. Her stomach churned.

B rie sniffed, her mind racing through a catalogue of aromas. A flashback of Toelachoc Prison on DerTah and the threatening ghosts of violent criminals made her cringe. *Is that sickening odor decaying flesh?*

Abarax growled. "I have never before encountered the smell of death in Mittkeer."

Penee sprinted to catch up.

La fluttered above her and darted away.

Luminous mismatched eyes widened as a shudder shook Penee's entire body. Tears streamed down her face. Collapsing to one knee, she vomited.

The semi-opaque figure of a man loomed over her. Its hideous, toothless mouth gaped wide. "Thank you for transporting me to the Land of All Time and No Time." Its malignant gaze fixed on Penee, it blew out a putrid breath. "You and your friend will come with me."

Abarax lunged forward. Penee's scream of horrific pain brought him to a full stop.

The creature's plasmic essence enshrouded her. Color leaked from her skin. She clawed her throat, struggling to breathe. A stifled gurgling sound rang though All Time as she crumbled to a death-still heap.

"Leave her alone." Brie handed Abarax Irstant's staff and faced the creature. "We'll do whatever you want."

The malevolent gaze devoured her. "Give me back my life, and I will release your friend unharmed."

Brie returned the penetrating stare.

"Not powerful enough, VarTerel?" The repulsive creature's snarl trembled through Mittkeer. It pointed a bony finger.

Pain double her over. Her breath hissed from between bared teeth. Resolve to end the conflict and save her friend surged up her spine. She shifted shape.

R ayna's attention locked onto the startled creature. Irstant's staff flew from Abarax's hand through star-studded night to hers. "Do you have a name?"

Hideous features twisted into an infuriated scowl. "I want VarTerel AsTar? What did you do with her?"

"I am the VarTerel." Rayna leveled the crystal tip of the staff at its chest. "Would you like me to prove it?"

Hollow sounding syllables sprayed from its mouth. A nervous cackle of laughter spewed after them. Conniving whines laced with deceit filled Mittkeer. "Please don't hurt me, VarTerel. If you help me, I'll help you."

The staff's crystal's center glinted blue. Rayna inched forward. "What do they call you?"

Bony fists clenched. Its chin jutted forward. "Dred is my name." A growl rumbled. "I am your worst nightmare come to haunt you."

She pretended to shudder. "What a *frightening* name!" Awe filled her voice. "How did you enter Mittkeer, Dred?"

He patted Penee's head. "The Girl with the Matriarch's Eyes carried me through the portal." More cackled laughter. "I waited close by. When time opened its gates, I hitched a ride. My master will be pleased."

Rayna beamed her appreciation. "Your ingenuity will indeed impress him. If you tell me who he is, I'll make sure he knows how you fooled a VarTerel and invaded Mittkeer."

Beneath a cunning stare, the toothless mouth puckered and smoothed. "You would do that for me?"

"Oh, yes! You are so scary, so smart, and so clever! He will reward you well."

"Furrnoce is my master." The creatures plasmic body quivered. "But, it is Skultar to whom you must speak. Now, VarTerel, give me back my life." Aggression blazed within the ravaged features.

A shaft of blue light shot from the Usolamet crystal, struck it mid-chest, and sent it rocketing backward. Its infuriated bellow echoed through Mittkeer. The shattered plasma reformed into a fearsome jungle puma. Orbs of flaming red focused on her face. It raised its hackles and prepared to charge.

Her gaze never leaving the phantom cat, Rayna spoke under her breath. "Abarax, get Penee." She released Irstant's staff to float at her side.

The gigantic puma launched through the air. She caught it by its massive neck, swung it in a wide circle, and released it. Quicker than a blink, she snatched the staff and took aim. Dazzling blue light ripped through the endless ever-night sky, hovered within the filmy body, and with a loud crack, ruptured it into a multitude of tiny pieces. A wave of her hand clustered the translucent specks together. She chanted,

"All Time, No Time, eternal land,
Give this puma a place to stand.
Let it shine a marker, a warning,
A Constellation rising in early morning."

The sparkling cluster rose high overhead, reshaping into the outline of the wild cat.

Rayna lowered the staff. "Eternal existence is far more than you deserve, Dred of TaSneach Penal Colony."

Neul Isle
Gisa Point
Timhé Valley
Tide Pool
Bholcáno
Sea of Canttila

Sea of Canttila
Plains of Cârthea
San Crúil River
Tibêth Cove
Rina Island
San Crúil Mountains
Baobo Forest
BOLCÁN MURLOCH
Elgnat Range
Valley of Tá Súil
Áfini Sacu
Forest of Deora
Lágosin Canú
Lake Chittârine
Créada Sacu

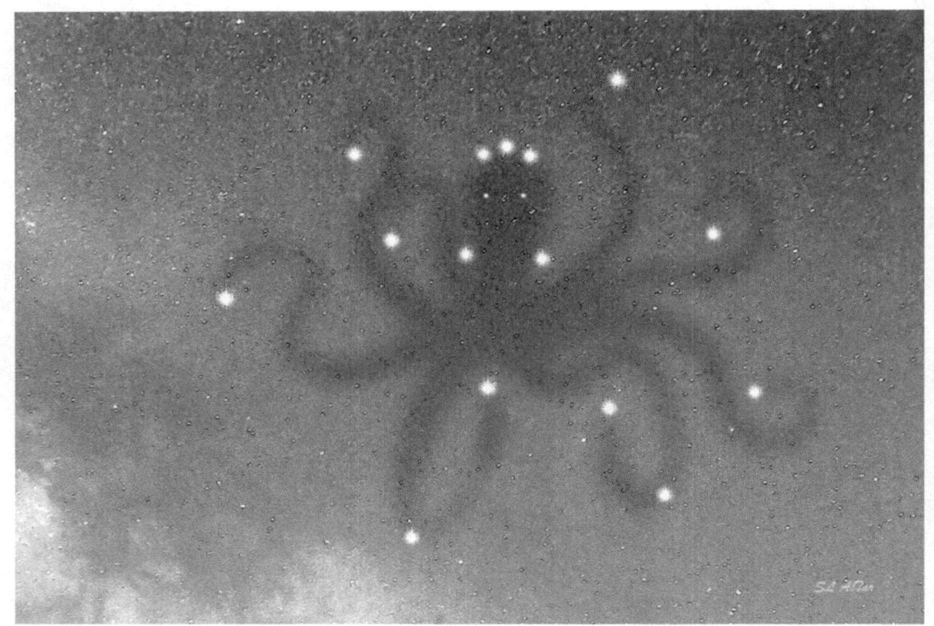

30

Brie resumed her true persona, regarded the constellation with a sense of accomplishment, and faced her astonished companions.

Abarax gazed at her with wonder.

Penee worked to produce a shaky smile. "Once upon a time, I doubted your power as a VarTerel." The slight smile steadied. "Never again, Brielle AsTar." Curiosity reshaped into an expression of awe. "Do you remember what happens when you are Rayna?"

Brie tucked long curls behind her ears. "The MasTer took control of a separate personality. In my case, I am Rayna and Rayna is me. I'm aware of everything that's happening."

The Astican cleared its throat. "How did that Dred-thing find us?"

Penee brush hair from her forehead. "I can the answer that. Furrnoce must have brought it to Soputto with him. He's well acquainted with my energy signature and programed The Box's seeker beam to find me. I thought something strange was happening when it linked to my mind. Dred used the beam's frequency to lead him to me. Does that answer your question, Abarax?"

"It does, Penesert. Although, I do not understand some of it."

A damp mouth locked onto Brie's wrist. The word *"Incirrata"* whispered through her thoughts. "Are you feeling strong enough to travel, Pen?"

Penee winced and scratched her arm. "How far?"

"I'm not sure. We need to find the constellation Incirrata. It's the signpost that points us at the portal to Neul Isle."

"How do you know where to go? It all looks alike—stars, stars, and more stars." She glanced down. "I guess your friend knows the way, right?"

Brie ignored the dig. "Incirrata is an octopus found in the deep waters of Soputto. Watch for a single bright star in an off-centered circle of eight stars. Fainter but still visible, you'll perceive four lines of smaller stars trailing from the lower curve of the circle."

Penee rubbed her forearm. "My arm burns like it did in the dream." She grimaced. "I wonder what's going on?"

"Let's find Neul Isle, so we can examine it." The warm mouth tightening on Brie's wrist herded her ahead of her friends. She called over her shoulder. "I believe we go this way."

"Wait." Penee searched the globe of stars. "I dropped Henri's staff, and I can't see it anywhere."

"Don't panic, Pen. Hold up your hand and call it to you."

"Oh, right. Sorry." The staff materialized. "I guess I'm tired."

Abarax grew taller, picked her up, and sat her on its shoulder. "You ride, Penesert. Brielle will lead."

Brie, an invisible fox at her side, a giant Astican at her heels, and a luna moth fluttering close by, raised the crystal, Usolamet. The star-scape comprising Mittkeer reminded her of the honor bestowed on her by the Galactic Counsel. *I love All Time and No Time. Thank you, Chealim and Relevart, for trusting me to be a VarTerel.*

She visualized the map of the island. A search of the lagoon's shoreline closest to the Forest of Deora helped her to pinpoint an exit location. *Good. What should we do first? Find the Stannag or the old man—*

"*Incirrata.*" Her invisible guide brought her to a standstill.

The constellation shone brighter. She lowered her hand to her side. "*Thanks.*"

A wet tongue licked her fingers. Abarax put Penee down and searched the eternal night sky.

Penee squinted up at the stars. "I can see it. Now what?"

"Hold on." Brie placed Irstant's staff upright in front of her.

Penee's fingers encircled the smooth shaft. A taloned hand gripped it below the crystal tip.

Brie drew in a calming breath. The portal opened. Stars blurred, and the gateway closed behind them.

No one moved. Not even La ventured from Abarax's protective presence.

A world of oppressive silence closed enclosed Penee. Air trapped in her lungs fought for freedom. Instinctive reflexes released it. Dampness creeping over her skin turned the itchy burn on her forearm to a sharp sting. Gritting her teeth, she focused on the landscape of Neul Isle.

Clouds covering everything as far as she could see thinned above Bolcán Murloch and the mountainous terrain surrounding it. The mirror-calm lagoon absorbed the soft gray of the mist. A slow pivot revealed little else. She shivered. "How will we find anything in this?"

Henri's staff tingled in her hand. A throbbing hum whispered around it. Brie's gasp of surprise echoed her own. Both of the VarTerels' staffs had vanished.

"We are in the right place." Brie peered into foggy grayness. "Henri and Irstant are nearby. That's the only reason their staffs would leave us."

Astican scales rustled a warning. "Something moves." It shifted to a bat and raced over the lagoon.

La flew after it into the clouds. She reappeared moments later. *"Incirrata comes."*

The bat darted from the cloud cover to touch down as the Astican. Abarax towered above them. "It travels beneath the surface." He pointed at the faint outline of an island near the far end of the lagoon.

Ridges of water moving their direction formed a path through the water's center. The closer it came, the more Penee's forearm burned. She sank to the ground, tears spilling down her face. "What is wrong?"

Pale-gold eyes, positioned on the front sides of a blue-gray bulbous sack, rose above the surface at the edge of a large tidal pool. Horizontal, black, rectangular-shaped pupils narrowed. A low-pitched buzz repeated several times.

Penee sobbed and cradled her arm.

The incirrata slithered into the shallow basin. A long, writhing tentacle lifted free of the water. The tip caressed her cheek, touched her sleeve, and hovered.

Penee made a soft sound in her throat and lowered the arm to rest on her thigh. Her gaze locked on the Stannag Incirrata, she peeled back her shirt sleeve and the protective mail Irstant had fashioned for her. The top side of the forearm blazed red.

Tiny clicks accompanied the tentacle as it came to rest on the bare arm. Suction cups kissing her skin eased the pain. The tentacle withdrew beneath the water.

She gasped. "Brielle, look."

As though drawn by an artist's brush, a tattoo emerged on her forearm. The bulbous body of an incirrata appeared on her bared arm below the elbow. Eight tentacles trailed down the arm, their tips curling over her wrist and the back of her hand.

Penee crinkled her brow and shook her head. "I don't know where—"

La landed on her shoulder. *"You listen."* She fluttered her gossamer wings.

The Stannag lowered beneath the water. A column of fog formed and misted away, leaving an opaque Aahana standing on the shore. Sadness dripped from the fire-opal eyes and quivered in her full lips.

"I have a message for the VarTerel and the Bearer of the Sign of Incirrata. Those you seek are with the K'iin in a hidden valley. You know what you must do to free Neul Isle and its people. Find my heart and soul. Free me to return to my homeland and my family. When you do, my tears of happiness will save your friends."

Aahana, Daughter of Abellona the Sun Queen of Soputto, misted into nothing.

La glided skyward.

The incirrata's tentacle touched Penee's cheek and came to rest on the tattooed forearm. A hissed buzz whispered. It withdrew the tentacle and dove from sight, leaving rippling water in its wake.

Penee rubbed her forearm and watched the tattoo fade. "Where did the tattoo came from, Brielle?"

"I believe I know. Think, Pen."

She pulled back her shirt sleeve. Irstant's flesh-colored mail stretched over her arm like a second skin. A faint memory snapped into focus. "Irstant."

Brie helped her to her feet and kissed her cheek. "We need to find a safe spot to spend the night. I can't imagine we want to be wandering Neul after dark. The Forest of Deora is a long hike northeast of here."

The Luna Moth alighted on Abarax's over-large hand. The Astican shrunk to human size. "In the trees nearby, La found a good place with a spring. She will lead us to it."

Brie trailed after the Astican.

Penee stared over the lagoon. A break in the clouds created a pool of light on the water. The incirrata surfaced at its center and slowly submerged.

I will find you, Irstant. I promise.

B rie stood in the grouping of oak and evergreen nestled into the curve of rugged, lichen-covered hills not far from the lagoon. The faint tingle of the Star and the warm breath on her hand suggested safety. Still, she checked and rechecked. Her mental scan confirmed the area would be safe, at least for the night.

While Abarax built raised sleeping pallets from fallen trees and evergreen boughs, Brie helped Penee harvest edible plants. Coranna's careful instruction had paid off for all of them. The shirt Penee had removed to use as a basket soon bulged with greens: kupa, Soputton spinach and celery, and horopito, a spicy yellow and red speckled leaf for Abarax.

By the time they returned to camp, the Astican had not only built two pallets, but had constructed a lean-to-shelter to protect them from the weather. Between the sleeping pallets, it had covered the ground with evergreen boughs. Angelic innocence accompanied the explanation that in ludoc form it would *rest* there and guard them.

Penee smiled at their winged companion and held up a horopito leaf. "I brought you a treat."

The Astican sniffed the yellow and red leaf, bit off the tip, and crunched it between its front teeth. Delight registered. "Spicy! Thank you, Penesert."

After washing their bounty in the underground spring they found gurgling up between a spill of tan stones and a gash in the hillside, Brie started a small fire in a pit Abarax had built. Its warmth drew her companions, and soon they gathered around it, enjoying a feast of fresh greens.

"Any idea why visitors to Neul are never seen again, Penee?" Brie tossed a stem into the fire.

"No one knows. People choose not to come here rather than risk their lives." She touched her forearm. "Do you think the Stannag is the culprit?"

Brie stirred the fire with a twig and reviewed their contact with the incirrata. "It is not a killer of men. What else inhabits Neul? Are there dangerous animals?"

Firelight sparkled in Penee's eyes, highlighting the amber specks in the green one. She blinked and straightened. "There is a spider called the ipōkat. Its bite is poisonous, but it's rarely seen. The K'iin believe it is a mystical being who takes the shape of a spider. Barlet used to read Soputton mythology to me. Stories of the K'iin where some of my favorites."

Brie tossed several small sticks on the fire. "Is there one in particular that has stayed with you?"

"My favorite is the legend of Kat and Ipō. Would you like to hear it?"

"I'd love it."

After staring into the distance for some time, Penee began.

"The ipōkat is named after two demi-gods, Kat, a female, and Ipō, a male. In K'iin mythology, the gods sent this young pair of demi-gods to Neul in spider form to spin the web of life and to create a sacred tribe to inhabit and protect the island. Each spider wove a web in a separate tree. When the time of mating arrived, the spiders danced their dance, and the male retreated to its web. The next morning, Ipō awoke in human form. Over the next several turnings, he watched and waited, longing for Kat to assume her human shape.

"As her time drew near, the female spider prepared her web to receive the eggs. Working feverishly, she spun an egg sac, pressed her abdomen to it, and deposited the thirteen eggs requested by the gods.

"While she worked, Ipō's anticipation grew. Soon, Kat would join him. Soon...

"Instead of returning to her human shape when the job was complete, Kat maintained her arachnid form in order to protect the eggs. Every turning Ipō arrived beneath the web. Disappointment turned to jealousy. In a fit of anger, he stole the egg sac and hid it in a hollow tree.

"Frantic to find it, the female spider spun a slender silk thread and dropped onto his shoulder. He begged her to forget about the sac and join him. When she refused, he threatened to destroy the eggs. Her stinger sank deep into his neck. He cried out, sank to his knees, and shifted. On his eight arachnid legs, he scurried into hiding.

"Angered by his treachery, the gods removed the female and the egg sac to a tree in a fertile valley on the opposite side of the island. The female secured the eggs to the tree and punctured a hole in the woven sac. One at a time, tiny spiders crawled through the hole, scrambled over her, and clung to a silk thread dangling from her spinneret. She spun the thread longer and longer. When it touched the ground, the tiny spider convulsed and became human. The first spider hatched was the shaman. He assisted each newly hatched spider until thirteen K'iin waited beneath the tree. The Shaman plucked the exhausted female from her perch and placed her on the ground. He knelt, cupped his hands around her, and blew the breath of life over her. A wave of his hand brought Kat's motionless human body into existence. The K'iin, six men and six women, knelt around her and chanted with their shaman. To the song sung by her progeny, Kat's spirit left the body. She hovered above them projecting her love and vanished. The K'iin buried her physical being and built a shrine in her honor."

Penee grew quiet.

Abarax's scales whispered with impatience. "Where did the goddess go? And the male spider? Did it live or die?"

"The legend says Kat returned to spider form and went in search of her mate and true love. It does not tell us much about Ipō. To this turning, Kat continues her eternal search. She has been known to wander in both human and spider form. The K'iin are the only people on Soputto immune to the ipōkat's bite."

"What a beautiful legend." Brie warmed her hands over the fire.

Penee followed her example, rubbed her hands together, and gripped her knees. "I'm not ruling out Kat as a danger. Stories abound about how terrifying she is. Neul has a few odd creatures like the tuatara, but nothing that preys on humans. If La will keep watch, we should be able to sleep without worrying."

Brie shivered. Mist drifted through the trees and nestled around them. She placed two more dry branches on the fire. After taking care of her personal needs, she lay down on her sleeping pallet, then nodded. "Surprisingly comfortable, Abarax. Thanks."

"You are welcome, Brielle AsTar. Let us sleep while we can."

Penee chimed in her thanks and curled into a tight ball.

At the end of her pallet, Brie felt the warmth of her invisible safety net nestle next to her ankles and gave herself permission to rest.

31

La reveled in the tranquility of the mist covering Neul. The only thing that could make her happier was moonlight. She considered flying skyward until the clouds lay below her, but something kept her near Abarax and her Humans. Flitting from tree to tree, she came to rest across from Brie's sleeping pallet.

Since her forced stay in Mittkeer, La noticed a developing talent for discerning the invisible, including Brielle's protector. Although the covert fox at Brie's feet remained unworried, La could not relax. A restless circle of the clearing ended as the fox's golden eyes blinked open.

Brie's protector lifted its head. Its pointed nose sniffed.

La flew to a lower branch. Her long proboscis flicked to its full length. Something unusual tainted the night air.

Black ears twitching, the fox pushed up to its haunches, eye fixed on the forest

An ethereal feminine figure floated free of the shadowy trees. Large, mint green eyes gazed at the fire pit, lifted to rest on La, and lowered to the fox. She drifted closer to the fire. Long, strawberry blonde hair glinted golden in the flickering light. Her attention returned to La. She lifted a hand. *"Come, pretty moth. I won't harm you."* A wistful expression wiped the sadness from her face.

La fluttered to the hand. Her feet tasted the filmy flesh. Nothing alarmed her.

"I have a favor to ask, Luna Moth. Your companions are here to rescue their friends. I will help if you promise to help free my friend, Aahana."

La's wings trembled. *"Who you?"*

Sadness returned to the lovely face. *"I am Kat, Demi-Goddess of the Small Creatures of K'iin. You heard my story from the Bearer of the Incirrata."*

La's wings quivered. *"How I help?"*

"You will know when the time comes, pretty moth." Kat floated to the foot of Brie's pallet. *"Be wary, Red Fox. Angry ghosts wander Neul Isle. They sense the power of the VarTerel and the Bearer of the Incirrata."*

Her luminous presence wavered. *"I will return with the rising sun to guide your friends to the Forest of Deora."* Mint green eyes, the last things to lose their luster, held a hint of secrets to come.

The fox curled up and rested its nose between its paws. La spiraled upward, landed on an evergreen branch, and gazed at her companions from multi-faceted eyes.

👁 👁

Penee woke early, slipped from camp, and walked to the shore of the lagoon. Dim light filtering through layers of tear-laden clouds tinted the surface a pale pewter gray. At the edge of the tide pool, she sat cross-legged, trying to imagine how difficult it must be for Aahana to have lost so much time with her husband and child. Half a centurial cycle had passed. Both her loved ones had moved beyond reach. She had missed taking part in so many special, beautiful moments of their lives.

The water at the pool's rim trembled. Two golden ovals rose above the surface. A pale tentacle writhed toward her, caressed her tear-damp cheek, and withdrew. The oval eyes swiveled to peer past her.

Penee picked out the glint of pale green wings and raised a hand. The tickle of La's tiny feet made her smile. "Good morning, lovely La."

The moth quivered. *"Kat waits."*

"Kat waits? Who? Oh. You mean the Goddess Kat, don't you? I hardly think she—"

The incirrata's soft buzz hummed. A wet tentacle nudged her knee.

La fluttered to her shoulder. *"Stannag say: She named Rina. Kat real."*

Penee stroked the tentacle with a hesitant finger. "I'm going, Rina."

The incirrata glided away from the shoreline and dove into deep water.

Penee found Brie and Abarax conversing with a filmy figure with strawberry-blonde hair and large, glistening eyes the color of mint leaves. "Kat?"

The elegant specter turned her beautiful head. Her high, breathy words whispered through the mist. "Bearer of the Incirrata, I am Kat, the Isle of Neul's Goddess of Small Creatures."

Brie handed Penee her pack. "Kat's leading us to the Forest of Deora."

Penee considered the goddess. "Why would *you* help us?"

"You bear the sign of my friend, Aahana. The VarTerel is the only one who can find the crystal jar and return Aahana's heart and soul." Sadness engulfed her. "To gain my freedom, I must help." Her filmy shape trembled. "Speaking aloud diminishes my ability to stay visible." She faded. A small spider coalesced in her place.

La hovered. *"Abarax carry her. She direct me."*

The Astican placed the spider in its cupped hand, and the strange procession trouped from the trees into a wide gully. Abarax hesitated.

La flitted to his shoulder. *"Kat say follow."* She caressed his cheek with a delicate wing and continued down the gully.

The Astican, muttering under its breath, trekked after her.

Penee hurried to keep up. The urge to glance back gave her a rare glimpse of a fox herding Brie ahead of it. She nodded to herself. *At least we are well-protected.*

Brie peered up at the sky. Clouds rolling down the obsidian mountainsides obscured the height of gray-black dunes. The desire to see Neul Isle beneath a blue, sunny sky overwhelmed her.

A fox nose nudged her. The Star stung. Searching the misty terrain, she sent a telepathic warning. *"We are about to encounter trouble. I'm not certain what."*

The procession came to a halt. La landed on Abarax's shoulder. *"Stay."* She flew deeper into the gully.

The Star's intense throbbing continued to warn of danger.

La shot back to Abarax. *"Beware!"*

Penee made a strangled sound. "By the gods of Soputto!"

Near the end of the gully, the opaque form of a brown and yellow spider, bigger than the fox, descended a rocky ridge. It crawled over the top of a boulder and leapt to the ground. Eight powerful legs ate up the distance between it and them. A steady clicking increased in frequency the closer it came.

La fluttered into the air. *"Kat say put down."*

Abarax placed the small spider on the ground and moved away.

La darted skyward and hovered. *"Beware, Goddess!"*

Enlarging to match its counterpart's size, the black and red spider stood its ground and clicked a response. Radiance engulfed it. Kat's ethereal being materialized. "Ipō! Why have you hidden from me?"

The brown spider whipped its abdomen around. A silk thread shot from its spinneret and wrapped around Kat's plasmic essence. A second thread caught her. Loop after sticky loop encircled her until, like a fly in a web, she could not move.

Penee started forward. Brie seized her wrist. "This is their fight. Watch."

Ipō's spider form reeled Kat in. Pushing her to the ground, it crawled on top of her, its fangs on either side of her throat.

Kat's loving gaze remained fixed on the spider. "I will not fight you, Ipō. My mother instincts could not allow you to hurt the eggs. Apologize to the Gods. They will set us free. End my immortal existence, and you condemn yourself to eternity in spider form."

Dense fog roiled up to enshroud them. A fox's mouth closing over Brie's wrist urged her toward the trees. Abarax herded Penee after them.

La squeaked a series of high-pitched sounds and flew to the far end of the gully.

Spider legs shot outward from the turbid fog. Wind blew over the lagoon, dispersed the murkiness, and tossed the opaque, brown spider free of its prey.

Tension sharpened. Aahana's shout from the lagoon floated down the gully. "If you die, Goddess Kat, Ipō will not stop at your death. He will end the lives of all who have befriended you."

The wind gusted one final time. In the ensuing stillness, Brie gripped Penee's hand. Every nerve straining, she stared down the gully.

The brown spider twitched and struggled to regain its footing. Aggression shone in its four black eyes.

Kat stepped free of her silken bonds. "Do not think I will allow you to hurt anyone else, Ipō. My love for you is unending. Even if I am forced to fight you, it will not die. Forgive me, Ipō. Forgive—"

The brown spider launched through the air. It hit only emptiness and tumbled thorax over head. Scuttling around to face her, it pressed its abdomen low to the ground.

Kat's shift to female spider left her towering above him.

Penee gasped. Brie rubbed the tingling Star.

The Astican's wings unfurled and wrapped around them. La streaked down the gully to alight on its shoulder.

The male spider leapt forward. Snagging it mid-air, the female flung it to the ground and clambered over its stunned body. Working her spinnerets with the skill of a master weaver, she encased it in a silken cocoon. Fangs sunk into head and thorax. Writhing in anger and pain, the male spider struggled to escape, fought for its freedom, and finally lay motionless.

The female backed away. A tremor shook its body. Kat materialized and hurried to the male's side. The silken cocoon fell away. A dull white light flared around them.

Brie strained to see. Dissolving light left two humans visible. A man as handsome as Kat was beautiful, lay with his head in her lap. Her tears dripped onto his ashen cheeks. The anger that distorted his expression into hate morphed to understanding. Love glowed. Kat kissed his forehead, his cheeks, his mouth. "I love you, Ipō. The gods come for you. May eternal time bless you and keep you."

His hand clutched hers. "I love you, Kat." Death-weighted eyelids closed. A shaft of iridescent light shot from the clouds, enclosed his body, and lifted it through a lightning-carved tunnel in the clouds. Ipō, God of Small Creatures, vanished.

Thunder rocked Neul Isle. The churning clouds calmed. Kat raised her face. A corona of light enveloped her. She bowed her head. The corona subsided, leaving her in a body of flesh and bone.

Brie sighed. The Star of Truth no longer throbbed. Penee sniffed and wiped her tears. Abarax furled its wings and cupped protective hands around La.

Wind from the lagoon dispersed the mist in the gully. The demi-goddess signaled them to join her. "We must go." Without waiting, she made her way to the end of the chasm through a coulee between a high plateau and a range of hills. After a short hike over easy terrain, they turned into a narrow gorge with towering escarpments on either side. High overhead clouds spilled over the rims and drifted down the rock face.

The uneven ground in the dim light caused a whimper of dread from Penee.

Kat performed a graceful about face. "I'm sure you are thirsty and tired. Let's rest. At the end of the gorge, you'll be able to refill your water bottles."

Brie perched on a boulder, pulled out her canteen, and deposited her pack on the ground.

Penee rummaged for hers and drank deeply. "Thanks for the break, Kat. I was parched."

Abarax, in bat form, darted down the gorge.

With a sigh of satisfaction, Brie wiped the mouth of her canteen and offered it to Kat. "I believe you might need this."

The goddess swallowed a sip, looked surprised and then delighted. She took a long drink. "I had forgotten how good water is."

Brie smiled. "Please drink your fill."

"Thank you, VarTerel." Kat quenched her thirst and returned it.

Brie contemplated the exquisite face. "Tell us what happened. I believe you have been a ghost for some time. Now you are human."

"The gods of Soputto have given me the gift of life for living up to my responsibilities, even though it meant ending my true love's existence." She hung her head. "I could not let Ipō keep killing."

"Oh," Penee breathed. "I understand. After the mist covered the island, he killed anyone who came here."

Filled with a plea for understanding, Kat's gaze met hers. "I tried to find him, to stop him..." She lifted her hands in a gesture of entreaty. "I failed so many." Tears splashed unnoticed. "I could not allow him to kill anyone else. Now, I have lost him forever."

Brie took her hands. "You have always trusted your gods?"

"Yes." The small word quivered with emotion.

"Keep trusting, Kat."

The slap of leather scales announced Abarax's return. "Can you use DiMensionery here, VarTerel?"

Brie repacked her canteen. "Why?"

"A rockslide blocks the gorge at the far end. It would be best if we could teleport."

Penee joined the group. "Wish we knew where Skultar and the Mocendi are."

Kat cleared her throat. "I believe I can help." Her eyes glazed over. Satisfaction animated her features. "No one has arrived on Neul Isle since you did. No boats have crossed into the island's sacred waters."

Brie studied the goddess. "To teleport us safely, I have to identify where I'm going. Can you place an image in my mind?"

"I can do better than that. Hold hands in a circled. La, please sit on my shoulder." She regarded the group. "Ready?"

32

A shaft of sunlight penetrated the clouds, shot straight down into the gorge, and pooled around the goddess. Kat clasped Brie's hand on one side, Penee's on the other. Abarax completed the circle. The light enclosed them. At a signal from Kat, the shaft opened a tunnel that transported them above the clouds covering the island. The endless blue overhead meeting a field of clouds below created a breathtaking panorama. Low in the sky to the Southwest, the sun stained fluffy white a deep gold. To the Northeast, the coming of night crept forward.

Penee caught her eye. "Beautiful"

They descended. Light pooling like a spotlight on the clouds intensified. The tunnel opened. Their feet touched the ground at the spotlight's center.

Kat raised her head. "You are at your destination." She caught her breath. "I must leave you here. My mother NáDúr, Goddess of All Nature, summons me to her side." The shaft lifted her upward. "Search near the foot of the mountains." She grew fainter. "Save Aahana and Rina, and you will save your friends."

The shaft and the goddess dispersed into radiant specks, floating like embers into the night sky. With a low rumble, the clouds flowed together.

La landed on Brie's shoulder.

Abarax wrinkled its brow. "Where did she go?"

"She returned to her home." Brie shivered. Kat had been a warming presence. With her gone, the return of the cloud cover leached heat and light from everything. "It is late." She surveyed the surrounding area.

They stood in a field on the shore of a small lake bordering a floodplain. One end cozied up to the mist-draped Forest of Deora, the other to a cluster of cloud-laden hills. Brie ventured to the edge of the trees.

"I'll make sure it's safe. Don't enter the woods until I come back." A fox trotted into the dimness.

Penee walked over to her. "Did I see your protector?"

"You did, Pen. I wish he hadn't promised to stay out of sight."

"So do I." Penee peered into the forest. "This place sure feels spooky. Why don't—" She pointed. "I guess he's changed his mind."

The fox darted from the trees. Esán materialized at Brie's side.

She shot him a penetrating look. "Aren't you supposed to stay hidden? Won't Relevart be angry."

He hugged her. "I'm happy to see you, too." When she didn't speak, he released her and offered his hand. "Hi, Penee, I'm Esán."

Her grin stretching from ear to ear, she touched her palm to his. "I'm delighted to meet you. I'll give you a minute."

"I *am* glad you're here." Brie shot him a tentative look. "Please don't put yourself at risk for me."

"The time has come for me to follow my heart; to pay attention to the Seeds of Carsilem. They guide my life's journey. Relevart will understand." He hugged her to him.

Her head on his broad chest, she listened to his muffled heartbeat. His love warmed her. He tipped her face to receive a quick kiss.

"We need to talk with your companions." Keeping one arm around her waist, he guided her to where Penee, a knowing expression on her face, waited beside Abarax.

The Astican touched a fist to his heart. "It is good you are here, Esán Efre. Do you join us, or must you still remain hidden?"

Esán returned the heart salute. "I will most often be in fox form, but tonight we will need all the masculine energy we can muster. Ghosts of the men Ipō killed haunt the forest. Their anger leads them on a search for revenge. Most gather at the foot of the mountains outside a group of caverns. Others roam the woods. I suggest we find a camping spot in the hills at the other end of the lake."

La fluttered from Abarax's shoulder to hover in front of Esán. Her eye spots deepened in color.

He offered his palm. "I am Esán." Her tiny feet touched down. Her wings trembled. "Thank you, La, for taking care of Brielle. She is important to me."

Hovering once more, she flicked her proboscis out and in. *"You love?"*

He chuckled. "I love Brie very much."

La fluttered to Brie. *"You love?"*

Blood rushed to Brie's cheeks. She managed a flustered smiled. "I love Esán."

Penee grinned. "This has been quite a turning. Let's find someplace to camp. You can build a fire. I'll scrounge up some food?"

A strange wailing drifted from the forest.

She shuddered. "Sure hope they won't be serenading us all night."

Glad for a distraction, Brie slipped her hand into Esán's and walked with him toward the hills. Tonight, at least, she would enjoy his company and his counsel.

❦   ❦

Penee walked into camp, her shirt bulging with Neul's bounty. Brie and Esán sat by the fire, their faces animated, their unwavering attention on each other.

Abarax stacked pieces of dry wood in a pile and added a log to the fire. It sat in the grass, its wings trailing behind it, tossing dried twigs into the pit. Each addition caused a burst of small flames that encouraged the bigger pieces at the center to burn brighter.

Penee watched, mesmerized by each flare of warmth. She glanced up at the Astican. "Where's La?"

"She is doing some scouting." It placed two larger sticks on the fire. "Soon she will join us."

Esán cast a hungry glance Penee's direction. "You found dinner?"

Penee arranged her shirt to show off the feast of greens. "Help yourselves. I'll grab the canteens."

The crunch of crisp Soputton celery and the crackle of dried wood burning drifted through camp. Penee drank from her canteen and wiped her mouth on the back of her hand. "Barlet used to tell me food never tasted as good as it tastes in the wild. Now, I believe him." Curiosity nudged. She looked from Brie to Esán. "You seem to have a lot to catch up on."

The warm flicker of the fire turned Brie's curls to burnished copper and highlighted her happiness. "Esán has been in seclusion on Myrrh for almost two sun cycles. I've been on DerTah training with Wolloh Espyro."

Penee tossed a twig into the fire pit. "What's it like, training to be a DiMensioner?"

Brie pursed her lips, then shrugged. "It's arduous, exacting work. You've been experiencing some of the same things I've gone through...learning to shift shape, telepathy, teleporting. Wolloh is a task master and perfectionist. I'm lucky."

Penee broke a stick in half and flipped a piece into the fire. "Guess *I* am in training." The other half followed and burst into flame. "What about you, Esán? Why two sun cycles in seclusion?"

He finished his wild celery. "My home planet is Tao Spirian in the Clenaba Rolas System. It's a small, ocean-covered planet with a scattering of islands. Residents are attuned to sacred law. The concept of living in harmony with all things directs their lives. Over the course of our history, the deities of my people bestow the power of the Seeds of Carsilem on individual Tao Spirians. My father carries one seed. I was born with dual seeds, which is rare.

"Seclusion allows the talents engendered by the seeds to quicken and mature. It also provides the bearer with the opportunity to come to terms with what Carsilem offers, and the responsibilities it brings with it."

For a time, he sat in a thoughtful silence.

Penee observed him with interest. She liked what she saw: shoulder length hair the color of honey straight from the hive, stormy eyes that seemed to shift from blue to gray as she watched. He was medium height and well built. What intrigued her, however, was not his good looks. The immense power clothed in velvet-soft gentleness, unprecedented in the men in her life, attracted her.

He intertwined his fingers with Brie's. His deep feelings for her were obvious and honest. Penee lowered her gaze to hide an unexpected stab of envy. She realized when she raised them that Esán understood. His knowing smile warmed her. She climbed to her feet. "Think I'll take a walk before bedding down."

Abarax stood and shook his wings. "We will walk together, Penesert. Then I will shift to ludoc cat, and we will sleep."

Walking beside the Astican, she could not help but marvel at how much her life had changed. *For the first time, I can choose my own friends and make my own decisions.* Not even the pressure to find Irstant and Henri or the enemies tracking them could take away her newfound sense of freedom.

Arm in arm with the Abarax, she strolled farther up the ravine. Fog rolling down the hillside turned them back toward camp. They reached it to find the fire banked for the night. Abarax shifted to ludoc cat and stretched out on its side. She curled up and nestled into its warm fur. Esán, in fox form, stretched out next to Brie. He sniffed the air, then rested his nose on his paws.

Penee ignored a jealous twinge. Fatigue dropped her into a restless sleep. Sometime later, she woke for the umpteenth time to a moaning lament floating over the island. Each time it woke her, it seemed closer.

The lament grew more demanding. She slipped from beneath Abarax's wing to squat by the fire. A low, wailing moan made her shiver. Warming her hands over the dying embers, she fought down her rising fear.

Forsaking the fire's warmth, she made her way to the mouth of the shallow vale. An oppressive quiet, both tactile and heavy, chilled her. The hair on the back of her neck prickled. Instinct developed over years of running warned her to retreat.

A silent about-face and soundless footsteps carried her toward camp. Something cold and clammy brushed her check. She sped up her pace. Further up the track, indistinct figures blocked her path. Behind her, she picked out several more.

Wind rushing down the valley thinned the fogged. An opaque male figure floated in front of her. Penee suppressed a shudder. "What do you want?"

A chorus of moans filled the night. The eerie companions crowded around her.

Fatigue nudged Brie into a fitful slumber. Dreams carried her deeper. The morose moaning of lost souls led her through a labyrinth of places and times, where unmitigated sadness tainted everything. Cries of horror filled her head. Human bones rained down on her and scattered at her feet. An abrupt awakening left her fighting to reorient.

A hand clamped over her mouth. "Don't make a sound." Esán's whisper grounded her in the present. "They took Penee. Abarax is tracking them."

"Who took Penee?" She noticed for the first time the pitch-black coldness.

Esán pulled her to her feet. His arms closed around her; his cheek pressed to hers. "La woke Abarax, or we wouldn't have known until morning."

Encircled by his arms, she reviewed the maze she had travelled in her dreams. Inspiration made her giddy. "The ghosts of Ipō's victims captured her. We have to go to Deora."

"I know." He squeezed her hand. "The Seeds will take us there. I'll be close by."

Everything blurred. She arrived, a red fox at her side, just short of the Forest's border. Evergreens and Dast oaks intermingled to form a place of shadowed mystery. A low chorus of moans, replicating the ones in her dream, added to the eeriness.

La landed on her palm. *"Penee need."*

Brie glanced at the fox. "You lead, La. We'll follow."

The Luna Moth shot ahead. The fox trotted behind her. Grateful for the white tip of his tail, Brie hiked after him.

They had covered a good distance when La alighted on the low branch of a pine. Brie knelt beside the fox and peered through the ominous darkness. At the foot of a mountain, Penee fumbled with an ancient kerosene lantern. The wick burst to life. A slight adjustment and she lowered the chimney.

The glow pushed four opaque male figures back into a scattered semi-circle.

She held up the lantern. "Thank you for the light." Her calm gaze moved from figure to figure. "Why did you bring me here?"

"We wish to be released from this existence. To do so, we need the help of a VarTerel. All we ask is that you hear our story."

More opaque figures floated into the clearing.

Brie counted fifteen. All were men. All wore the clothing of different eras. They had died, and yet their sorrow lived in them, a thing as tangible as the fox at her feet.

Hopelessness filled Penee's voice. "I am not a VarTerel. I'm so sorry."

Moans of disappointment shook the mountainside and trembled through the treetops of Deora.

Brie, with Esán at her side, stepped free of the trees. Sorrowful faces turned her direction. The moans ceased.

"I am a VarTerel."

Her words incited a cheer of relief. The ghostly figures floated apart, opening a passage to Penee.

Esán's hand on her elbow gave her the courage to walk into the lantern's glow. Fifteen ghosts gathered around them.

Penee whispered, "I'm so glad you're here."

Brie stood between her companions. "This is my friend Esán, the Bearer of Dual Seeds of Carsilem. He wields a power similar to mine. You have sensed Penee's gifts. Tell us your story."

The oldest man spoke up. "We must confer." The ghosts floated into a grouping at the edge of the forest.

La fluttered to Brie's shoulder. *"Abarax near."*

"Thank you, La."

The moth flew to an oak tree where a bat clung to its rough bark.

"Let's sit." Esán guided her to a large, smooth rock. Penee chose one near it and set the lantern on ground between them.

Grateful for the company of friends, Brie watched the ghosts drift her direction.

33

The oldest man hovered in front of them. "We call ourselves the Púca. It means ghost in the language of our ancestors. My name is Sia Ceari. Once upon a time, I owned a boat and supported my family by fishing the waters off the coast of Dast. Most of my companions were fishermen. Others came to Neul out of curiosity. Some came to find lost loved ones. All of us met our deaths at the hands of a male ipōkat, a spider controlled by a member of the K'iin, a would-be shaman called Tura.

"Tura's anger at his people and the Stannag smoldered for the almost half of one centurial cycle. His goal—to make certain anyone setting foot on his island never left it alive—eventually drove him to madness."

Sia Ceari beckoned a younger ghost to join him. "This is Ardtús. He was the first to perish at the hands of Tura. He left behind a son, a daughter, a lovely wife, and a community that valued him."

Ardtús wore his sadness like a badge of honor. He bowed his head and floated to the side.

Another ghost drifted closer.

"This is the last man to die. We call him Bás. He is the youngest. His family deserves to know he died an honorable death.

"All of us have a personal story, lives filled with loved ones, and the desire to join them in the ever-world. Until you return the Stannag's heart and soul and complete the ceremony of release, we're trapped in this dimension on Neul Isle.

"We want it understood the Stannag incirrata of Neul had nothing to do with our deaths, nor did she cause our boats to sink. She honored us by burying our dead bodies in an undersea cavern. We are as attached to our bodies as we are to Tura. You, VarTerel, and your friends are our last hope."

Quiet settled over those at the foot of the San Crúil Mountains. The Púca gathered together to one side, their figures less distinct in the dim light penetrating through the clouds. Brie ached for each one and for the families who had never achieved closure.

Penee's brooding expression suggested questions to come. Brie stared at her hands. *I need space to digest what they have shared—time to determine if I can help. Where are you when I need you, Relevart? Wolloh? I wish I could talk to you, Aunt Henri.*

La's wings whispered next to her ear. *"Come."*

Brie gazed after the Luna Moth, removed a hand-light from her pack, and came to her feet. "I require some time alone. I won't be long."

La's pale green wings stood out against the granite gray of the mountainside. She hovered and flew on. Brie trained the hand-light's beam on the rough ground and hiked around a cascade of volcanic rock resembling a waterfall.

La waited by a narrow crevice tunneling under the mountain. Her soft squeak urged Brie to hurry.

Brie picked up her pace. Rough stone gave way to smoother terrain. The fissure widened into a dim open area lit by a wide crack high overhead. Playing the beam of the hand-light from walls to the ground, she inspected a space the size of a small entryway.

In a gaping cave mouth opposite her, an iridescent oval materialized and transformed. Henrietta held her spectacles in one hand and tapped the palm of the other.

"It is good to see you, niece. Although Irstant and I are not yet in danger, time is growing short. *You* have the power to save us; to release Tura and the men he has killed to the Soputton ever-world."

Her tapping grew less distinct as she became translucent. "Penee and Esán will assist you. Trust your heart, niece." Henri pocketed her spectacles. Her staff flashed into her hand. "You will have need of this." She leaned it against the arch and shimmered into nothing. Her voice floated from the darkness. "You are every bit the VarTerel I am, Brielle AsTar."

P enee, despondent for several reasons, shivered in the damp cold of dawn. Gazing up at the cloud cover, she wondered if she would ever see the sky again. Her left arm, aching for the first time since Rina touched it, distracted her. *Where is Brie?*

Across from her, Esán gazed up at the cloud-covered mountainside, his expression dreamy. His calm acceptance of Brie's lengthy absence should have eased her concern. *Should—I hate that word. She stifled a groan. I hate not knowing.* She ruffled her hair. "Aren't you worried about Brie?"

"She's fine, Penee. In fact, I expect La to come for us at any moment."

"You're alright with her being alone somewhere unprotected?"

Amusement made his eyes gleam steely blue. "Brielle can take care of herself. She would resent it if we decided she couldn't."

"Where's the Astican? I saw it fly by." Penee reined in a desire to wink. "You didn't, by chance, send it after her?"

He laughed. "You're good, Penesert! I sent Abarax, but don't tell Brie."

His merriment eased her tension. "I like you, Esán Efre."

He picked up the lantern. "I think we're about to be summoned." He pulled her to her feet.

Sia Ceari approached with the Púca clustering after him. "The VarTerel is ready."

La shot to Penee's shoulder. *"Brie say come."* Flying parallel to the steep granite face, she rounded a cascade of lava frozen by time and disappeared into a crevice leading under the mountain.

Penee hesitated. The Púca floated past her. Esán clasped her hand. "It's alright. Brielle is just out of sight. Let's find out what she's discovered."

Grateful for the lantern's warm glow, Penee hiked over the rocky ground. A slight curve in the trail deposited them in a space much higher than it was wide, where Brie waited amidst the murmuring figures of the Púca.

At their approach, the ghosts opened a path.

Brie hurried to meet them. "Aunt Henri was here. She says the three of us working together can free the Púca and the Stannag. Sia Ceari knows where Tura hides with the jar. The Púca can only guide us part way. Then we'll be on our own."

A small bat squeaked from its place on the cave mouth behind her. She shot Esán a coy look. "I noticed you sent a bodyguard."

Innocence cloaked him. "Only because I love you, not because I don't trust you to take care of yourself."

Brie blew him a kiss. "I need to confer with Sia Ceari. I promise to stay in sight."

Penee witnessed the exchange with a sigh. *Someday*— "Ouch. My arm is hurting. What do you suppose that means?"

Esán reached for the arm. "May I touch it?"

She held it out. The gentleness of his examination surprised her. When he released it, it no longer burned.

"What did you do?" She cradled it next to her chest.

"I asked the Seeds to ease the pain. They told me your tattoo holds much magic. It ties you to the Stannag and to something else that is unclear. Once you learn the complete secret, the tattoo will cease to hurt. Right now, it's a signal we're closing in on the crystal jar."

A human-sized Astican materializing created a startled reaction amongst the Púca. Some flashed from sight, some floated out of range, others crowded together and stared.

Brie waved them over. "Don't be afraid. This is an Astican. It is our friend."

Abarax bowed his head. "I am Abarax, an Astican from the planet of TreBlaya. The Universal VarTerel appointed me to protect Brie and her companions. It is my honor to stand at her side and to help you move on to your ever-world."

Sia Ceari responded. "We are grateful for your help, Astican."

Ghosts shimmered back into sight. Sia Ceari motioned Ardtús to his side.

"The cavern where Tura hides lies some distance from here. In the past, it was a violent place. I suggest Ardtús show the Astican the way. Once they make sure the approach to the cavern is safe and all is quiet within, we will lead you to it."

Ardtús nodded. Abarax assumed his bat shape. They streaked through the cave opening into the darkness.

Penee edged closer. "What made the cavern violent?"

Sia Ceari faded and steadied. "Before the time of the clouds over Neul, a group of younger K'iin worshipped the demon Scáth of the Soputton netherworld. Feranni Caverns became their playground. The Scáth withdrew many cycles ago, but rumors suggest they reappear during times of upheaval and change."

Esán drew Brie into the circle of his arm. She rested her head on his shoulder.

Penee stared at the cave entrance. Her arm stung. Her heart ached. *Why do I feel so alone? I am with friends who care about me. Why—*

Abarax and Ardtús reappeared, chasing her gloom into hiding.

👁 👁

The cave mouth, gaping and dark, did not invite entry. Brie hesitated. Aunt Henri's words—'You are every bit the VarTerel I am, Brielle AsTar'—strengthened her resolve.

Sia Ceari, La, and the Púca floated ahead. Esán ducked through and held the kerosene lantern higher. She stepped into its yellow glow, drew a breath, and moved into the darkness beyond. When Penee and Abarax were beside her, Esán once again took the lead. Sia Ceari had warned them the hand-light might attract unwanted attention. The lantern, more common to Neul, would be less apt to invite danger.

Close to the mouth, the cave narrowed to a tunnel. The slope of the low ceiling became steeper, forcing them to crawl on hands and knees.

Sudden darkness and Esán's frustrated exclamation halted their progress. "Brielle, follow my voice. The lantern's gone out. You are almost here. Keep coming."

Heavy darkness intensified her anxiety. Rough stone walls crept closer; the ceiling pressed lower. Penee's panicked breathing right at her heels didn't help.

Brie swallowed the fear lumping in her throat. She forced herself to keep crawling.

The walls falling away and Esán's hands guiding her to standing, helped her to regain her composure.

A windy howl increased to a full-fledged wail. Sia Ceari shouted over the roar. "Hurry. It's not safe to stay here for long."

Abarax called from the tunnel. "Go. I will shape a bat and follow."

"Sia Ceari, I need to use the hand-light." Penee's voice shook. "I'll set it to dim."

"No light." Sia Ceari's words felt cool on Brie's cheek. "Make a single line. We'll guide you. The grotto is not big. Once we are on the far side, you can relight the lantern."

Esán squeezed her hand. "Grab my belt, Brielle. Penee, hold on to Brie."

Surrounded by Púca, they advanced one step at a time through the pitch-black tempest cycloning around them. Sia Ceari, at the head of the cavalcade, called out. "Púca, ahead!"

Feathers of coolness brushed Brie's face. Wind gusts plummeted her back. Esán pulled her around a corner into stillness so intense it stole her breath. She doubled over, gasping.

Penee stumbled into her. "Where did *that* wind come from?"

The lantern sprang to life. Esán held it high. Púca gathered at the edge of the pool of light. Sia Ceari hovered closest.

"The wind rises from an underground grotto. It fights to be free of its prison." The Púca faded. "We must leave you here. The passage behind us will take you to the Cavern of Feranni. The Astican knows the way. Ardtús scouted ahead. All is quiet. You'll find Tura on the far side. Beware. His anger heightens the power he wields. We will rejoin you when you have Aahana's jar, and you are clear of the cavern." He raised a hand in farewell.

The Púca had vanished.

Penee peered at her. "Do you know what to expect in Feranni?"

"No. Abarax, where are you? La?"

A bat flew down the tunnel and landed in Astican form. "The cavern is not far. It is high ceilinged near the mouth and lower and narrower the further in you go. Something stopped me about midway across."

Brie frowned. "What kind of something?"

Scales shushed around its body. "I do not know."

The Luna Moth fluttered to Penee's shoulder. *"Cave not good."*

Smoothing her hair back from her face. Brie straightened her shoulders. "We're committed. Stay close together. Esán, since you have the lantern, take point."

Silence fraught with uncertainty followed them into the tunnel.

34

Esán sensed the strangeness long before they arrived at the Feranni Cavern. His sixth sense buzzed with the persistence of a fire alarm. He motioned Penee and Brie behind him and crept closer to the entrance. The stench of something rotten assailed them.

The companions came to a halt. Brie gagged. Penee covered her mouth and nose with her hands. Tears streamed between her fingers.

Abarax snuffled. "I smell death."

Esán raised the lantern. "What is the Star doing, Brie?"

She grimaced. "It's quiet. The danger seems to be that we'll be asphyxiated before we even enter the cavern."

He set the lantern on the ground. Pulling his handkerchief from his pocket, he tore it into triangular halves for the girls. "Cover your noses and mouths."

Brie finished tying hers. "What about you?"

"I think I'd better change shape. It will be easier for me to sense danger in fox form. Abarax, you can show me where you encountered the strangeness." He handed her the lantern. "Stay here. I'll call when I know it's safe."

His fox form skirted the entrance. Nose high and ears alert, he walked into the cavern. Nothing shouted a warning. Grateful for the fox's talent for blending in, he followed Abarax over sand and stone to the midway point.

Astican wings shook and settled. "The strangeness stopped me about here." Its brow furrowed.

"Wait here, Abarax. I'll scout ahead."

Nose to the ground, Esán trotted toward the back of the cavern. A thin stream of water trickled down the rock-strewn center of a creek bed. At its source, he discovered what had once been a permanent campsite, complete with a woodpile next to a fire pit. A sniffed search further back turned up the remains of a Human. Fox ears twitched. *Is this what alerted my sixth sense?*

Sensitivity honed by the Seeds picked up the vibration of past events, events which had not been pretty. Nothing in the present raised his hackles.

Esán shifted shape. "Abarax, it's safe."

A soft breeze caused the rustle of wings furling and announced its arrival. "I am here, Esán Efre."

"That was quick." He glanced up at the full-sized Astican. "How well do you see in the dark?"

"I have excellent night vision." Abarax scanned the area. "We are in a campsite. The odor of death comes from there." Two long strides and he stared down at the human remains. "I believe a fire would help us see better. I'll build it while you bring the others."

Esán jogged to the entrance. "We didn't find what stopped Abarax, but we might have found Tura's corpse."

Penee repositioned the torn handkerchief. "I'm sure edgy."

Brie handed the lantern to Esán and draped an arm around Penee's shoulders. "The unknown does that. Are you ready to make it the known?"

"I am. Lead the way, Esán."

Brie stepped into the cavern and shivered. Uncertain as to the shiver's origin, fear or cold, she moved closer to Esán. The lantern lit the path only a few steps ahead. Firelight on the far side of the cave enlivened mica flecks in the granite walls. The pearlescent glint drew her like a moth to a flame.

Speaking of moth... Her search left her unsatisfied until they reached the campsite. Abarax sat on a large rock, feeding wood chips to the flames. La perched on the top curve of its wing.

The stench of death, much stronger on this side of the cavern, penetrated the handkerchief and grabbed at her throat. Stifling the desire to throw up, she walked beyond the fire.

Her shadow joined by Penee's fell across a morbid sight. Esán held the lantern higher.

Human bones draped in tattered clothing framed skeletal hands clutching a crystal jar. Between two ribs, a hand-chipped obsidian spear head gleamed. The skull lay on its side, vacant orbital cavities staring into space. Its mandible dropped open to expose broken and missing teeth. The flicker of the fire's light created the illusion of movement.

Penee cringed. "Those bones are stripped clean, so why does it stink like rotting meat."

Abarax rose to its towering height. A long taloned finger pointed to one side at a dead animal in an advanced state of decay. "Over there, Penesert."

Penee shuddered and returned her attention to Tura's skeletal remains. "How do we retrieve the jar? *I'm* not getting near that thing."

Abarax reached out to touch the quartz crystal jar. A long, windy howl bounced off the cavern walls. The skull floated upward to hover over the scatter bones. Echo by echo, they reassembled into a sitting human skeleton.

Abarax jerked its hand away. Brie pulled Penee backward. Esán, the only one to remain unmoved, continued to illuminate the animating skeleton.

As though a clay artist worked, a balding head took shape. A wrinkled face with a glob of a nose formed. Muscle and skin covered the bones beneath the tattered clothing and molded themselves around the obsidian spearhead in the barrel chest. Faded eyes fought to focus. The disoriented gaze fastened on Brie.

Her soft inhale ended in a question. "You are Tura?"

The tip of a pinkish-gray tongue poked through a hole between front bottom teeth. Drool dripped from the corner of his mouth. "I am Tura, the Shaman King of Neul Isle." Suspicion deepened the profusion of wrinkles defining his narrowed eyes. "You came to steal my prize possession."

Esán moved to Brie's side. "We came to learn your story."

Lifted brows smoothed the multitude of lines. He peered from Brie to Penee to Esán. Shaggy brows snapped together. Flaccid skin draped the corners of his eyes. The jar clutched to his chest with one hand, he pointed at Abarax. "What is that thing?"

The Astican bowed its head. "I am an Astican. I, too, would hear your story."

His tongue poking repeatedly through the hole in his bottom teeth, the old man hunched his shoulders. Cradling the jar, he rocked back and forth. A long sucking sound echoed through the cavern. The expression on the wrinkled features grew distance, then wistful. At last, he straightened. "Sit. I will tell you the truth of the crystal jar."

T ura waited until the visitors had settled. Hugging the jar tighter, he licked his lips.

"I always wanted to be a shaman. I pleaded with my mother to let me speak with our wise man—to ask him to teach me. She finally gave in. Koati, our shaman, informed me our Stannag must select me. He only trained those she allowed to ride on her back.

"A few turnings later, Koati and the village elders escorted me to Bolcán Murloch. They sang the Song of Choosing, then instructed me to swim to the center of the lagoon. I treaded water until numbness claimed my body. Roiling currents engulfed me. The Stannag's tentacle snatched me up and dumped me on the beach. I had failed. Inconsolable, I ran away and hid.

"It was Koati who found me. He told me my destiny led a different path and left me at our hut. My mother scolded me. She called me stupid for embarrassing her and our clan. My father returned from the hunt, listened to my story, and banished me to live in the communal home. Disappointed, miserable, and angrier than I had ever been in my life, I swore to hurt the Stannag."

The pain of remembering choked him. He stared past the firelight, then cradled the jar tighter.

"Since my relations had abandoned me, I spent my spare time spying on our wise man and his new apprentice. One turning, Koati shared the story of

Aahana, the Sun Queen's daughter, and described her importance to our people."

Tura stroked the jar and slurped drool from the corner of his mouth.

"He disclosed that each moon cycle as the hump-backed moon began its transition to full, Aahana sealed her heart and soul in a quartz crystal jar and secreted it in a hidden cove. It was the apprentice's responsibility to stand guard, to keep the jar safe. Aahana returned to the incirrata's lair, went into a trance, and slipped into a parallel dimension to be with her loved ones. As the moon waned, she awoke from her trance state, reclaimed her heart and soul, and merged with the incirrata to resume her duties as Neul's Stannag."

He cackled softly.

"From that moment, I watched the apprentice's every move. One night he fell asleep. I stole the jar and its precious contents. Aahana arrived to collect it—"

He flashed his audience a wicked grin.

"I trapped the Sun Queen's daughter on Neul. She could no longer visit her loved ones.

"Koati suspected me from the beginning. I did not give in to his pressure, even when the clouds of sorrow obscured the isle.

"One turning, I left the village in the valley to escape Koati's anger. While I was gone, the Stannag's wrath roared long and loud. The island quaked. Huge rocks tumbled down the mountainside, blocking the mouth of the K'iin's valley and locking them inside forever."

Memories held him quiet. Sadness almost caught him. He sucked air through the gap in his teeth. "There was a time when I considered returning the heart." His gazed darted from one visitor to the next.

"Before my tribe became isolated in the Valley of Tá Súil, I fell in love." He snorted. "In the language of the K'iin, Tá Súil means hope." The snort grew into a crazed giggle. "Imagine that—hope."

He squeezed his eyes shut. Lost dreams flooded his mind. A sigh hissed. Lids fluttered open. He focused on the red-haired girl.

"Cailin and I grew up loving each another. She had soft, brown skin; dark, silky curls; and bronze eyes that gleamed like stars. The pain of missing her drove me to return the crystal jar. I carried it to the shore of the lagoon. My reflection in the water frightened me. I had grown old. Not only that—I am a criminal."

Light flickered brighter. He glared at a blond boy who adjusted the lantern's flame.

The boy clasped the hand of the red-haired girl next to him. His attention focused on Tura. "Please tell me and my friends what happened to those who visited the island after you stole Aahana's heart and soul?"

Hideous laughter overtook Tura. He smacked his lips together, cutting it short. "Neul Isle is *mine*. Anyone who trespasses must pay the price." Through squinted, flesh-draped eyes, he studied his visitors, then threw his head back and chortled with glee. His gaze snapped to their faces. "Do you think listening to my story will keep you safe from punishment? No! You will die as all who have come before you died." He set the jar on the ground, held out arthritic hands as though in supplication, and pointed at them one by one.

"How dare you set foot on my island. How dare you enter the Feranni Cave, my personal domain." His voice shook with rage. "You will pay with your lives. My ipōkat spider will kill you. I will dump your weighted bodies in the lagoon. When I find your boat, I will sink it."

His audience didn't flinch or shrink away. The red-haired girl leaned forward. The sympathy in her expression surprised him. He leveled his gaze at her.

"You, girl. Why do you look at me that way? I do not need sympathy from you or anyone else. My life is my own. Neul is mine. I am—"

"You are dead, Tura."

Her words stabbed deep. Anger choked him—brought back memories. "I lied to the Demi-Goddess, Kat. I promised to help her find her true love." A nasty laugh erupted. "I knew her bite would not kill me, so I betrayed her." A growl rumbled in his throat. "I needed her mate to kill people like you." He sucked a breath. "She caught me in my lie. Moon cycle after moon cycle, *she* tracked me. I got careless." Crippled fingers caressed the spearhead. "She took my spear—my weapon—and ran it through my heart."

The tip of his tongue travelled his top teeth. "I betrayed two women—the Goddess of Small Creatures and the Sun Queen's daughter. Aahana ties me to my dead body. She traps me in this cavern, hoping I'll return the crystal jar. Kat refuses to let me cross to the ever-world unless those I killed are free to go with me." He touched the spearhead. "Kat left this to remind me of my betrayal."

He rested a protective hand on the crystal jar and dropped his chin to his chest.

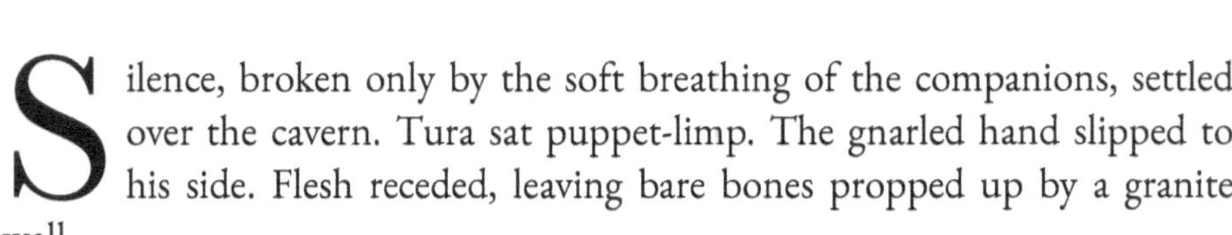

35

Silence, broken only by the soft breathing of the companions, settled over the cavern. Tura sat puppet-limp. The gnarled hand slipped to his side. Flesh receded, leaving bare bones propped up by a granite wall.

Esán caught Brie's eye. She nodded her understanding.

The fox materialized and crept forward. Skeletal fingers twitched. Crouching lower, the fox waited.

Penee inched backward. Brie moved beyond the skeleton's line of vision and climbed to her feet.

The skull's chin jerked up.

The fox froze, its nose touching the jar.

Empty eye sockets stared straight ahead. In the fire pit, crackling flames leapt higher and went out. Only the pale-yellow light of the lantern illuminated Tura and Aahana's crystal jar.

Esán's tail lifted. Brie stepped closer. He shifted, snatched the vessel, and passed it to her. "Go!" With it clutched to her chest, she jogged after an already sprinting Penee.

Moans of dismay propelled the skeleton to standing. Esán gripped the spearhead in its chest. A quick jerk freed it. Bones clattered to a heap on the ground. The skull rolled to a stop. He set it at the center of the pile of bones. "Rest, Tura. We will free those you killed. When their spirits pass into the ever-world, yours will follow."

A woman's deep shout echoed through Feranni. Lantern in hand, Esán raced with Abarax toward the cry. They braked to a stop where the cavern ceiling arced high and the walls fell away into the darkness.

Surrounded by a shimmering shield of protection, Penee and Rayna stood back to back, trapped in a circle of chanting shadows.

Esán's wards shot up. Abarax, full sized, and menacing stepped to his side. "*Scáth.*" The single word buzzed in Esán's mind.

Scáth, demons of the netherworld, danced around the women. "We want the jar, the heart, the soul. Give it to us and remain whole."

The demons lifted into flight. One by one, their devil faces afire with desire, they snapped their wings closed and darted at the shields.

Abarax, its attention riveted to the circling shadows, growled deep and low. "Demons. I will do this, Esán. Move away."

Its huge wings unfurled. Taloned hands lifted. "Flammé!" The shout echoed through the cavern.

A curtain of cascading sparks fell like red rain surrounding the Astican. A blazing sword flashed into the it's hand. The demons ceased their wild dance, whipped around to face their new adversary, and snarled.

Abarax swung his weapon left, then right. Astican features morphed into a mask of unmitigated horror. "Come if you dare, Scáth."

Shadow demons hovered. Menacing, ember-red eyes fixed on the Astican, they shot toward it. One by one they skewered themselves on the thrusting sword and executed a plunging return to the netherworld.

Four Scáth clustered together. Hatred-fed fury erupted into high-pitched screams. One after another, the demons rocketed toward Abarax.

Wielding the sword with the skill of a seasoned warrior, it intercepted each one. Writhing and screaming, they returned to the world of death.

"Abarax, duck!" Penee's screamed warning came too late.

The sword flew from its hand. A Scáth slammed into its chest, pierced its neck with razor-sharp fangs, and vanished. Reddish-blue blood flowed over shuddering gray scales. Abarax fell to its knees.

"Run Flammé through my heart—" It toppled onto its side, one wing trapped beneath; one extended behind it. Cherub features twisted. Horns sprouted amidst blond curls that burst into flame and shriveled.

Esán took command. "Penee, take the jar. Rayna, help me. Watch out for its wings."

With Rayna's strength added to his own, he rolled the Astican onto its back.

Penee, the precious jar cradled in her arms, stared in horror at Abarax's tortured features.

Abarax spit blood from a fanged mouth. "Hurry."

Rayna gripped the sword's hilt in both hands, straddled the Astican's chest, and raised it. One strong downward thrust ran the heart through.

The bloodied body jerked, shuddered, and lay motionless. Rayna pulled the blade free. Stepping to the side of the body, she held the sword high. Flames blazed. Sparks showered down on Abarax. Flammé, the Demon's Fire, flashed into another dimension.

La landed on Esán's shoulder. With a fearful squeak, she fluttered to the Astican's chest. Her wings drooped. *"My first friend gone."*

B rie materialized and knelt. "Oh, Abarax, I am so sorry. I wish Ari and Efillaeh were with us. I wish…" Bowing her head, she let the tears come.

Penee whispered, "Efillaeh?"

Esán started to explain, grew quiet, and gave a soft laugh.

Murmuring of voices across from her penetrated Brie's sorrow.

"Perhaps if you stopped crying, Brielle, we could get to work."

Brie's head came up. Her eyes fastened on her twin, kneeling across from her. "Ari! How did you—" She laughed. "Never mind how. Let's help Abarax. Penee, kneel at its feet. Esán move to its head." Brie tipped the Remembering Stone from its pouch and positioned it on the Astican's forehead. She knelt opposite her twin. "Ari, are you ready?"

"I am." Ari laid the sacred healing knife next to the wound on Abarax's chest and offered her hands to Brie.

Wisps of purple light from the amethyst cabochons in Efillaeh's hilt penetrated the wound. Blue light from the Remembering Stone engulfed the motionless body.

Abarax did not respond. The stillness of death cloaked him. La came to rest on the knife. Her tiny squeaks of sorrow were the only sound in the cavern. She fluttered to the blue stone. Her proboscis flicked out. A droplet of fluid fell onto the Stone and dripped onto the Astican's forehead.

Brie held her breath. Across from her, Ari closed her eyes. A tremor moved from the Astican's head to its feet. The fangs withdrew, leaving in their place a rosebud mouth. Horns shrunk, the blistered scalp smoothed, and blond curls grew in their place. A peaceful expression settled over the cherubic face.

When nothing else occurred, Brie remembered Corvus and Wolloh and their return from death. Trusting her instincts, she stabbed the sharp blade into Abarax's heart.

A shock wave ran up her arm and into her chest. Numbness crawled over her body, paralyzed her lungs, and formed a constricting band around her heart. Distantly, she noted the Star of Truth's faint tingling. Esán pouring his love into her essence held her motionless. Penee released Abarax's ankles to pick up the crystal jar. Radiance flowed from its contents, illuminating the Astican. La lifted into flight. Taloned fingers closed over the hand holding Efillaeh. Together, Brie and Abarax removed the blade. The wound healed.

The radiance from the jar dimmed. Blue light from the Remembering Stone faded. Efillaeh's amethyst cabochons no longer glowed.

Ari returned the knife to its scabbard. "I'd say that's a job well done. What about you, Abarax?"

The Astican did not respond. Its deadly pallor lingered. The girls exchanged glances. La lifted into flight and hovered. The enormous body quivered. A gossamer aura shimmered around it. In succession, Abarax's mental and etheric bodies floated to sitting. They merged. Pale blue eyes blinked and examined the transparency of an upraised hand. The rosebud mouth curved up, then frowned. It sighed. "I thank you, Ari and Brie, for bringing me back."

La squeaked. "You ghost?"

Its expression grew sadder. "They gave me a choice, my beautiful Luna Moth—die and become a demon Scáth or remain a half-being on Neul Isle."

Ari rested a hand on Efillaeh. "I am so sorry, Abarax."

Its physical body came to sitting and integrated with its astral partners. Long, taloned fingers curled and uncurled. It stretched its neck and yawned. "Until we complete our work here, I have the use of this physical container. When you leave Neul, I must drop it."

La squeaked, fluttered to the rosebud lips. Her proboscis flicked, and her wings trembled. With another soft squeak, she alighted on the gray-scaled hand.

Abarax smiled, its expression so full of love, Brie's eyes filled with tears.

"I am glad to see you, Abarax." Ari's tone held a note of sadness.

"It is good to see you, Arienh. Thank you for bringing the sacred knife." Its gaze sought each of the companions. "I did not understand friendship until this adventure. Thank you."

Ari jumped to her feet. "I have to go. So do you, Esán. You're needed on Tao Spirian." Grasping Brie's hand, she pulled her to standing. "I wish we had more time. Take care of yourself, little sis." She gave her a hug.

Brie hugged her back and grinned. "I'm glad we're speaking, Arienh AsTar."

"So am I." The three words, weighted with emotion, expressed the depth of her feelings. A dismissive shake left her grinning. "Hey, did the information I sent work?"

Brie laughed. "It did. I have a big surprise for you the next time we meet. Tell Relevart after we return Aahana's jar, we'll rescue Henri and Irstant."

"I will. You better say goodbye to Esán. I need to talk to Penee."

Brie moved into Esán's embrace. "I know you have to go, so I won't make a fuss—"

His gentle kiss engraved his love in her heart. "I'll find you wherever you are." He released her.

Ari joined them, the black pouch with the recorder disc in her hand. "I'll take this back to the library and ensure the information is safe." She looped the ribbon over her head.

Brie gave her a hug. "Thanks for everything, Ari. Take care of yourself."

"You, too."

Esán clasped Ari's hand. "Relevart brought you, right?"

"He did, but you're to take me back to Myrrh. Mother needs to speak with you before you go to Tao Spirian."

They stepped apart from the group.

Ari waved. "I'll make certain Elf knows you're safe, Penee. Goodbye, Abarax. Thanks for taking care of Brie."

Mittkeer's star-studded portal swirled opened. They vanished into Mittkeer.

Brie sighed. "I wish they could have stayed."

A rush of dread left Penee fighting for breath. "We need to leave the caverns." She cradled the jar to her chest and cringed. "I don't know why..."

The ground shuddered. Rocks and pebbles trembled. A sharp jolt preceded a series of waves that sent them stumbling into one another. A second tremor shook the cavern.

Brie shouted. "Hang on to me." Henri's staff flashed into her hand.

Abarax gripped her arm. The entire cavern rocked, rolled, and roared. Stones ricocheted off walls. Shattered chunks flew through the air.

Mittkeer's gaping mouth swept them up like autumn leaves in a storm and closed to the thunderous boom of the cavern's collapse. Astican scales hummed. An agitated La flitted from companion to companion.

Brie whistled. "That was close! Good instincts, Pen."

Gulping down her nausea, Penee produced a shaky smile. "I'm uncertain what alerted me." She flinched. "Oh. My arm burns. Do you think Rina warned us?"

Brie rubbed the back of her neck. "Whatever it was beat the Star. The question is: did the quake hit the entire island, or was it localized in the cavern?"

Penee chewed her bottom lip. "Let's exit Mittkeer at our campsite by the lagoon and see what we find." She held up the jar. "We can also return this." The pain in her arm stopped. "I think Aahana and Rina will be happy about that."

Brie searched the stars. "Help me find the constellation Incirrata."

"Up there." The Astican pointed. "I'll exit first and determine if it's safe."

Penee groaned. "Hurry, Abarax. The jar is getting hotter." She shot a pleading glance in Brie's direction.

Brie strode over the carpet of midnight stars to take up a position facing the constellation. It faded. Trees and water solidified. With La fluttering at its side, Abarax stepped into the world of Neul Isle.

Penee fidgeted. "Where are they?"

"*All safe.*" La landed on the jar, fluttered upward, and darted ahead of them.

Mittkeer left them on the beach, gazing over Bolcán Murloch. The mist thinned. A breeze ruffled the lagoon's surface. A sea bird squawked a welcome.

Brie walked to the water's edge. "Doesn't appear that the quake hit island-wide. I wonder what triggered it?"

Sia Ceari, the Púca leader, floated from the trees into her line of vision. "Fí, the king of the Scáth, ordered Tura's soul brought to him. Your promise, VarTerel, that his soul would follow those he killed into the ever-world made their task impossible. In a fit of rage, Fí swore to trap Tura and you in the cavern forever. He created the quake. Your escape did not make him happy."

Penee hugged the jar. "Can he cause a quake out here?"

Ghostly eyes twinkled. "The Stannag presides over the upper-world of Neul. Fí dare not attempt to harm her domain." He shifted his attention to the jar. "The incirrata comes. I will rejoin my comrades until she returns to herself."

Warmth flowed over Penee's left forearm. The jar's contents stained the quartz crystal with a poppy-red glow. A soft splash announced the Rina's arrival. Her bulbous, sac-like body trembled.

La's pale wings beat a gentle rhythm. "*Place jar in pool.*"

Penee knelt. A quivering tentacle encircled the glowing quartz container. The Stannag and the jar sank below the surface of the lagoon. Penee rolled back her sleeve and gazed in wonder at the shimmering tattoo.

36

A hush fell over Neul Isle. The sensation of every animal and plant, mountain and plain, and particle of soil and sand anticipating change tingled over Brie's skin. The clouds hung lower and heavier as if they, too, waited.

Penee came to her feet. Its leather scales made no sound as Abarax moved to stand behind them. The Luna Moth, pale green against the grayness, faded into the mistiness as she flew over the water toward Rina Island.

Penee cradled her arm. The water's usual pewter gray sheen intermingled with the muted colors of a sunny turning. "What's happening? Where is she?"

"Shhh. Give her time." Brie dared not speak aloud for fear of breaking the spell.

Abarax pointed a taloned finger. "Look!"

The oppressive clouds churned and thinned. Those resting on the banks of the lagoon grew hazy. An ocean breeze blew down the channel behind Rina Island over the water, dispersing the low-hanging clouds to rest on the tops of the mountains. Half a centurial cycle after Aahana shed her heartbroken tears, the slopes enclosing Bolcán Murloch glowed with faint sunshine.

Brie held her breath. Penee beamed. The Luna Moth dropped from the misty ceiling and fluttered to Abarax. Her telepathic message reached them all. *"She comes."*

A rippled path from the small island cut the lagoon in two. A gleaming body broke the surface, dove, and reappeared a short distance from the tide pool. Vibrant gold ovals rose above the water's surface. The bulbous body of the Stannag incirrata, resplendent in the orange-red of the rising sun, pushed upward. Deep ocean secrets scented the air. Jeweled, salmon-tinted tentacles lifted it into the tide pool. Radiant golden light engulfed it. The spirit guardian of Neul stepped free.

Aahana regarded them from luminous fire-opal eyes. Long braids fell to her waist in a cascade of ebony fire. Her slight smile melted into sadness. "You have given me back my heart and my soul. I am grateful. I promised tears of happiness to help your friends." A regretful shake of the head foreshadowed a sad sigh. "I do not feel happy. I have lost my life, my family of origin, my daughter and husband." She caught a teardrop on her fingertip. "This will not serve your friends." It merged into the lagoon.

Aahana sought Brie. "I wish to see my daughter, to watch her grow, to experience the beautiful blessing of her children. I yearn to see the man I love. Please, VarTerel, take me back in time. Do this, and happy tears will flow." She raised a graceful hand. "Tears that will leave Neul in the sun's light and free the K'iin from the Valley of Tá Súil. Please, VarTerel, help me heal my loss and my sadness."

Brie clutched the Remembering Stone. "I understand how to travel from one dimension to another, but..." She swallowed a lump in her throat. "...I have never traveled into the past. I'm not sure I can."

Aahana pressed her palms together. "Please try."

Brie heard the pleading in her voice, saw it in her beautiful face. She glanced at Penee for support.

Her steady gaze held only confidence. "You are a VarTerel. Chealim would not have chosen you if you were incapable of doing this. And, Brie, *you* have *Henri's* staff."

A seed of hope blossomed in Brie's heart. "We mustn't leave Neul without a guardian."

Aahana offered a hand to Penee. "You are the Bearer of the Incirrata. You will protect the isle in my absence."

"Do I need to become one with Rina to be the Stannag?"

"You do not." Aahana gazed at the incirrata. "She will work with you until I return."

Penee frowned. "What if Skultar and Thorlu arrive, and you're not here?"

Abarax touched his heart. "La and I agree to serve as your protectors, Penesert."

Expectation enhanced Aahana's beauty. "Do not fret. Your enemies search for Neul, but they have gone astray. Until they discover their mistake, they will continue to wander." She knelt beside the tide pool. The tip of a tentacle encircled her wrist. "Rina wishes you to join us."

Penee knelt. A salmon-tinted tentacle encircled her tattooed arm. Aahana pressed a shimmering aquamarine gemstone into her hand and raised her voice in song.

> *"Incirrata, hear my request.*
> *The Bearer serves at my behest.*
> *She will protect and honor Neul*
> *Until I return your magic jewel."*

The Inciratta's glorious new salmon color intensified. A scarlet tentacle unwound from Penee's arm and writhed to rest on her forehead.

Penee's eyes rounded. "Oh my. You are the most beautiful creature."

The jeweled tip of the tentacle touched her lips, caressed cheek of the Sun Queen's daughter, and withdrew. The incirrata submerged.

Aahana rose, offered her hand, and helped Penee to standing. "You are now the Stannag guardian of Neul Isle." She bowed her head. "Thank you!"

Brie raised her hand. Henri's staff appeared, delicately carved and gleaming. Anticipation cloaking her, Aahana clasped the wooden shaft. One breath and Neul Isle blurred into the Land of All Time and No Time.

The stars of Mittkeer enclosed Brie and Aahana. At first, neither spoke.

Aahana stared in wonder. "So many stars. How do you know where to go?"

Brie handed her the staff and pulled the blue velvet pouch from beneath her tunic. "Constellations act like compass points. The Atrilaasu tribe in the desert of Fera Finnero on DerTah taught me to use dreaming tracks, songs you create to keep you on the right path. I have used this method to remember the pathways of Mittkeer."

Curiosity replaced Aahana's sadness. "How do we go back in time?"

With Remembering Stone warming Brie's palm. "I believe the best way is to access your memories. Tell me what you're hoping to see."

Aahana lifted elegant hands in a gestured plea. "I wish to see how my daughter and her husband age." She pressed her palms together. "I long to walk the streets of my village and to stand in the forest where I played as a child." Pulling a braid over her shoulder, she stroked the weave. "Abellona, the Sun Queen of Soputto, is my mother. I wish to petition her for release into the ever-world, so I can join my family."

"What of your responsibility to Neul?" Brie asked without censure.

"It is my hope the Queen will send a replacement. I won't know her mind until I ask."

Brie reviewed what she had learned from Wolloh and Henri about time travel. "A portal window is our best option. Through it we can watch a condensed version of your family's past." She drew a large, upright oval with the Remembering Stone. "I'll take the staff, Aahana. You hold the Stone next to your heart. Concentrate on your memories before Tura stole the jar. Once we have established a connection to the past, we can move forward. Let me know when you're ready."

Aahana took the Stone, drew in a breath, and nodded. "I'm ready."

The tranquility of Mittkeer settled over them. Brie tuned into the memories being absorbed by the Stone and repeated the charm taught to her by Henri.

"Portal window, open wide.
Let us see the world inside.
Into the past let us travel,
Aahana's memories to unravel."

Sparkling stars blurred, leaving the oval devoid of night.

Her heartbeat quickened. Sun warmed her face. Summer flowers perfumed the air. Gleeful, childish laughter brought her gaze to the portal window. She lowered the staff.

The main street running through the middle of a Soputton village came into view. A horse attached to a wagon nibbled grass and flicked flies away with its tail. A tall, handsome man stacked boxes in the wagon bed. Down the well-traveled road, a little girl pulled her hand from an older woman's and ran straight into his arms.

Aahana caught her breath. "Do they know we're here?"

"No. We remain in this dimension. The window portal allows us to view theirs. Who are they?"

"The little girl is Alta, my daughter. The man is my husband, Thad. We met at a village dance." A dreamy smile crept over her face. "He stole my heart."

"You are a demi-goddess, correct?"

"I am." Her brow crinkled. "I grew tired of gods and goddess. One night, I ran away from home. This village was the home of my mortal father, who died when I was a child. It seemed an appropriate place to begin a new life.

"I forgot my former existence and the responsibilities that came with it. We took part in a commitment ceremony. Alta was a wee baby when my mother summoned me home. I considered disobeying, but thought better of it. She sent me to Neul Isle to live up to my life pledge. It was the last time I saw my family."

The image in the oval moved as though they walked along the village street. Aahana pointed out the shrine to her mother, her favorite park, the general store, livery stable, and schoolhouse. She closed her eyes. A narrow lane dotted with small cottages took shape. Flower boxes and border gardens added bright spots of color. At the end of the lane, a stone cottage surrounded by trees steadied. "This is our cottage. Thad's father built it as a young man. He presented it to us the day of our commitment ceremony. I loved every moment I spent here." She brushed tears from her face. "I'm ready to move forward, if you are."

"Although I'm uncertain how this works, I know how to return to our present. Moving through your family's history is more elusive." She placed a hand on Aahana's shoulder. "Your memories are the key. Concentrate on what you desire. The Stone will help you."

The scene in the window morphed. A teenage Alta walked from a new shrine in the village square, a shrine dedicated to Aahana. She ambled along the flower edged pathways. Every once in a while, she knelt, pulled a weed, sniffed a blossom, and smiled. The window showed a close-up view of the shrine.

Aahana stared in amazement at her likeness carved from Soputton obsidian. Sheltered in a building made of field stones, the statue gazed over the village from fire-opal eyes. Candles flickered around it.

Brie read the plaque over the entryway. "Aahana, Daughter of Abellona, the Sun Queen, graces the Village of Sonas with light, love, and healing."

Tears slipped down ebony cheeks. The village blurred. A forest filled the oval. Alta and a young man walked hand in hand. Moments of their life together flitted by: their commitment ceremony; the births of their three children; an illness that befell their oldest daughter; her passing into the ever-world; on it went until they too passed, leaving behind a son, a daughter, and several grandchildren.

The scene shifted. Thad's life sped by. He remained faithful to Aahana, worked hard at training horses and helping on his family's farm. His journey to the ever-world preceded Alta's. They buried his wooden casket in the family burial ground behind the cottage.

The portal window filled with night and stars. Tears streaming down her face, Aahana kissed the Remembering Stone and returned it. "Are we back in the present?"

"We are." Brie slipped the Stone in its pouch and tucked it beneath her tunic. "Your family is beautiful. I feel privileged to have seen them through your eyes. Are you still committed to finding your mother?"

"I am. We must go to Mount Dia Bandia on the continent of Nira. If we exit Mittkeer on top of the mountain, the gateway to Shió Ridur, the world of the Gods, will open."

Brie peered into the distance. "We are looking for Altair, the brightest star in the sky. It marks the way to Nira."

37

Penee sat beside the tide pool with Rina's jeweled tentacle resting on her tattoo. The swoosh, shoosh of the incirrata's breath blended with the call of seabirds and the incoming tide. Pale scarlet tentacles floating on the water's surface rose and fell with its gentle roll. Faint sunlight penetrating the thinning cloud cover made the shoreline glow.

Nature's natural rhythm soothed her edginess. Soon, Abarax and the Luna Moth would return from patrolling the island. She relaxed and luxuriated in the serenity of Neul Isle.

"You look beautiful, Penesert."

She jerked around. "Den?" Suspicion choked her. "What are you doing here?" Her gaze darted past him. "Is Skultar with you? Furrnoce? The Mo—"

"No. No. And no. I came because the incirrata called me." A charming smile almost obliterated her mistrust. His hand on her shoulder kept her from jumping to her feet. "Please don't get up on my account." He sat beside her. Rina's tentacle touched his hand and returned to Penee's arm. Rolling up his shirt sleeve, he rested his right forearm on his knee. "It seems we have something in common."

Penee gawked at the tattoo of an incirrata identical to her own.

Rina's shoosh increased in volume. A gentle glide from the tide pool into the lagoon submerged her up to her oval eyes. Bubbles surged upward as she dove deeper.

Den tilted his head. "You seem surprised." He traced the length of a tattooed tentacle tattooed. "I discovered it about the time you did." Resting his arms on his knees, he scanned the lagoon and then angled to look at her. "Like you, I did not realize I bore the sign of the incirrata. Irstant has marked our lives. We, you and I, have always shared a connection." His expression grew distant. "I remember you as a little girl." Blue eyes with sparkles of amethyst flooded with memories. "The moment I saw you, the need to protect you overwhelmed me." He rested a hand on her arm.

His touch caused a tirade of emotions, jumbled her thoughts, and tangled them like Ipō's silk threads had tangled around Kat. "You work for Skultar."

"How else could I discover his plans for you? I had to be close to our enemies so I could protect you and others I care about."

She yanked her arm away, scrambled to her feet. and shot him a withering glare. "How can I ever trust you?" Two long, angry strides put some distance between them. Folding her arms, she glowered at the trees skirting the clearing.

The sounds of him standing, the crunch of his boots, his exhale as he turned her to him made her wince. "Penee, I swear I'm on your side and the side of the VarTerels."

She stared at his broad chest and pressed her lips together.

He ducked to see her better. "Please look at me. I understand it looks bad, but I had to keep my genuine feelings hidden. Skultar is someone to be reckoned with. I needed him to believe I was his lackey."

Her head jerked up. "*Was* his lackey? Aren't you going back to lick his boots?" Scorn slathered the words. Hope tugged at her heart.

"I'm here to stay. Even if I wanted to go back..." Amusement flashed. "Skultar, Furrnoce, Thorlu, and Vygel are wandering the ocean because I recalibrated their compass." He shrugged. "I also provided the wrong charts."

His hands rested on her shoulders. "I helped you escape from TaSneach, remember. Henri and Irstant are out of harm's way because I learned of

Skultar's plans to kill them and got them to safety. I put my life at risk to save Relevart. You can trust me, Penee." He released her.

The absence of his warm contact made her shiver. She walked to the tide pool. Small fish darting back and forth mirrored her inner turmoil. A crab scuttled over the rocks into a dark crevice. Penee squeezed her eyes shut. *I wish I could hide, too.* She blinked, raked her fingers through her short hair, and turned to study the man who had haunted her dreams since she was a child.

Den did not approach. He waited, she assumed, for her to make the next move. "So, you're here. Now what?"

"Freeing Henri and Irstant is at the top of my list. Tell me what you have discovered."

Her brow arced. "Wait. You moved them to Neul Isle, and you don't know how to free them?"

"I teleported them to—"

Abarax dropped from the sky like an angry god and landed next to her. Its scales whispered a warning. It took an aggressive step toward Den. "You are the enemy. I suggest you leave."

Penee looked from its combative stance to Den's wary posture. *I need your help, Brielle.*

⁂

Mittkeer's exit portal closed, leaving Brie and Aahana staring at the clouds resting on the top of Mount Dia Bandia. "Do you think your mother is aware of our presence?"

"She knows." Aahana apprehension changed from a simmer to a boil.

The clouds flowed apart, revealing a palatial staircase. Two uniformed attendants descended to stand at attention. The Sun Queen's crest emblazoning their uniforms shone like the star it represented.

Aahana's sharp inhale directed Brie's gaze to the top of the stairs. A woman stepped into view. Her flawless beauty surpassed that of her daughter. Ebony skin, fire-opal eyes, hair coiffed into an intricate style depicting the sun, and a shimmering gown radiating fiery light marked her as royalty.

Her regal descent left a trail of sparks in her wake. Upon reaching the bottom step, she inclined her head. "Welcome, VarTerel Brielle AsTar, to Dia

Bandia." Each word held a melody. The queen's gracious smile washed over Brie, warming her as though the sun had appeared after a long, cold winter.

Brie touched her heart. "It is my honor."

The Sun Queen's radiant gaze moved to Aahana. "Dearest daughter, it has been far too long." She offered a hand. "Come. We have much to discuss." Her benevolence warmed Brie for the second time. "Your friends require your presence on Neul Isle. I will return Aahana to you at the conclusion of our business. Thank you, Brielle, for bringing her home."

Aahana took her mother's hand. The two women ascended into the clouds. The attendants vanished along with the staircase.

Brie raised Henri's staff and arrived in Mittkeer below the Incirrata constellation. She stepped free of Mittkeer to find her companions in a debate about to get ugly. Den and the Astican faced off. Penee, at a loss, glared from one to the other. La, the only calm presence in the clearing, alighted on her shoulder.

Abarax took a menacing step. "I told you to leave."

Den shrugged. "I have nowhere to go. I am not your enemy, Astican, nor am I Penee's."

An aggressive rumble shook the Astican. Its wings shivered.

Brie walked into their line of vision. "I suggest a truce. Fighting won't help us accomplish anything. Abarax, thank you for guarding Penee." She looked at Den. "You are on our side, correct?"

Penee folded her arms. "He says he moved Henri and Irstant to this island, but he doesn't know where they are." She shook her head. "Does that sound truthful?"

Brie sank onto a makeshift sleeping pallet. "Perhaps, we should let him clarify his position. Abarax, calm down. Penee, sit by me. Den, explain yourself."

A small Abarax flew to a branch above Brie's head. Penee plopped down beside her.

Den sat opposite. "I have been with Irstant for ten sun cycles since my mother turned his care over to me. Prior to that, I would go with her to his home whenever I could. Irstant fascinated me. I followed him everywhere. One turning, I told him about meeting a little girl with mismatched eyes and my promise to find her. To my surprise, he knew your story, Penesert. I had been his apprentice for about four years when he sent me to infiltrate Skultar's ranks and gain his trust. I believe that was about the time your cousin moved you to TaSneach. Irstant realized Skultar would discover how talented you are. It was my job to keep Irstant informed about your safety and your whereabouts."

Penee looked puzzled. "Why would Irstant care about me?"

Den studied her intently. "Relevart is his best friend."

"But Relevart didn't meet me until recently."

"I don't have all the answers, Penee. We need to rescue Irstant and Henri so we can ask him." Den tossed a small rock from hand to hand. "Which brings me to why I sent them to the K'iin and why I don't know how to free them."

He dropped the rock, shoved up his shirt sleeve, and showed his arm to Brie. "Not long after, I started my training as a DiMensioner, I had a dream about a scarlet incirrata. My arm burning woke me up." His gaze moved to the tide pool. "I shared the dream with Irstant. He explained that the incirrata would help me save people I cared about." His gaze returned to the girls. "I almost forgot about the dream. A few turnings after you escaped, Penee, Skultar and Furrnoce were discussing how to gain control of the Universal VarTerel. Irstant and Henri topped the list. It also included you, Penee, and Elf, as well as you, Brie, and your twin.

"When they kidnapped Relevart, Ari, and Elf, I dreamt about a tribe on Neul Isle who could induce a coma-like state to hide their mental signatures. The incirrata was my key to the K'iin." He exhaled a frustrated breath. "I didn't discover Furrnoce's plan to sedate Irstant and Henri with the bite of a luna moth until after the fact. The best I could do was teleport them to the Valley of Tá Súil and hope the K'iin would care for them." A sardonic grin flickered. "A side note: Skultar was furious at Furrnoce for what he had done with the moth."

Smoothing his sleeve over his tattoo, he looked from Brie to Penee. "Hope that helps."

Brie turned to Penee. "What do you think?"

"I think it's nice to have help, especially since Esán had to leave." She stood up and peered down at Den. "Never make me regret trusting you."

He came to his feet and embraced her. "That's a promise."

She relaxed against him, caught herself, and stepped away. To cover her confusion, she busied herself stacking wood in the fire pit. "I think we need a fire. It's almost sunset."

Brie caught Den's eye, saw a raw spark of emotion, and bent to help Penee with the firewood.

A human-sized Abarax landed and folded gray-scaled arms across rippling chest muscles. It regarded Den with more interest than animosity. "You are not the enemy?"

Den's extraordinary smile flashed. "I am your comrade, Abarax. Together we will protect Brielle and Penee." He held out his hand.

The Astican looked taken aback. The cherub features crinkled in a full-fledged grin as it shook the hand. "Comrade." The word rolled from its tongue a letter at a time. The grin grew even bigger. "*I* have a comrade. It is good."

Brie looked from human male to Astican. *What an amazing life I am living.*

38

Lightning zigzagged across the clouds enshrouding the island. Thunder rumbled over the lagoon. Aahana materialized in all of her radiant splendor. The tide pool at her feet pulsated with Rina's jeweled tentacles leveraging her bulbous body onto the pool's sandy bottom.

Aahana knelt. Unshed tears slipped down her cheeks. "Please, Brielle. I need the crystal vial. It is time to honor my promise."

Brie removed the jeweled stopper and passed the vial to Aahana. Tears spilled down her cheeks. The incirrata leveraged its body above the water. Glistening droplets leaked from golden eyes. A mixture of their tears dripped in the vial. Aahana rose to her feet and lifted it above her head. Her magnificent voice rang out.

> *"Clouds of sadness and remorse*
> *It is time to change your course*
> *Allow the sun to reappear*
> *Rid Neul Isle of Aahana's fear."*

The clouds dissolved. Late-turning sun washed the island with gentle light. Flocks of birds rose into the color-streaked heavens, their cries of joy echoing over the lagoon. Deer, rabbits, and squirrels ventured onto the shore, their noses lifted high. Silvery fish jumped above the water's surface and sent a rain of sparkling droplets into the air as they returned to their ocean home. The inhabitants of the Isle of Neul absorbed the light and love offered by the Sun Queen's daughter.

Aahana faced toward the Valley of Tá Súil.

> *"Hidden valley, the time is here*
> *To release the spell rendered by fear*
> *Entrance open, release the K'iin*
> *Allow them out and others in."*

A muffled rumble shook the island and sent waves rolling over the lagoon.

At her feet, the incirrata trembled. Salmon and blue faded to white. Her tentacles reached for Aahana. A shudder rocked the bulbous body. Tentacles quivered. A long hiss filled the clearing. Color flooded Neul's incirrata. Rina, resplendent in her new scarlet sheen, slid into Bolcán Murloch. Leaving bubbles in her wake, she swam a large circle beneath the full brightness of the sun and returned to the edge of the tide pool.

Aahana regarded the vial with wonder and handed it to Brie. "Tears of happiness to bring your friends back to this life." Her radiance increased the magnificence of the sun's returning. "Mother has given me permission to pass into the ever-world—but not until you return from the Valley of Tá Súil, and we have released the spirits of the Púca." She smothered a yawn. "One more thing... Neul is now visible. Your enemies will not remain lost much longer. Rest. Tomorrow we visit the K'iin."

A mist spun around her. The scarlet Stannag blew a long, low buzz and disappeared into the depths of the lagoon.

Brie sealed the vial with the jeweled stopper and tucked it away. La lifted into flight.

Abarax bowed. "We will keep watch, VarTerel." A moth-sized Astican flew after her.

Den and Penee cradled their tattooed arms and gazed skyward.

Night crept over Neul. TaSneach rose with ultimate grace, soaking the land in moonlight for the first time in half a centurial cycle.

Púca gathered at the tree line, their opaque bodies shimmering in the iridescent light. Sia Ceari floated to Brie's side. "Hope infuses the air tonight. We will also stand watch. Rest well, Brielle AsTar." Like wisps of mist in the wind, he and his comrades drifted through the woods.

After a dinner of greens, Den cut fresh pine boughs for the two raised sleeping pallets and banked the fire. Penee helped him to prepare a bed on the ground between them before curling up on her own.

A nagging restlessness kept Brie from settling down. She strolled to the water's edge and attempted to enjoy the moonlight's sparkling dance, the stars glittering in the exposed sky, and the tranquility of a moonlit night. A premonition made her remove the Remembering Stone from its pouch. As she curled her fingers around it, memories stirred...the tourmaline Throne of Netydis glowed in its amethyst cavern. Her heart wrenched. She tucked the stone away and hurried to Penee's side.

"Penee, wake up. We can't stay here." She shook her. Nothing happened.

Den strode to her side. "What's wrong?"

"The SorTech has tapped into Penee's energy signature. She's unresponsive. I saw this in a vision, Den. Skultar and the Mocendi are closing in. We have to leave here, or they'll find us. As long as The Box remains connected to Penee, we can't use DiMensionery."

Den scooped the unconscious girl up in his arms. "But they can, right?"

"Right."

A frantic La flew into the clearing. *"Wicked men."*

Abarax landed in Astican form. "They found the inlet. It won't take them long to reach Rina Island."

Light flashed at the lagoon's center. Vygel hovered above the surface, his cape flaring. A tentacle encircled his ankle and yanked. Frantic shouts echoed off the mountains. The MasTer's Mocendi hit the water with a resounding splash. A choked cry gurgled into nothing.

Brie urged Den into the woods. Abarax's bat form darted ahead of them. La flew at their side. They emerged from the woods to find the ludoc cat crouching in the gully. Brie scrambled onto its back. Den climbed up behind her and wedged Penee's limp body between them.

The ludoc winged its way over the gorge, the wetlands, and the lake. The Forest of Deora shrunk to a small patch of green as the flying cat banked over the San Crúil Mountains to land on the eastern slope in the cool light of the Soputto's second moon.

Brie jumped from its back. Den slid Penee into her waiting arms. He climbed down and helped to lower Penee to the ground.

Abarax shifted and sniffed the air. "Are we safe?"

Brie glanced back toward the lagoon. "Not unless I can disconnect The Box from her mind. Please keep watch. Send La to discover what Skultar and Thorlu are up to."

Astican and Luna Moth took flight.

Kneeling beside her friend, Brie pondered her options.

Den dropped to his knees beside her. "What if we work together? I'll create a distraction that will free you to release the connection."

She peered up at him. "What level of DiMensionery have you attained?"

"That's information I may not disclose." His steady gaze did not waver. "I believe you understand."

She controlled her desire to snap at him. "But you can tell me who besides Irstant oversees your training?"

"We have little time, Brie."

An Ari-like obstinacy kept her from giving in. "Answer my question, so we can get to work." She waited, alternative choices lining up in her mind in the event he denied her the information.

"Chealim oversees my training."

A breath she did not realize she'd been holding escaped, taking the tension building between them with it. "Good. Create that diversion, Den."

He grew silent and bowed his head. "Ready."

Brie explored Penee's mind, found the SorTech's connection and, with a surgeon's precision, released it. Penee's breathing changed; her face relaxed. Den sat back and blew out a long breath.

Abarax landed. Malicious glee animated his features. "They rescued Vygel.

He's back at their camp by Rina Island. Furrnoce puzzles over the behavior of The Box. It isn't performing as expected."

Brie glanced at Den. "What did you do?"

"I rewired it."

His bland stare made her laugh. She grinned. "Thought so."

A dark brow arched. "You thought what?"

She shrugged and bent over Penee. "Penesert, it's time to wake up."

B rie's muffled command roused Penee from a chasm cut deep in her psyche. The effort it took to drag herself back to consciousness left her gasping. Pain ripping her brain in two launched her upright.

Den's warm embrace eased her panic. Brie's cool hands on her temples turned the sharp pain to a dull throb.

Penee murmured, "What happened?"

"Skultar and gang found Neul." Brie grimaced. "The Box found you."

Penee's hand flew to her neck. "Wait. Henri removed the disc. How—"

"You were under Skultar's thumb for quite a while." Den cradled her closer. "Furrnoce had plenty of time to learn your energy signature."

A tiny Abarax landed and shot up to human height, its expression harried. "Thorlu located our camp. He knows we are near."

Brie sighed. "On the run again." She squeezed the bridge of her nose, lowered her hand, and studied the Astican. "Do you still need sleep even though you're not connected to your physical body?"

La's agitated flutter distracted him. "It is alright, La. I am content. Do not worry about me." He offered his palm. The tip of a talon touched her wing. "Go check the camp. I will stand guard here." Forcing his attention back to Brie, he heaved a heavy sigh. "To answer your question, Brielle... This physical container needs rest. My etheric body does not. What of tomorrow?"

A stab of grief surprised her. "We can't descend on the K'iin in the dark. Our best bet is to teleport into the valley after sunrise."

Penee observed her companions with interest.

Den's expression questioned Brie's choice. "I thought you said no overt DiMensionery."

Brie gazed up at the moon. "If you and Abarax create a distraction, Penee and I can teleport without being detected."

La, wings glowing in the moonlight, flitted to Brie's upturned palm. *"Wicked men sleep. One guarding."*

Brie shared the message.

Penee squeezed Den's hand. "I need some sleep." She looked hopefully at Abarax.

The Astican shifted to ludoc cat and stretched out on a dry patch of ground. With a sigh, she nestled close to his furry belly and slept.

B rie and Den sat in a companionable silence, watching the moon Chearra paint the sky a soft glowing red. "We've only been on the island a short time, but seeing the moons rise is like a miracle." Brie hugged herself. "I wonder what the K'iin are feeling tonight? The clouds have vanished. Their valley is no longer a trap." She studied her palm and remembered Ari's fascination with her lifeline. "Did they know this turning would come? Will they greet us as friends or enemies? Will they help us save Henri and Irstant?" She pressed her palms together. "So many questions only time can address."

Den flashed a smile. "Tomorrow will arrive faster if you sleep. La and I will stand guard."

Brie didn't move. "Will Skultar and Thorlu bed down, or try to find us?"

He angled his head to see her better. "You *are* full of questions, aren't you?" Fingers interlaced, he rested his elbows on his knees and stared at the moon-soaked landscape. "Stories abound about the deaths on Neul Isle. Ghosts and deadly spiders are rumored to roam. Night is the worst time to be abroad. Skultar values his hide. Thorlu always protects his. Vygel, from what I can tell, acts without considering the outcome, so he might be a danger." A humorous look twinkled. "He took a nosedive into the lagoon, so he may think twice before venturing off on his own. As for Furrnoce, with his arrogance and overblown ego, he would let his best friend die to save himself. Does that address your concern?"

She stood up. "Time to get some sleep. Wake me in a couple of hours. I'll stand watch, so you can rest." Not waiting to hear his reply, she crawled under the ludoc's outstretched wing, snuggled into its warm belly fur, and slept.

The murmur of voices woke her to a glorious dawn sky. The ludoc cat's cloudy gray eyes gleamed close to her face. Scooting from under his protective wing, she climbed to her feet and stretched. A short distance away, Penee and Den emerged from their conversation only long enough to acknowledge her presence.

Behind her, Abarax shifted. "You slept well, Brielle AsTar. La reported all quiet several times during the night. Our enemies stir as we speak."

She stifled a yawn. "Did you get some rest?"

"The *body* rested." Its rueful smile held a touch of dejection.

She noted the lack of ownership he attached to the body and walked over to Den. "You rewired The Box, correct?"

"Correct. Why?"

"Thorlu and gang are awake. Will it pick up DiMensionery at this distance?"

"If I accomplished what I set out to do, it won't pick up much of anything."

Brie held out her hand. Henri's staff materialized. "We need to go to the valley. Which is the better option...teleport or use Mittkeer?"

Den's brows bridged. "If I miswired something, teleporting will create less of a ripple effect."

La streaked down the mountainside. *"Wicked men closer."*

His brow smoothed. "Did either of you sense them teleport?"

Penee blinked. "I felt nothing."

Lips pressed lips together, she let her senses roam. "I felt a minor tremor, only because I have the staff." She rubbed her neck. "The Star's burning. We need to go. Please hold onto me."

Den moved to her side. Penee gripped her shoulder. Abarax shaped a bat and landed on Den's hand beside La. A ripple of energy rolled over the mountains. Brie teleported them to the foot of the San Crúil Range with Deora Forest at their back.

Penee mouthed, "What the—"

They stood on Rina Island above the subterranean lair.

Sia Ceari flashed into view. He put an image of San Crúil Valley in Brie's mind and faded.

Mittkeer opened. Neul vanished. Penee groaned. Brie met Den's questioning gaze. "Thorlu's hunter instincts are highly developed. I needed him confused, so we could disappear. Hold on."

Both moved to grip the staff. Abarax and La clung to their shoulders. Brie pictured the fertile basin. Star's blurred. Time regressed.

They stepped from Mittkeer into the San Crúil Valley of yesterday. as the clouds overhead roiled and misted away. The ground shook. Boulders exploded outward, leaving the valley open at both ends.

From a long, low building, an ancient man walked toward them. Eyes as bright as a child's looked from Den to Penee, paused on the bat, moved to La, and ended peering at Brie.

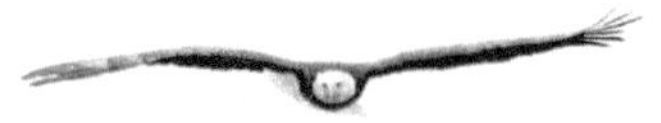

39

The man assessed Brie with such intense scrutiny she knew he missed little. She examined him with a similar earnestness. Her gaze moved from the hides worn around his waist and over one shoulder to the tattoos on his arms that told the story of the incirrata. Those on his calves depicted the setting sun, the moon, and the stars. A feather adorned his white, frizzy hair. The wisdom of many sun cycles lined his tanned cheeks and filled the deep-set dark eyes. She detected the hint of a smile as his attention expanded to include her companions.

His husky voice worked to pronounce an introduction in the language of his guests. "I am K'iin. I am Dri Adoh, the shaman, tribal leader." He touched his head, then pointed at Brie's. "May I learn?"

"You may, Dri Adoh. I am called Brie."

Shamanic power washed over her. Dri Adoh's perceptive presence searching her thoughts recalled memories of cool, fresh rain in spring. His reverential bow, when he withdrew from her mind, humbled her.

The shaman moved to Den. They examined each other with candid interest. Dri Adoh seemed satisfied with what he saw, ran his fingertips down Den's right arm, and switched his astute attention to Penee.

He indicated her tattooed arm, placed a hand on his heart, and inclined his head.

Surprise brought a whispered gasp. She returned his reverent bow.

He did not speak but beckoned them to follow. Their trek through the village went unnoticed by the tribe's men, women, and children celebrating the return of the sun. Inside a long, low building, the shaman led them past a series of tables to a partition behind which Irstant and Henri lay on narrow cots.

"I learned your language from their minds, VarTerel Brie." He checked his sleeping guests. "We must work together; we must work fast." His penetrating gaze fastened on hers. "You must remove the enchantment which suspends them between life and death. I do not know its origin." He stepped aside.

Brie sandwiched Henri's hand between hers. Shutting her eyes, she explored her aunt's psyche. Threads of SorTechory wove a web of forgetting around her. Brie continued her careful search. The SorTech had primed the intricate workings of the trap to kill if anyone tampered with the threads.

She faced the shaman. "The enchantment is twofold." She explained what she had discovered. "If we trigger the trap, Aunt Henri will die. Thoughts, anyone?"

Dri Adoh studied the elder VarTerels. "Your instincts are attuned to do this work, VarTerel Brie. Trust them to guide you."

Wolloh's voice in her mind steadied her resolve. "Penee, Aunt Henri's staff is the key to unraveling the trap. Please take it and stand at her head. Den, maintain a safe space for us. Be prepared to step in if we need you." She blew out a breath. "Here I go."

Attention concentrated on the threads of SorTechory, she sought a way to reverse the trap. The rose quartz crystal topping her aunt's staff hummed. Brie whispered a command. A shaft of pale pink light streamed into the crown of her great-aunt's head. With meticulous care, Brie guided it to the trap. Stillness encased her aunt. Brie maneuvered the light to enclose the trap's trigger. Henri gave a soft moan. The crystal hummed louder. Light flared brighter. Another moan and the trap dissolved. Brie glanced up. "I disarmed the trap. Penee, concentrate on the web."

She refocused her mental control on the intricate weave and studied the threads of SorTechory. A charm breaker Henri had taught her jumped to the forefront. *Lavrune!* The web unraveled, puffing into nothing. She exhaled. "It's done. Now, Irstant."

Penee moved to Irstant's feet. Brie stood at his head, his staff in her hand. A search for the trap unearthed a different trigger. Like a jigsaw puzzle, its pieces fit perfectly into place. She stepped back, aimed Usolamet at the crown of Irstant's head, and directed her intent. "Irstant!" His hand jerked. "Usolamet!" The trigger gleamed. One at a time, the puzzle's pieces exploded into nothing. His hand jerked a second time. The web of SorTechory unraveled. Breathing easily at last, she stood the staff upright.

Dri Adoh explained what he required to bring them back to consciousness, positioned Penee opposite him next to Henri and Den at her feet, each held a VarTerel's staff. He called Brie to his side. "You carry a special stone to help them remember. Yes?"

"I do." She offered him the smooth blue stone.

"It is your power which enlivens it, VarTerel Brie. I will work with the crystal vial." He accepted the vial and touched Henrietta's forehead. "Please position the stone here."

She placed the Remembering Stone.

Removing the jeweled stopper, the shaman held the vial up to the light.

> *"Tears of joy and light and sun*
> *Rejoin this body and soul as one.*
> *Banish all that does not give*
> *Her freedom, sight, and will to live."*

Penee parted Henri's lips. The Stannag's tears of happiness wet her lips. Eyelids twitched. Her chest rose and fell. A rush of blood tinted her cheeks, dispersing their paleness. A long sigh later, she stared up at the grass roof.

Brie removed the Remembering Stone and kissed her cheek. "Rest, Aunt Henri."

Violet eyes drifted shut. She slept.

After repeating the ritual with Irstant, Dri Adoh led them beyond the partition. He addressed Den. "You sent these souls to me for their safe keeping. I have protected them, nurtured them, and helped to bring them back. Den Zironho, you must pay a price for the danger to my people."

"Tell me what I must do, Dri Adoh, to repay your kindness."

The shaman's stern gaze included Penee. "As bearers of the sign of our goddess Incirrata, you must bless the K'iin with a child from your joining."

Penee stiffened. "I can't promise something I don't know will happen."

Den placed a gentle arm around her.

Dri Adoh waited, his demeanor uncompromising.

A tremor pulsed through Henri's staff. Brie's hand groped for the Remembering Stone. "I believe I have a solution. May I speak?"

Interest gleamed in the shaman's eyes. "Please share, VarTerel."

Brie explained the process of protariflee and gave him a minute to assimilate its potential. "Penee is a daughter of this process."

"Den is a son of protariflee." Henri, supported by Irstant, walked carefully to Brie's side.

Den's handsome features hardened. "Would you care to explain?"

Henri shook her head. "Irstant will tell your story at the appropriate time. Thorlu, Vygel, and Skultar are closing in on the valley." Her weak voice quivered. "Brie, explain your idea."

Den assisted the elder VarTerels to a bench. Brie waited while he maneuvered onto one next to them. "We will soon return to TreBlaya and the ship El Aperdisa, which has a protariflee lab. If Penee and Den agree, I suggest, Dri Adoh, you select a young woman to go with us. Penee has eggs stored already. Den can contribute sperm. When the Protariflee Team has successfully implanted an embryo in your tribeswoman, we can bring her back to Neul Isle."

The long house grew silent. Dri Adoh stroked the fur piece on his chest. "Even if they agree, I cannot ask one of my tribe to do what you are suggesting. They have never been outside this valley. How can I ask them to go through dimensions, to carry another's child?"

A young woman stepped from behind the partition, smiled at Henri and Irstant, and spoke haltingly. "If you agree, I will go, Father." After a difficult discussion, the shaman kissed her forehead and brought her to the table.

Pride balanced Dri Adoh's apparent distress. "This is my youngest daughter, Inōni. She has been visiting our guests. Her shamanic gifts helped her to learn their language and to understand the depth of their power. If you agree, Penee and Den, she says she will go."

Den escorted Penee to one side. After a brief discussion and a quick hug, they rejoined the group.

Penee took Inōni's hands. "You honor us with your desire to carry our child for your people."

Inōni looked relieved. "It is good."

Brie caught a movement beyond the shaman, saw her aunt raise spectacles, and Irstant swivel his twisted body to look over his shoulder.

All conversation ceased.

Henri peered through her lenses. A beautiful woman walked between the long tables. Strawberry blonde hair formed a shining aura surrounding her. Mint green eyes flashed an urgent message.

Brie, the first to find her tongue, called out. "Kat!"

Dri Adoh bowed. "Offspring of NáDúr, Goddess of All Nature."

"Dri Adoh, Shaman Leader of the K'iin, I come to you at my mother's behest. The enemies of your guests have imprisoned Aahana and the incirrata. They also threaten the K'iin. Dri Adoh and Inōni, you must prepare to protect your people. You, Brielle, and your companions must return to the lagoon.

She held out her hands. "Brie, take my hands. We will work together. Everyone else, form a circle around us."

Henri accepted Penee's help to navigate between the tables. Den guided Irstant into place.

The goddess bowed. "Please, VarTerels, call your staffs."

Henri lifted a hand. Happiness coursed through her as fingers closed around the delicately carved rowan wood.

Usolamet appeared in Irstant's gnarled hand. His twisted body straightened; his bronze eye's gleamed. "Thank you, Kat!"

Humming energy racing from person to person rocked the long house.

Kat inhaled a long breath. "Brie, we must enter Mittkeer. Hang on, everyone. Now, Brielle!"

The room vanished. Unending night focused, trembled, sharpened. At a word from Kat, a column of light enclosed the circle. "Picture the campsite by the lagoon." She took a breath. Mittkeer vanished. The lagoon and the tide pool steadied. A warm breeze diffused gasps of surprise.

Usolamet glowed. Irstant swung to face Bolcán Murloch. Henri moved to his side.

On Rina Island, shields of energy refracted their light to shafts shooting below the water's surface.

Henri raised her spectacles and peered over the lagoon. "Our enemies imprison the Guardian Stannag in the incirrata's lair. Shafts of light form bars across the entrance. To free them, we must destroy our enemies' shields." Alertness enclosed her. "We are about to have a guest. Irstant and I will make ourselves scarce. I suggest, Kat, that you do the same. Surprise is much better unannounced."

"I will return soon." Kat faded.

Henri caught Brie's eye. *"Remember, Brielle, what I told you."*

Thorlu Tangorra's overabundance of pride preceded him. Brie rubbed her arms and grimaced. Avarice drifted ahead of him over the lagoon. A villain's shrewdness tainted the air, sparking a warning response from the Star.

Penee and Den, one on either side of her at the clearing's center, reacted with uneasiness. Their shields shimmered. Brie waited until the vibration of Thorlu's wards permeated the clearing. Hers snapped into place.

He materialized a safe distance from them. "Ah, Brielle. A moment longer and I would have had you." Eyebrows raised, he pinned his shrewd gaze on Den. "Den Zironho, Skultar will be so disappointed his favorite aide is a traitor." His sarcastic grimace became an enchanting smile. "Your cousin, Penesert, will be most delighted to have you back under his protection." He glanced beyond the trio. "I could have sworn others arrived with you." A hard stare drilled into Brie.

She ignored it and his sneer. "What do you need from us?"

He flipped his cape behind his shoulders. "I require all of you to come with me. What do you say?"

Penee scowled. "Why on Soputto would we do that?"

"Because, Penesert, if *you* refuse, *we* will cut off the Stannag's tentacles one by one."

She flinched.

"I gather you don't like that? How about you, Den?"

Den's right arm trembled. "What you do with the Stannag is your business."

Thorlu pursed his lips. "We shall see. Let me tell you what else your refusal to join me will cause. I haven't decided what to do with the Sun Queen's daughter, but I promise that the K'iin, Henrietta Avetlire, and Relevart's good friend Irstant will wish they were still trapped in the valley." He glanced around. "Where is the Universal VarTerel, anyway?"

Brie folded her arms, lifted her chin, and shrugged. "I have no idea."

He faded, then solidified. "How is The MasTer's gene treating you? Vygel fears you might find it troublesome."

"Tell Vygel I appreciate his concern." She turned her back.

Penee and Den stepped together, hiding her from view.

"I'll give you some time to discuss your options. They are fewer than you imagine. If Brie doesn't respond by sunrise, we will cut the first tentacle from the Stannag." Thorlu whipped his cape and disappeared.

Stillness reigned in the clearing, but not in Brie's mind.

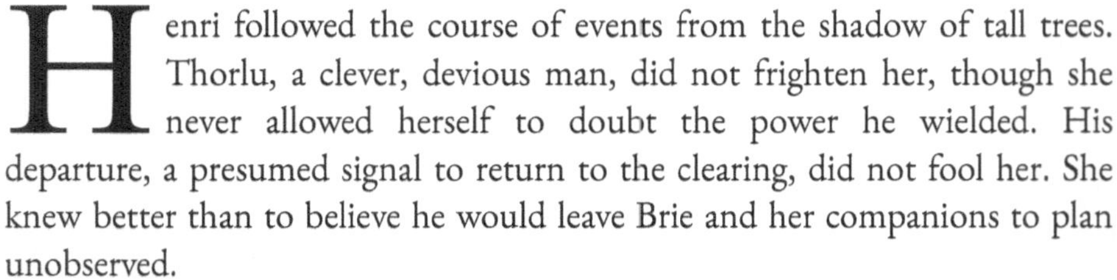

40

Henri followed the course of events from the shadow of tall trees. Thorlu, a clever, devious man, did not frighten her, though she never allowed herself to doubt the power he wielded. His departure, a presumed signal to return to the clearing, did not fool her. She knew better than to believe he would leave Brie and her companions to plan unobserved.

Irstant had withdrawn his power. He stood, his body crooked; his eyes blind. His thoughts masked, he used subtle telepathy to communicate. *"Be watchful."*

Henri responded by squeezing his hand. Their time together in the longhouse had introduced them. She understood Relevart's desire to help his dear childhood friend, a VarTerel whose power and wisdom matched his own.

Irstant's energy shifted. Usolamet glimmered within its rowan cocoon. Eagle alert, his piercing bronze eyes searched. His hand shot out. Strong fingers closed around her arm.

The Mocendi flashed into view.

Vygel cackled. "You thought we didn't know you were here."

Thorlu's scathing stare raked Irstant from head to foot. "You look rather imposing, old man."

Henri's rose quartz crystal glowed brighter. The hand on her arm tightened. With Irstant, she rocketed upward, tailed by Thorlu's angry shouts. Mittkeer snatched them into its star-studded maw.

A tall shadow emerged from the celestial backdrop. "What a pleasure to see you both!"

The well-loved voice inspired everything from relief to delight. Henri walked into Relevart's embrace and lifted her face to receive his gentle kiss.

Usolamet glittered a moment longer before Irstant moved into the circle of friendship. The crystal dimmed. Irstant's body contorted. Brilliant bronze irises turned to milky white. He rested his balding head against Relevart's shoulder. *"Friends—a rare and treasured gift."* A shaky step away ended with him leaning on his staff, an aura of expectancy draping him.

Henri looked up at her lifemate. "Do we go back..."

Relevart kissed her forehead. "This is a fight our heirs must win on their own."

Henri peered at him through her thick lenses. "Can we at least watch them?" She chuckled. "I sound like Arienh."

He laughed. "Indeed, you do." With his staff, he fashioned a bench from the fabric of time. A hand on his old friend's arm, he guided Irstant to it. "Please be comfortable, my dear friend."

Henri, seated at the opposite end of the bench, peered at her life-mate, her magnified eyes questioning. "A Time Window?"

His sparkled. The crystal tip of his staff glowed. Wielding it like a huge paint brush, he drew a large oval. "A Time Window, my dear, through which we can see the present unfolding." He sat down between her and Irstant and tapped the center of the oval.

With a hand resting on Irstant's knee, he recited:

> *"All time, no time, clear our sight,*
> *Let us observe the coming fight.*
> *We will watch, but not add fire.*
> *Lessons given will inspire."*

Irstant touched the hand on his knee. His sighted eyes gleamed with delight.

Spectacles in one hand and staff in the other, Henri glued her attention to the clearing on Neul Isle.

Thorlu's frustrated howl whipped over Bolcán Murloch. Brie, a hand shading her eyes, saw her great-aunt and Irstant rocket above the trees. She whooped with delight when Mittkeer engulfed them.

The proximity of the Mocendi vibrated in the clearing. Half expecting them to return, she stiffened. Penee moved closer to Den, whose expression exposed little.

Light flashing at the end of the lagoon and the abating of Mocendi energy eased Brie's angst.

Penee pulled back her sleeves to expose her arm. Her tattoo burned blood red. "We have to do something. What if their threat to cut off a tentacle is real?"

Abarax landed on the shore. "Four men just arrived in Skultar's camp. They are assembling winged harnesses. They have strange canisters, too. What are they planning?"

Den scowled. "The canisters are bombs. The robotic wings will enable the soldiers to fly over the island and drop them. We have to warn the K'iin."

La fluttered close. *"I go to K'iin."* She whizzed from sight.

Brie paced to the shoreline. Ideas formed; ideas crumpled. One floated on the surface. She hurried back to her companions. "The first shape I ever shifted to was a DerTahan Water ConDria. I'm not sure I can make this shift on Soputto. If it works, I'll help you change to a ConDria. Then we will deal with the winged soldiers."

Den pointed across the lagoon. "Something is happening in Skultar's camp. Better hurry. Tell us what to do."

"If I manage the change to ConDria, I'll fly over you. Water droplets helped Esán shift, so cross your fingers it will happen again. If it does, you distract the soldiers. I'll head to Rina's lair."

"Wait, Brie." Penee grabbed her arm. "What's a ConDria?"

Penee's worried expression made Brie laugh. "It's part condor—part dragon—and composed of water." She stepped away. "*You* will *love* it. Here I go."

Focusing on the desert of Fera Finnero brought to mind the delight of her unexpected shift. Coolness flowed over her. Her heart beat a new rhythm. Huge watery wings carried her into the air.

Brie heard Penee's gasp of surprise and Den's deep laugh as she circled back to the clearing. A low swoop sent droplets of glistening water raining down on their upraised faces. Not waiting to see them shift, she soared high above the lagoon.

Two dark shapes rose from behind the Mocendi's shimmering shields. She folded her wings and dove into the lagoon. Gills on the sides of her neck controlled her breath. Gliding deeper, she angled her massive body toward the wavering bars of light securing the incirrata's den.

B rie's shift to the dragon-sized Water ConDria happened so fast chills piggybacked on Penee's astonished gasp. "Den, it's beautiful. Can I shape that?"

Water droplets from Brie's wing tips dripped down Den's chin. A dragon shaped head with a condor's beak began his shift. His husky laugh transformed to a gurgling squawk. Water-formed wings lifted his massive aqueous body above the lagoon. He made a swooping circle.

Penee watched with a mix of awe and disappointment. Den's ConDria banked over her. Water rain down on her uplifted face. Dizzying coolness washed over her. Exquisite fluidity carried her into the air. A breadth of beingness she had never imagined left her breathless.

"Penee!" Den's telepathic shout focused her on two winged soldiers streaking their direction. Two more shot skyward from behind the Mocendi's shields.

Penee inventoried her new shape's abilities, soared upward, and leveled off above the two winged men. A spewed stream of water hit a soldier broadside and left him struggling to remain airborne. A direct hit sent the second man head over booted feet. The water snatched at his wingtips. He righted himself and flew back toward the island.

Penee circled upward. A soldier lay unconscious on the shore, shattered pieces of his robotic wings strewn over the ground. Abarax deposited another man further up the beach. La fluttered to his shoulder, bit his neck, and left him in a drugged stupor.

Den's wings fanning the air held him suspended, a man dangling from his talons. A soldier closed in. Hovering upright, he aimed a black cylinder. Penee raced toward him, whipped sideways, wrapped her long tail around a wing, and threw the man away from Den.

Another circuit of the lagoon sent her soaring above Den's floundering prey. Heavy robotic wings dug at his body. He struggled to release them. Den swooped low. His water talons gripped the man's harness. Powerful wings carried the ConDria and its burden over a tree-covered ridge.

Above her, Abarax made a final circuit of the lagoon and soared back to camp.

Den streaked from behind the ridge. A long, graceful glide brought him to her side as she prepared to touch down. Together, they landed in human form, breathless and exhilarated by their experience in the shape of a DerTahan Water ConDria.

Abarax greeted them with an appreciative grin. "We did well."

Penee threw herself into Den's arms and laughed with childish delight.

❦ ❦

In Mittkeer, Henri and her fellow VarTerels observed the younger generation battle the enemy. She cheered each success of the Water ConDria brigade. The men on either side of her nodded their approval when Den carried the last soldier over the ridge.

Relevart touched the Time Window. The scene changed. Brie had almost reached the incirrata's lair.

Henri patted Relevart's hand. "You read my mind."

"I anticipate your every wish, my dear." His soft laugh made Irstant smile.

Engrossed in the activities of her great-niece, Henri found herself mesmerized by the ConDria's grace underwater. Wings pressed to the sides of the body and a rolling motion from the head to the tip of the long tail propelled the massive creature to the incirrata's lair at a surprising speed. Her inspection of the bars ended with a swooping about-face.

Swimming below the surface to the far end of the lagoon, she thrust her powerful wings downward and soared from water to sky in one extraordinary move. She landed in human form by the tidal pool, where Den, Penee, and Abarax waited, their eyes shining with admiration.

Penee grinned. "That was amazing! I love shaping a Water ConDria."

Brie acknowledged her delight with a happy grin. "Me, too. What happened with the soldiers?"

Abarax summarized its story, then lifted a hand to welcome the Luna Moth. "La is the hero. She drugged the men."

La fluttered. "Sleep long, long time. I go check."

Penee's eyes twinkled. "Den, where's the last soldier.

"I left him in a valley to recover. He won't make it back to camp any time soon." He pursed his lips. "I'm concerned about the soldier who made it back. Skultar won't wait long to retaliate. We need to rescue the Stannag. What did you discover?"

"I found the lair secured by bars of light radiating from Thorlu's primary shields. To free the Stannag, we must destroy the light bars without alerting Skultar and his men."

Den looked intrigued. "You want to leave the primary shields in place?"

"Yes. Just long enough to confuse our enemies. What I need from you, Penee and Abarax, is a distraction."

La flew to the Astican. It frowned. "La has been spying. One soldier is unharmed. Skultar and the Mocendi want retribution. They have several bombs and are preparing to construct a catapult."

Den offered his hand. La alighted. "Well done, Luna Moth. Are you willing to help free the Stannag?"

Her wings palpated. *"Help. Yes."*

"Good. You and Abarax keep watch at the enemy camp."

Henri tapped her knee with her glasses. "I wonder what plan they will devise?"

Penee regarded Brie, her mind humming with ideas. *What type of distraction will give you time to rescue the Stannag?*

Den cleared his throat. "I might have an idea."

She shot him a startled glance. "Were you reading my thoughts?"

He looked surprised. "I wouldn't invade your privacy that way without permission."

Brie interjected. "What's your plan, Den?"

"If I walk into camp like nothing has happened, I'm betting chaos will erupt. Thorlu and Vygel saw me with you. The last time I was with Skultar, we were at the seaside village where he picked up the boat. Since then..." He shrugged.

Penee gasped. "Den, they'll capture you! Then what?"

"Freeing the Stannag is the important thing. What happens to me is immaterial."

She gripped his arm. "Not to me, Den Zironho."

His dazzling smile drowned her. She put some distance between them. "So, you walk into camp. What do I do?"

"Stay out of sight. Watch for a chance to snatch one of those canisters. If my plan doesn't work, drop it on the shore. Better yet, drop it on Skultar's boat. Don't shape the ConDria, and DON'T get caught." Shaping a gray hawk, he soared skyward.

Brie hugged her. "It'll all work out. Go. Keep him out of trouble until I have time to reach the lair."

Penee caught her hand. "Be careful, Brielle AsTar. Friends are hard to come by. I don't want to lose you."

"You be careful, too." Brie climbed onto a large rock. "See you soon." Her splash-less dive carried her effortlessly through the water.

Penee couldn't shake off a chill of foreboding as Brie shaped the Water ConDria and disappeared into the dark depths of the Bolcán Murloch. *Take care.* She shifted to Soputton swift and raced over the lagoon. *With luck, I'll beat Den to the camp.*

The solitary flight gave her time to calm her anxiety and prepare for whatever happened next. Halfway to the island, she flew toward the shore. A circuitous course inland allowed her to approach the enemies camp from the back and land in a Neul pine within listening distance of her enemies.

Skultar paced the clearing, his bald head gleaming, his nostrils flaring. Anger raged in beady, dark-eyed gaze that flashed from Furrnoce, cowering to one side, to the Mocendi.

"How could you allow this to happen? Three pairs of robotic wings destroyed. All the time and money to create them wasted." He marched up to the Mocendi. "Why didn't you tell me about the Water ConDria?" A huff of exasperation ended in a leer. "Did you plan to inform me the VarTerels escaped?"

Vygel opened his mouth.

Skultar sneered. "DiMensionery—" He spit. "Prove your worth, gentlemen. Make sure those shields of yours don't fail, or I will make you sorry you ever sought me out."

His gaze fastened on the soldier. "Suit up. Drop a bomb in the lagoon. I want those pretentious young fools to know they haven't won." Rounding on Furrnoce, he growled, "Is The Box fixed?"

The SorTech scuttled backward. "No, master."

Skultar glowered. "No is *not* acceptable, you idiot. Get busy." He reeled around to glare at the Mocendi. "One of you mind the shields. The other bring me those girls—and find Den Zironho."

"I'm right here, Skultar Rados." Den strode into the clearing.

Skultar froze. Hatred spewed from every pore in his body. "What are you doing my camp, traitor?"

Den produced a satiric smirk. "I thought you called."

The Governor of the TaSneach Penal Colony bristled with a desire to do harm. He marched one step in Den's direction. The Mocendi closed ranks behind him.

Penee ignored her inclination to act.

Den did not move. His expression showed no fear.

Skultar, violence screaming, took another step.

With a mechanical whine, the soldier lifted into the air. All eyes turned his way.

Panic propelled the Soputton swift into flight. *Brie is underwater with a bomb on the way. How do I save her?*

41

Henri rose from the star-spangled bench in Mittkeer with her heart in her throat. "Brie is in the lagoon. We have to warn her."

Relevart eased her down beside him. "This is their battle, Henrietta. We cannot interfere." Dejection shadowed his hopeful features. "All we can do is watch. They will figure it out."

A rebuttal left a bitter taste in Henri's mouth. Hope fading, she focused on the Water ConDria floating in front of the Stannag's lair and Penee's petite swift chasing a bomb-carrying, winged soldier over the lagoon.

Penee waited until she cleared the shields to shift to a ConDria. The shock of the change mid-air left her reeling. Confusion fogged her mind. Her vision cleared. The soldier hovered, ready to drop a glossy black canister. A hard, downward thrust of her wings hurtled her toward him.

The soldier's head whipped her direction. His hand hit the release. The bomb sped to its target, pierced the water's surface, and detonated—all as her beak closed on his wing.

The explosion hurled their limp bodies through the air. Ripped from her grasp, the soldier plummeted, one broken wing dangling. Penee righted her dragon-sized body, slowed its descent, and banked into a wide circle.

I n Mittkeer, Henri, spectacles on her nose, peered at the time window. The scene shifted.

B eneath the water, a muffled roar opened a cavernous space surrounding the debilitated ConDria. Undulating underwater waves pitched the limp body into the light bars, sucked it backward, and pitched it forward again. Water slamming together propelled the unconscious ConDria into human form. Rock-heavy, Brie plunged downward, bubbles of escaping air forming a trail behind her.

Henri gripped her staff, ready to interfere. The light bars shattered and freed the trapped Stannag. She reminded herself to breathe.

The phantom incirrata shot to Brie's side. Its long tentacles enveloped her. Jet propulsion carried incirrata and human through roiling currents to the lagoon's surface.

A ConDria, legs extended, dropped from the sky. The incirrata released Brie's waterlogged body. Penee's watery talons snatched it from the lagoon. Powerful wings pressing against the air, she carried the Universe's youngest VarTerel to safety.

High tide and the aftermath of the explosion lifted the Stannag into the tide pool. Aahana materialized as the ConDria deposited Brie gently on the ground at the clearings center.

Penee materialized and sank down beside her.

Aahana knelt to brush wet curls from Brie's pale forehead.

Penee gulped in a shaking breath. "Is she alive?"

Aahana met her frightened gaze. "Barely."

A Soputton gray hawk landed at Brie's head. Den eased to sitting. "You did well, Penesert. Please introduce your friend."

Penee managed a shaky introduction. "Aahana, Daughter of the Sun Queen, meet Den Zironho."

An explosion rocked the opposite end of the lagoon. Den, his attention fixed on Brie, nodded. "Sounds like Abarax hid a canister in The Box."

Penee laid a trembling hand on his arm.

He examined the twin. "She hasn't given up. Let's see what we can do to help her. Penee, place the Remembering Stone over her heart."

She retrieved the pouch from under Brie's soaked tunic and placed the Stone.

"Good." He looked from Penee to Aahana. "You are both healers. Cup the stone between your hands. Picture life flowing from hands to stone to Brie."

Focused intent soaked the clearing. From the birds in the heavens to the fish in the sea, everything on Neul Isle seemed to hold its breath. In the tide pool, Rina's bulbous blue-gray sac floated part way above the water, her horizontal irises opening and closing, her tentacles lifting and falling amidst fat-leafed seaweed.

I n Mittkeer, three VarTerel's, attention riveted to the scene playing out in the time window, forgot to breathe.

B rie lay suspended in memory: the roar, the explosion, the deep cavity engulfing her, the compression wave throwing her into the light bars. She relived every repeated bubble pulse that surged through her watery body. The realization that if she had been in human form when the blast detonated, she would be dead kept her a hostage to unconsciousness. Fear of what she might discover imprisoned her as surely as the bars of light had imprisoned the incirrata.

Her thoughts drifted. *Is the Stannag free? Did the explosion kill her?* A vague memory flickered. *Something enfolding me. What?* She used her concern for the incirrata to obscure her fear for herself. *Where am I?* Her fingers moving over hard, dry ground, oxygen flowing in and out of her lungs, the wet hair sticking to her neck and cheeks brought a wave of relief. *I'm not at the bottom of the lagoon.*

Warmth infusing her chest acted like the thrust of her wings against air. She soared upward, embracing a return to awareness. Her eyes darting beneath her lids admitted a flicker of light. Hands on her temples thrummed with life. Her heart picked up its rhythm. Blood pulsed through her veins. An upsurge of energy enlivened every part of her body.

She heard a groan. The realization it was her own released her last vestige of fear. Her eyelids fluttered open, revealing a trio of anxious faces. Her memory provided their names: Penee, Den, Aahana. La's tiny squeak brought a genuine smile. An attempt to move shattered it.

Pain throbbed in every joint and muscle. Her right ear popped. She pressed a hand to her aching left ear. It came away sticky with blood. Panic tiptoed closer. A quick mental inventory of her body let in a ray of hope. "No bones broken." Gratitude made her giddy.

Den leaned closer. "Do you want to sit up or lie still?"

His question sounded crackly and far away.

She croaked a whispered response. "Sit."

He slid an arm under her shoulders. "Are you ready?"

"Yes." She tensed. A deep inhale exited in a groan. Wooziness forced her to clutch his hand harder. A steadying moment later, she regarded her friends with a growing sense of relief.

Penee's guilt was tangible. "I didn't know if you'd survive." She hiccuped a gulp of air. "I tried to reach the soldier. I'm so sorry." Tears trickled down her face.

Brie reached for her hand. "You brought me here, right?"

A tiny nod. "I did. But the Stannag rescued you."

"The incirrata is alright?"

Penee moved aside. The gray-blue incirrata floated in the tide pool. When she saw Brie, color flooded her body and jewels bedecked her scarlet tentacles.

Brie flashed a smile. "You *both* saved me! Thank you."

As the image in the Time Window faded into the unending night sky, Henri tucked her spectacles away. She studied her life companion. "You knew they would make it, right?"

He sandwiched her small hand between his larger ones. "I knew they had the potential and the skills."

Irstant's gaze darted over the starscape. *"Relevart, I can see."*

Relevart released her hand to squeeze Irstant's shoulder. "Mittkeer has given you a gift, my friend."

The old man tugged at his braided beard. *"I believe the charm you created helped. Thank you."*

Henri stood up. "What now, Universal VarTerel?"

"You go to Neul to check on Brielle." He helped Irstant to his feet. "Irstant and I have some unfinished business with two Mocendi. We'll come to you when it's complete."

The star-studded bench melted back into time. Henri gripped her staff, focused her intention, and walked from the night stars into the late afternoon sun. Cool shadows helped to calm her slight nausea.

Brie leaned against the end of a raised sleeping pallet. Penee sat on one side with Den. Aahana had just risen.

"Aunt Henri!" Brie croaked her delight. "I am so glad to see you. Where's Relevart? Is Irstant alright?"

Henri examined her through amethyst-rimmed spectacles. "You sound like your sister. A little patience will provide all the answers, my dearest niece." She tucked her specs in their pocket.

Penee jumped to her feet. "I am so glad you gave the Mocendi the slip!"

By the time Penee had hugged her and introduced her to Aahana, Den had climbed to his feet. He offered his hand. "I am Den Zironho." His smile flashed. "You are the life-mate of the Universal VarTerel."

Good looks which would have made her giddy in her youth received a perceptive examination. "Den, I owe you a debt of gratitude. Thank you for rescuing me from Skultar's clutches." She studied the handsome face, the curve of his mouth, the thick, wavy hair. A fleeting moment of recognition passed between them. "I have heard so much about you. It is nice to meet you at last." She glanced toward the trees. "Ah, Abarax, I thought that was you. I don't suppose you could find a seat for this older soul?"

The Astican placed his favorite upturned stump next to Brie. "It is good to see you, Henrietta Avetlire."

La fluttered to her hand. *"La hurt you. Sorry."*

Henri smiled. "I forgive you, dear Luna Moth. As you see, I am well."

The lovely creature fluttered to her shoulder, brushed a wing against her cheek, and flew to Abarax.

A soft buzz from the lagoon called to her. Staff in hand, she walked the short distance to the tide pool. A red tentacle extended toward her. Holding out her hand, she allowed the jeweled tip to rest on her palm. Her world faded; the world of the incirrata enfolded her. An exchange of love and understanding passed between them. "Thank you, Rina, for saving my niece."

Aahana walked to her side. The tentacle withdrew beneath the water. "Rina says you are a gift to Neul Isle."

Henri kissed the salty dampness on her palm and beamed. "As are you, Aahana."

The Sun Queen's daughter sighed. "I only wish to go home."

Rina blew a long hiss. Aahana stepped to her side and faded.

Henri walked back to the sleeping pallets. She sent her staff into hiding and sank onto the stump. Brie's obvious pain made her heart ache. "You are lucky to be alive, Brielle AsTar." She tapped her niece's forehead. "Better?"

Brie sighed. "Much better. Thank you."

Henri scrutinized Den from beneath half-closed lids. Another flash of recognition tempted her to ask if they had ever met. She resisted. "Tell us, Den, how you escaped being captured by Skultar. He appeared to be most disappointed in you."

⁙

Henri might have plucked the question from Penee's personal desire to know. More interested in Den's answer than she wanted him to realize, she kept her expression bland.

Den turned to Henri. "I had no idea you could see what was happening."

Henri held a single lens to her eye. "Time windows come in handy, if one has escaped into Mittkeer." She lowered the specs to her lap.

"Ah, well..." Den inclined his head. "Fortunately for me, the soldier who released the canister lifted off at an opportune moment. The distraction allowed me to put some distance between Skultar and myself. Aftershocks from the bomb he dropped too close to Rina Island sent Skultar, the Mocendi, and Furrnoce scrambling to stay upright. Their fumbling gave me an opportunity to dash into the woods. I shaped a gray hawk and flew here. No one followed, so I assume the chaos kept them busy enough not to miss me right away."

Relevart and Irstant materialized. "That and The Box exploding." The Universal VarTerel smiled. "Outstanding work, Abarax." He knelt by Brie. "You frightened us, Brielle. How are you?"

"I'm sore, Relevart. My left ear won't clear. Other than that, I'm just tired and happy to be alive."

He examined her for a long moment. "We are most glad Penee and the incirrata could assist." His expression softened. "You can rest soon, my dear."

Leaning on the staff, he climbed to his feet, his attention fixed on Penee. "Penesert, you are proving to be a genuine leader. Do not doubt yourself. Brielle would not have survived if not for your quick thinking. Thank you."

Penee's cheeks grew warm. She stuttered, "You're w-w-welcome."

His appreciation encompassed the group. "You have all done excellent work. Irstant and I have a meeting with Dri Adoh to discuss what needs to be accomplished before we are free to leave Neul Isle."

Henri tapped her specs on her knee. "What of our Mocendi?"

Irstant narrowed his bronze-brown eyes. "It seems they sensed we were coming."

Relevart's eyebrows bridged. "Vygel and Thorlu have disappeared. I'm certain an opportunity to search for them will present itself." His brows relaxed. "Enough of the Mocendi."

"What of my cousin and his SorTech?"

Penee's worried question brought a sly expression to the VarTerel's features. "Skultar and Furrnoce sailed back to Dast." A mischievous twinkle suggested the trip would not be uneventful.

42

Brie yearned for sleep. She smothered a yawn. Relevart had just announced it was the time to adjourn to Rina Island. Jaw clamped shut, she clasped Den's hands. A steady pull eased her to standing. She bit back a squeal of pain and slumped against him. His protective arms kept her from falling.

She managed a weak smile. "Thanks, Den."

Henri offered her staff. "Lean on this, niece. We're about to teleport."

Brie closed her eyes. Concentration brought a clear image of the Stannag's island. She held her breath. The clearing vanished. They arrived on the lair side of Rina Island. A celebration already in progress overflowed onto the mainland, where the joyful sound of children's high-pitched voices exploding into giggles carried over the water. On the island itself, K'iin adults worked to complete preparations for the upcoming ceremonies.

Wooden benches formed a semi-circle facing the lagoon. Several lean-tos constructed for the elders sat under a group of trees. The aroma of a deer roasting on a spit over the fire made Brie's mouth water. Women attending to the cooking laughed and chatted as they worked.

Brie watched with interest. *I wonder how it feels to be outside the valley after being trapped for so long?*

Relevart interrupt her with a gentle touch. "Irstant and I are meeting with Dri Adoh. Do you need anything?"

Den draped an arm over her shoulders. "Go ahead. We'll take care of her."

Feeling somewhat like a troublesome child, Brie sank onto a bench. "I'm fine, Relevart. Please go."

At the workstation, Inōni accepted two wooden cups from a smiling older woman and walked over to the new arrivals. Relevart and Irstant greeted her and departed.

Henri sat down and accepted a cup of brewed mint.

Brie lowered onto the bench. "Smells good, Aunt Henri."

Den rose to his feet. "I believe Inōni has something for you, too, Brielle."

Penee kissed her cheek. "La will fetch us if you need anything." She and Den ambled to the shore nearest Rina's lair.

Inōni acknowledged Henri with a shy smile. "You are looking refreshed."

Henri held up her cup. "I am, thanks to your special tea."

"I'm glad you like it." She offered Brie the remaining cup. "Valerian and devil's club root for the pain. You drink."

Laughter drifted their way. Inōni's joy reached out to touch everyone. "We are so happy! Thank you for freeing us from the valley."

Brie's left ear crackled, distorting the words. Disheartened, she touched her ear. "I'm sorry. I didn't understand what you said."

Inōni pointed at herself. "You show me?"

Brie placed the healer's hand on her forehead.

The tingle of a mental touch elicited a nod of understanding. Inōni withdrew a small vial and a funnel-shaped leaf from a pouch at her waist. "Silva oil. Good."

Brie held the funnel in place. Inōni put several drops of oil in her ear and stuffed it with white, filmy moss. "Drink your tea." She nodded to Henrietta and left to enjoy the sunset.

Deep in conversation, Irstant and Relevart walked up the path toward them.

Irstant glanced ahead and waved. He limped to Brie's side. *"You look better, Brielle."* He eased onto the bench. *"How do you feel?"*

"I don't hurt as much." She showed him the cup. "Valerian with devil's club root. It works."

Relevart sat next to Henri, leaned his forearms on his knees, and pitched his voice for Brie to hear. "You are looking stronger, my dear. Time will be the healer."

Henri regarded him with interest. "Did you meet with Dri Adoh?"

"We discussed his plans for the upcoming ceremonies. He told us how we can assist."

A twinkle danced in violet eyes. "Care to share?"

Relevart put and arm around his life-mate. "Tonight, we have a feast to celebrate the return of the sun and the K'iin's release from the valley. At dawn tomorrow morning, we release the souls of the Púca and Tura to the ever-world, then we welcome the new Stannag. When we have discharged these responsibilities, we are free to depart."

Brie finished her herbal mixture as Den and Penee approached from the shore with a distraught Aahana between them. Tears shimmered on the ebony cheeks. Defeat cloaked her with the heaviness of iron.

Henri made room on the bench. Penee helped the sobbing woman to sit. "Aahana has asked me to explain her distress, Relevart. Her mother sent word no substitute has come forward to replace her as Stannag. The messenger also told her Den and I cannot leave Neul until they have found one."

Henrietta put an arm around the Sun Queen's daughter. "I am so sorry, my dear. I know how much you wish to return to your home."

Penee plopped on the ground. "I can't stay here much longer. I have responsibilities elsewhere." She looked at the group. "Please think of something."

La flew to Brie's hand. A human-sized Abarax strode up the hill from the incirrata's lair. "We have a solution."

Aahana blinked away her tears. "Tell us, Astican and Luna Moth."

Abarax sat on the ground with its wings spread out behind it. La settled on the tip of its long, taloned finger. "We have been talking with Rina." Sadness flickered in the angelic face. "I must soon leave my body to remain on Neul as a half-being or become a Scáth. If the Sun Queen and Dri Adoh agree, I will replace Aahana as protector of the Isle of Neul."

La's wings trembled. He continued. "My beautiful friend, La, is coming to the end of her life cycle. If you grant her an eternal after-being, she will join me." Earnestness curved the rosebud mouth. "It will be unnecessary for another daughter of the Sun Queen to leave her world and those she loves."

Brie sorted through what she thought she had heard. "What do you think, Aahana?"

The Sun Queen's youngest daughter swallowed a sob, wiped a tear from her cheek, and rose from the bench. "I think I must confer with my mother." She looked dazed. "I must go to Dia Bandia. She will want to consult with Dri Adoh. I..." The magnitude of what she must do left her shaking.

Bracing herself for pain, Brie forced herself to her feet. "I'll take you to Dia Bandia." A flinch turned to a gasp.

Relevart moved to her side. "Sit down, Brielle. Den, please ask Dri Adoh to join us." He held out a cloth handkerchief. "Dry your tears, Aahana. I will escort you to the mountain."

Surprise registered on the exquisite face. "You would do that for me?"

"It would be my honor." His staff flashed into being.

A smiling Dri Adoh strode to his side. "I have always desired to experience the Land of Time."

Relevart inclined his head. "Please hold on to my staff." With solemn dignity, he offered Aahana his arm. "Shall we step into Mittkeer?"

She wiped her tears, straightened her slumped shoulders, and shook her long braids back from her face. Before they settled, Mittkeer embraced them.

Brie leaned her head on Henri's shoulder, glad to be on the bench next to her aunt and not in the Land of Time.

Relevart and Dri Adoh escorted a radiant Aahana from Mittkeer. Abarax came to its feet so fast its scales hummed. La hovered, anticipation quivering her delicate wings.

Aahana, flanked by the Universal VarTerel and the Shaman of K'iin, stopped in front of them. "Abellona, the Queen of the Sun People sends you this message, Luna Moth and Astican." Swirling light surrounded her. The Sun Queen stepped from the iridescent mist, a fiery scepter in her upraised hand.

"Astican of TreBlaya, you honor me, Aahana, and my daughters to be. I accept your offer to become the Stannag Guardian of Neul for *All Time*. The incirrata welcome's you in my daughter's stead. From this moment forward, all will know you as Sirlaa Grá, Heart Flame in the language of the Sun People."

Cool blue flames engulfed Abarax. Its heart glowed red in its chest. Air unfurled its blazing wings. It lifted into the dusk-tinted sky. Far below, Neul Isle encircled by the fire of the setting sun filled it with love.

The Queen's summons brought it to the ground. "Kneel, Sirlaa Grá." She tapped each shoulder with the blazing star topping her scepter. The blue flames faded. Motioning Abarax to stand, she pressed the star against the gray scales over its heart. A mist roiled into a cloud and cleared, leaving Aahana in her place.

Abarax willed chaotic thoughts into stillness. "I am grateful to you and your mother." It summoned all its love for La. "What of my lovely Luna Moth?"

Aahana's happiness lit up the coming night. "Tomorrow at sunrise, Kat, the Goddess of Small Creatures, will preside over La's passing. She will then resurrect the Luna Moth's spirit to bless it with the gift of eternal after-being."

La's soft squeak of love filled Abarax's heart. Her wings caressed its cheek.

Dri Adoh moved to Aahana's side. "Sirlaa Grá, the K'iin will bury your physical bodies on Rina Island and build a shrine in your honor." Jubilance surrounding him, he faced his tribesmen. "It is time to feast and celebrate!"

Cheers filled the coming night. Sounds of drum and flute and voices raised in song accompanied the last rays of dusk below the horizon and welcomed the soft beginnings of the moon's rising.

In the flickering flame of torchlight, Relevart studied the Astican's chest. "Abellona has given you another gift, Abarax."

Taloned fingers explored the spot where she had pressed the scepter. "What is it?"

Aahana beamed up at him. "She left the imprint of the Sun over your heart. In the tradition of our People, she has marked you as her offspring. By doing so, she fulfills her obligation to provide an heir to serve with the incirrata as Stannag." Aahana's fire-opal eyes gleamed. "I honor you as family." Blowing a kiss, she ran to join those gathering for the celebratory feast.

Relevart's emotions overflowed. "I'm so proud of you, Sirlaa Grá. You have done well."

Henri linked arms with her life-mate. "I wonder, Abarax, what Rayn would think of this adventure? I know she would be proud of you." She smiled. "You and La need some time." She drew Relevart down the path.

With the Luna Moth at its side, the TreBlayan Astican, head high and heart full, walked to the incirrata's lair.

P enee and Den had helped Brie to a lean-to, brought her a large leaf filled with deer meat and roots, and left her to rest. Another time, the sounds of celebration would have enticed her. Tonight, fatigue kept her prone. She stared at the crest of TaSneach topping the mountains. *I wish you were here, Esán. It has been quite a turning.*

Penee's soft voice woke her. "Brielle, the Púca await us."

Stifling a yawn, Brie eased her sore body to the edge of the cot. "Tell Relevart I'm on the way."

She sat, allowing herself to wake up. A slow ascent to standing left her breathing a sigh of relief. "Not as painful as I expected. I can do this."

Den met her outside to escort her to the semi-circled benches. Relevart, Henri, and Irstant greeted her with appraising looks. Penee slid onto the bench beside her aunt.

Tribesmen holding flaming torches lined the shore. Women in ceremonial dress waited to one side. The Púca, their opaque forms already beginning to dim, clustered on the other. A lone figure drifted apart from the group.

Penee nudged her. "Isn't that Tura? I wonder if he realized he'd have to face those he had killed?"

Dri Adoh conversed with Sri Ceari. The Púca leader conferred with his men. Bás, the youngest fisherman, drew Tura into their ranks.

"That's good." Penee sighed.

Compassion thrummed in Brie's heart. "It is the way of Trilemma, the expelling of DosWah, the shadow of evil." She laughed. "I sound like a VarTerel."

"You are one, Brielle AsTar."

Penee's solemn response made her stop to consider how accepting the role of VarTerel had changed her life. Her aunt's understanding pat on the hand reminded her she wasn't alone. Setting this weighty topic aside, she stretched to ease the pain in her back.

The darkness before dawn, broken only by torchlight and the pale gold of the rising sun tinting the horizon line, seemed full of secrets. The tribe waited behind the row of benches. Children, rubbing sleep from their eyes, sat cross-legged on the sidelines. Three drummers and a flutist waited to enter. Brie felt the emotion building.

The shaman, his sacred shepherd's crook in hand, moved from group to group greeting the members. He completed his circuit facing Relevart.

"The Ceremony of Passing is about to begin. You and your companions honor us with your presence, Universal VarTerel. We prepare to circle. Please join us."

Dri Adoh took his place at the circle's center. Silence settled over Rina Island. The drummers produced a steady, whisper-quiet roll. The flutist raised her instrument and played a series of long, breathy notes that faded with the soft sound of drumming into the stillness of dawn.

In the language of the K'iin, Dri Adoh began the ceremony. "We honor the Four Directions: Air! Fire! Water! Earth! We call forth the ancestors of the sacred Isle of Neul, of the K'iin, and of those whose spirits are preparing to pass into the ever-world."

The drummers' roll whispered over the island. The flute's glorious sound joined with it. Those in the circle raised their arms. A low humming grew louder. Inōni walked to stand with the musicians. At the Shaman's signal, the Púca and Tura floated into a circle. The musicians played. Inōni's voice rose in song.

> *"Peace to the ancestors of all the deceased.*
> *On this morning in time, they will be released.*
> *We welcome your presence, the solace you bring;*
> *We lift up our voices, your praises to sing.*
>
> *Ancestors, we honor your stories, your grace;*
> *Your feet that have walked in this glorious place;*
> *Your hands that have worked on the land and the seas;*
> *Your breath that has moved through the winds and the trees.*

> *Be with us here in this circled farewell;*
> *Escort those who pass to the land where you dwell.*
> *We celebrate all and the lives you have lived;*
> *We honor your passing and all that you give.*
>
> *Ancestors, we honor your stories, your grace;*
> *Your feet that have walked in this glorious place;*
> *Your hands that have worked on the land and the seas;*
> *Your breath that has moved through the winds and the trees."*

With each verse, the Púca and Tura grew fainter. The K'iin swayed to the music. Their voices rose as they sang the second chorus with Inōni. The song faded. The K'iin blew out a long breath. Sri Ceari and his companions floated into a sky tinted coral by the rising sun and vanished.

The women moved to the circle's center and danced a beautiful farewell. Brie saw Penee's tears. Her own made a silent journey down her cheeks.

The K'iin grew quiet. Aahana and Kat approached from the shore on either side of a full-sized Astican with the Luna Moth on its shoulder. Their time had come.

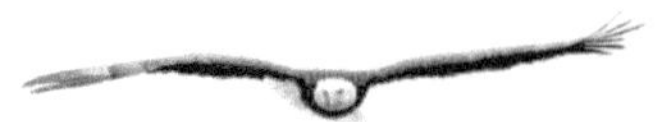

43

Penee plodded after Kat and Aahana to a cleft between two forested mountains where Dri Adoh had consecrated a grave for the burial of the Astican and the Luna Moth's physical bodies. At the end of their week of celebrating, the K'iin would construct a shrine at the gravesite to honor them.

Only close friends attended the Rites of Release. Tribesmen would join them by the incirrata's lair to witness Aahana passing the Stannag's baton to Abarax and La.

Penee plodded along the path, resisting the urge to turn back. She'd said her goodbyes. All she wanted was to mourn in private. She understood the choices the friends had made. Still, she ached with loneliness. Her life would be emptier with the loss of the Astican and the Luna Moth.

On the far side of the grave, Den stood with their companions. He excused himself to join her. "Do you want to go back? You've said your farewells."

She gave the towering Abarax and the moth an appraising look. La, perched on its finger, appeared minuscule in comparison. "They love each other. Do you find that strange?"

The amethyst in his blue eyes sparked in the morning's early light. "What gives me the right to define someone else's love?"

They joined the circle forming around Kat. Brie squeezed her hand. Everyone grew quiet.

K at cupped the Luna Moth in her hands. The fragile wings quivered. Life leaked away. The Demi-Goddess lifted her hands to the heavens. "Nature's Mother, I carry out your wishes. Please bless the transition of this Luna Moth from living to after-being." She spoke a few words in the language of the gods, bowed her head and recited a simple verse:

> *"Wee moth in my hand, I grant you long life.*
> *In a body of light, you'll exist without strife*
> *To join with the Stannag and Neul Isle protect*
> *Your reward will be love and mutual respect."*

From the upraised hands a translucent moth rose and hovered. Abarax gazed at La with so much love Penee found it hard to breathe. At Kat's direction, the Astican reclined on the consecrated ground. The Demi-Goddess placed the Luna Moth's physical body on the emblem of the sun burned over its heart. Enclosing them in its wings, Abarax breathed its last breath. Its spirit left its body, floated to La, and infused the Luna Moth with its love.

Kat touched her heart in farewell. A shaft of light lifted her skyward until she faded from sight.

Penee slipped a hand into Den's. The ordination of the future Stannag was about to begin.

Aahana, with Abarax and La, led the group to the shoreline. K'iin gathered to witness the exchange of power. The Sun Queen's daughter directed Den and Penee, the Bearers of the Incirrata, to stand on either side of the spirit couple. She knelt at the water's edge. The incirrata surfaced. Pale blue tentacles encircled her waist.

Above them, the sky opened. A palatial staircase appeared. Radiance unrolled in a carpet of light. The majestic Abellona descended, scepter in hand. Hair the flaming red of the sun formed a glowing halo. Her fire-opal gaze moved from her daughter to Abarax and La and came to rest on Penee and Den.

Her melodious tones infused the morning with wonder. "Bearers of the Incirrata, show us a sign."

Penee's tattooed arm tingled. She pushed up her sleeves. The tattoo glowed. Opposite, Den exposed his arm. His tattoo matched hers.

The Sun Queen's gaze swept over the crowd. "We gather to witness the changing of the guard. Aahana, my youngest daughter, I absolve your pledge of lifelong service." Her regal radiance brightened the lagoon. "Abarax and La, please repeat after me:

> *I accept the decree of the Queen of the Sun*
> *To join with the Stannag and become as one;*
> *To protect all that's sacred will be my reign's rule.*
> *I will honor the K'iin and the Isle of Neul."*

She lifted her scepter. Luminous rays of light flooded the sky, enveloped Abarax, La, and the incirrata. When the rays withdrew, Aahana stood on the staircase beside her mother. The trio had vanished.

Sunlight pooled at the center of the lagoon. A scarlet Stannag Incirrata surfaced, jeweled tentacles tossing sparkles of light over the water. To the cheers of the K'iin, it circled Bolcán Murloch and dove from sight.

The staircase and its occupants faded into the light of the sun. Penee rubbed the tattoo on her arm and accepted an embrace from Den.

Relevart gazed over his flock. Their responsibilities on Neul Isle had drawn to a close. Their enemies were busy elsewhere. The CoaleScence prepared to move forward, and so must they.

He searched the gathering and found the Shaman talking with Inōni. "It is time to bid your farewells, Dri Adoh."

The ancient one sighed. "Inōni, are you certain you will make this journey?"

She touched her forehead to his and hurried away.

Dri Adoh watched her go with deep sadness. Turning to Relevart, he held up a leather pouch. "I learned from Henri of the Galactic Library on Myrrh. This contains a codex, a screenfold, of the K'iin's history since the coming of the clouds. Please deliver it to the librarian. I included a gift for Inōni in the pouch. When her child is born, please give it to her."

Relevart accepted it with a slight bow. "I promise to do both. I also pledge to return your daughter and grand-one to you safely."

Inōni returned with her belongings in a woven basket. She kissed her father's cheek and hurried to join Brie and Henri.

Taking his leave of the shaman, Relevart gathered his group together. A head count assured him everyone was present. It felt strange not to have Abarax in the group. He looked over the lagoon. Happiness filled his heart.

The scarlet incirrata circled Bolcán Murloch, jeweled tentacles trailing behind it. Diamond sparkles scattered over the water. With a quiet splash, it submerged, leaving its memory in ripples on the lagoon's shimmering blue surface.

Satisfied all was well, Relevart nodded to the group. "Time to go. Staffs ready."

Four rowan wood staffs snapped into view, their crystal crowns glowing. Brie touched the tourmaline topping hers and beamed. "Thanks, Relevart."

"You're welcome, Brielle."

Mittkeer's portal spun open. Enclosed in the land of stars, he guided them away from Neul's constellation, Incirrata. They passed the moth, Actias. Bilar, the sign of balance, glittered up ahead. He brought the group to a halt beneath it.

Brie smiled up at him. "I know where we're going." She repeated a songline she had created. "Bilar is to Myrrh like a door from afar."

Mittkeer opened, their staffs vanished. They walked into the garden at the Guardian of Myrrh's cottage. Ari, Elf, and Torgin waved from the back porch.

Relevart responded to the hope in Brie's face. "You may share your status, Brielle."

Excitement glowed in her upturned face. Grabbing Penee by the hand, she ran to meet her sister and friends. Her exuberance reminded him of the child she had been.

Henri's gentle presence pulled his attention to her beloved face. Everyone else had gone. He gazed down at her. "Yes, my dear."

She dimpled like a girl. "Before we all go our separate ways, Irstant has something to share. He and Den are waiting inside."

Matching his long stride to his life-mate's shorter one, he escorted her across the garden. They entered the kitchen to find Den and Irstant conversing with Sparrow. Relevart bent to pat Majeska, then offered his palm to Myrrh's Guardian.

SparrowLyn touched hers to it. "Thank you for bringing my daughter home." She poured her guests a glass of water and placed a full pitcher on the table. "If you need anything else, I'll be in my studio with Allynae."

Relevart lowered his lanky height onto the kitchen chair next to Henri and looked from Irstant to Den. "A closed meeting?"

In response, Irstant gripped the edge of the table and came to his feet. His staff appeared in his free hand. Usolamet engulfed him in an aura of crystal light. His body straightened. He cleared his throat. "I have a story to tell, one that cannot wait any longer." Bronze eyes rested on Den. "Although this tale involves both you and Relevart, I will direct it to you, Den Zironho."

The braided beard on his chin quivered. Usolamet gleamed brighter. "After I was initiated to the level of High DiMensioner, the Order of Esprow assigned me to Soputto to oversee a situation in the capitol of Reachti which required a delicate hand. One morning, a young woman knocked at my door. She introduced herself as Miram and presented me with a handwritten message from Rasiana Diōn, a friend of Rayn's. The brief letter stated that Miram had been smuggled to Soputto from TreBlaya. It requested that I protect her and her unborn son. As you can imagine, my curiosity was peaked. I took the girl under my wing with the promise to myself I would learn more about Rasiana and her friend, Rayn.

"Soon after you were born, Den, my enemies captured and tortured me. Relevart came to my rescue. I returned to Soputto and your mother's excellent care. You and I developed a close relationship. It didn't take me long to realize you carried the gifts of DiMensionery, not average gifts, but those that would someday raise you, if you did the work, to the rank of VarTerel.

"You were about thirteen when Relevart paid us a visit. Enchanted by him, you spent every spare moment in his company. DiMensionery became your passion.

"Just short of your sixteenth birthday, your mother asked to meet with me. We adjourned to my study, where she swore me to secrecy. Her life was in danger. That night she planned to leave Soputto. Her existence, yours, mine, and Relevart's depended on my discretion. A promise that I would take care of you prompted her to tell me the following story.

He wiped the fatigue from his face with a shaky smile. Trembling fingers lifted a glass to his lips. He quenched his thirst, sank into a chair, and continued.

"I had always known Miram was more than she seemed, so it came as no surprise that she had been a protariflee expert attached to a ship called El Aperdisa. I was, however, taken aback that she was the granddaughter of Katareen, Rayn's sister."

Henri sucked in a soft breath. Her gaze darted to her lifemate. Relevart kept his attention fixed on his friend.

Irstant tugged at the braid on his chin. "Miram told me about The MasTer's power over Rayn. She shared what had made Rasiana ask her for help.

"One night, Rasiana found Rayn sobbing. The MasTer had discovered her desire to have her birth-mate's baby. He swore that if Rayn pursued this course, he would kill the child.

"Rasiana and Miram put their heads together. Without Rayn's knowledge, they hatched a plan to grant her wish. She would know nothing about it, thus The MasTer would remain ignorant. Miriam was impregnated in the lab and smuggled onto a visiting ship. Rasiana planned to tell Rayn when a safe time presented itself."

Relevart could contain himself no longer. Feelings, guesses, memories all slammed together. "What are you telling us, Jaime?"

The childhood name brought a rush of blood to Irstant's pale cheeks. His staff slipped from his weakened grasp. Relevart and Den hurried to his side. Their eyes met in a flash of recognition.

Irstant's body twisted. He looked from one to the other, mouthed father and son, and slumped in the chair.

Henri hurried to Sparrow's studio and returned with Allynae and Sparrow.

Relevart moved aside. Den and Allynae lifted his unconscious friend to carry him to a bedroom down the hall. When he lay propped up on a down pillow, Allynae slipped away. Relevart clasped Irstant's icy hand. The sound of quiet breathing assured him his childhood friend lived.

Den moved to his side. "Irstant's gifts to me have been many. He raised me, groomed me to be a good man, and trained me to be a VarTerel. Today he has given another incredible gift, the most important one of all."

They faced each other. Relevart saw Rayn and himself in Den's features. The truth of their familial relationship settled in his heart. "My life has been full, except for the emptiness in my heart." He placed a hand on his chest. "It is now overflowing. I am honored to learn you are my firstborn."

Den raised a single brow. "Don't get sentimental on me, old man." He grinned. "I have wondered at my connection to you. Now, I understand. Yes, VarTerel, I am glad you are my father."

Henri arrived in the doorway, her amethyst framed spectacles resting on her nose. Magnified eyes gleamed with understanding.

Relevart beckoned her into the room. "Allow me to introduce my son."

👁 👁

Henrietta had sent Den and Relevart to take a walk in the garden. She sat alone, holding Irstant's hand. Blindness had returned with the end of Miriam's story. His eyelids fluttered open. He turned blind eyes in her direction. *"Henri, Den is a Palmira."*

She squeezed his hand. "The eyes give it away. I have wondered if we're related. Thank you for sharing. It must have been difficult to keep this secret."

"Painfully so. I realized the ramifications if I revealed it."

"Why now, Irstant?"

Mixed emotions flowed from his hand into hers. Henrietta experienced them as if they were her own.

"My life is slipping away, Henri. I didn't want the secret to die with me."

"Can I do anything?"

He pressed her hand to his lips and sighed. *"You can love Rethdun and mother his son."* He drifted to sleep.

Relevart tiptoed into the room. Sadness held him silent for a long time. He gazed down at his old friend. "Did he say how long he has?"

Henri stood up. "I would guess a turning, maybe two. No more." She hesitated. "He's ready to go, Rethdun. You must let him. I gather Den has gone to find Penee. I'll give you and Irstant some time to yourselves. Sparrow has something to show us when you are ready. I'll see you in her studio."

At the doorway, she glanced back. Relevart, sat, head bowed, holding his best friend's hand to his heart.

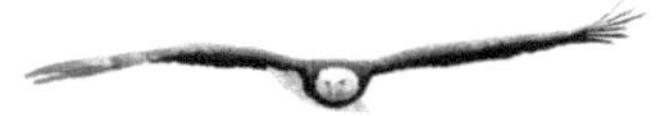

44

Penee perched on a bench by the pond, casting intermittent glances at the cottage. Elf sat in the grass with Torgin, discussing the research Relevart had asked them to do in the Galactic Library. She watched their animated expressions with a touch of impatience. What she wanted was to see Den. Her instincts told her that whatever Irstant had to share was important.

She flipped a piece of grass into the air. The sudden freedom sent it fluttering to the water's glassy surface. Across the pond, the twins walked hand in hand, absorbed in each other. Seeing them together made her realize how close they were.

Brie stopped to look at her twin. Her staff materialized. Ari's hands flew to her mouth. Astonishment left her grinning. Penee caught herself smiling at their burst of laughter and shared delight.

She glanced at the cottage. Her heart skipped a beat. Den strode toward her, his expression more alive than she had ever seen it. She jumped to her feet and ran straight into his arms. He rested his chin on her head. Chuckling, he released her. "I have just received the most unexpected news." His eyes sparkled. "I never knew my father. Mother refused to talk about him. Now I understand why."

Penee couldn't contain her excitement. "Who is he? Tell me."

He grinned. "You're smart. Guess."

Concentration wrinkled her forehead. "Irstant had something to share— Oh! Relevart is—" Her head tipped; brows lifted. "How can that be? Ah! Protariflee. You are a child of protariflee. Relevart is your father. Who's your mother?"

He grabbed her hand. "Let's get the others, and I'll show you." He started across the garden.

She pulled him up short. "How can you show me?"

He released her. "Come find out."

Intrigued by the mystery of his mother, she ran with him to the pond. He introduced himself to Torgin and Elf and explained that a surprise awaited them. On the way to the cottage, he intercepted twins and invited them to come along.

Soon they were all trouping up the back steps with excitement and expectation bubbling.

Brie brought up the rear. Ari's excitement at the news that she was a VarTerel surprised and pleased her. She had given her twin permission to share the news with Elf. They trailed after the others up the back stairs. Elf glanced back and grinned.

The last time everyone gathered at the cottage, they had celebrated the conclusion of the Unfolding. She cast a wistful glance at the barn. Esán's surprise appearance at that event had thrilled her. "I sure miss you, Esán Efre."

"I missed you, too, Brielle AsTar."

She spun to find him on the swing in the ancient maple tree. He jumped, landed on two feet, and caught his stride. "I heard about the party. We'd better hurry."

Hand in hand, they ran up the steps to the empty kitchen. Allynae peeked into the room. "Let's go. You're holding up the show." He hastened down the hall to Sparrow's art studio.

Esán received a warm welcome as they joined those already assembled. A cloth-draped easel at the studio's center was the subject of the excited buzz filling the room. Brie inventoried the people she loved. Ari drew a shy Inōni into the group. Relevart guided Henri next to Den and Penee. Her parents took their places on either side of the veiled painting.

SparrowLyn addressed the newly united father and son. "I had a dream..." On cue, Allynae stripped the cloth away. On the canvas, parents Relevart and Rayn were surrounded by their children: eldest son Den, his brother Rethson, his half-brother Elf, and Penee, his protariflee sister.

The room, at first silent, exploded with exclamations of wonder. Brie caught her breath. Penee gurgled in surprise. Den's hand flew to his heart. Henri's spectacles appeared in her hand. A bemused smile lit Relevart's face.

Brie and Esán made their way to Penee's side. "What a handsome family!"

"Can I claim to be one of them?" She sounded dubious.

Relevart swept her up in a bear hug. "You are every bit as dear to me as a blood daughter." He kissed her cheek.

Happy and smiling, she hurried to Den's side.

Henri peered through her spectacles at Relevart's face. "SparrowLyn included Rethson in the painting. You realize what that means?"

The Universal VarTerel studied the painting, his gaze intent. "It means he lives. I *will* find him, Henrietta."

Brie watched her Aunt Henri and Relevart standing arm in arm, elder eyes fixed on the portrait of the family they hadn't known existed.

With a lingering glance at the painting, Brie followed Esán from the room. She glanced back to find her mother observing them. Blowing her a kiss, she turned to Esán. "Mother's amazing, isn't she?"

F or Penee, the following two turnings passed in a blur of shared news, getting to know everyone, and basking in the realization she belonged. She had a family. Friends surrounded her. Her life hummed with a sense of love she had never known.

She took it upon herself to make certain Inōni met everyone. Elf and Ari showed them the Guardian's acreage. Ari shared stories of Myrrh's history. She told them about the pony, Tam, and Majeska, the gray, amethyst-eyed cat. Tears glistening, Ari described how the dog, Buster, gave his life for the twins. A trip to Nemttachenn Tower via the Intersect reminded Penee of traveling through Mittkeer. CheeTrann, the Sentinel of Myrrh, welcomed them to the Terces Wood. Wood Tiffs, Sibine and Tibin, gave them a tour of their TreeOm. In a clearing filled with tiny, fluttering Nyti, Kieel, the Nyti leader, landed on Inōni's hand and introduced them to his daughter, Reana. Although the time flew by, she thought often of Den and his vigil at Irstant's bedside.

On the third morning, she woke to find him in her bedroom chair, gazing at her with over-bright eyes. Pushing herself to sitting, she brushed her hair back from her face.

"Irstant?"

Den sighed. "He passed as the dawn birds welcomed morning to Myrrh. Torture left its mark, Penee. Death took him too soon. Thankfully, he slipped away with no pain." A tear trickled. "He was my mentor, my friend, my pseudo father. I will miss him."

Penee padded across the room to kneel beside his chair. "I can't make you feel better, but I'm here."

His fingertip brushed her cheek. "He told me to take care of you. You just met him, but Irstant watched over you from afar most of your life." Arms encircled her. They held each other in silence until Den's sigh tousled her hair. He sat back to study her with such intensity she blushed.

"What?"

"Relevart, Henri, and I are taking Irstant's body to Persow for burial before we travel with Inōni to TreBlaya. I wondered whether you would like to come?"

She released a soft breath. "I would love to. When do we leave?"

"We'll have a ceremony by the pond this afternoon. We'll depart right after it."

Esán held Brie's hand, his gaze on those assembled around an open casket crafted from the silvery wood of a Tirips Tree. With Henrietta by his side, the Universal VarTerel presided over the ceremony honoring Irstant, his lifelong friend. Den and Penee stood opposite them. Ari, Elf, and Inōni waited to one side; Allynae to the other. A quick search alerted him to the absence of SparrowLyn and Torgin. The desire to honor Irstant held him silent but did not cancel the urgent buzzing in his mind. Brie's inquiring look focused his attention on the end of Relevart's words of praise.

Henri drew Inōni forward. "Before Irstant passed, he asked that Inōni sing the song of passing sung by the K'iin on the Isle of Neul.

Inōni lifted her delicate face to the Myrrhinian sun.

> *"Peace to the ancestors of Irstant, the deceased.*
> *On this morning in time, his soul seeks release.*
> *We welcome your presence, the peace that you bring;*
> *We lift up our voices, your praises to sing.*
>
> *Ancestors, we honor your stories, your grace;*
> *Your feet that have walked in this glorious place;*
> *Your hands that have worked on the land and the seas;*
> *Your breath that has moved through the winds and the trees.*
>
> *Be with us here in this circled farewell;*
> *Escort Irstant to the land where you dwell.*
> *We celebrate him and the life he has lived;*
> *We honor his passing and all he did give.*
>
> *Ancestors, we honor your stories, your grace;*
> *Your feet that have walked in this glorious place;*
> *Your hands that have worked on the land and the seas;*
> *Your breath that has moved through the winds and the trees."*

To the strains of Inōni's beautiful voice, everyone placed a small sunflower, Irstant's favorite, in his weathered hands. The serene melody melted into the breezes of Myrrh. Everyone filed by the casket to whisper their goodbyes. Den and Relevart fastened the casket's silvery lid in place. The portal into Mittkeer opened. Relevart, Henrietta, Penee and Den rested a hand on the Tirips Tree casket. Star-spangled night engulfed them, leaving those left behind gazing at sunlight on the garden pond.

Esán scanned the area. SparrowLyn hurried across the garden with Torgin in tow. Allynae led Ari, Elf, and Inōni up the path to the cottage.

Esán pulled Brie into a gentle embrace. "I can't stay, Brielle."

SparrowLyn joined them. "Neither can you, Brie." She handed her a note. "Chealim asked me to give you this. Please be careful. I'll tell Ari and Penee. Don't worry about Inōni. I'll take good care of her." She gave them all a quick hug, then hurried away.

Brie turned the note over, broke the seal, and read out loud. "The council requests that Brielle AsTar and Torgin Wilith Whalend accompany Esán Efre to the planet Tao Spirian, where you will attend a meeting concerning an urgent assignment. Your presence is required post haste. Chealim."

She looked up. "This sounds serious."

"It is." Esán linked arms with Torgin and held out his hand. She clasped it. Her staff whispered into being. Mittkeer embraced them in a whirl of stars, constellations, galaxies, and planets.

Secrets well-hidden, secrets unknown,
Many are searching, none are alone.
Seekers of power driven by greed
Make killing and sacrifice a personal creed.

The CoaleScence has begun.

GLOSSARY LINK

A searchable glossary for the
VarTerels' Universe™ is available online at:

www.skrandolph.com/glossary

ACKNOWLEDGMENTS

ABOUT THE AUTHOR
FROM DANCE STAGE TO WRITTEN PAGE

STORYTELLER

Dance, humanity's most ancient narrative art, captivated S.K. Randolph as a child living and dancing in the British Crown Colony of Bermuda. After graduating from the University of Utah with a BFA in Ballet, her dance career spanned four decades of performing, mentoring, teaching, choreographing, and directing. Over sixty of her original choreographic works were brought to life for theatre audiences around the globe, establishing her deep foundation in pacing, movement, and narrative structure. She was the Ballet Mistress of the Colorado Ballet and the Alberta Ballet as well as cofounder of the Bermuda Dance Theatre. For the last two decades of her dance career, she educated the next generation of creatives, as Director of Dance at Interlochen Center for the Arts, named the "#1 Best High School for the Arts in America", and at St. Paul's School.

S.K. at the helm of her forty-foot boat leaving Seattle, Washington on a transformative seventy-five day voyage up the Inside Passage to Sitka, Alaska. Then a decade writing while living afloat swinging on the anchor rode in one remote Alaskan cove or another. 2010

DIGITAL ARTIST

S.K., a pioneer in the digital art sphere, has been creating original digital art since 1997. Utilizing a unique, self-taught technique, she transforms photographs into vibrant, otherworldly masterpieces using Adobe Photoshop. Today, her VarTerels' Universe™ series features nearly 500 of these hand-crafted digital illustrations.

VOYAGE TO WRITING

In 2010, S.K. retired from the dance world to live with her partner on their boat in the world's largest temperate rainforest along the remote and rugged coast of Alaska. Isolated in nature, she spent a "gap decade" afloat honing her writing, refining her digital art style, and mastering shipboard skills (including catching dinner). It was during this creative voyage that she transitioned her storytelling from the dance stage to the written and illustrated page, self-publishing her first novel, *DiMensioner's Revenge*, in 2011.

TODAY

Now, in 2026, S.K. is currently writing the twenty-first installment of her saga. She and her partner reside in the lower-48 states, living on the side of the largest flat-top mountain in the world. From her mountain studio, she continues to cultivate her "Illustrated by the Author" Science Fantasy series, VarTerels' Universe™, dedicating her life to the timeless journey of a true storyteller.

S.K.'s website
www.skrandolph.com

Facebook
facebook.com/skrandolph11

Substack
skrandolph.substack.com

Lessons

VarTerels' Universe™ Book 12
Part II- CoaleScence
Novella
26 pages

On the desert planet of DerTah, blind oracle WoNadahem Mardree must overcome devastating loss and her deepest fears when a mysterious shape-shifting DiMensioner arrives seeking knowledge, challenging everything she believes about fate, power, and love.

Available in the paperback *Agothany 2* and as an individual eBook.

An epic science fantasy saga told through art and words
in companion shorts and illustrated novels,
available as paperbacks and eBooks.

Illustrated by the author, color in eBooks
and black and white in paperbacks.

Presented in suggested reading order.

DiMensioner's Revenge

Illustrated by the Author
VarTerels' Universe™ Book 1
Part I - UnFolding
Novel
642 pages, 73 illustrations

Four young people from a regimented city discover their destiny when they journey to Myrrh—the hidden remnant of Old Earth—only to find themselves hunted by a vengeful DiMensioner, his death shadow, and alien mercenaries determined to destroy everything they've come to cherish.

Available as a paperback with black & white illustrations and eBook with color illustrations.

Gifts

VarTerels' Universe™ Book 2
Part I - UnFolding
Novella
34 pages

A pregnant art student must deceive a ruthless surveillance state about her twin daughters' true father, the brother of a powerful Guardian, or become the perfect hostage in a deadly political game.

Available in the paperback *Agothany 1* and as an individual eBook.

Discovery

VarTerels' Universe™ Book 3
Part I - UnFolding
Novelette
32 pages

Fourteen-year-old Torgin must choose between protecting his passion for music and spying on the only friends who understand him in a dystopian city where the government controls every aspect of life.

Available in the paperback *Agothany 1* and as an individual eBook.

Rescue

VarTerels' Universe™ Book 4
Part I - UnFolding
Novella
31 pages

In a dystopian city where surveillance is constant and conformity is mandatory, twin sisters Ari and Brie must navigate secret portals and evade ruthless patrollers to rescue a lost boy and return him home before their forbidden act lands them all in the dreaded Five Towers.

Available in the paperback *Agothany 1* and as an individual eBook.

ConDra's Fire

Illustrated by the Author
VarTerels' Universe™ Book 5
Part I - UnFolding
Novel
504 pages, 59 illustrations

Kidnapped to a hostile desert planet, Esán must survive while his friends race to rescue him, unaware that their rescue mission will unleash ancient powers and reveal family secrets that could destroy three worlds.

Available as a paperback with black & white illustrations and eBook with color illustrations.

Encounters

VarTerels' Universe™ Book 6
Part I - UnFolding
Novella
29 pages

When a vengeful DiMensioner forms an unholy alliance with a death shadow to steal a legendary crystal and destroy the Guardian who banished him, he discovers that the children he saves along the way may hold the key to his own redemption—or his ultimate damnation.

Available in the paperback *Agothany 1* and as an individual eBook.

Metamorphosis

VarTerels' Universe™ Book 7
Part I - UnFolding
Novella
31 pages

Wrongfully banished from his home planet and left disfigured by a catastrophic magical accident, Laurent must shed his arrogance and accept his broken reflection before he can master the ancient art of dimensional magic and discover his true purpose.

Available in the paperback *Agothany 1* and as an individual eBook.

MasTer's Reach

Illustrated by the Author
VarTerels' Universe™ Book 8
Part I - UnFolding
Novel
686 pages, 60 illustrations

As the UnFolding reaches its climax, teenagers wielding legendary artifacts must evade deadly hunters across multiple worlds while uncovering shocking truths about The MasTer's identity and a centuries-old conflict that threatens to destroy the Eleo Preda people forever.

Available as a paperback with black & white illustrations and eBook with color illustrations.

Wanted

VarTerels' Universe™ Book 9
Part I - UnFolding
Novella
33 pages

A fugitive with a dark past escapes prison only to discover he's being hunted by a powerful mystical league that wants to control his untapped ability to bend reality itself.

Available in the paperback *Agothany 1* and as an individual eBook.

Jaradee's Legacy

Illustrated by the Author
VarTerels' Universe™ Book 10
Part I - UnFolding
Novel
336 pages, 51 illustrations

Separated as children during a brutal genocide, birth-mate twins Rayn and Rethdun must survive across galaxies while carrying the genetic legacy that could save their dying civilization or destroy them both.

Available as a paperback with black & white illustrations and eBook with color illustrations.

Agothany 1

An anthology of
the Companion Shorts
*Gifts, Discovery, Rescue Encounters,
Metamorphosis,* and *Collision*
in VarTerels' Universe™
Part I - UnFolding
256 pages

Available as a paperback.
Each Companion Short also
available as an individual eBook.

Incirrata Secret

Illustrated by the Author
VarTerels' Universe™ Book 11
Part II- CoaleScence
Novel
428 pages, 45 illustrations

Racing against ruthless enemies across mystical dimensions, the Universe's youngest VarTerel and a prophesied leader with legendary eyes must rescue kidnapped mentors from a cloud-shrouded island where a phantom octopus guards secrets that could reshape their world—or destroy it.

Available as a paperback with black & white illustrations and eBook with color illustrations.

Lessons

VarTerels' Universe™ Book 12
Part II- CoaleScence
Novella
26 pages

On the desert planet of DerTah, blind oracle WoNadahem Mardree must overcome devastating loss and her deepest fears when a mysterious shape-shifting DiMensioner arrives seeking knowledge, challenging everything she believes about fate, power, and love.

Available in the paperback *Agothany 2* and as an individual eBook.

Corps Stones

Illustrated by the Author
VarTerels' Universe™ Book 13
Part II- CoaleScence
Novel
438 pages, 52 illustrations

A young VarTerel and her friends journey to 1969 New York City to recover three stolen Corps Stones before their entire solar system collapses into chaos.

Available as a paperback with black & white illustrations and eBook with color illustrations.

Fishing

VarTerels' Universe™ Book 14
Part II- CoaleScence
Novella
30 pages

A twelve-year-old boy with extraordinary powers must survive slavery, betrayal, and the relentless pursuit of a deadly league that murdered his parents and will stop at nothing to control him.

Available in the paperback *Agothany 2* and as an individual eBook.

Duplicity

VarTerels' Universe™ Book 15
Part II- CoaleScence
Novella
30 pages

A sworn protector with shapeshifting abilities and a future Guardian destined to unite worlds must outwit a ruthless League of sorcerers determined to claim her before she can fulfill her destiny.

Available in the paperback *Agothany 2* and as an individual eBook.

Mocendi's Gambit

Illustrated by the Author
VarTerels' Universe™ Book 16
Part II- CoaleScence
Novel
328 page, 35 illustrations

Stripped of her protective Star of Truth and held captive aboard an enemy ship young VarTerel Brielle AsTar must trust an unlikely ally—a former enemy seeking redemption—and escape through folded time before The MasTer's followers destroy everything she loves.

Available as a paperback with black & white illustrations and eBook with color illustrations.

Destiny

VarTerels' Universe™ Book 17
Part II- CoaleScence
Novella
32 pages

Brielle AsTar, the youngest VarTerel in the Inner Universe, must hide her genetically engineered babies and their surrogate mother from ruthless spies while battling a dangerous gene threatening to resurrect an ancient evil.

Available in the paperback *Agothany 2* and as an individual eBook.

Cimondeli

VarTerels' Universe™ Book 18
Part II- CoaleScence
Short Story
12 pages

Sixteen-year-old Desty has never seen the sky, but when she ventures beyond her underground refuge for the first time, she discovers her telepathic gifts, befriends a majestic flying lizard, and learns that healing a poisoned world may begin with bridging the divide between enemy tribes.

Available in the paperback *Agothany 2* and as an individual eBook.

Queen's Quest

Illustrated by the Author
VarTerels' Universe™ Book 19
Part II- CoaleScence
Novel
420 pages, 44 illustrations

A young VarTerel, a bearer of cosmic seeds, a musical genius, and a street-smart boy with magical spectacles must unite their extraordinary powers to shatter an impenetrable dome, defeat a rogue demi-god, and complete a universal cycle before time runs out.

Available as a paperback with black & white illustrations and eBook with color illustrations.

Collision

Prequel to VarTerels' Universe™
VarTerels' Universe™ Book 20
Part II- CoaleScence
Novella
64 pages, 14 illustrations

A genius physicist barely out of university must lead a team of Galactic Guardians wielding ancient instruments of power to rescue Earth from total annihilation, even as enemies from his past conspire to ensure the planet's destruction.

Available in the paperback *Agothany 2* with black & white illustrations and as an individual eBook with color illustrations.

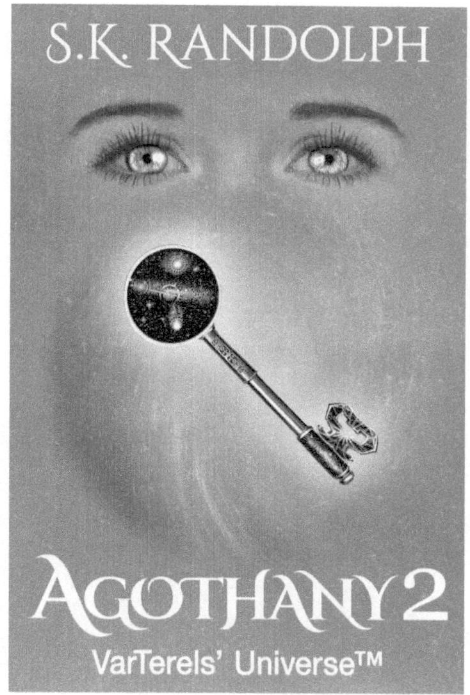

Agothany 2

An anthology of
the Companion Shorts
Lessons, Fishing, Duplicity
Destiny, Cimondeli, and *Collision*
in VarTerels' Universe™
Part II - CoaleScence
284 pages

Available as a paperback.
Each Companion Short also
available as an individual eBook.

Divided Destinies

Illustrated by the Author
VarTerels' Universe™ Book 21
Part III- QuicKening
Novel
a Work In Progress

Divided Destinies is a work in progress with a targeted release date of late 2026. An illustrated novel, it starts QuicKening, Part III of the VarTerels' Universe™.

See www.SKRandolph.com for current status and subscribe to S.K.'s newsletter to receive progress updates.